# _Bandita Bonita_

### Romancing Billy the Kid

# *Bandita Bonita*

## Romancing Billy the Kid

A Novel

## Nicole Maddalo Dixon

SANTA FE

Sunstone books may be purchased for educational, business, or sales promotional use.
For information please write: Special Markets Department, Sunstone Press,
P.O. Box 2321, Santa Fe, New Mexico 87504-2321.

Cover art by Ed Larson
Book and Cover design › Vicki Ahl
Body typeface › Aparajita
Printed on acid-free paper
⊗
eBook 978-1-61139-211-1

---

Library of Congress Cataloging-in-Publication Data

Maddalo-Dixon, Nicole.
 Bandita Bonita : Romancing Billy the Kid, a novel / by Nicole Maddalo-Dixon.
  pages cm
 ISBN 978-0-86534-973-5 (softcover : alk. paper)
 1. Billy, the Kid--Fiction. 2. Western stories. 3. Love stories. I. Title.
 PS3613.A283466B36 2013
 813'.6--dc23
                    2013038902

---

**WWW.SUNSTONEPRESS.COM**
SUNSTONE PRESS / POST OFFICE BOX 2321 / SANTA FE, NM 87504-2321 /USA
(505) 988-4418 / ORDERS ONLY (800) 243-5644 / FAX (505) 988-1025

To my husband, Wallace, who has always understood my heart when no one else could.

# PART I
## Lincoln County

# 1

## August, 1877

I am sixteen. Taking me toward what was to be the unavoidable conclusion of my maidenhood was the Union Pacific railway as it sped me along to this undesirable milestone after a wearisome, long steamship journey around the eastern coast to the Gulf. I was on my way to be with the man my parents had arranged for me to marry.

The first class compartment was filled with smoke from the cigars and cigarettes of the other first class passengers and this caused my eyes to glaze. I blinked and a tear fell, rolling down my cheek and surprising me. I was stronger than this, or so I had thought. I had been planning for this unfortunate moment, albeit against my will, for all of my life. Sixteen years' worth of wrapping my feelings in an emotional corset of whalebone while constantly reminding myself that I was meant for nothing more than the plans my family held for me. Now, the thing about whalebone…it hurts.

Though arranged marriages were largely out of fashion, my father and mother refused to take any chances with me and opted instead to ensure that my match would be a good one: a marriage that would transact continued wealth and position. They did not want to risk a repeat (and another scandal) of what my elder sister, Ginelle, who was twelve years my senior, had done. In not having a son, my father turned to his daughters to marry well and carry on the family business and our good family name and social standing, but Ginny fell hopelessly in love and eloped with a boy born well below Ginny's station and who was gravely disapproved of by my parents. But Ginny was in love. And because of this, because of love, she had been excommunicated from the family and stricken from the will. This left her and her family impoverished.

I was merely a pawn in my family's designs which God himself seemed to approve of, and there was no doubt that one should do as they were told as it was accepted by all that His will should not be refused, even if one were to vehemently disagree with His will, as I myself did.

I wiped the little tear away and no more came. Wheel against track hummed a lullaby and I allowed it to calm my mind into thinking of some other place in some other time where I could do as I pleased, though I could not fathom that such a place even existed.

Accompanying me on this journey was my governess, Colleen. I loved her more than I loved my own cold and distant mother. Colleen cared for me during the past ten years since leaving Ireland after her husband passed away from cholera. She was only twenty-one then. Though I had never known her husband I grieved silently for her, yet. She never spoke of him, but I know she loved him absolutely, and I was affected by her loss of a great love as I imagined they must have had, and in allowing my imagination to run wild with thoughts of this, I envied her.

Outwardly, I had a role to play; I was not to yield to governesses as if they were contemporaries. But, alone with Colleen, I could behave as freely as I wanted. When I was younger, I could laugh and play childish pranks which Colleen only played at being irritated with. Yet, she never spoke about her husband, and I took my cue from her silence on the matter, never asking her about something so personal. In the books I read and kept secret from my family, books which were considered refuse among my kind, where love was rampant and passionate, and women swooned for men who caught them, I imagined that this is what it must have been like for Colleen and her husband. I romanticized them, envisioning them clinging tightly to one another out of love. The same sort of love I had wanted and prayed I would receive when I came of age and it was time to do my duty for my family and marry the man of their choosing. I prayed so very hard that he would by chance be a man with whom I would fall hopelessly in love, and he with me, and we would live a life of happiness, fulfilling both my dreams and the plans of my family.

I wondered if Colleen still thought of him, her husband; if her heart was cracked beyond repair, for she never loved another, not to my knowledge, and she still wore her ring. Though I had never experienced love outwardly, I certainly had inwardly. It spread like wildfire from the chest throughout the limbs making one weak with pleasure. In my books I was the heroine, and the male protagonist the lover who chased me until I could stand it no more and must give in to him and my own desire. I wanted it to be like this for me, but alas, it was not.

I knew these romantic dreams of mine were merely innocent childish whimsy that were entirely impractical and purposeless in reality, so instead, I was to marry a man whom I did not love; a man who exemplified the valuable credentials necessary to receive my hand, and I was to marry him in a place far away which was the one variable I had never considered. I was to wed a man and live by his side in a place far from home; a place which loathsome stories of horror were told: Indian massacres, brothels full of diseased women who gave their bodies to mean men for a meager sum, men who shot each other dead in the street over a suspected cheat during a game of poker, and the raping and pillaging of white women—is this really the life my father wanted for me? No…it was what he wanted for his already considerable wealth. I was hardly a thought in the matter.

My father was a retired Union general and a steel and lumber magnate—a venture capitalist who came from old money. There was land to claim in the west, land on which to build, where people were settling much faster than they could construct lodgings. One's head could spin at the thought of how fast one could make a great deal of money by having a stake of the west and simply building upon it. My father would be a great man of industry in the west with his daughter firmly planted there, married to a man who, like himself, was also a venture capitalist and saw the potential in such a place. The potential was known by all. People constantly and consistently travelled west in the hopes of striking it rich, expending themselves under hard labor only to find themselves penniless and unlucky. But those with means would rule the land out there with ease. And there was gold to be had! Gold that was said to be so abundant that the earth released it generously from its grasp without much effort. There were hills, mountains made of the stuff! Or so they said. And there was silver, too! Metals that had the potential to make one rich, gratis! It was no wonder, then, that so many were making their pilgrimage out west when one could acquire something for nothing and gain so much if they found themselves among the lucky few. My father would have many prospects to enjoy at my expense.

My father was giving me away to an Englishman nine years my senior whom I had met twice and whose family still resided in England. Upon their death, they would divide their land with my father and their son, giving my father space to transcend the eastern coast and reach across into Europe just as the Tunstall's had done, straddling the Atlantic and raising their businesses in Canada. And then there was the land out west that my father would procure and my future husband would receive upon our marriage. My husband would receive an additional stipend in order to acquire more cattle and lumber to ensure that his empire thrived to further shape his domain as it expanded. My husband would also be in the business of selling lumber to the towns in need of building supplies, receiving the materials from my father, and there was no end to the supply of settlers in sight. There was so much land to obtain and so much wood to sell. The profits seemed endless. The opportunity for this extended wealth depended upon me. I found this a heavy load for a girl so young to carry. John seemed kind and was fairly easy on the eyes, but I felt nothing for him outside of genteel measure, and I was certain he felt the same. My prayers had not been answered.

John left England for America in 1872, landing in New York where the business deal was struck for my hand upon my seventeenth birthday. Having the security of my hand in marriage, though six years away, made no difference to John as he was happy to live as an unattached bachelor for as long as he could with the security of a wealthy marriage on the horizon. He was interested in the ladies, and so the gap of time between then and our marriage left him completely free as an eligible bachelor. During this period of time he left New York for Canada to operate his family business, then left to pursue and conquer in California. When that did not pan out, John decided to begin settling his monetary pursuits in the true west as planned in order to start early in broadening his fortune by being a cattleman and an entrepreneur. He was at present settled in a place called Lincoln County in New Mexico, and I was sent packing to join him there where I was to stay with John's partner and lawyer, and his partner's wife, Mr. and Mrs. Alex McSween, until our wedding in June, 1878. It was now only August, but June felt to be only a short time away. It was too close, all moving too fast. The inertia of my life made it hard to catch my breath.

I stared through the window of the car looking out at the landscape and watching it go by, putting more and more distance between me and my home. It had been two days since Colleen and I first stepped onto this train and in almost as much time I hadn't seen much civilization out there. It only served to heighten my misery. Many people were leaving the east for the west to find land and make them a homestead, and the newly built rails were a benefit for them as it obliterated the need for the treacherous trails. But for me, the train was a hated convenience cruelly carrying me to my fate which I privately contested and was repelled by. I was miserable.

And *oh*, but there was oil out there, too! Crude so rich and abundant that a man could haul in the money it promised for generations to come. Even in death my father would be a man to be reckoned with, and for my part in all of this, I would be all but forgotten. My father would live on in history through his daring efforts of grappling with the earth until it yielded its fruits, making him a pioneer hero. People would know his name for decades, and his family would carry on that name living parallel to his past existence, making it all but certain he would be a person to be dealt with even as his bones broke down into dust. He would be a great historical footnote, and I would help get him there. I would merge two worlds of fortune and make babies who would continue it all. *My God*! The thought of a man seeing me at my most intimate vulnerability made me shiver, let alone allow him to touch me in the manner that God meant for us humans to procreate. My mother took the liberty to discuss my wedding night before I left New York as I would not see my family until I was to marry. She spoke straightforward without emotion of this factual event despite my evident horror, sparing no detail.

I swallowed the threat of bile at the thought of what I had learned, lest I relieve my stomach of such disdain right here in this very car and embarrass myself in front of all these fine people. I'm positive that wouldn't do.

"Geangáire, Mo Mhuirnín," Colleen said in her Irish brogue. *Smile, my dear.* I gave her a small one, a smirk at best.

"It is best not to know the love you want. I pray this for you so that you never know the sadness of losing it," she said.

So then, my grief for her all these years was not unfounded. She grieved as I imagined, and I hoped she'd say more, but she remained silent.

"I would rather have love and lose it than to never know what it felt like," I replied.

I looked sideways at her and saw her lips peak at the corners for just a second as she looked down into her lap, hands crossed delicately there, one over the other.

"I want to be on fire with passion," I blurted out.

"Hold your tongue, child! It's not proper for you to speak so plainly!"

*Then I shall think it.*

"A man would take advantage of a pretty girl like you if you'd let him by talking like that. You should feel fortunate to be marrying a man who will respect you and keep you safe."

I looked at her.

"Men have desires much stronger than that of our own! Our bodies are merely a means to an end for that desire, dear. It is best to allow that satisfaction to the man who will treat you with admiration and give you a good life."

*Do not be a whore,* is all I heard. How funny, considering my love was for sale by my keeper, and it was bought and paid for by a man I cared for, not. In this way, the prostitution of my body was acceptable. Could they not see this?

I wanted only to give myself to a man whom I would love and who would love me the same. It made sense to me not at all to lay with a man I care nothing for, even if it was in the marital bed.

Did God not mean for us to share ourselves in love? This is what I've been taught all my life. Things of this nature may not have been spoken of so casually but I could read between the lines of overheard conversations. And, more than that, I could read. And the things I read made it seem perfectly fine, right, and just to give one's self to a man when the bond of love was shared. I had no intentions of letting just any man touch me, though I suppose those intentions were of poor use to me considering my fate. It would seem that my father's plan outstripped God's and my own by far. I lived in a world of hypocrisy. Love thy Father, behave under the example He has given you, but do as your father wishes though it may be against the grain of your maker. What lies! And I am a lie. I will be a false wife. Is that not a sin? I feel it is.

My thoughts turned darker still as disturbing aspects of the new country I would inhabit came to the surface of my mind. My father, on the privacy of our own land, had taken me into the woods to hunt and to teach me to use a rifle. My mother of course disapproved, but my father assured her it was necessary in the event I may need to protect myself. Hearing this had worried me.

My father, the general, the consummate soldier, thought nothing of teaching a lady all about shooting, especially in the absence of a much desired son. I was to behave in the manner of a proper lady in public, but his eyes gleamed at reliving part of his glory days as he showed me how to hold the rifle properly and sight my target, treating me as if I were the son he did not have, settling on bonding with me.

"You're almost a natural!" he said, patting me on the back as if I were his boy, a look of pride upon his face. "You'll do just fine!" he proudly assured me.

My stomach faltered.

"Father…"

He looked at me; eyes still alight and smile unwavering.

"What is it you mean by saying I'll 'do just fine'?"

His smile folded and he looked at me seriously.

"I know such things are not proper for you, but in battle you must always be prepared."

"Battle?"

This word had launched an illness within me. Perhaps this particular word was simply an overzealous one, as my father often spoke like a soldier. The troubling part, however, is that my using a rifle would not be an issue if there were no true dangers I might have to face, and it seemed apparent that there would be.

"Tell me, father, the truth, please. Where am I to go that I should be prepared for battle? I am no soldier. I'm a gentlewoman. I should not have to worry over such things as these."

He seemed vexed at my question and opinion, and I realized my tone and attitude would be considered out of line. It was not my place to tell my father what should or should not be.

"Elucia, do not be insolent with me! You will do as you are told for your family's sake! In this life one must make sacrifices. It is best that you are equipped to handle any unfortunate events should they find you."

*One must make sacrifices, but it is you making the sacrifice! Not I! You are sacrificing me!*

I was being sacrificed for things that were of no concern to me and considered by someone else. Was no aspect of my life my own?

My father turned back to the task at hand, firing at a small animal that had wandered into his line of sight. I winced at the rifle's report. The conversation was over. It seemed worth it to him to forfeit his own daughter for the chance to accrue extra money and land. This was inherently clear. And sending me off to a place where I must learn to use a rifle! The incense I felt with my father had grown to a height I had never before experienced.

I had always done as I was told, things I did not want to do, and never did I become cross. I was never one for gossiping like a hen when called upon, or calling upon others to gossip like hens, yet I did so, and all the while sitting around with our needlepoint. But these things were necessary for my family's societal status—keeping up with the inner-circles. How I hated needlepoint! All my life it was piano, voice lessons, and *needlepoint*! How I hated this life that restrained me from the freedom I preferred! I wanted to live as a man and do as I please, not sit with some Godforsaken canvas held in place by an embroidery hoop, sewing petit point of an object I couldn't care less about while the other girls chatted idly away at the prospects of men they hoped would court them and eventually ask for their hand, and the scandalous behavior of other girls we knew of, which, quite frankly, always seemed tame and unimportant to me.

*Martha Gabler was out late with that Jennison boy without a chaperone!*

*How terrible for her reputation!*

And then the laughs and smirks would follow the believed ruination as if for our own amusement. How sickened I was of it all. And as one could imagine, I was excellent in needlepoint (I spent the majority of my life practicing at it endlessly, mercilessly, as my fingers cramped and stiffened and my time revolved around the inane task of putting thread to needle and needle to canvas) and music, the latter of which I was called upon to perform constantly so that my mother and father could make an exhibition of me before their guests. I felt as though I were a performing monkey. My life in its entirety was fashioned to please others—all but myself. And now I was being whisked off to a place where my own life might be threatened all in the name of money and the happiness of others. And here, I thought marrying a man I did not love would be my biggest disappointment and worry! Now I would, that I could, be happy to marry such a man but remain in New York! But out west where the country was expanding is where the money could be made and a man could extend his empire, and it was my misfortune that my father knew of a man who was as greatly ambitious and eager as himself to make his mark in a land where such opportunity was practically being given away if one had the means. And John had the means. Therefore, it was simple enough for him to claim the land in the west, and so there I must go so I could be with a man whose ideas relied on that sort of pliability. My father preyed off of John Tunstall's enterprises using myself as the bait, and John Tunstall preyed upon the bait that would help further his own ambitions. With all of the preying my poor carcass couldn't possibly remain intact.

We were on the Southern Pacific and would pass through El Paso Texas before arriving at the New Mexican border. There, just over the threshold, we would disembark and unload our belongings, of which there were many. From there we would have a long journey that would no doubt be tumultuous. This caused me fear, for I have heard tales of Indians scalping not only men but women, and blond women were considered a prize amongst the savages that roamed the prairies. I reached up and caressed a golden lock that had tumbled from my woven hair as I considered this notion. I swallowed in anxiety.

I turned to Colleen, "How much longer must we bear this ride?" as if I were in a great big hurry to jump out of the pan and into the fire.

"I believe we have another three or four days of travel ahead of us by train."

Three or four days before I could even begin to hope to get the worst part of my journey over with; the far more vulnerable journey through the desert. As much as I loathed the thought of being in Lincoln County I prayed to God that we would be there before we knew it. If I had no choice but to marry John and be placed there, well, better sooner than later.

A steward passed by offering refreshments. I took a cup of tea and a biscuit. Colleen had the same. I lifted the cheap china to my lips and jolted. Jesse James! He robbed trains! Trains were robbed and its passengers murdered! Was there no end to the horror of this journey in sight? It was as if my mind were forced to walk over hot coals, jumping from one scald to the next. *Did they kill women?* I wondered. I couldn't recall. Or I didn't know. I didn't know if I had ever read anything of the sort. I did not know exactly where in storage my valuables were placed on the train, but I was sure if we were threatened I'd direct them myself to the thousands of dollars that were aboard if Colleen and I could be spared. This reminded me of the outlaws running loose amongst the plains. Thousands of them! Dirty, greedy, vicious, horrible men without scruples of any kind! Humanity was simply rife with these pitfalls and I would live among them. If I made it past them first.

I couldn't breathe. My corset restrained me. I began to pant and Colleen tried to soothe me. She didn't ask any questions, just told me to relax, *relax*. It was nothing for a woman to pant so heavily in the heat. In fact, it was quite common as our innards were squeezed nearly to the point of being crushed. What a cruel thing it could be, being a woman. I should have been born a man.

We stepped off the train onto a dusty platform somewhere in the far southeast of New Mexico. A ridiculously large caravan waited alongside the train station, the sort that drew unwanted attention. I knew that ne'er-do-wells would be drawn to something like that. A guarded dessert train that large could only mean that valuables were on board.

I saw men with shotguns standing by the coaches and watched them talking casually. I watched men walk by with guns strapped by their sides. I saw men, toothless and dirty bearded, bellies protruding beyond the band of their pants, spitting brown fluid at a pot and missing. There was no shortage of disgust already. And the guns. *The guns!*

Everything I've heard, it was all true, and I saw it all spread out before me like a twisted ballet of dreadfulness.

The heat emanating from the train mixed with the dust in the air and the sun beating down. It dizzied me. I spied a bench along the wall of the station.

"Colleen, I need to sit down."

She took me by the arm, a source of support, and walked me to the bench, sitting with me. I fanned at myself furiously in an attempt to cool myself and flail away the dust all at once. She, too, began fanning.

There had been men travelling with us from New York—hired hands to assist with my belongings. I watched them as they pulled pieces of luggage from the storage car and rolled them over towards the caravan, handing them off to the men there who stowed them away upon carts and wagons. There was a stage coach, dusty, black, and weather beaten, parked in the middle of the other open and covered wagons in the train. Its leathery makeup reminded me of the wings of a bat, or some other undesirable creature. There would be no travelling in style anymore, not here. Back east you couldn't have paid me to step foot inside that thing. It looked beyond used. Its wheels seemed rotten and the whole vehicle itself seemed rickety. It was a leathery-black ugly looking thing.

I noticed the women and their attire. Plain. I looked at myself in the window of the train depot, admiring my French, tailor-made silk dress. And these women were wearing bonnets that tied beneath the chin. I reached up and felt my silk, wide-brimmed velvet trimmed plumed hat. I abhorred those plain, southern sun bonnets. I refused to refer to my head accessories as anything but hats as they were fashionable and were nothing like those ugly, chuck-wagon headgear. Sun bonnets were horribly provincial. But then again, they were right at home here.

The men finished loading the wagons with my effects and we were ushered over to where our new party awaited. The men whose money my father bought to bring us out would be heading back to New York on the next available eastbound train. I felt a twinge of homesickness and a bit of jealousy. As I approached my ride, a rough looking man offered me a canteen of water for the journey. Ordinarily I would have turned up my nose at such a clumsy artifact, but I was thirsty, and just looking out at the dusty plains was enough to make me think twice.

He lifted his hat and I acknowledged by bowing my head and lowering my eyes. In some sort of country-twang he introduced himself as Bailey Hanover and offered me his hand which I graciously accepted and thanked him for as I attempted to step into the coach. I was impressed by the way he helped me so skillfully. I found, however, the shotgun he was holding in his other hand rather intimidating. They all had them, and pistols at their sides. There must have been twenty or so men. It alarmed me more than it comforted. So many hired guns meant preparation for trouble.

I sat down in the coach and, after Colleen made it in and sat across from me with a canteen of her own, Bailey Hanover closed the door. I quickly took inventory of our transportation; no windows, only gaping squares where the glass should have been and yellowed canvas shades rolled up above. The seating was covered with lightly padded, torn leather, but one could still uncomfortably feel the wood beneath. I leaned forward and out of the windowless pane to catch Mr. Hanover's attention.

"How long will it take? The drive to Lincoln County?" I asked.

In his twang he replied, "Might could be long as a week. We'll have to make a few stops t'git the horses watered or changed, git us somethin' t' eat and some rest. By my account it might be a bit longer."

"Longer?"

"Well ma'am, we're down here 'long the border and we need to move about one-third slightly northeast. There'll be some harsh terrain to cover, and like I said, we got the horses to worry 'bout and gettin' good rest. It'll be slow going what with all the wagons an' them bein' loaded up. We'll be as accommodatin' as we can. I'll be ridin' up top, and Lawrence here will be ridin' 'long the back," he pointed to a slight, clean shaven man who tipped his hat at me and nodded. "If you need anythin' 'long the way an' need for us to stop, jes' stick your arm out an' pound along the side."

He winked and turned to walk away, and I was left staring incredulously at the spot his face had previously been. *Stop?* Why on earth would I want to stop? Was he mad? I didn't want to stop until we reached Lincoln. He didn't seem the least bit concerned about our long, strenuous trek.

"My God...we're meant to live as barbarians," I said aloud, staring down at the dirty floor of the compartment. Colleen chuckled heartily. Dubiously, I looked up at her.

"They expect me to reach my arm out of a moving vehicle and pound upon it like some fish monger's wife! And do you know that they haven't any running water here?"

She sat with her hand covering her mouth, attempting to mask her amusement at the idea of a pampered lady of position having to live like a plainswoman. A farmer's wife! To be sure, I felt certain that my next statement would end her fun at my expense and horrify her just the same.

"And if one must relieve themselves, they must..." I lowered my voice, "...they must use a privy. Do you know what that is? A small wooden shack out of doors used when one must evacuate..." I was already considerably embarrassed. "...themself!"

At this Colleen burst out, laughing loudly. I puckered my lips as if a lemon wedge had been placed between my teeth. To me, this wasn't funny in the least.

"Can you not realize how primitive and uncivilized it is?!" I whispered loudly. "Inside there is a wooden plank with a hole in the middle! If the thought of that isn't horrible enough for you, you should know that I hear the smell is unbearable. We shall be as animals, sitting upon the waste of others!"

I thought it impossible, but this only made her laugh harder. I set my lips and folded my arms in frustration. She was truly enjoying my discomfort. What a riotous moment for her, indeed!

"I doubt you'll laugh when you find yourself running out in the middle of the night in your under things to sit in a tiny wooden shack. And every time you go in there everyone will know what it is you're doing. All the men will be milling around while you do your business!"

She put her head down but kept her eyes on me, fingers still pressed to her lips which remained in a smile.

"My dear," she replied, "do you think I've lived my life as you have all of my thirty-one years?"

I thought on this as she went on.

"In Ireland things were no different. In fact, I believe they may have been worse. Much of human waste was freshly released right into the town's drinking supply."

I shrank at the thought of this and, somehow, managed to keep down the contents of my stomach.

"So I guess it will be a delight for you to see me live in such squalor then. I can tell by the way you're carrying on."

I looked away from her and out the windowless pane.

"I'm sure the thought of me lifting my skirts in a box the size of a coffin while men stand around just outside the door must please you so!"

What fresh hell awaited me?

"I am not laughing at your imagined misfortune, Lucy. I'm laughing at your real-izing of it. Though it *should* prove very entertaining to watch a lady such as yourself try to avoid the inevitable."

I looked back at her in derision, and then turned to look back out the window.

"We'll be surrounded by men. There'll be nothing to do but try to remain a lady under such impossible circumstances. I shall stave off any disagreeable...tasks for as long as I possibly can."

The carriage ride was awful. My back began to ache almost immediately and my neck was sore. The coach rocked brutally back and forth and we could feel every bump the desert had to offer. So far there was nothing to quell the unpleasant feelings I had about my unfortunate situation. If only there were one thing that could distract me from it even for a moment I would welcome it. Every turn on this trip proved bleak. Even a man locked away in darkness who has accepted his fate would pray for just one sliver of sunshine, if only to have it a moment's worth of the day.

# 2

## October, 1877

I had been settled in Lincoln County in the Mc-Sween residence for nearly two months. It was now October. What happened to September? For all my prayers the world refused to slow down. Upon my arrival I took note of my temporary dwelling and it turned my stomach in knots. It was built like a fortress, with slits through the stone walls so one could shoot out while being kept safely hidden. I remembered more and more fervently my father's instructing me to shoot a rifle. John had given me a gift; a pair of nickel-plated Schofields with an emblem of the Irish symbol of a turned horseshoe for luck inlaid upon the mother of pearl grips. I didn't know what to say as this was not the sort of gift I was used to receiving. But I supposed it was appropriate here, which only served to frighten me all the more. I was tired of being so damn terrified!

Instead of thanking him all I could do was ask why he would give me pistols with an Irish symbol of luck when we were of English descent. And was it not the Irish who were so devastatingly troublesome here?

He only chuckled at me. It was not meant to be mean—I could see affection in his eyes as he studied my bewilderment.

"True, we are English, but we are in a place that is primarily made up of the Irish. And luck is luck, is it not? Considering the large Irish settlement, I thought it appropriate. It's exceptionally recognizable. One of the most famous symbols of luck in the world!"

I nodded but I disagreed. I disagreed with the whole goddamned gift! But I did not know how truly fortuitous those emblems would become.

"I meant them as a sporting gift—to welcome you to the west. But I have considered that it might not be such a bad idea for you to learn how to use them. For two hours a day you will practice with them. A few of my men will be there to educate you each day."

I was losing my mind over all of this!

"Why must I learn to shoot, John? Surely it is unnecessary."

"One can hope. Yet I want you to have all the amenities you need to live out here. In case you hadn't noticed, this climate is harsh."

I snorted; a sound which had never before escaped me. Yes, I not only noticed the climate, but I had been warned of it long before I reached my destination. Any hope that the talk of this place was simply overzealous was long gone. I was now witnessing all of it with my own eyes. I imagined that it could get much worse and prayed the bark of my thoughts were much worse than their bite.

"Many women know how to use a gun out here, my dear. I only want for you to be educated in the use of firearms as well."

I had been practicing vigorously with my pistols for nearly two months' time. A man by the name of Josiah Scurlock, known as "Doc" among the men, spent much time with me. I found him pleasant and well educated. He had practiced to be a doctor. I did not ask how he ended up here; it seemed people of different sorts ended up here. I only needed to look at myself to know that the how was unimportant. A man by the name of Charlie Bowdre also took his turn in showing me how to fire upon targets, and I had become quite adept at handling the dreadful things themselves, but I continued to miss my marks more than hit them home. Still, I managed to miss them only slightly during the better part of my lessons.

I began to look forward to these two hours each day. It was a break from the monotony of the routine of woman's work. I could not abide the needlepoint that Susan McSween enjoyed so much while we prattled away frivolously in the parlor. Here I could play in my mind. My imagination had always been the key to whatever happiness I could capture. Of course I found it all so unusual, but what difference did it make? Evidently, it was necessary. All of this was strange—why should firing six-shooters be any different?

In spending so much time around the men, I began to feel as though I was missing out, as it was easy to notice that they seemed to have so much fun just working in the yard or the fields, and I was nothing but envious! They laughed even while they worked laboriously out of doors all day, though they were not always in sight, scoping out the land and maintaining the cattle. They would take off to town in the evenings and I wished I could go with them. I wondered what fun they were having there while I was trapped in my own personal hell.

Sometimes they would pass through on the McSween's property when they had finished with their accountabilities, and I would often hear them as they headed into town hooting and hollering and generally being merry. By nine o'clock at night as I prepared for bed, I'd hear them running off to make a grand time of the night. To be a man in this world meant freedom. I spent my days, with the exception of those two hours a day, in a fog, awaiting and dreading June.

Each morning, late, a chaperone would drive me over to John's where I would visit with him, and in the early afternoons I was allotted my two hours, shooting, and most evenings John would visit with me at the McSween's and dine with us. My affections for him neither grew nor shrunk. I simply felt nothing for the man with the exception that I found him to be generally kind and generous towards me. But, to be sure, he had much to gain from our union, and truth be told I found him a bore. He was all about business. There was no courting or any sort of romantic excitement of any kind on his behalf. I was simply treated as I was; there to marry him; lucrative chattel.

Frequently, he would take me to his store in town where I was able to pick up needlework supplies and anything else that I wanted or needed. On occasion, we dined in town while his hired guns waited. Always we were escorted into town by men with guns, and I was overwhelmed as I could understand the need for them.

I began to recognize that there were certain men who stared John down, hands on their guns as we drove past, leaning in closely and speaking to one another as they watched him go by. I had been told that there was something of a dispute between John and his competitors, J.J. Dolan, and L.G. Murphy, who owned the store opposite his. It was explained to me that the men who stared ominously at John were hired by Dolan. This supposed quarrel often caused unbearable tension within the town and the danger was tangible.

The only thing that I enjoyed about this place was those two hours a day spent firing at targets. Two hours of having the sweet liberty I craved that men won with such ease. And after realizing the easy trouble to be found in Lincoln, I began to take my lessons even more seriously.

Often, Colleen and I spent many nights talking before bed in which I wept on her shoulder, telling her of how miserable I was. She would try to comfort me as she always had. She truly felt for me, I know this. I was so terribly homesick; I felt I could die from a broken heart. She'd brush my hair lovingly, calming me, and braid it before I climbed into bed.

"Colleen, I am so happy you're here. You are the only thing that keeps me tethered to something familiar. This place is so awful, and I do not love John. I have not begun to feel a thing for him. He spends most of his time discussing industry, and when we are busy dining we have not a thing to talk about. Well, I don't. He, on the other hand, talks of cattle and his store and of expansion. I am not interested in any of that. John doesn't love me, either. This is an abysmal business contract and I hate my life for it! My heart breaks each day!"

"Sshhhh….Mo cuisle. You don't know what it is you are saying. No. You are far better off than many. We all have our crosses to bear, but at least you will know you will be taken care of. I promise you your heart is not broken, it is only hindered."

I made an unintelligible sound against her shoulder.

"Think on this, love—you don't love him, and he does not love you. There is no pressure but to survive, and you will survive with ease. The point is to live, mocuishle. You will learn to respect one another and exist. Love fades. You and John will develop a satisfying relationship, I promise you."

I whimpered and looked up as if into the heavens, wiping my nose with the back of my hand.

"You make it seem as though it's ridiculous. But you haven't bothered with a man in ten years! What I feel is of no consequence to you! You don't seek out what I do, how can I accept your promise of just existing?" I laughed sarcastically at her foolishness. "I am getting advice from a woman who wants no more out of life than to get out of bed each morning and have nothing to look forward to with the exception of existing with the love of a dead husband! And then to sleep on her own each night with no one special to share her bed!"

It was out of line for me to say, but I felt as though she was proving to be a hypocrite in an attempt to make me feel better. She had the good fortune to experience a love so great that no other man would do, and I could only guess she lives well on those memories. She has more than I ever will, dead husband and all!

"Lucy, you know nothing of what you speak of! If anything, my life ought to be a cautionary tale to you. I live for a dead man and am shut of all other men. You and I are not so very different at all. We both have our burdens to bear, and we shall bear them together! It seems to you impossible to love John, and I believe it impossible for me to love another. Either way, what difference does it make, other than I live every day in the past? I wouldn't want that for you. Better for you not to feel so deeply for your husband. If you lose him you will go on and live a normal life. You will not be cursed by the memory of love."

"Perhaps I would not lose a husband whom I love dearly to a wretched disease! I should stop wanting because you say I should expect to lose what I want so badly because you have? How selfish and stupid you can be!"

At this she stood up and wordlessly left the room, closing the door quietly behind her. I had hurt her. She never spoke about her husband. She kept whatever remained of him to herself rather than squander her memories of him in bits and pieces. Yet tonight, she had shared something of him with me, had hinted of him because I was a brat, complaining of my own circumstances and she wanted to soothe me. Perhaps she was right. Maybe it was better not to love. Apparently, when love was lost, one felt worse than I felt at this moment. She had been right; we were in the same boat, her and me, with the exception that she was living off scraps of memories of love and nothing more, and I was living off of scraps of what I had hoped for but was not to be. We were both empty inside, but I did not miss anyone so desperately as she. I did not have to live with the pain of losing love. In her, this night when she had spoken of him, I saw that my heart was in fact not broken, only numb. Perhaps that was better. I made a vow to myself that upon waking I would change my outlook. I would accept what life had planned for me and appreciate that I would never suffer the heartache that Colleen bore silently each and every day. If I felt tortured for a love I would never have, then she must be tortured by a love she had lost, and therefore, must be by far worse for the wear.

Tomorrow would be different, and I would apologize to Colleen with the utmost sincerity I could manage. I should have known better. While I wanted love so badly, I had cast hers off as foolishness and made it seem absurd. It was I who was selfish and stupid, but I hadn't meant any of what I said. I only felt poorly and sorry for myself and took it out on poor Colleen who has never been anything but good to me. If I yearn for love so desperately, then how could I have cast hers off so callously as if it should have meant nothing? The truth was, what she had is what I wanted. Yes, I would be better tomorrow.

By the next morning I had woken up earlier than usual. When I had first come to Lincoln I was always forced awake by the crowing of a rather irritating rooster roaming about out in the yard, but today I beat even him by dawn. I sat up in bed and waited for Colleen to come and help me dress. When she came in I'd be ready with an apology, but two hours later, when she knocked and opened my door, nothing came to me. It had dawned on me at that very moment that saying I was sorry would not be good enough. I imagined her lying in bed last night, weeping as I did. Weeping because of me; because of what I had said. I deprecated the love she had for her husband. How does one atone for something such as that?

She came towards me in silence and I pulled the covers back, stepping out of bed and sitting down before my dressing table. I felt tense and insecure; the room so dense with Colleen in it. I begged my mind to bring me words of regret but it would not. Was it my imagination, or did she tug at and brush my hair much more ferociously than usual? Perhaps she only felt careless; I could not gauge a situation of this nature as one had never before in my life occurred.

When my hair was finished and tied up expertly by Colleen's hand it was time to dress. I chose silk, my favorite, but Colleen refuted my preference wearisomely, stating simply that silk was too fine for morning, and that it was late October and I would wear a wool dress.

"But it is warm enough here!" I protested.

"It has not been warm in days!" she snapped. "We are six-thousand feet above sea level and it is nearly November! You'll wear light wool."

Wool! Light or otherwise, she was being impossible!

"Silk is too fancy for you to wear this time of day, Lucy. The light wool will keep you warm enough. It is chilly this morning. You must watch your health out here. The doctor is not directly at your disposal and who knows how late he may come."

I looked at her, trying to read her face which was turned entirely away from me.

Finally she turned to me and said, "All right...the French lace morning gown."

Relieved, I watched her pull the pretty white gown from my wardrobe.

"The people out here don't know the difference of when and where to wear what anyway," I said with a degree of smarm. Colleen grabbed my forearm.

"You mustn't put down others who haven't your education because you think them stupid! The people who live here have all made pilgrimages from the east just as you have. They are not ignorant. Often they may be simple, but John and the McSween's come from well-respected families. It is not attractive for a woman to look down upon her contemporaries, regardless of the class. Do you think me ignorant because my job is looking after you?"

I looked down "No," I replied in a small voice. "I only prefer certain things and wish to get away with it. It is a small thing, but silk is my favorite. I thought the least I could have was that one thing."

"This is not about wearing silk in the morning; you and I both know that; it is about your vanity."

She seemed exhausted in expressing this to me.

She removed my nightshift and helped me into my chemise. She reached in my trunk for my corset. Light pink with delicate embroidery around the top.

"You haven't eaten well these past two months. I must reset your corset and blouse."

I stood straight and rigid as she pulled harshly at the cords. I closed my eyes and grabbed helplessly at the back of my dressing table's chair for support each time she'd yank. She pulled so tightly I could barely breathe. I wanted to tell her so, but I knew I deserved this. I must figure out a way to show her the regret I felt for my poor behavior. In the meantime I would receive my punishment and let her troubled mind take it out on me.

By the time she was finished I was breathing shallow and in small measures. I could not bear it and yet I said nothing. She yanked at the cleverly blended buckles along the back of my sides on the brocade dress to affix it against my small waist. It was all too much; I knew not how I would sit, let alone eat. Fortunately, my entire life had been conditioned around discomfort. I approached the dining room and took my place beside John. I dreaded the insurmountable job it would be to sit down in my chair. Would I be able to bend? Slowly, I sat.

"Are you all right my dear? Did you not sleep well?"

"Yes John, I had. Why is it you ask?"

"You move as one who is sore. I have seen it aplenty among the men coming in from the fields."

He and Alex laughed and I hid my aversion to this statement. It was not humorous to make fun of hard working men who received low enough wages. I also did not care for the embarrassing remark; to make fun at the expense of a lady was reprehensible at best.

Unmoved by his manners I thought, *Go ahead, make fun you English prat*!

Colleen was helping the McSween's woman in the kitchen, bringing the food to the table. Colleen and the woman would eat separately in the kitchen once our table was prepared. I did not want her out of my sight, especially today of all days. If I could not verbally repent, I could, at least, act it out.

As we began to eat I found I could not. I was barely even able to sit naturally. My corset was too tight! I excused myself and left through the next room, crossing it to reach the hall where my bedchamber was situated. I ran in and closed the door behind me and began fumbling at the buttons of my dress. Once I had it undone I tore at the clasps on the front of my corset, releasing them over my belly. Finally, breathing room! I reached around back and loosened the buckles on the dress as subtly as I could. I did not want it to be evident that my waist would be oddly shaped as the dress would certainly not lay right now. I felt all but sure of John's audacity at bringing attention to that. The horror if he did!

I buttoned back up and looked at myself in the floor-length mirror. The adjustment had made a slight mockery of my waist, however, I was fairly certain that I had managed the adjustment well enough, and Alex and John would have business matters to discuss and be firmly entangled in that, and Susan, near Colleen's age, usually joined in the discussion between her husband and John. Whenever she did speak with me out of politeness it was to talk about the latest fashions. There was boredom all around. At this point it couldn't possibly matter anyway. Even if I had wanted to, I could not have hooked my corset closed again upon my regret as it was wound so tightly. I grabbed a long shawl and wrapped it around my shoulders, assuring that it hung properly over my stomach. It would make a good excuse for my up and leaving the breakfast table if I made the point that I felt a chill.

While the men spoke and Susan chimed in, I waited for a pause. I had conjured an idea as a way to perhaps mend the rift between me and Colleen. When finally there was a lull in the conversation I took the opportunity. "John?"

"Yes Elucia?"

"There is a certain needlepoint pattern I am interested in working on. I was wondering if you might consider ordering it to the store for me."

"Certainly. We'll go to town this afternoon and take care of it. It will give me a chance to check on some things. I'd like to take a look at the books."

I tried hard to avoid rolling my eyes at this last statement. Fine. If I must suffer through the boorish nightmare that is John going over the store numbers then I shall endure it. I could make it part of my grand, self-inflicted punishment for Colleen.

While in town I noticed the usual sights; unscrupulous men staring at John and the hired guns surrounding John glaring back. Being helped down out of the buggy I walked quickly into the store. I did not wait for an escort; I wanted only to come in from the street.

I walked to the clerk behind the counter and told him what it was I needed and he placed my order. I was told it could take up to two weeks, if my pattern could be ordered at all. This stalled my enthusiasm. I wanted to thread a four-leaf clover for Colleen and, as deft as I was with freehand, I was unsure I could make it perfect, and it *must* be perfect! I thanked the clerk and hoped for the best, but two weeks was a long time to wait to offer an apology. But what I had in mind would come from the heart and mean something in which I felt words could do no justice. In as much of a rush I was in to repair the damage I had caused, I was sure that, with time, the fence between us would mend well enough, and I would be so wonderful to her from this day forward! If I began to notice that I behaved selfish and spoiled I would simply withdraw the behavior. The only difficulty in this was that my ego was drafted a certain way for sixteen years now and I worried if I would even recognize this unpleasant behavior in myself. I decided that I would study those around me. If, in this place, I could not find one selfless individual, then God must intend for me to be as I am, and therefore, I could do nothing about it—I would be doomed in vanity. But these people, aside from those committed to making trouble, seemed goodly and kind. I avoided the women up until this point, not only because of my belief that they were of the plain sort, but also because this town was up-and-coming and I was beyond them; they were moths and I the flame. The women hinted inelegantly as they sought an invitation from me for a visit, and made crude invitations to have me visit their homes which I shirked simply because I did not care to be used as a catalyst to make others feel more important than they were. I abhorred the thought of being the epicenter of a whole new social class. But if I must, I could tolerate these provincials if it would help me improve my bearings on the subject of the mannerisms of regular people and, in return, I could endure their superficial gossip and their need-to-know about the latest fashions and travel, raising their status by association if it pleased them so. Quid pro quo was fair enough, I must concede.

I had met Mr. John Chisum's niece Sallie a few times. Mr. Chisum was a well-off cattleman, benefactor, and partner to Alex and John. His cattle ranch and estate sat about thirty miles to the south. Sallie, however, was what one could consider my western counterpart. That is not to say that she was deserved of this consideration as she was by far outstripped by my pedigree, but of all the people here she was the only young lady my age I knew who was above the western class average. Her family money was new, but I supposed I could manage a visit with her to attempt to pick up western conduct.

And then there was Phyllis Dillinger. Good God, Phyllis Dillinger! She was a relentless little opportunist! She had tried considerably to ingratiate herself to me since I first stepped out of that awful stage coach onto McSween property. In town, if I saw her, I made an attempt to conceal myself, a feat in-and-of itself. She'd follow me around like a lost puppy, asking me the trivial questions I strictly wished to avoid. Where did I get my clothes? How should she curtsey properly and make it look flawless? And *when* should she curtsey? Did all my clothes come from Paris? What was New York society like? Could I show her how to walk as gracefully as I did? And other things of the sort. Her only interest was in frivolity. I found her foolish at best, and at worst, a bore. I did not have to look too hard to see that Phyllis was beyond even my help. Her demeanor was a lost-cause. Her figure was bust, and she had nothing useful to talk about, and when she did speak, all that came out was an annoying voice that sounded as though a sock had been stuffed down her throat. High-Society etiquette would appear ridiculous on her even if she *had* been flawless; she simply did not have the pedigree to substantiate the favor of class. It would be as pointless as a thoroughbred donkey.

When caught speaking with her, I consoled myself in the knowledge that the sound of her was better than that of a bell peal, even if only. She desired my friendship because of my prominence—what a wonderful accessory I would make to any woman in town, indeed. Phyllis never spoke of anything but what I could do for or help her with. Ah…the only trace of a true social climber! Congratulations, Phyllis! You're not completely bereft of worthiness.

I wondered if I could turn the tables, however. I was an educated woman, not to mention of the lessons in life I had been taught regarding the art of being woman. If I could not wrest the knowledge I sought from Phyllis, then I should be considered just as useless as she. The problem was, however, paying any attention at all to Phyllis meant opening the door and being charitable towards her. She had better provide what I sought out if I were to attempt the trouble, and after all, she seemed the simplest of them all.

It was too bad that she was not the much less irritating Candace Kelly. Candace seemed shy but confident. She approached me on occasion when she'd find me on Wortley Street as I browsed or waited for John to finish up his business with the store. I found her pleasant. She never pushed or seemed to want anything from me but polite conversation. She had golden locks like mine, always swept up under something resembling a fashionable hat, and always looked pretty in her frocks. She had freckles that swam across the bridge of her sloping, pointed nose and cheeks, and she was blessed with bowed lips—a pretty specimen. She was pleasant all around, I should say. I didn't mind speaking with her so much.

But Phyllis! Unkempt Phyllis, with dark, wiry curly hair that could not be tamed and always managed to escape whatever dreary accessory that sat atop her head, was short and squat and wore ugly colors that did her complexion no favors. I never saw the girl without a face bespeckled with red blotches. She knew not the first thing of primping! It may be that she knew this and was the reason she pursued me so relentlessly, though I could not believe a girl as naive as she was would even recognize these flaws. She was the type of girl who, at home, I would dare not associate myself with.

But in this matter, I was willing to accept her company for the sake of Colleen. I wanted to change for her. Maybe Phyllis would be a surprising keynote in that endeavor. I would make it a point to ask her questions about Lincoln and its people and western living in general, though she struck me as empty headed and a poor mentor. But I would also ask the woman who cooked for Alex and Susan to show me how to bake, and though the activity would be objectionable for a lady to do, it might help to impart humility on my behalf. Perhaps I should bother to ask the woman her name. It was unexpected of and considered unnecessary for me to know these simple people and their country eloquences, but being over a thousand miles away, who in New York would know of those whom I acquainted myself with? And here, the social politics were much different than those back east. If I were to be a westerner, then perhaps I ought to know their customs.

During the days while I waited to see if my specially ordered pattern would arrive, things between Colleen and me seemed to revert back to normal. I still, however, had to make my apology. While visiting with John one afternoon, I asked him if we could go to his store to see if my pattern had arrived, but he seemed troubled.

"Whatever is it, John?"

He walked towards me, placing both of his hands upon my upper-arms.

"Elucia, dear, it is nothing for you to worry or concern yourself with."

"Yes, John, but I can see that you are distraught. If I am to be your wife, I would appreciate it you felt you could confide in—"

"Eight of my horses have been taken from Mr. Brewer's residence! All of this after forcing his cook to feed them—an extra slight!"

I stood and stared at him a moment, searching for something useful to say so that I did not seem idle but, unfortunately, I knew not what to say or how to comfort him in this instance.

"Is there a chance you may recover them?" I asked.

He sighed and ran his hands over the back of his leather chair before using it to sit at his desk with his head down and resting over his crossed hands—the sign of an exhausted man. Perhaps I had been too harsh in judging him; In this moment I only felt sorry for him.

He looked up. "I don't know…I doubt it. They left with a promise never to steal from me again. I suppose that is something. Just your average horse-thieving criminals to be found at every turn out here. I should have seen it coming sooner or later, such fine horses as they are. I should not have expected them to go unnoticed."

He looked down and shook his head in sorrow, sighing again.

"Horses are stolen all the time. I suppose it was rather chivalrous of them to promise never to steal from me again. That leaves me with some comfort, as I'll only need worry about the remaining thieves this territory has to offer."

"Then that is something."

I smiled kindly at him, though I recognized his sarcasm. Eight horses! Eight expensive horses, gone. The promise not to steal from him again meant very little as they had stolen from him already.

"They seem so very brazen, these men," I remarked. "When did such a thing happen?"

"Just before dawn this very morning."

At these words a man I had seen on occasion came running in.

"Seven Rivers, John!"

John looked fast up from his desk.

"What?"

Seven Rivers! The goddamned thieves were caught. Well one, anyway."

The man turned to me contritely in turn for his language, "My apologies, ma'am."

I only stared back.

"Send the sheriff down, Fitzy. I want my horses brought back to town!"


I was fortunate! The clerk was able to find the sort of pattern I applied for and I began working on it in earnest. As I sat in John's parlor I heard his buggy pull up out back. It was only early afternoon and already I felt I had been stitching for hours. Eyes strained and exhausted, I rubbed at them and I put down my needlework, heading towards the back door, interested, of course, in what John must have contended with during his visit at the jail. He had gone to speak to the man who had stolen his horses as the thief requested his presence. I don't know whether it was out of courtesy or curiosity that John went, but he decided he would go and speak with him.

I stepped onto the back porch and saw a boy sitting next to John in the buggy. His head was down, his clothes fairly soiled and coming apart at the seams in places. His boots were well worn. The brim of his hat was tipped low; I could not see his face in its entirety, and when he stepped from the buggy he kept his head down. I could, however, see that his hair was flaxen as it was much too long and his hat was completely unable to conceal it. I would have wagered that each of the soles of his boots were a stitch away from liberating themselves.

John stepped down and walked around the front of the cart until he was standing next to the boy. He looked up at me and introduced the stranger.

"Elucia, this is William Bonney," he said, lowering his face mischievously before jauntily adding, "the thief who took my horses."

Judging by his youthful appearance, I wondered, was this truly the boy who had stolen John's horses? And if so, why on earth would John want to bring here to his home, trusting him amongst his property? I was annoyed and upset that John should not think of my safety, placing me in close enough proximity to a creature such as that. I should not be made to feel so uncertain in my own home. The west was a truly remarkable place, accepting and entertaining such scoundrels. I would have guessed that such a slight, tender aged boy, who could have been no older than I, should have lacked a mountain's worth of experience in the career of a true horse thief, or any kind of thief for that matter. The boy looked up at me reluctantly when John introduced us.

"William, this is my fiancée, Miss Howard."

"Hello, William," I dispassionately offered.

His demeanor was shy and not at all what I would expect from a criminal. I extended my arm to him in the customary way one might in offering a greeting. At first he seemed both perplexed and full of trepidation by my gesture as if uncertain how to respond. Then tentatively, he took my hand and reservedly said, "Hi."

He respectfully removed his hat and lowered his head, and I smiled at him in spite of myself. I would not have counted on his manners being so intact.

I admit his looks appealed to me. His blue eyes were made vivid by the early afternoon sun's glare, and he had such delicate, feminine features set in the context of a man's face which gave him an appealing countenance. I noted his lengthy eyebrows, the same flaxen color of his hair, and how dramatically they framed both eyes. His slightly aquiline nose gave his face a satisfactory sort of character, especially when coupled by the other aforementioned attributes. I noticed that his white teeth entertained a hint of an overbite, his front teeth slightly bucked. His skin was fair, but his cheeks and the bridge of his nose were colored by the sun. His boyish good looks were, without argument, very pleasant.

He returned my smile and I could not help but to find this simple, rustic creature utterly engaging. I could not help but like him immediately at the outset.

"Please, call me Elucia," I offered, surprised by my own cordiality and suggestion of familiarity.

We all three stood silently a moment after the introduction. I looked again to William and attempted to meet his gaze, but no sooner had we made eye contact did he timidly lower his eyes, nervous.

John explained he would be keeping William on at the ranch and taking him to his store in order to arrange for him the necessary supplies he would need, but the boy, William, still only looked down, staring at his boots, holding his hat in his hands anxiously as I stood alongside him and continued to stare, wanting to talk with him and make small conversation. When I spoke I saw that he tried to hold my gaze, but it would slip and he would look down before attempting to again look at me. He appeared fretful, and I suppose this was because my stare was so inadvertently impolite. My manners were indeed much better than this, but I felt incapable as I was taken aback by my own feelings of interest for the boy. I was taken aback even further when he looked down again for a mere second before looking up at me with a slight grin that had found its way across his lips. My stomach felt fluttery. I could see straight away why John had brought this thief home. His charisma and charm were arguably difficult to disregard—they were hard to overlook, and harder still to ignore.

When John had come back from town with William I was shocked by the latter's transformation from street drifter to civilian. Such a sweet face he had! The late sun shone sharply, lighting it up and making those blue eyes ever more brilliant! He stood before me, remarkably put together in a gleaming, crisp white shirt, black bolero jacket and hat, black corduroy pants, and light colored duster. His hair had been cropped neatly; he was so visibly proud. John had given him a gift of two brand new revolvers which he had strapped down and buckled around his waist, giving him such an air of confidence that his attitude became much more self-assured and his posture all the more poised than when we had first met. From the first, I could see that this young man was only too familiar and right at home with such treacherous things.

His transformation, and by association, his demeanor, was impressive when compared to the shy boy I had been introduced to not more than three hours prior. Self-respect seemed to suit him as if it were his true nature.

I found, however, despite his seemingly replenished self-assurance, he would still drop his gaze from mine. Immediately I was enchanted by this southwestern boy, bringing the first twinges of excitement to my life here in Lincoln where there hadn't been before. I had decided that I should like to get to know him.

It soon became clear enough that William exhibited unexpected intelligence which pleased John greatly. He found him clever, and felt that William could only flourish under the proper tutelage and, considering this, John enlisted him as my pupil, not only because of my exceptional education, but because, in being a lady, John hoped that William might benefit from the exposure of feminine influence which should help improve the mannerisms of this boy from the streets. I was to spend an hour with him two to three days a week, and in return, I would be made to study under William for the two hours put aside for targeting as it was soon discovered that his expertise with firearms was considerable, and he far outperformed any of the others.

As a direct result of this, William was removed from doing labor in the fields all day in order to serve as John's personal hired-gun in no time at all, joining the ranks of the other men John kept in his protective guard who were meant to follow along on his journeys and short trips into town. I was, of course, no stranger to this way of life by now, as I, too, was often accompanied by a squad of armed men on orders from John when escorted into town by Colleen.

As uncomfortable as I was living in a place such as this where one's life could be in danger simply by going about one's own business, and taking a stroll into town for innocent reasons could prove hazardous, I did not mind being expected to spend time with William for two hours some days, even if those hours were to be spent learning a vicious trade. His shy disposition ingratiated him to me, as he seemed a very pleasant boy indeed, and his boyish good looks were too pleasing of a distraction to pass on.

Before dusk fell I stood waiting on the back porch for the ride that would take both Colleen and I back home to the McSween's, and there I saw William stride by. I had not seen him today as he, instead, spent it with John. He was sitting atop a new horse and what looked to be a brand new saddle. He was wearing spurs, new, and he had a Winchester holstered in its side-scabbard upon the animal, and he wore a white flannel shirt with a brown buttoned up vest and brown pants. He also sported a brown roughrider hat. The boy was positively beaming as he came toward me.

"Hi Miss Howard," he said as he dramatically and gracefully swept his hat down and along the side of the animal.

"Hello William. And *please*, call me Elucia."

He nodded his head in recollection.

"Do you see what I've got?" he asked excitedly.

"The horse and saddle?"

"John gave it to me as a present! I'd never known anyone like him, giving something like this to a person like me."

"I think he must have much faith in you, then."

I'll work hard for him, I can swear to you that!"

"I'm sure you will, William."

Colleen came out to let me know our driver had arrived.

"I'll be right there Colleen."

"Where is it you're heading off too? McSween's?" he asked.

He didn't pronounce his "ing's", so it came out sounding like, headin'; another charming aspect I had come to adore. I felt absolutely smitten and sorry to leave. I had to admit this to myself.

"Yes," I confirmed.

He smiled and looked down, then back up at me. In the short amount time we had gotten to know each other we had grown more relaxed with one another.

"I must say, you certainly cut a positively handsome figure up there Mr. William Bonney."

I smiled at my own shocking audacity, and he smiled back, genuinely pleased.

"I'll see you tomorrow?" he asked, sounding hopeful.

"Of course, if you'd like."

He seemed happy at the prospect. Spending two hours with him alone pleased me greatly, but it caused an irritating flurry in my stomach.

We looked at each other a moment.

"I should go. It was truly nice speaking with you, William. We'll speak again tomorrow."

He smiled at me and before he turned to go said, "I look forward to it."

I turned and walked through the porch door, a smile of my own upon my blushed face.


As I climbed into the carriage Colleen looked at me curiously.

"You're taken with that boy."

I kept smiling and staring ahead until I found the cautious words that I would be careful to say. I trusted Colleen more than anyone else, but I wanted to tread lightly.

"I find him interesting."

"You hardly know him."

"Yet already I'm captivated. In such a short time he has fascinated me, which is more than I can say for most of the people I've known for years as they bore me so," I switched tacks, "What difference does it make anyhow? I'm set to wed John before I know it. Some field-hand is not going to change that."

But with John incorporating William into his personal guard and in having him stay close to my side as well, my acquaintance with him could only develop which served to keep my interests all the more buoyed. I began to count on this.


In need of some fresh air and to be free from the walls of captivity, I wanted to walk through the town's orchards and admire the scenery and enjoy the peace to be had there. William, of course, was my escort, and as we prepared to cross the street, I placed my left hand upon his arm, just above the elbow. He seemed surprised by my gesture, and out of the corner of my eye I caught him turn to glimpse me curiously. I did not know any other course of action as it was only proper for a man to help a lady across. If I was not mistaken, he seemed thrilled by this gesture and appeared to take it in earnest. He appeared proud. The innocence of his response towards my action ingratiated him to me even more and, if it were in fact true that he had been pleased by my gesture, then I was nothing if not happy to oblige him.

On another occasion we had gone into town to procure supplies. We took the wagon, Josiah driving, myself in front between him and John with William in the back. When we were through collecting our wares and prepared to head back, William offered me his hand to help me into the wagon and politely I accepted, deeply wishing I hadn't the misfortune of wearing gloves as his own hands were unsheathed and I wanted an excuse to hold his hand.

I found myself unable to look directly at him, feeling awkward and anxious as I was certain that he could see through to my sinful thoughts of him. Never before had I been rendered self-conscious by one so far beneath me. But rather than allow him to see that he had affected me and caused my cheeks to flush in his presence, I decided to keep my head down and expression calm; this was the best tactic I could employ to help me cope, though I'm sure the end result made it seem as though I coldly failed to acknowledge him altogether when the truth was my thoughts were filled with him.

# 3

## November, 1877

I sat working on the pattern of the four-leaf clover which had been intended to aide me in making my amends with Colleen. It was fortunate that I did not need to concentrate greatly on the task as all of my concentration was, at present, monopolized by William Bonney. I did try to focus on the pattern because the whole idea of waiting on this design was to ensure that I accomplished it correctly. But William would not go away—my mind demanding that I meditate upon him. I even cherished his name, Billy Bonney, as the boys called him, the alliteration pleasing to me; like a poem. When at John's, I found myself counting down the very minutes to when it would be time for William to come for me.

One day in particular it was still early in the morning and John had not come to the McSween's for breakfast as he was out on business. Still, I had insisted that I visit his ranch straight away as I was impatient, the truth being that I had hoped I would run into William.

I will admit that my burgeoning feelings for William had irritated me on occasion. A part of me had wished he'd go away, and better yet, that we had never met. He was not good enough for me and, even still, if this had not been so, his arrival was by far too late. It was my heart that fought my mind's logic. I must believe the irritation was caused by the conflict of what was expected of me and what it was I wanted, as opposed to William being the true source of my internal struggle.

"John!" I shouted a bit too loudly as he walked in at ten o'clock.

"Yes Elucia."

I could hear the exhaustion in his voice.

"Why are you so excitable this morning?" he asked.

"Am I?"

"Yes."

"Is William with you?"

He seemed curious by my zeal. I thought quickly and, looking to the book I had been reading, though I had read it before as it was one of my favorites, I said, "There is a book…this one."

I raised it up before him and made a great show of waving it about in a gratuitously aggressive manner.

"I'm eager to give it to him," I explained, "I have just finished it for the second time and I think he would enjoy it."

I made an attempt to sound calm when I asked, "Where is he?"

"He's gone out to see about the cattle."

I was disappointed at this and hoped that I had not appeared too deflated by the news.

"He is due to come in at noon and will escort you back to Alex and Susan's. I am going to have him stay with you this afternoon into the evening. There's a very good chance that I will not be back until tomorrow, late afternoon."

My spirits lifted, but I looked at him, confused.

"Where is it you're to go?"

"I must visit with Mr. Chisum. Alex and I are preparing to make our way there shortly."

"Why haven't you mentioned this before now?" I wondered.

"These things come up, Elucia. Alex and I only realized this morning that we must make an emergency meeting. We're subject to many hurdles here."

I nodded, pretending to understand.

"I see. I only was not expecting news of a sudden departure," I said, acting as though I was sorry he must go.

"We will be back before you know it. And you will have your companion, after all," he said, smiling.

John now referred to William fondly as my "companion". He had put his complete faith in him and this pleased me greatly. However, my private friendship with William was consigned only to the open grounds on which we were assigned as it was considered inappropriate otherwise. In public, he was only to accompany me about town.


I found him sitting alone on the porch outside of the McSween's.

"William?"

Slightly startled, he looked up at me.

"Would you care to come inside with me? Colleen is down with a headache, and everyone else went into town for supplies. I thought maybe you could keep company with me."

He smiled and shyly nodded, as though he seemed a bit uncertain.

Once inside, I asked him if he would like some tea, and when he replied that he would, I directed him to the parlor and excused myself in order to put the kettle on. When the kettle whistled I prepared and brought in a tray of refreshments, placing it down upon the table. I then moved to sit down alongside him. After pouring us both a cup, I picked up my needlepoint and began stitching. We were awkward but polite together. As he picked up his saucer and raised the teacup to his lips I asked him to tell me where he was from, interested in wanting to know him.

"A few places. I guess at this point you could say I'm from Silver City."

"Is your family still there?"

He placed the cup back upon the saucer and lowered his eyes to it, wearing a sad, semi-smile. Quietly, he replied, "No. My mother passed away when I was fourteen, and my step-father went to Arizona. I have a brother, but I don't see him."

He looked at me with those doe-eyed blues of his, a fleeting sadness within them. My heart instantly went to him.

"I'm sorry," I offered, "I didn't mean to pry."

"It's okay," he assured me, "it was a few years ago. I've gotten used to it."

I smiled at that.

"You're from New York?" he asked.

"I am. How did you come to know this?"

"I heard it around. I was born in New York."

"Oh? Which part?"

"I'm not sure. The poor part, I'd think."

I chuckled at his frankness, clearly meant to diffuse the tension, and said, "I'm from the borough of Manhattan, the north side."

"What is that?"

I smiled sweetly at him and replied, "It's a very wealthy area of New York."

We became quiet for a few moments.

"Do you read, William?"

"You mean *can* I read."

He grinned at his own jest and I returned the smile, impressed by his cleverness in catching my true curiosity. I appreciated his good humor despite the obvious insult, though I did not mean it as such.

"Yes," I contritely replied.

"I love to read. I used to spend all of my time reading."

"Used to?"

"Well, I haven't exactly had as much time on my hands as I once did. My life hasn't been as carefree as those days."

We grew quiet again and I took the opportunity to busy myself with my cup of tea, taking a sip while thinking of other topics to discuss. I thought to ask him which works he liked to read when, suddenly, I blurted, "It must be awfully dull having to stay here with me—"

"It's okay," he enthusiastically interrupted, "I mean…I'm flattered that John would trust me with you—to stay with you."

I smiled, appreciating his uninhibited admission.

"It's like I told you; he's very impressed with you," was my reply.

"Yeah?"

I nodded and added, "I suppose that it *is* remarkable, given that you have only been with him for such a short while."

It was clear that he was pleased.

"Yeah…I guess so," he humbly replied.

Once again, silence had set in. I placed my cup and saucer back down on the tray and I stood, taking my needlepoint from my lap and laying it upon the arm of the sofa. I asked if he would please excuse me for a moment. He nodded, put his cup down, and respectively stood as I left the parlor to go to my room where I located my copy of The Adventures of Tom Sawyer. I brought it back with me and offered it to him.

"It's one of my favorite books," I confided, "I feel you might enjoy it as well."

Like an obedient child he said, "Okay. If you think so, I guess I will."

He placed the book on his lap and rested his hands atop it as he smiled grandly at me, making no attempt in hiding how desperately he wanted to please me. His devotion felled me irrevocably.

It was this very moment when my love for the boy formally began. Despite his meager background it had become apparent that he embodied all that I had wished for in a husband. He was easygoing with a natural sense of humor, and he was easy on the eyes, having such a lively appearance highlighted by those beautiful blue eyes and the near permanent smile he retained. I adored his bright expressions; the way he loved to laugh, the way he smiled when he looked at me, and how his blue eyes caught and reflected the light. I especially enjoyed the way he focused his attention on me, unlike John. He was certainly a happy and welcome diversion.

I would often find William as I did that very first day we met, staring at me then looking away, reticent and bashful when I would meet his gaze. I found him hopelessly endearing and became firmly attached to him. I was not used to men treating me as though I was something to be revered. The men of my social class did not necessarily find me exceptional as they were constantly surrounded by women of my financial position and therefore expected nothing less than perfection. They were pompous and arrogant, concerned only with which woman made a proper match for financial reasons rather than considering the woman herself. The women of my class were not all that different from the men as they knew they must fulfill their duty towards their families and equally choose a proper match. But like me, most of them wanted to be courted. They wanted to be flattered and enticed, and to swoon from overwhelming love. In that world it was a rare thing to court a man who made one feel cherished.

But here was William, who seemed to admire me. It was as if my prayers had been partially answered. Certainly, it was not a perfect situation, but neither was John. And I could make do. I would take my happiness and accept it as it is. I would appreciate and make it work to my advantage. As long as he stayed close I would scheme to have my cake and eat it, too. I would fulfill my duty to my family and still satisfy my own wants and desires through having him.

Soon we fell into an easy cadence and spent the rest of the morning in uninterrupted conversation with one another, seeming to never run out of things to talk about. He spoke to me of his family, how his father died before he was born, his step-father's indifference to him and his brother after the death of his mother, subsequently abandoning them. He explained how he was turned out as a result of this and left to fend for himself at the young age of fourteen. He told me how he had gotten into a small scrape in Silver City and left for Arizona to seek help from his step-father who claimed that he wanted nothing to do with a troublemaker for a son, refusing to care for such a boy who would shamelessly destroy his name.

Though at first he understandably exhibited trepidation in telling me these things, he finally managed to trust me enough as it was clear I had only sympathy for him as opposed to condemnation. I accepted him rather than recoil from him. This encouraged him to grow bold enough to confide in me his stint with the outlaw band known as The Boys, an outfit I had incidentally heard off. They were a vicious group; I had heard plenty of horrifying stories. I had a hard time reconciling this agreeable, respectable youth with such boyish looks as being part of such a gang. This was no hardened criminal before me. Sitting here with him, I could only think of him as gentle.

William explained his reasons of association, assuring me that he took up with them because it was the best option for him at the time. He not only needed the protection they could provide him, but the surrogate family he found in them. He made no excuses for himself, admitting that he had done things he was not proud of, and he expressed that, due to the ferocity of the gang, he was only too happy to beg John that he please give him an opportunity to start over and have a chance at a normal, decent life. He did, however, express some gratitude to The Boys for taking him in, nonetheless. If they had not, he was uncertain what may have happened otherwise. He admitted that he knew he did not belong with such a band of brothers—that they were a means to an end, and so he took the first chance that came his way to get out, and that was John. He admitted, too, that Jesse Evans, the leader of the gang, harbored bad blood against him, making it all the more necessary for him to find a way out.

After explaining all of this to me, a contemplative quietness seeped in and enveloped him. William looked as though there was something on his mind but seemed unsure of whether or not to confess his thoughts. However, I could honestly say that, so at ease was I with this boy, and so much trust did I have for him already, that I felt it would have been impossible for him to say anything that would have caused an adverse reaction on my part against him. I was not a simple girl, and I knew without his telling me that he must have been involved in some less than respectable deeds. In addition, my living here in Lincoln County and being subjected to, for the past three months, the horror of prejudice and injustice that ran rampant as the way of life here, I was certain that any negative thing about himself that he could confide in me would seem par for the course. And the simple fact was, whatever he could have possibly done would have been outshone by the decent boy I had come to know him to be.

"What is it, William? Please…you can tell me."

He looked at me, studying my face. Finally, he decided to own up and divulge the secret he was too ashamed to speak aloud.

"I killed a man."

With great unintentional horror I looked at him. It was an admission I was not expecting, though it did not cause me to fear him.

He read the look on my face and I watched his expression change to regret. Quickly, I reached out and placed my hand upon his shoulder to reassure him.

"Go on William…please. You've only surprised me. I promise you I won't hold any of what you might say against you."

He looked at me, assessing my face again, wondering if he could indeed trust me.

"He was coming down on me pretty hard. He had forced me to the ground, held me there by the weight of him. He struck me despite my protests—I begged him to stop."

His face was fixed in a look of recollection, and I wondered to him, "Why would someone do such a thing?"

He looked at me keenly, "He was a real obnoxious sort, a real son of a bitch—he was big, too! Mean…"

He looked down and surveyed himself to emphasize for me the slightness of his build so that I could imagine this giant of a man bearing down on someone like him. Chuckling awkwardly, he added, "As you can picture, the fight wasn't very fair. I had been minding my own business. One minute I was standing at the bar, the next minute I was flat on the ground."

So struck was I by this tale that I shamelessly blurted out, "How did it happen? How did you kill him?"

I realized my error, although too late, and felt my face burn in embarrassment due to the crudeness of my enthusiasm.

Undaunted by my impolite and ill-mannered behavior, he impassively explained, "I had found work as a farmhand in Arizona. After my father had turned me away and refused me help, I began trying to make my own way. But before leaving my father's lodging, I went through his things and found his six-shooter put away in a closet in the room he occupied."

This detail of his life caused my heart to break for him. I surprised myself by feeling ever more determined to remain by this fair stranger's side as someone he could rely on. In my mind, there was just something about him—something that told me to "hold on".

"I took whatever money I could find and I got out of there right quick." He spoke to the room as though he were lost in thought. "Once I found work I was able to buy my own guns and some new clothes. I dressed as respectably as I could. I tried to make a straight go of it, but I don't think it was in the cards for me. I wish I could say that my waywardness ended there, but, not having a horse, I stole one. It turned out to be the property of the U.S. Military, and, well, they caught me up and I was put in the stockade."

"Again?"

He laughed at my wide-eyed, childlike exuberance.

"Yeah…" he nodded, as he continued to laugh, "but I escaped. Funny, though, how they found me. A friend and I were having breakfast when the sheriff came in pretending to wait on us, not wanting to spook us into running."

I laughed harder at the thought of this charade.

"The first time I caught trouble I was in Silver City. A real trouble maker I knew, went by the name Sombrero Jack, he stole some clothes from a laundry and asked me to hide them in my room at a boarding house that I had hired. I worked there, and I worked hard, so my room, board, and meals were free. I was able to save whatever money I made because of this; it wasn't too bad of a set-up. I didn't think it was such a big deal, hiding those clothes. After all, *I* didn't lift them. For my favor he offered to let me keep some of them for myself and I jumped at the chance to have some new clothes."

What must it be like to be in such dire straits that the promise of used clothing could appeal to one?

"I was so thrilled at the thought of having new clothes that I ignored them being stolen. I didn't think much on it."

Demonstratively, I replaced my hand upon him, this time on his forearm, letting him understand that he was in the presence of a friend who would not judge him on his past, no matter how adverse it may be. That was then, and this was now. I understood that nature had played this boy as a wicked instrument, but I would be sure to guide him and keep him on the straight and narrow. I would make him my personal crusade and pet-project.

"And so what about that man you killed?" I asked.

"Oh, that…"

He took a moment to consider and choose his words. "Well, having me pinned to the ground, beating on me, I managed to wrench one arm free, reached for my gun and pulled the trigger."

"You shot him?"

He looked to me, grinning. "Got him off me, didn't it?"

I looked down and nodded slightly, moving my hand down his arm to place it over his hand which still lay upon the book I had lent him. I was struck by how warm it was and how his skin felt against the palm of my own hand.

He shook his head absently. "It wasn't my intention, killing him," he looked at me, searching my face to see if I believed him, "I only wanted it to stop."

"Then what?"

"I got the hell out of there. I met The Boys and wound up here. So here I am."

He smiled matter-of-factly.

We heard a commotion at the front door. Susan and the others had come back. It was nearly late afternoon and dinner would soon be served.

He stood, preparing to leave, but I hurriedly stopped him.

"William, stay."

It was all I wanted, for him to say, but I realized my eagerness for his company was audacious and so I hastily followed it with, "For dinner."

"Oh, no… I don't want to impose. I don't think I should. I don't think they would like—"

"Of course you should! You are not an imposition! Are you not my friend and guest and also my pupil and teacher? Etiquette compels me to extend the invitation, and to refuse it would be to insult me. You are my constant companion; this puts you in a prestigious position," I smiled up at him and he smiled back.

He nodded, and then sat back down next to me.

"And will we begin again tomorrow? My lesson, I mean," I asked.

"If it's what you want. At one o'clock."


It was 12:45 p.m. in the afternoon and I was so very anxious at the thought of seeing William after sharing the confident intimacies and easy familiarity of yesterday, yet I worried that he would not come. His flirtations of yesterday may have been imagined; a desire culminated in my head as my desperation for a great romance grew in the face of a disappointing nuptial binding. To remain calm I reminded myself that it was worthless to think about this boy. His societal standing was by far beneath my own and, therefore, I should think of him no further than the hired help that he was. Still, my heart did not seem to know the difference, or for that matter, care, and my stomach would not untie its knots.

He rode in from the fields with a boy not much older than himself, Quinn, who had been christened "Minxie" because of his surname, Minx. Minxie had come here with his family from Manchester and spoke in a low-end British accent, an attribute that drew attention as his regional tongue sounded odd and interesting among the men, especially to William as it amused him. It was strange to imagine him coming abroad from the same land as John but sounding so completely different. It was easy to differentiate how polished John's speech was when one compared it with Minxie's own accent.

They dismounted and William leaned against a post by the barn, taking a pull from his canteen and wiping the sweat from his brow with the back of his hand. He spied Lucy standing, or more precisely, gracefully pacing along the back porch. He stared at her, thinking on her perfection. She wore a gown of a light brownish color with a matching hat and plumes; her abundant golden locks curled and swept up impeccably. She reminded him of royalty. Her clothes were so fine, her face unadulterated, unfettered by labor in the sun. Her skin was as if it was made of delicate porcelain and this had captivated him along with the way her gold spun hair accented this feature. She was lovely. He thought of her much today, though he felt as though that, even in only thinking of her, he was wrong to do so, she being so far above him, and his employer's bride at that. He was a fool; he knew his place.

Suddenly, he felt a push from his left side that jolted him from his reverie and, in his native Cockney, Minxie warned him.

"Don't even fink about it, mate."

"About what?"

"'er," *Her*. Minxie lifted his chin to indicate Lucy.

Billy laughed it off.

"I don't know what you're talking about."

"Hell ya don't! I know that look. Most of the bloody men have it when she's 'round, but most of them have been here long enough to know better. Don't fin' I don't know what you're finkin'. You're quite obvious. That alone is nervy."

"You're imagining things. I'm simply looking in her direction. I'm taking her down for targeting in a few."

"Bollocks! C'mon Billy. Lay off 'er. She's your boss's fiancée for Christ's sake! There're plenty of other women in town who I'm sure you'll have no trouble in gainin' the attentions of. Ya make me nervous as I have spent all of five hours wif ya and yet somethin' tells me you'll go for what ya want."

Billy only grinned playfully. He reiterated, "I was just looking in her direction, Minxie. As for those other women in town, the mere sight of her ruins a man for the likes of them," he winked.

Minxie didn't smile and looked him over cautiously.

"You can't tell me you see a beauty like that and easily forget it," Billy challenged.

"I can tell ya I'd forget it right fast if it were the goddamned boss's wife!"

At that moment Lucy turned their way and noticed them standing there. She waved and both boys waved back. Gesturing to Billy, she indicated to him that she wanted him to come over to where she stood, which he happily did.

With a sly grin on his face he looked at Minxie.

"Well…see ya, Quinn Minx. The boss's wife is calling me over."

As he walked away he looked back and smiled mischievously at Minxie, who stared back with a wary expression betrayed by his own slight smile.


As Billy approached Lucy her smile widened, which in turn caused him to smile even more from sheer elation. He removed his hat.

"William! Would you mind if we sat together today? We can talk about the book I have lent you."

Billy tried to keep himself in check, but still he smiled with pronounced interest.

"Of course, if you'd rather we did that than practice targets."

They smiled timidly at one another and tried to meet one another's eyes. Minxie had him figured all right. He'd have to watch himself.

"I *would* prefer it! And as you can see, I have not dressed for a day in the fields. Have you been able to do much reading?"

"As a matter-of-fact, I have. I read it when I lay in bed at night."

"I had thought to lend it to you because I considered the protagonist, Tom Sawyer, as being very similar to you. He has many adventures!"

So she thought of him, then. This was an amusing surprise. He had also noticed she said this with an air of awe. He thought back to his own adventures and didn't picture them quite like she must have. Maybe at the outset there were similarities, but his world was much uglier, darker by comparison. Either way, he'd be happy to give in to her imagination.

"Well, adventures I've certainly had. But I don't think they'd be suitable for a woman such as you to read about."

She smiled widely at the intimate understanding that lie between them on this subject, and then her expression seemed to change. Instead of idly discussing the contents of the story, she decided, ultimately, that she *would* rather see him in his element.

"I think I would like to have you teach me today after all. Would you mind taking me back to the McSweens'? I'll need to change into my riding clothes. You can take me there in the buggy, and then you could come back here to get your horse. Mine ought to be ready by then."

Up close she looked positively grand, and he could breathe in her scent which he found affecting. He often had much on his mind, and Lucy was part of the amalgams running through it. But today he could focus solely on her. He was looking forward to the couple of hours they would spend together. He wanted to know her more.

"Whatever you want," was his reply.

○○○

I saw him ride towards me while I stood outside the McSweens' barn waiting for their farmhand to finish adjusting my saddle. He was a Mexican and I did not pay him much attention.

For my trip out west, I had two identical riding outfits that had been specially tailored for me in England so that I could sit astride during a hunt. I usually wore the black suede jacket with the dark cornflower suede lapels and matching dark cornflower wool mackinaw vest with the tight fitting black wool, pinstriped pants, which completed the outfit. Incidentally, it was my favorite between the two, but it was at the laundry as I wore it often. Today it was the light sepia brown suede jacket with dark red suede lapels and dark red mackinaw vest. The fitted riding pants were of an ochra brown. It wasn't such a terrible fashion, I admit, though I would have preferred to wear the black as it looked considerably more fetching on me, but it was of no matter. At this moment my thoughts were turned to William as I watched him walk his horse towards me.

"Howdy", he said while lifting his hat.

I responded by curtsying playfully.

"I'm only just waiting for my saddle to be fitted," I informed him.

He walked into the barn and watched the saddle being strapped.

"La correa en ese caballo es demasiado apretado," said William.

*(The strap on that horse is too tight.)*

The Mexican replied, "No, señor, se ajusta el caballo!"

*(No, sir, it's adjusted to the horse.)*

"Ella es incómodo. ¿No te das cuenta?"

*(Can't you see she's uncomfortable?)*

I watched William, amazed. He could speak to these people? I wondered what the problem was.

William walked towards the Mexican hand, "Dar la caballo aquí, para mí. Yo lo hebilla!

*(Give the horse to me. I'll handle it.)*

The Mexican relinquished the strap and William loosened and re-strapped it.

The Mexican walked away mumbling in Spanish as William made the adjustments.

"What was that all about?" I wondered aloud.

"He was girthing this saddle too tight. The horse will become difficult; she'd have no room to breathe comfortably. Her agitated disposition should have made it obvious she wasn't happy, but he just kept tightening it on up. The horse could buck you right off! Where'd they get that guy anyway?"

"I don't know. I don't know him."

"You have a man doing things for you and you don't know anything about him? Not even his name?"

That seemed about right, so I nodded.

He laughed in disbelief.

"What?"

He shook his head. "Nothing."

He waited for my horse to fill up her lungs before tightening the buckle to allow her comfort and breathing room.

"What was it he said when he walked away?" I asked.

He looked at me suspiciously, as if he shouldn't relay this information, but then he seemed to relent, deciding that he could tell me without insult.

"He was muttering something about goddamned gringos who know everything… something to that effect. I don't know. I really wasn't paying attention."

"How is it you've come to speak Spanish?"

"Spent a lot of my time with them growing up. Still do. I admire and respect them, the Mexican population—I consider myself one of them."

"Why?"

He looked at me and cocked an eyebrow, patted my horse, then leaned against her.

"Tell me why you like the Mexican population," I said.

"Why? Does it surprise you?"

"A little. They're *Mexicans*."

"Yeah, well, Mexicans are people, too."

His statement bore a sharp edge and suddenly I felt an anxious desire to make an effort to correct the violation. I was unaccustomed to concerning myself over how I affected those beneath me, but William was different. I found myself wanting to please him.

"Yes, I understand. Maybe you could enlighten me," I proposed.

He laughed lightly. "Me? Enlighten you? Your Majesty, you must be joking."

"Well, yes. Clearly I've missed the point of the Mexican people and have offended you. Why don't you share with me why it is they should be respected so?"

"Shouldn't all people be respected?"

I thought on this and answered him honestly. "No."

He laughed at my candor.

"There are people I am acquainted with who are nothing but shallow and selfish. I do not respect them much," I explained.

"Yeah, well…I guess exceptions are allowed. Here, let me help you up." He offered me his hand. "Your mare got a name?"

"Of course she does."

I gave him a peculiar look in regard to what I considered a strange question. He looked back at me as he waited on the answer.

"Viola," I said, finally.

He nodded, entertained. "You named your horse like she was a lady? Why do that?"

"Have you ever seen the play Twelfth Night? By William Shakespeare?" I asked.

"No."

"Oh, it's wonderful! One of my very favorites! Its protagonist is Viola, an aristocratic castaway in a new land who must disguise herself as a man, putting on pretenses to make her own way in the world. It's a very fascinating play, I assure you. And she speaks French, as I do."

"You speak French?"

"Yes. And German, as does John."

"But not Spanish?"

"Of course not."

"Why do you say it like that?"

"There is no such use for me to know such a lowly language," I said instinctively, my words full of disdain. Immediately I was sorry, as I had promptly offended him once again.

"You think so, huh?"

The acerbic tone of his voice was unmistakable—he was vexed.

I checked myself this time before responding, and as politely as I could I asked, "What makes you wonder so? That it should be silly for me not to speak Spanish?"

"Well, you're in New Mexico, darlin'. Most of the people here speak Spanish."

"Oh, I see. Well then, that is something else I have you for as well."

I gave him such a charming smile that he had no choice but to let his guard down, chuckling despite his previous impatience with me. I changed the subject back to our prior conversation.

"So, you must see the play. Perhaps the theatre will hold a review."

He laughed emphatically. "Theatre? There ain't any theatre any place near the likes of Lincoln County, but I think I can take you at your word that it's a good show. Okay, then, let's head out of here."

With William's help I sat atop Viola. After he had mounted his own horse I said, "Isn't."

"Come again?"

"It's 'isn't', as in 'is not'. You said 'ain't'."

"Well now, I guess that's what I have *you* for then, *isn't* it?"

He returned the same charming smile I had given him moments before, and at this it was my turn to laugh with delight.

As we began to ride he turned to me and said, "There's something I want you to do for me."

I looked him over warily, wondering if he had a presumptuous, imposing proposition.

"What is it?" I asked, cautiously.

"Call me Billy."

"You don't prefer William?"

He smiled to himself and replied, "Darlin', you could call me anything you like and it'd sound just as sweet coming from your lips, but all the same, my friends call me Billy."

I nodded so that he understood I respected his request, but my cheeks flushed hot at his flirtatiousness.

He led us to the empty horse ring where we always practiced; John used this ring to break in new horses. My horse followed his and when he stopped he dismounted and, like a true gentleman, assisted me down from my mount. I watched him walk to the far opposite side from where we stopped, which was *much* further than usual, and saw him set out the bottles we would use as targets.

When he walked back to me he said, "Here, give me your gun."

He held out his hand and I removed the revolver slung on my left hip out of its scabbard and handed it to him. He studied it, turning it over and over in his hands. Watching him caress that pistol so fondly and carefully caused me such sinful thoughts. I began to wonder what his hands would feel like if it were me he was stroking. My thoughts were unbearably intense as I watched the way his hands slid effortlessly over the smooth metal of the firearm, and I had to tear myself away from those thoughts immediately—I should not think of such things. And though I knew I was being irrational and foolish, I forced myself to look into Billy's face to ensure that he could not have guessed what had gone through my mind. I was embarrassed by the mere thought that he could read my mind and come to know my wicked feelings, and so full of anxiety was I over this invented concept that when he clicked open the chamber it jolted me and I snapped-to when he spoke.

"They show you how to clean these things?"

I shook my head, my cheeks burning.

"You need to learn. If you don't, these Schofields won't do you much good eventually."

He looked at me oddly. "You okay?"

I nodded, rapid and silent.

"You sure? You're looking a little flushed."

I looked down and shrugged.

"How'd somebody like you come to have these things anyway?" he asked.

Still unable to look directly at him, I looked at my boots when I answered.

"John gave them to me as a gift. I thought it peculiar."

"Well, you are in the west. Maybe he was being... what's the word?"

"Allegorical?"

He stared at me silently a moment and furrowed his brow, not understanding the word. "Yeah, sure, that'll do. Either way, they're fine-looking, decent guns. Looks like he spent a pretty penny. Even got a horseshoe inlay right here on the handle—for good luck, I bet. I thought you said you ain't Irish."

"Aren't," I corrected. "And no, I am an Englishwoman," I said rather proudly.

He looked back at the gun. "This is an awful lot of gun for a girl to handle, especially one of your size."

"I'm not sure John truly meant for me to use those, but I handle it okay."

"It? I notice you got two there. What's the other for? Decoration?"

I looked down at the gun slung on my right hip, then looked at him, smirking at the joke.

"I am not so terribly good with this one. In any event, it evens it out so I don't appear lopsided." I smiled at my own simple joke, but he didn't appear entertained.

In fact, his light eyes darkened, taking on a shade of impatience. He handed me back my gun and I put it in its holster.

"I didn't mean to upset you so—"

"Lucy, I don't consider something like this a joke. You need to know how to use both of them pistols. John may have given you a present of these guns in jest, which, to be honest, makes me consider him a fool, and they look ridiculous on you, but it's apparent that he wants you to learn how to use them. You should take this as seriously as I do. Take out the left gun."

I did as he told me.

"We're going to use just this one today. See that green bottle there, in the middle of the two brown?"

I nodded.

"Fire at it."

"It's too far away and too small"

"Fine. Hit the green bottle with your right gun."

"I told you, I don't think I can." I placed my left gun back on my belt.

"Then you shouldn't get to have guns like the ones you got if you don't know how to use them and don't want to bother to learn! Guns like them belong to someone who intends to use them properly!"

His tone was serious. This was a different Billy—one that I had displeased, and this disturbed me as I sought terribly to gratify him. His disposition had become severe so suddenly and I quickly lost any quixotic thoughts I had in favor of concentrating on my desire to please him. He no longer seemed at ease, and all traces of his good humor appeared gone, and though I wanted to do as he bid me I hesitated. He leaned down and looked me in the eyes acutely. I couldn't help but notice the flecks of white in his irises as they were picked up by the sun.

"Lucy," he said, his voice ominous, "skin that expensive accessory and use it like I tell you too. Now! Pony up!"

I couldn't help but stare back at him before moving. He was making me nervous.

"Quit looking and shoot that goddamned pistol!"

I turned and pulled the gun back out of its holster. I held it at full arm's length and tried to sight the barrel. He looked at me.

"Open both your eyes."

I turned to him. "What?"

"Your right eye is shut. If you want to learn to properly shoot then open both your eyes. No gunfighter worth his salt shoots with one eye closed unless he's missing one. Excepting certain circumstances, most can't draw a bead in the time it takes to sight an object in a fight. There isn't any time to aim! That's what the rifle is for! Long range shots where you sight your target."

"Draw a bead?"

"Aim, Lucy! The bottle! Draw a bead on that bottle with your gun and fire!"

I still stood there, stupidly.

Losing his patience he said, "Sight the goddamned bottle and pull the goddamned trigger!"

I did as he told me. I was so nervous the kick-back bucked my hand and I missed completely. I looked at him, slightly terrified. What would he say now that I've missed it outright?

"That's what I thought" was all he said.

When he looked at me again, the seriousness disappeared and was replaced by a countenance that was sweet and tolerant. He looked into my eyes again and placed both of his hands upon my upper arms, wrapping his fingers around them as far as they would go.

"Lucy," he began softly, "these aren't for show. They're not adornments. They're not baubles. One of the truths out here is you can always tell a man who goes heels but doesn't know how to use them. He's the loudest mouth in the crowd and he usually winds up bucked out in smoke. It's an insult to those of us who know how to use iron and make it count when we fire them. You're wearing very serious weapons around your waist and you ought to know how to use them both. Otherwise, you're just a fraud. I want to show you proper. But I won't stand here and argufy with you. Do you want me to show you?"

I nodded obediently and listened to every word he'd said. I was delving further beneath the surface of who this boy really was. My previous considerations of him not having the wherewithal to be any kind of man to be trifled with were quickly altered.

Before I knew it, he'd pulled his right gun and blew the bottle off the post. It happened so fast that it had shaken me. I put my hand to my heart in an attempt to still it and stared in awe at the place the bottle had been. I then looked at him and gave him a wide smile with a matching wide-eyed stare. He grinned back, and before I realized it, he pulled his other gun with his left hand and shot the rest of the bottles off of their posts.

I was utterly mystified by the sensation coursing throughout my veins, and even more confused at feeling what could only be an awakening of lust. I was hanging in the balance, believing that searching out an attraction to a man with wealth and the right breeding seemed dull. This man was…no, he was a boy. But it was of no matter—it wasn't of any consequence how I should think of him because I could not even begin to reconcile how to conceive of him yet. I only felt the excitement he instilled in me. I knew my feelings were primitive at best, and that I should ignore and overlook them, but how could one forget the body's basic needs when they are screaming from within every corpuscle? He may not have been a gentleman, but even better it was as though he were a sentry—a protector. He would watch out for me, and I liked that better. I began to feel truly safe for the first time in Lincoln.

When my admiration had ebbed enough I found him staring out across the ring where the bottles had been, gun in his hand still smoking.

"That was my left hand, Lucy."

"I—I know it." I stuttered. I had lost my ability to speak articulately, unaware that I was still staring at his face and admiring him.

"You're wearing two guns. Out there," he pointed out to nowhere in particular, "if a man sees you strapped like that, then he's gonna expect that you know how to use what you have. It's no use arguing with me over how far the target is. Next time, shoot when I tell you to. What the hell have I been teaching you out here? Cause I know them boys ain't been teaching you a goddamned thing."

He turned away from me, put his gun away and placed his hands on his hips. He shook his head as he looked up and mumbled something. Then he turned to face me.

"How do you know how to shoot like that?" I asked.

He only stared at me, then looked off somewhere to the side as if in contemplation. He stepped away a very short distance.

"Billy?"

I walked and stood near him, placing my hand on his arm. He turned to look at me.

"Lucy, you wouldn't understand what it's like for me. You're all "Your Grace" and whatnot, but I'm a scavenger. I wouldn't have meant to be but I didn't have much choice in the matter." He grew quiet and looked down. In a near whisper he said, "I don't want to talk about this again with you. Not right now."

I looked down and somberly replied, "There is no need; I remember well what you have already said."

Unamused, he stared at me, and I then felt the need to reassure him. "I will never repeat anything you have said to me in confidence."

He smiled slightly and stood matter-of-factly, hooking both thumbs in his gun belt and jutting his right hip before light-heartedly responding, "I haven't led a very respectable life for the past three years and I don't want to relive it now. I want to head someplace else in my life, make something right of myself. That's probably all you need to know from now on."

At this, I sighed rather audibly and shook my head. I turned from him and sat down on the grass.

He lowered himself next to me, resting on his haunches and clasping both of his hands before him.

"What is it?" he asked.

His question surprised me. I've never known a man to be concerned with my feelings after he had spoken so firmly; a man so honest and careful. The men I knew always passed my frustrations off as women's issues and unimportant, but Billy showed me thoughtfulness. His actions were unexpected. He made me falter at every turn.

"Men. That's what. Men."

He laughed but it was sympathetic.

"Yeah…we're a real bitch. Get it?" Then he laughed again like he did earlier, only not as heartily. He was trying to lighten the mood, make me feel better.

I looked to him without amusement.

"Okay, what about us men?" he asked.

My comfort with him was such that I thought nothing of offering my thoughts on a subject which would be improper otherwise. Women did not complain to men, especially when the complaint involved their own gender.

"Men think we are delicate. It is as though they believe we will shatter upon hear-ing anything disagreeable. They believe we ought to be kept in the dark and hidden away from the ways of the world, though not all women need to be in the protection of men this way. We can handle more than you realize." I sighed. "Bearing that in mind, it is a sick idea, then, to give me a present of guns! Why bother? If trouble should arise, the men can shut us out before the killing rampages commence, coming to our rescue. Perhaps they can pretend it isn't happening so that we will not notice."

I put my head down and heard him chuckle. I turned and looked at him in earnest. "If we're to be shielded from such things, why then should my father have had me practice with a rifle, and John give me a pair of guns—with an insignia of luck no less!" I thought a moment and then went on. "Did you know that plenty of women have not only ridden into battle, but have lead it? Princess Isabella of France, for instance. And the Indian princess Rani Lakshmi Bai—"

"Who?"

"—who brought her child to war. And of course St. Joan, everyone knows that! And there are plenty more!"

Billy stared at me curiously. "Okay. I imagine that a woman like you, you'd be kept in the dark. And you're right; a present of guns is a strange decision if they want you to stay ignorant. But I know plenty of women out here who can hold their own. The thing is, Lucy, they're not so innocent as you are. Many of them are coarse and lead rough lives. Most times they need to know how to handle a rifle to help protect their land."

I tilted my head thoughtfully and looked at him as he went on.

"There are plenty of California widows around, and so they know a thing or two about picking up a shotgun. But the women I mean to refer to? They're…hard. You're very refined and elegant, and…well, I wouldn't want to ruin you with the awful truth either." He gave a slight smile. "The sight of you dressed like that with those side arms seems peculiar."

I smiled at that, but still I scoffed. "What's a 'California Widow'?" I asked.

He laughed but ignored the question. "I've seen the wealthy Mexicans plenty, but as far as eastern white women like you? You're the first. And you're certainly the first to pay any attention to someone like me. Someone like you, paying any attention to me—just sitting here with me now, making time for me, wanting to get to know me—it's unsettling, to tell the truth. I've had girls interested in me, but interested with me? And trying to understand me? That's new."

"Unsettling?"

"Maybe that's the wrong word. It's strange to me."

"Then it's too bad you don't see yourself as I do. If you could, it would not prove too daunting to imagine why I might like you as I do." He smiled at me and I continued, "I find you remarkable. And it just so happens that, in the very short time I've known you, I find I want to know about you all the more. Some people are like that, no matter their background. And I'll tell you something else…I've been out here since August, and you're the first person I've connected with. If you only knew how miserable I was before you came! I hadn't any friends but Colleen. Overnight it changed for me. I found someone that kept my interest—"

I stopped myself, embarrassed. I had revealed too much—I'd been too honest with him and it upset me to wonder what he must think of me! And if others should know how I had dispensed of my personal feelings so wantonly, admitting my admiration to the very object of my affection so informally, it would be decided that I was shameful and possessed such shallow dignity! But like a true gentleman, he allowed the slip of my tongue to go by without mention.

I rolled onto my side, bending my knees and propping myself up with my right arm, hoping that he would not think less of me due to this lax behavior of mine. But even as I thought this I could not stop myself—I was far too comfortable with him.

"Women are stronger than men think we are. I think I can handle knowing of your past. After the things you have told me already, I would think you would understand that."

Billy was to my right and now sitting upon the grass as well. He grinned widely, "You make a very good argument. All right…" he relaxed and made himself comfortable, leaning back and propped up by his elbows, "I'll talk to you. But you have to promise me you keep it between us," he looked at me solemnly yet playfully, tantalized by our sharing of secrets.

I nodded, "You know it is. Strictly between us, I cross my heart." For dramatic effect, I crisscrossed my heart with my finger. "I should like to know everything about you, no matter what; I'm fascinated!" I widened my eyes and smiled devilishly.

He looked at me with the strangest expression; I could not read it. I think perhaps he was thinking on what it was I had just said, the faintest smile gracing his lips.

"I'm not used to anybody caring enough about me to want to know anything."

I rolled onto my stomach and ran my hand over the grass. "You should become accustomed to it—if we're to be friends. It's necessary to know as much about one another as possible, and you should know it is immaterial to me, the things you have done once upon a time.

I sat up again and, leaning on him, wrapped my arms around his and affectionately placed my head upon his shoulder.

"You know, they used to call me 'Henry'?" he admitted.

I lifted my head, "No! You haven't always been Billy?"

"Sure I've always been Billy, but my step-father's name was William, so they took to calling me by my middle name, Henry. Henry Antrim."

"I know that name, 'Antrim'."

He stared at the grass and asked, "Yeah?"

"Yes! Of course! Kid Antrim! That must be you! And you stole our horses with that gang of men! Oh…there wasn't much in the paper about you but isn't it funny?"

"How so?"

"I'd read the little bits of information they'd post about you, a young boy. I thought it a thrill! I imagined you to be this romantic, swashbuckling figure living a life of adventure!"

Billy laughed whole-heartedly at my naiveté. "Swashbuckling?"

I looked up and batted my eyes at him melodramatically as I placed a hand over my heart and feigned a swoon.

"Of course," I breathed. "What else is a girl to do? I imagined that you'd come along and steal me away."

This made him laugh harder. "It never seemed like any adventure. When my mother died the only family I had ever known was gone. Then I was on my own just trying to survive."

"Whatever happened to that Jack person?" I asked. "The one you had told me about."

"Sombrero Jack?"

"Yes! That's him!"

"He took off, so the sheriff put me in jail to hold me over night. I was terrified of what would happen to me, so I climbed up and out of the chimney, looking black as coal when I come out."

"You've been in jail three times! And you escaped through the chimney?" I was wide-eyed and absolutely beside myself.

"Yep." He seemed completely at ease now. My fascination seemed to amuse him.

"I was scared as hell and wanted the fastest way outta there, so I scurried on up there." He pointed his finger toward the sky and made an upward spiraling motion as he said this, "My only way out."

A rebellious laugh escaped me, which in turn made him grin.

"You are an adventurer, all right. You truly are!"

"I wasn't always like this. Once upon a time my mother and step-father owned land. Not much, but as far as frontier life goes, we were doing quite well. My mother had her own laundry service—the City Laundry. It got a real nice write-up in the paper and everything," he beamed.

He looked at me, but I remained quiet, waiting for him to continue.

"This was in Wichita, Kansas. Our land was filled with fruit trees that we had planted. My brother and I would pick and eat the plumbs that grew. They had purchased other tracts of land," he trailed off.

He became thoughtful and I left him to his mind, not wanting to utter a word.

"My mother saw to it that me and my brother could read and write and figure out numbers. We didn't go to school until we made it to Silver City. But a heavy rain caused the mud roof of the school house to collapse."

"I could tell you were educated, Billy!" I smiled and propped my chin in my hands, infatuated.

"Better than most around these parts, anyway."

He pulled at the grass around him and shook his head regretfully before blurting, "I bragged about killing that man." He looked at me soberly. "I had to. That's how I got in with The Boys. Killing a man gave them all reason they needed to make me part of their gang. I needed to belong somewhere. Being on my own wouldn't have been so very wise. But I've never told anyone out of guilt before, that it was an accident. Not until now."

He looked at me and again I wrapped both of my arms around his in consolation, resting my head upon his shoulder once more.

"I'll never tell, Billy. You can tell me what you want and I'll never tell anyone the truth of how you feel about it."

"I believe I was right to let it out to you. You believe I didn't mean to go bad, don't you?"

I nodded against him. "You are not bad, Billy. It's this place. It's...wrong. I was frightened to come here. I only feel better now that you are here."

We heard hoof-beats and he looked up.

"It's Brewer," he said.

We quickly moved away from each other and stood up, brushing ourselves off.

When Richard approached Billy asked, "What is it Richard?"

"John asked me to ride out and see how things were going."

Richard Brewer was John's foreman and the man from whom The Boys had demanded breakfast after they had stolen John's mares from his property while Billy still rode with them and I could see that Richard distrusted Billy, and I knew John was checking up on me. I wondered if he had sent Richard because John knew he would give an objective report. Richard was a fair enough man.

"Things are just fine," Billy replied. "And for the record, for all her lessons, Lucy doesn't know a nickel's worth about shooting her guns."

"How do you figure?" asked Richard.

"Well Richard, I watched."

"Didn't look like you were doing much shooting by the way I came."

"We had finished for the day," I said, my tone imposing, "and if it is okay by you, Richard, Billy and I were conducting a friendly conversation."

Humbled, Richard accepted this. The manner in which I had spoken was a subtle reminder to dare not question me, the fiancée of his employer and future lady of the household.

"Well, you two ought to be getting back. We're settling on an early supper tonight, and John wants us to run barbed wire. We're expecting a pretty long job out of it."

Billy nodded. "We're on our way back then," he assured.

Richard nodded then turned his horse, riding back the way he came. Billy and I looked at one another, and I felt his hand slide into mine. I felt him run his thumb over my knuckles. He smiled at me and I smiled back.

# 4

## November, 1877

$F$or two weeks I practiced with Billy in the afternoons and worked on Colleen's gift in the mornings. Having completed it, I intended to give it to her at the first national Thanksgiving celebration to be held on Wortley Street.

Forlorn and melancholy, I had been sulking on the chaise outside the door of John's office. I lay back upon it, feeling sorry for myself as I could hear the boys out in the yard and here I was, locked away inside on a dreary, chilly day. I propped myself upon my knees to look out the window at them, pressing my hands and face to the glass in an unladylike fashion. Feeling guilty, Colleen refused to entertain me, opting instead to spend the day keeping company with John's housemaid, Hannah, helping her in doing woman's work. I could smell something delicious cooking in the kitchen where the cook was working.

Colleen didn't feel at all comfortable sitting with me while another woman flitted about the house. "But," I told her, "governesses are above housemaids, and I am your charge." However, her lowborn Irish birthright kept her from feeling comfortable in simply sitting and spending the day being idle with a lady of leisure. In addition, she insisted that being of an industrious nature was a far better indicator of a good, solid character. I chose to ignore such an obvious slight, intended or not. I may have loved Colleen like a mother, but to acknowledge her belittlement of my lifestyle was beneath me.

I leaned back from the glass and noticed I had left a print of my face and hands. I used my sleeve to wipe them away just before the office door opened, surprising me as if I were a child with its hand caught in a cookie jar. It would be unacceptable to find me cleaning windows with my dress.

When John had come out of his office I had quickly turned to sit properly, twisting my skirt in the process. As I endeavored to smooth it, he looked reprovingly at me, but only in jest. I begged to be able to go into town, but both he and Colleen forbade this, saying it was too damp and cold outside. I had finished all of the books I had brought with me and, therefore, had nothing to do. The boys who stayed in the bunkhouse often cooked their own meals, but I sometimes brought them freshly made biscuits from the kitchen. Today I would not be doing even that. I supposed with a sigh that I would not be doing much of anything today.

Just then I heard laughter outside and on impulse I turned my head to again look through the window and out into the yard, longing to know what the joke was. Earlier when the boys had come in from the field I heard shots and much yelling as they were having a grand time playing at target practice and killing their own brand of time, though, unlike me, I could see that they were enjoying themselves. I looked at John who stood looking out the window as well.

I plead with him, "Can we not simply go to the store? I only want to buy some ribbon for my hair. In 6 days' time will be the Thanksgiving celebration."

He sat down next to me and sighed, saying, "You have plenty of things to be worn that day. I do not believe you need any ribbon." Then, sympathetically, he looked at me, "I know how you fidget so, but you must trust me that this weather would do you far worse for the celebration than not having any ribbons for your hair." He smiled at me and I taxed myself in order to gratify him by offering a half-hearted smile in return.

I thought I had a brilliant idea when I said, "Alex and Susan live just next to the store. I can be taken there on my way home."

"I don't think you'll be going home tonight, Elucia. You and Colleen will stay here. We're expecting a rainfall and I'm afraid there is too much of a chill. It's not appropriate weather. I don't want to have to call on the doctor and have you down with a cold. It's best to be wise."

Spend the night? *Here*? Scandalous! I would not need to go far at all. Why attach such fragility to me? *Perhaps*, I thought, *he wants to protect his meal ticket*.

I nodded my head pretending to agree and turned again to look out the window after hearing another bout of laughter. I wondered what was so funny because I'm sure I wouldn't know being stuck indoors so far away. The window started to spot with rain and I saw the men move just inside the safety of the barn. They had a fire going out there; perhaps that's why *they* did not feel a chill.

Bored and upset, I indulged myself with thoughts of Billy as a pleasant escape from such tedium. I longed for the two hours we had with one another on the days we would practice, though they were mostly spent with Billy telling me everything I was doing wrong and correcting my behavior, becoming frustrated and even vexed with me at times. He could also be difficult when his attention was entirely upon how I was holding my revolver and how fast I could draw and shoot it and hit the target. He was strict. But I had made some progress and could now shoot with my left hand, even if not very well.

Sometimes, when evening fell, he would ride by my sleeping quarters at The McSweens' where he knew I liked to bundle up and sit outside on the porch reading. Often, he would stop and talk with me, asking about my life back home; about my family: one older sister; days spent on end bothering about the latest fashions and endless fittings and a lack of eating so measurements could be sent to Paris for the next season's new fashions; women and girls blathering about the who's-who of polite society; girls becoming worrisome over suitors and sitting on their hands so as not to bite at their nails when they began to fear he might not propose after all. I complained about wasted time spent bent over canvass and thread and charity work. He hesitated at this last thing, but I explained that it was not the charity itself that was bothersome, but the reason behind it, making any fulfillment of the work null-and-void; the poor are in fashion. Providing to the less fortunate was merely another outlet for the wealthy to show how grateful they could be for all they had. This was the purpose the poor served us.

I assured Billy that I'd much rather hear about his life as it was far more interesting, to which he agreed it was, but then he assured me that he'd rather have the stability of my life. I pointed out that it seemed as though, perhaps, we each fulfilled one another with something we felt missing in our own lives and he believed this was possible. I longed for his freedom, and he wanted the reliability that my life provided. This seemed to be the solid foundation of our bond.

We had grown so accustomed to one another that, one afternoon in particular, he had broken from the others to come sit with me a moment on John's porch before we were to go to the ring. He sat closer than would ordinarily be acceptable for a man, and this action caused some stirring of conversation among the other men standing near enough to notice. It was easy for us to be so innocently familiar with one another emotionally that it allowed for our physical proximity to one another to be easier still. We spoke often with our heads bent towards one another, conveying an air of intimacy that was frowned upon by his contemporaries. I realized then that men were hens as well as they spoke of my showing him favor and placing him in the good graces of John. This was not altogether untrue; I did speak highly of Billy to John, but it was John himself who had realized Billy's usefulness and potential and quickly moved him up the line. I did not need to prod the matter much at all, but the others had made up their minds that Billy was my pet and that this was the reason for which he advanced and they took liberties, chiding him on occasion. It was somewhat distressing to me, but only because I did not like to think he was being troubled, but he calmed me by assuring me it did not bother him all that much, and that it was his matter to deal with solely. I was determined to help Billy however I could which served to dissatisfy his pride, but to complain to me was to receive no benefit as I would see to it that I attempted my level best to secure for him a place and a future.

But as we sat together, he rested his hand on the wooden bench and had flinched upon being speared by a rather large splinter that sat deeply in his left forefinger. Gently, I lifted his hand in mine to examine the damage, planning to tend to the tiny wound. This act stunned the boys, who observed us ever more closely. To them, this "inappropriateness" was a sure sign of prejudice that would guarantee Billy's place even above those who had been working John's land much longer which irritated them considerably.

Distressing as it could be, ultimately, I could not be bothered with what they thought as the help's bitterness was at last no concern to me. It was Billy who must tolerate their resentment and the occasional derisive remark. I did not bother about it when Billy protested my favor, either. I had my plans and my sights set for Billy; the others and what they thought be damned. However, it was not all bad as the boys did genuinely like Billy and so generally they left him alone.

Before taking me to my lesson, I had him come with me into the house and had gone down to my room to get my kit. When I had come back I saw that he had removed his hat and was seated on the couch in an attentive manner, his hat resting on his lap. I sat down very close to him, taking his left hand in my own, slipping my fingers between his. This was, of course, by design. I removed the tweezers from my kit and began to carefully pluck the splinter from his finger. I felt him looking at me; my face must have betrayed the burning that was there beneath the skin which only made me too happy to have a task to busy myself with so as to seem oblivious. I pretended to focus intently on the splinter, though no splinter could ever need such attention—as deep as it was, the tweezers would pull it out with ease. Finally, I decided that it was no matter as I desired the moment to last. Upon plucking the splinter from his hand, I reached back into my kit and pulled out a small pot of lavender liniment. I removed its lid and dipped my finger in. Gently I rubbed the ointment on the spot where the splinter had been.

"This is lavender—"

Almost immediately he jolted, as if he remembered something, and stuttered a bit as he exclaimed, "That's it! That's the scent!"

"I beg your pardon?"

"I recognize it; you wear it often."

I was delighted that he knew my scent. But I thought it best to try and ignore the sentiment as I found the idea of it seductive.

"Yes…In New York I often wore a fragrance of violet, but it's so terribly difficult to buy in Lincoln. In fact, I believe I'd have to send for it back east. What I have left of it I'd like to conserve. But I find lavender nice as well."

"Well," he began, "I ain't—*haven't*—ever smelled anything violet, but I surely do appreciate the lavender."

I blushed even more and waited a moment before I cleared my throat and promised, "This will help protect and heal the wound."

"I'm sure it'll do all right," he said.

I was sure the tiny wound would, too, but why end the moment when there were so many excuses to carry on? I turned his hand over, my fingers still entwined with his. "Your hand is wind burned—it is so dry. You're not wearing your gloves outdoors, in the fields, are you?"

He shook his head, "No," he quietly replied.

"You should, Billy. By January they'll be far worse."

His hands were delicate, almost aristocratic in that the fingers themselves were slight and thin, the feel of them between mine heady. His hand was warm, and he made no move to fix its position, allowing me to hold his hand as I pleased. But I considered our circumstances; we were alone in the parlor, sitting side-by-side on the couch as lovers, and the feeling came upon me that this was too bold and I reluctantly let go and replaced the lid on the pot of ointment. Someone could have walked in at any time and found us like that.

After we had quit our lesson that afternoon, he relaxed with me as usual, and the more comfortable he became, the more he talked.

He told me that a man working for Dolan by the name of Buck Morton had it in for him over an issue involving Buck's sweetheart. At this I was not so surprised. It was not Billy's fault that he often caught the eyes of the girls—they all preened for him. But there was no one else to blame but Billy for entertaining such attentions. I was, however, concerned, as my feelings for Billy were, by now, profound, and though I hated to admit it, I understood the reason men kept things secret from women. Buck Morton had a deep hatred of Billy and, being an extremely jealous man, he tortured Billy with wildly abusive behavior prior to his coming here. It didn't help things for me when Billy let slip that he was lying in wait to return Buck's abusive favor.

He had no sooner told me of Buck when he told me about Jesse Evans, who also was currently in the employ of Dolan, and how bad blood was thick between them two as well. Things began to converge. I knew of Jesse Evans and how he led The Boys. Stories of him abounded in the press; he was notorious for his violence, and I knew The Boys were a ferocious gang as the papers were rampant with stories of their depravity. I had known that they had given Billy up to John for stealing his horses, though I thought this acceptable as I imagined the circumstances for Billy were now far better, but he himself didn't care for the betrayal at all. It was of no matter that it turned out to be a fortuitous occurrence, pride, as usual, being the culprit. He did not bother to consider how Evans had, in reality, done him a tremendous service. Had Jesse Evans not pointed the finger at Billy for stealing John's mares, where he would be now instead of working his way to a better life one could only imagine. Despite their being mortal enemies now, he wasn't so terribly worried about Evans, and from witnessing first hand his firing prowess, I felt maybe it was Jesse Evans who had better tread lightly.

Regardless of the stories Billy had told me I still could not manage to reconcile this rather gentle boy with being what they would call a "hard case" out here. He was good-natured and truly loved a good joke. He was always smiling or laughing, except when I complained during a lesson, and I had considered him thoughtful and sensitive.

But I thought more about that and remembered how suddenly his disposition turned remarkably dark that first day we practiced with targets. And, too, there was that quick temper of his. And after paying close attention to him when he demonstrated his expertise during our time spent at the ring, I had observed the edgy coolness of his character as he concentrated on the task at hand, handling the charge with rigor despite the fact that we were only shooting at bottles. I reminded myself that he was a boy who could not trust the future and felt that at any moment the ground could fall completely out from under him and he'd be put right back out into nowhere fending for his life. I was ever more determined to establish him, and if I played things just right, and he continued to impress, there would be much potential for him.

Still, I sensed that something was broken within him, and I wondered if this might possibly cause a hindrance as his trust in people must be tenuous. But he had a loyalty in him that ran deep, though after I had truly considered him I could make no mistake that he was not one to be trifled with.

He was damaged in the way that he was so young and had already lost everything, gaining only a working knowledge of the hate found so often in this part of the world and what it was worth as a result. I couldn't decide if this broke my heart for him or if, considering the unforgiving climate out here, made me all the more fond of him. There was something to be admired in a young man who learned to survive under those conditions and become fearless, but not necessarily recklessly so. Billy was kindhearted, respectful, mindful, sweet, and very profound, but yes, he had an unmistakable viciousness in him. He was full of vengeance in response to what he found unjust, and, admittedly, I found this attractive in him. I thought him thrilling.

During the last fifteen minutes of my lesson he would quit his concentration to sit in the grass and talk with me. I especially enjoyed when he happened by the McSweens' and would sit with me there as we could talk past dark without interruption before I'd retreat into my room through the door that connected it with the porch. In the passing of three weeks' time I found I had come to know him so very well, and effortlessly we grew all the more closer as we spent more time together; words flowed easily between us.

He would often play with me, teaching me to dance as the Mexicans did, or show me Irish steps and how to dance the Polka. In my social arena we did not dance this way and I found it stimulating. He and I would laugh over how difficult this could be for me. As graceful as I was, I had remarkable trouble keeping up with such quick steps and having to turn so freely, being tossed about.

He was charming and charismatic, and so extraordinarily clever! He drew people in. The girls in town had begun to whisper their fancies of him. Phyllis Dillinger was especially bold in her fondness. He was kind to her if she caught him unaware but, if he had the good fortune to discover her in his path, he'd find a way to quickly slip away. But for pretty Candace Kelly he took the time to flirt favorably. I was, at times, jealous of this if I should be near enough to notice, and I would make an excuse to leave the company of whomever I was speaking with and make my way to him in order to be pleased greatly at how he would then turn the lion's share of his attentions to me, satisfying my anxiety.

But, he had not met Sallie Chisum yet. The boys were very taken with her, and she would be here for the celebration of our first Thanksgiving where she and her uncle would be put up alongside me at Alex and Susan's. This caused me concern as I did not know if I could compete with a pretty girl who shared his western culture, but I had to remind myself that I was promised and so Billy was free to like whom he pleased.

Still, I did not want to lose any time I had with him to anyone else—I simply did not want to share him. I began to love New Mexico because of him and would miss him terribly at times. We had a bond that I believed was more than just friendliness, but with John between us I knew it could not move beyond that. Still, I selfishly wanted no other girl to replace me in his eyes.

But, though I began to love my new home, I knew that love revolved strictly around Billy as otherwise I could not reconcile the place with that of New York. It was uncertain here. Many people who were maleficent mixed in with benevolent, honest men—the mixture was volatile. I feared for John. I knew he was just as ambitious as Murphy and Dolan and, like them, was not devoid of greed, but for all intents-and-purposes, he was playing by the rules. Things became more ominous and I was not oblivious to this, for how could oblivion be possible while the troubles were omnipresent? I would overhear alarming talk about something referred to as the Santa Fe Ring, and Billy would often speak of the town's sheriff, Brady, being a "back-shooting bastard". I don't think he realized exactly how much he was letting on during our casual exchanges, nor did he know exactly what it meant to me, which was fear, for if he knew, he would have remained reserved. I don't think he considered hiding anything much from me in view of my being a soul he found reliable and trustworthy and, feeling as comfortable with me as he did, he managed to fill in the gaps enough to cause me plenty concern. I feared so much more for Billy because of Buck Morton and Jesse Evans being in the employ of Dolan. With Billy employed by their boss's adversary, it wouldn't take much of an excuse for them to go after him. I suffered guilt because of this, knowing I ought to reserve my utmost concern for John. It was awful of me, I knew, but in such a short time, Billy had begun to mean far too much to me, and despite my guilt I now resented John for using Billy as his personal sentinel, placing him in the way of harm in order to avoid any trouble directed at him. This way, Morton and Evans could find him for certain.

Billy and I both clung to one another as ballast. I needed him, and even more so than I had before, I entertained lustful thoughts of him and dared to wonder if he thought the same, and then I silently scolded myself as usual for even allowing myself to think of it.

The sky had begun to grow dark and dinner was placed out for me and John, breaking my daydreams of Billy. We ate in silence.

When the celebration had finally arrived on the twenty-ninth, I gave Colleen the gift I had been making for her while she attended me and helped me dress for the evening's festivities. She seemed thrilled by my small gesture and I was happy that I had taken the time to manage it for her. I still had not the courage to come straight out and apologize for my cruelty and convey that I had not meant to be hurtful, but yet I still could not come to terms with the wisdom she tried to impart; I could not accept living a placid life with a placid man whom I had only placid feelings for. I still wanted all the things I was not meant to have, the things I had read about, the things that my companionship with Billy had given me a taste of.

I sometimes felt that it was terribly unfortunate that I should have met him. Knowing him made things all the more worse and I was much more saddened than I had ever been. In the least, I was resigned to and had accepted my life's purpose prior to knowing him, and for this, I admit, I held bad feelings towards Billy, taking my frustrations out on him. If it were not for him I could stand my fate! His flirtatious mannerisms were unacceptable as they made it all the more difficult for me, but by my life, I wouldn't quit things with him. I couldn't now, for I was far too attached and would miss him terribly. Now, in this instant, I felt as though I hated him! My feelings for him made it seem as though I were that much more closed in than ever before. I wished to ignore him, I wanted to pull back, and tonight would make a good excuse for that. I would focus on and welcome those whom I hadn't before in order to occupy myself to keep from thinking about or talking with Billy. The social climbers had hit a stroke of luck!

I had a brilliant dress for the Christmas celebration and found it unfortunate that it could not be worn tonight. How resplendent I would have appeared, making quite the impression! I'd wear a white sable hat, with a diamond band and a matching white sable cape that tied with a twisted silk, silver rope. The dress was of a white silk cuirasse bodice, lavishly intricate with silver studding, and bustled train with a silver organza overskirt. I was breathless merely thinking of it. But for tonight, a gown so plain by comparison that I balked at the thought of wearing it as I wanted so much to stand out tonight, setting out the milk for the social climbing kittens. What a sight I would have been otherwise! I would have worn my diamond eardrops to compliment the ensemble—they couldn't have resisted me! I would have appeared as gleaming white, virginal snow! Tonight it was a mint green wool dress with a sage green plaid pattern and matching solid sage green velvet, fur-lined cape, my only adornments being emerald baubles for my ears and a simple emerald to be worn around my neck. *I might as well be a milkmaid!* I supposed Thanksgiving was simply not terribly important, after all.

I thought of Billy and I wondered if he might be one of Sallie's admirer's after to-night. I decided that, most definitely, he would. I was more than confident that she would be taken with him as well, and so, if he should cater to her charms, then I would work that much harder towards procuring for him a future in which she would find acceptable. As there was nothing of myself that I could offer him, then I should craft him into a desirable bachelor so that he could make a fine match.

Though I was considered handsome, Sallie was vivacious and pretty, and more importantly, unattached; there was no reason that Billy should not want to make a match with her. All the king's men were keen to pounce upon her, and as John became more and more impressed by Billy's willingness and competency (he had declared that he would "make a man of him yet!") the easier it should become for me to shoehorn him into a marketable position. I would do what I could to ensure him as a proper suitor—a man with something to offer a lady. *A lady of the plains, but a lady no less*! Sallie was considered upper crust in a place such as the likes of Lincoln, and to that end, she would be ideal for Billy to pursue on his rise, and so I set my mind to work and prepared to use my societal wiles in order to impress her with him.

To my great satisfaction, Sallie wore clothes which, to my trained eye, were slightly ill-fitting. This betrayed her social status as this meant they were to be worn as long as possible, being let in or out, whereas my clothes, with the exception of my morn-ing and afternoon dresses, were to consummately fit properly while in fashion. Small things like this gratified and put me at ease as I knew that Billy would never do better than me; wanting something I could never have, this was all I could do to comfort myself. I wore finery and she was unadorned, and this further allowed a lift in my spirits. I was much more of an impressive sight, my mind always harboring the thought that this might continue to bring Billy's attention to me regardless of the deterrents that separated us. The difficulty of my situation at present was this: I did not love John, I loved Billy, and so it was a struggle to let him go entirely. And so, though she was still by far better suited for Billy than I, I could not deny that I still hoped that, since all appealing aspects attributed to a woman of means were in my favor, his head would remain turned in my direction. After all, the disparities of comparison between Sallie and I were stacked in my favor. My education far outstripped hers, she was outdone by my singing voice, I maintained better posture and grace, and I had a broader knowledge of the world and was better read.

Though wealthy, her father, who partnered in the cattle vocation with her uncle, was still considered only a common tradesman by the association of my class, and being a man of new money, he held no place with the true elitists, and so when my thoughts would settle upon Billy as I attempted to push him from my mind for the sake of my own sanity, I would ask myself, if a prominent cattleman was only all of that, then what ought William H. Bonney mean to me?

When John and I had arrived at the celebration on Wortley Street he helped Colleen and me down out of the buggy only for me to find Phyllis waiting there in the ugliest shade of green I had ever seen. What a mess she was, as usual. The boys had not yet arrived, and I wondered how she would impart her attentions to both me and Billy at the same time since I had decided to keep him far apart from me tonight so that I might try to dispose of my feelings for him. How would she corner us together, killing two birds with one stone?

Alex and Susan were directly behind us in their own buggy, and after Alex helped his wife down, he and John began to discuss business.

"Elucia! How I love that dress!" Phyllis shouted like a fishwife.

I smiled forcibly and summoned as much politeness as I could. There was nothing pleasant about her appearance to which I could return the compliment (now I saw the splendor of my own dress), and in the spirit of evading impossible compliments, I simply said, "Phyllis, how do you find things this evening?"

"Oh," she replied, "I am having such a wonderful time!"

I smiled, pretending that I appreciated her enjoyment of the festivities. I wanted desperately to break away from her; she was so overly excited that she overwhelmed me, which was made worse by her standing much too closely. Worse, I had not much to say which, to my dismay, concerned me. I had been trained to endure the things I found disagreeable, especially people, always able to raise suitable, if shallow, conversation. But my dislike of Phyllis made this task challenging. I was supposed to be adept at hiding my true feelings while under the guise of civility. The roughness of this town must have begun to affect me. I suspected that spending so much time with Billy and his western commonality, learning to fire pistols, was an even larger offense as it was already such an improper trade for a lady; my polished disposition was beginning to tarnish. Billy's openness and candor was invading and undoing years' worth of pretentions which, in turn, fed into my discontent at being a kept pet of refinement. I began to grow bolder and rebel as I passed the days with him. It could only be a better reason to avoid him.

Before I could attempt a reply to Phyllis the sound of hoof beats and shouting caught our attention. We turned our heads in unison towards the commotion to see that the boys were riding up and, after setting their horses in the stable, one by one they walked toward the group of us. There was a crowd of them, and I noticed Billy among them. He looked at me happily, but just as quickly frowned upon noticing Phyllis standing there with me. This caused me an amused, sly smile. Perhaps I should stick by her for all of the evening, then, as it was sure to cause him to keep his distance from me. The thought of being stuck with Phyllis caused me to choke on air, but it would have to be endured, and I was reminded that I had resigned myself to becoming more acquainted with, and therefore more accustomed to, the sensibilities of this place, and this included poor, disordered, dowdy Phyllis. I was thinking on this when Billy approached. Was he braving this bore to say hello to me? I accidentally smiled genuinely at him which caused me frustration. How would I ever get over this boy? It seemed an insurmountable feat as I adored him so!

Smiling despite my will, I nodded and said hello to him. He removed his hat and smiled at me, but looked nervously towards Phyllis, the rabid skunk. Instead of her noticing his hesitancy, being unable or unwilling to read the expressions of others, she beamed. I turned my head away, feigning indifference, when I heard her exclaim excitedly, "Billy!"

Her ecstatic shout drew my attention back again. He smiled at her and, impressively, impeccably returning her pleasantry. I simply looked off again as though I were bored, which, if not for Billy being so terribly close, I almost was. My face was still turned away when I heard him tell me I looked dreadfully pretty. I couldn't help but look at him after his compliment, and as I was preparing myself to respond, Phyllis resounded with, "Elucia always looks magnificent!"

How vulgar! What poor manners! A woman ought never draw attention to another in such an ill-mannered way, and far worse, ignorantly monopolize another's response by blurting her own in its place which was so very out-of-line. It was solely upon me to accept and return his compliment! I gave her a tight-lipped, disapproving smile.

"Billy, will you ask me to dance later?" she followed up, rudely.

I imperceptibly closed my eyes out of irritation and embarrassment at her lack of decorum.

Billy stuttered, "Sure, I suppose so. That'd be okay."

It was all I could do not to look at him and laugh at his misfortune.

"Oh, I look forward to it so much!" she replied, delighted.

Mocking her I said, "That is a nice bonnet you wear, Phyllis."

Her face lit up at the notion of my complimenting her. She truly did not understand that I was being facetious.

Unable to help himself, as it was unlike him to relish such undeserved cruelty towards a lady, Billy's eyes sparkled at the insult, the corner of his lips turning up into a wicked grin, being in on the subtle joke knowing how much I detested her and this particular accessory and, despite my awareness of Billy's disinterest in poking fun at women gratuitously, I was encouraged to make another elusive, nasty remark nonetheless after his surprisingly favorable reaction to the last one as I was unable to resist sharing another personal inside joke with him.

Furthermore, I already felt ill-tempered at having to share Billy's presence with her which only served to embolden my nastiness whereas ordinarily I would have held my tongue in check. It did not matter how I told myself I wanted to distance myself from him; it was a lie.

"Tell me wherever do you buy your clothes?" I asked.

"Oh, these?" she smoothed out her skirt.

"Yes, of course those," *you dolt.*

"I buy them at the local shops here in town."

How finely my dress managed by comparison to not just Phyllis' dress, but all of the girls here. Though initially plain to my jaded eyes, it now occurred to me that it was indeed grand.

Dispassionately, I replied, "I figured as much," I fanned my face and looked away, haughtily. "Of course you would."

Phyllis cleared her throat uncertainly. She managed to pick up on my intended spitefulness but was still unsure as to whether or not it was imagined. Billy, who knew damned well that I was being unkind, now wore an expression of shock. Perhaps I'd gone too far, then. At home I never would have spoken this way—to anyone. Usually my false sincerity impressed even me. I was losing the grand etiquette I carried here with me from New York, and I imagine with no one of my class to keep me in line, there was nothing to halt my cruel affectations.

"What is the name of the color?" I proceeded.

She fretfully and sloppily grabbed at her skirt, glancing at it.

"Oh," she replied timidly. "I'm not sure. I don't believe it has a name."

"All colors have a name," I rudely snapped, "though I suppose that I, too, would have a terrible time of it if I were made to name whatever color it is that you are wearing."

Her cheeks flushed red at this and she looked down at the ground, unable to look anywhere else out of humiliation. Billy stared at me in disbelief, stunned at my poor behavior. He quickly went to Phyllis's rescue.

"Phyllis…" he began, "Would you care to dance now?"

Her face lit up again at this.

"Yes! I would! Thank you!"

His eyes bore into mine as they walked past, and I looked down in shame. He had wordlessly chastised me for my ruthless conduct. I had never displeased him before, not in this way; I was regretful. I don't know which disturbed me more, that I was able to be so mean, or that I endeavored to seek Billy's approval at all turns.

There was a long table that ran the entire length of Wortley, and when it was time to dine we took our places, the boys sitting much farther down from where John, Alex, Susan, and myself sat, along with John Chisum, his niece Sallie, and his brother, James. Sallie was not yet present in her place at the table, and I decided to take a walk along the rows of chairs until I came close enough to make out Billy sitting with Minxie, Jim, and Charlie, with George standing behind them looking interested. They were laughing, Billy's face hidden in part by shadow, and there next to him sat Sallie Chisum, fanning the heat from the flames that bordered the street for warmth and flirtatiously touching him upon the arm. I felt my own heat simmering beneath the surface of my cheeks at this spectacle. I closed my eyes and tried to ignore this jealousy, but my mind was already overly consumed with knowing how I had disappointed and upset Billy. How I wished I could take back what I had done to Phyllis!

I kept my attention on Billy, observing my best friend longingly, who was as eagerly involved in the conversation with Sallie as she was with him. I studied him, there in the dark, his face lit partially by the nearby flames, and concluded that I would have expected these charming manners from him, and although he wasn't yet inspired to speak with her as intimately as he often did with me, he was plenty more excitable than he had been upon our first meeting. I imagined it would be soon enough when they, too, would be found in private conversation. My concern was that I had turned him off to me, and I could not say that I blamed him.

As the night wore on I found that I'd search Billy out and note where he was. I hated that I did this. I saw him dance a polka with Sallie and discovered that she was quite adept at this. I wondered if perhaps he might have asked me, too, had I not disenchanted him, but then I prayed thank God he would not, lest my graceful disposition be given up at the sight of my own inability to keep up. I began to feel the guilt at what I had done more acutely than I had earlier, and I felt the urge to perform in some satisfactory way to recover his approval, but then, indignantly, I refused this urge outright as I refused to yield to one beneath myself in order to seek clemency. But even as I thought this I knew I was only fooling myself. I wanted Billy's forgiveness. His thoughts of me were the only thoughts that mattered.

The very next afternoon I sent Hannah to find Billy with a note stating that I would not go with him to the ring today; my humiliation was too great and I did not want to face him. But foolishly I sat on John's porch reading and this made me vulnerable. I had been outside only twenty minutes when I heard hoof beats. I looked up to see him galloping towards me very deliberately. He was wearing the bolero hat and jacket he had gotten at John's store on that first day of his arrival and he was looking particularly fine. My stomach dropped into oblivion and an ache spread itself out wide over my chest. I began my day resigned to the task of avoiding Billy and feeling full of strength in my decision, but upon seeing him it took only a moment to have my fortitude betrayed by my emotions. However, as good fortune would have it, I remembered myself, and what was more, never before was I so aware of myself. My attention was paid to every aspect of my posture as I stood ceremoniously: back straight, shoulders back, jaw set, head lifted high so that I could look down my nose at him as he approached the bottom of the steps upon dismounting. He tilted his hat back atop his head exposing his face to me, stopping at the bottom step and propping one booted foot upon it, hooking his thumbs onto his cartridge belt.

Seeing him so unmoved and unimpressed by my arrogance nearly caused my strength to wane. For him to ignore my state of being only reminded me of what hung heavy between us; he was not afraid of me in the least. The tears were just behind my eyes and I prayed they would not fall as I missed him already and wanted desperately to beg for his mercy. I wanted him to smile at me again and talk to me as a friend, but his usual, natural good-humor was lost on me. My heart begged that I stop all of this and break down for him, that I welcome him and beg for his compassion, but I had to put an end to what was happening as a result of our increasing closeness. I had to stand firm. There was nothing else to be done.

He held out the note I had given Hannah. "What's this?" he asked, before crumpling it and throwing it down. "What came over you? What did you do that for last night?"

"Last night?" I pretended. I stood there, wishing this were already over. I was not sure I could maintain the strength I needed. I wished him away before I lost my composure.

"You know exactly what I'm talking about! You hurt that girl's feelings!"

"How dare you?" I sniffed. "What gives you the right to stand there and speak to me so insolently?"

"I thought I was your friend. A friend would warn another of their bad manners."

"Bad manners?"

I now felt a confusing mixture of both anger and desire—anger that he could dare approach me in this way, and desire that he had the nerve. I so desperately wanted to concede to his displeasure so we could go back to the way things were supposed to be between him and me. I wanted to reach to him and hold on for dear life. *Billy*, I silently prayed, *please don't hate me.*

"You, Mr. Bonney, are not my friend. I am your employer. My husband-to-be pays your wages, and yet you approach me as if I were some housemaid. Before you warn others of their bad manners, you should check your own in addition to remembering your place!"

His eyes were a brilliant blue as they looked up at me. He bit at his lower lip and stepped away, backing up without turning so that he still faced me.

"*My* place?" he began in a semi whisper, "*You're* the one who's out of her whole goddamned country! You come here and you treat the people as if they're insects! Who do you think you are?"

I stood there, physically trying to intimidate him despite recognizing it was absolutely useless and impossible to cow him; it was a futile endeavor. My heart barely beat, dying for him. I wanted to collapse at his feet and prove that I did not look down upon him or anyone else, that I wanted to go away with him and belong with him like one of his own. But I could not. I could not allow myself to weaken, though my knees trembled.

He hated me in this moment, and yet I loved him—and so there it was—the truth. Colleen was right. It would have been easier if I did not feel so much for this boy. The hurt was not worth the passion when his arms were not there to comfort you.

I stood there, fading before him though he did not notice, or possibly he simply did not care. Surely he knew me well enough to recognize that I was coming apart at the seams, trying desperately to hold myself together. This should have been obvious to him, yet he only threw his hands up in defeat, determining that I was not worth the trouble.

I watched him as he remounted his horse and looked at me contemptuously, lowering his hat so that his face was concealed in shadow. He backed his horse up and kicked it, angrily commanding it to ride, pulling its reigns to to run it back from where he came, never looking back at me. I walked quickly into the house and into a nearby closet where I collapsed, crying. I would no longer have him to look forward to, I knew. It was all done, and I was a fool.

**5**

# December, 1877

I sat outside the stables at John Chisum's in the afternoon on a crudely made wooden bench while Viola was being saddled. We had come here for the week over business matters; it had been nearly five days since we had arrived. Chisum's home was large and sat on a great expanse of land here in the territory.

Billy and I had not bothered with one another since we argued the day after Thanksgiving. We would not as much as look in each other's direction if it could be avoided. Twice he had escorted me to the store in town and did not look at me, let alone utter a single word. I was sure he did this to make a point—to compound the words I had spoken against him, that he was my servant and I his mistress.

I made excuses to John as to why I was not practicing my lessons. I'd either have a headache or allude to my being indisposed due to women's nature in which case he wouldn't press. I hid my depression when in his or Colleen's company, only allowing myself to submit to sorrow when alone.

Today I explained that I wanted to go for a ride but John was concerned over this as I was unfamiliar with the land, and a woman riding out alone under volatile conditions, such as these times were, was frowned upon. He tried to insist that Billy accompany me, but I refused, telling him I wanted to be alone. I was able to calm his concerns by promising that I would not go far, staying only along the creek bed, and by pointing out that I would be among the many armed men that Chisum employed on his land to survey its parameters for any signs of trouble, and the men whose sole job it was to stand guard over the ranch itself. This placated him enough to allow me to go alone.

I was wearing my black wool and silk blend riding habit and a lace accented top hat, a white chemisette beneath the tailored jacket. I favored this habit over my dark grey as it was a much more handsome garment and looked particularly both fetching and dramatic on me. I might not have appreciated the tedium that was my existence in my social strata, but I did enjoy the fine garments it provided me. My lavish wardrobe never failed to lift my spirits and, this was something, as my moods had easily dampened over these past few days when, not only would I find Sallie flirtatiously teasing Billy, but would notice, too, his proclivity for her diversions. They spent much of their time together, and I knew they spoke to one another well into the night as he and I had done so often once upon a time.

They were, at this very moment, out riding together, and I had been in the middle of hoping my path would not cross theirs when I saw the pair come riding up the creek bed, racing their horses through the wash and laughing as they did so. They were heading in my direction as they approached the stable and, as they came near, Billy coolly tipped his hat to me while Sallie said hello before being helped down from her mare by Billy, giggling coyly as he assisted her. I studied her closely as he aided her and saw how she reveled in the attention he gave her, repaying him with her own full-on exploits of affection, using time-tested artifices such as touching him gently upon the arm every chance she could manage, allowing her hand to linger as long as she dared. She would laugh charmingly and timidly smile all while batting her little eyelashes whenever he would glance at her.

But, I saw, he did not place his hand discreetly upon her waste or the small of her back as he did with me when helping me down. I smiled at that.

When he took the horses and led them inside the stable she came over and sat with me upon the rickety wooden bench. I noticed that she looked particularly pretty as her cheeks were flushed with pleasure. She complimented me on my dress and I reached up intuitively to touch my hat before thanking her and complimenting her in kind as I took in her own outfit. Hers was the color of gold with black lapels and, here, too, loose fitting. She was wearing a very large brooch on her collar. It was garish in the way I'd expect from new money as it was extremely ostentatious, made of gold dressed up with large, tacky, inelegantly cut rubies and cultured pearls—far too dramatic for so early in the day, or any time of day for that matter. I asked where she had received it and she confided in me that her uncle had given it to her as a Christmas gift. I smiled as if I thought it was sweet, which I suppose I was. Worn at the collar of my high-necked white chemisette was my own brooch; a tastefully simple onyx.

Billy came out of the stables and said goodbye to Sallie. She turned to him and smiled, delicately waving as he walked by, and I imagined that they had shared a special look. Paranoid or not, I turned my head away from this display as I felt the pressure on my heart that had recently become so familiar. When I looked back I saw that he was looking at me as he walked, waiting until I caught his eye before he turned away. I thought this action odd considering our behavior towards one another over the past week.

I turned my attention back to Sallie, admittedly feeling generous towards her now as his acknowledgement had buoyed me.

"Are you faring well here in New Mexico?" she asked.

She was kind and affable, this one, and I found it to be a pity as I did not want to like her, being envious by the garnered attention she received from Billy, attention that I seemed to have lost. I found that she had a pleasant, southwestern drawl, not unlike

Billy's, and it reminded me that this might be a good chance to discuss and understand southwestern customs.

"I'm doing well, thank you," I replied, "but I find it a bit difficult to maneuver out here at times." She looked at me curiously and so I added, "The people here, they're very different from those of New York. I'm not certain I fit in here, though I would very much like to."

"I'm afraid you may find you'll never quit fit in," she said neutrally.

"Why do you say that?" I replied, truly interested to know how it was that I could never find my way here.

"You're not like them. You are educated and from one of the finest families in the east. You reside within your own circle of friends there, I'm sure; friends who share the same background and social standing."

"To be sure," I agreed.

"You'll always walk among them here, but not with them. You're far more cultured and refined; much too sophisticated."

I was sure she spoke to me with esteem rather than spite, though I was convinced that she appreciated the concept that I would always be an outsider and, therefore, present little competition in regard to upstaging her when it came to trust and familiarity. I would bet that she counted on the locals' inability to communicate with me, though it would be a poor hope on her behalf as my status alone spoke volumes above her. Whether or not I could bridge the gap with these people mattered not at all; they would still look to me for influence if not true friendship.

However, in response to her supposition I stressed, "But if I must live alongside them, then I should like to be able to relate to them."

"How could you when you'll always know far more than most of the people in this whole territory ever will? You are educated while so many of them cannot even read, let alone write. They live a tough existence, here. You've never known a hard day's work in your life, I'm sure. It's likely there will always be a rift between you and them, great or small."

I was confident that she was pleased by this belief of hers and, hearing this, I was saddened as it served only to remind me of the distinct gap that currently divided Billy and me. Prior to our dispute, I hadn't felt as though a great precipice separated us, but perhaps this was only an illusion because, as Sallie had pointed out, I would never truly fit in, and if this were to be the case, it could only mean that Billy and I were fated to remain estranged due to the unseen barrier of position while conversely, made obvious to me by the circumstances I witnessed, he and Sallie would always maintain an easy connection as they shared the same cultural background. I imagined, then, that it was inevitable and only a matter of time that he and I would eventually drift further apart.

Thinking on this, though it saddened me, it encouraged me to selflessly make this an opportunity to pave the way for Billy and so I seized upon it.

Quietly I cleared my throat. "Actually, I have spent much time with William. He and I managed to get along quite well from the first; it is no secret that he is my favorite."

I looked steadily into her eyes after saying this to see if my sentiment found meaning. When I was sure it had I continued, "John is very impressed with him. William has been doing exceptionally well—he's rapidly ascending with John's own endorsement. I cannot help but express my admiration for him as it is my opinion that he will go far."

She smiled avidly at this observation of mine. "I have heard that you favor him so, but how far could he possibly go as a farmhand?"

She asked this question with optimism, though I detected the slightest hint of incertitude in her tone and saw it drift into her eyes, causing me to become vehemently defensive of Billy and emphatically inclined to challenge her.

"He is *no* farmhand, and as for his escalating potential, I can assure you he may go *very* far. He is a natural born leader, a trait that is not lost on John. William is clever and savvy, and it is only a matter of time before he has reached his pinnacle of success.

He is not yet even eighteen and already he is progressing, and it is no small thing that he has only been in John's employ for just over one month. At this rate, I wouldn't be surprised if someday, during his youth, he found himself at John's right hand. John already relies heavily enough on him as William has proven himself to be extremely competent. He moves quickly up the ranks, impressing John on a daily basis."

Now I must plant a seed of urgency to ensure her determination.

"There isn't a girl in town that does not have her eyes on him. He is besieged at every turn."

"Do you truly believe he will make something of himself?"

"How could I not? I know unquestionably that he is well on his way. I can assure you that his future is promising." I wanted to underscore this point, and so I added, "If he were not an exceptional boy, someone of my position would not bother with and endorse him as I do. It is plainly evident that he has tremendous potential and much to offer. And what clever wit he possesses! It makes him all the more appealing. Such an outstanding individual as he ought to be nurtured and groomed in order to prepare him for a future of prospects, an endeavor which I fully and happily intend to help cultivate. As I have said, in such a short time already, William has proven quite the valuable asset."

I could see that her interest was piqued and so I congratulated myself on the supremacy of my manipulative skills.

"He's quite remarkable, really," I finished.

She now seemed preoccupied in contemplating the sentiments I made during our discussion as she reflected on what I had articulated, and so I offered another calculated element. "You seem to get on with him well. Do you not agree that his company is by far more amusing than any other, and that he is quite agreeable as well?"

She established that she did in fact agree, and it was easy enough to see that I had persuaded her to consider him. And though I knew that Billy's God-given charm and charisma made him naturally engaging, I realized it would take my influence for him to be taken seriously and to get him past the gates of never. If I could persuade her that a girl of my station could be impressed by such a boy, then how could someone such as Sallie Chisum not be? I had made it abundantly clear to her that my reverence for him counted for something, and I had made it even more clear that, because he had my favor, Billy had received my full endorsement. It would not be a fool's belief to assume that I could make or break a man in John's eyes, and because I set my sights on Billy he was as good as successful. I could rest assured that Sallie Chisum was now aware of this.

But then, seeing how her thoughts labored over the possibility of such an opportunity, I was surprised by how my own thoughts turned troubled as I observed her mind function greedily. It was only natural for a woman to want to marry a man with the ability to care for her, and I could not begrudge her this—but my biased mind reasoned otherwise.

She was willing to accept him only if he were made a respectable enough suitor. I could read her heart with the intuition that God had blessed us women with, and at this I understood that she did not deserve him. How I cared for him, truly, despite his low-born standing, and the truth of it was it would not take much coaxing to get me to leave Lincoln with him and leave my riches and all the superfluous superficiality that had plagued me for sixteen years behind. I found Billy to be extraordinary, and I could attest to the fact that financial means did not make one exceptional all on its own. Money did not make a man great; a man either was or he wasn't—money only served to exacerbate his flaws or highlight his good character. With this, it occurred to me that, wealthy or not, it was she who, with her greed and success scheming, was not good enough for him.

I began to feel guilty; I was campaigning for Billy the same way in which I despised how others campaigned for me: Pre-contraction. I shamelessly promoted him which, in turn, had in fact shamed me. Still though, my actions were consummated out of thoughtfulness rather than financial prospect, and so there was some comfort after all. I wanted him to excel into a better life but I realized that by contriving and scheming to make him seem an appropriate suitor meant that I had inadvertently couriered the belief that in reality I did not think him good enough. But the truth was that I believed him to be better than most people, common or otherwise. He did not place value on one because of what one had or from where one came. These traits alone made him desirable, but I imagined what he could do if only he had the financial power to force others to notice that he was the very model of integrity, and I suppose it was this dilemma that accounted for my actions. He may have possessed a good, solid character, but he would need means to exact such an example.

Viola had been standing at the ready for some time now, whinnying, as she was anxious to be let out. Taking her cue, I expressed to Sallie my enjoyment in speaking with her and apologized for having to end the conversation. I received a warm goodbye from her in return.

The stableman helped me onto my English sidesaddle and after adjusting my skirt to lie attractively I strode off, bringing Viola to an easy pace once I reached as far as the house. Between the stable and the house there was a fairly steep grade, but upon reaching the crest I could see fully the beautiful grounds of the Chisum property as it stretched far and wide and seemed as lovely as a Church landscape painting in the early afternoon light. The land looked as if it were interminably open and made one feel small by comparison, causing me to think of John and his concern over my being out here on my own and the lie I told by promising him that I would not go far.

I desperately needed to be on my own and away from Billy and Sallie and the distress her coquettish behavior had caused me, and so I brought Viola to a full gallop quickly and imagined that I was running away. Unfortunately, however, I could not outrun nor discount the thought that Sallie and Billy were doubtlessly spending time together at this very moment, and the pang in my chest which I had grown accustomed to was insufferable but, nonetheless, I would be pleased to know if the kernel of thought I had planted within Sallie's mind had begun to grow. Though it would pain me to see him with another, much worse was the thought of him drifting for all of his life alone and, worse still, drifting afar from me. Honestly, I wanted for him to have both a happy life and the stability he longed for. His competency made him an excellent candidate for Sallie should he rise through the ranks, and this would be worth his falling in love; I could give up my passionate thoughts of him for this. If he and Sallie succeeded together satisfactorily, then chances were Billy would always be a part of my life. I could therefore ensure his survival as well as my own vicariously through him. Better to see him with another, especially one of worthiness, than to not see him at all. I should like to see him have a decent, happy life.

I slowed Viola when I heard the hoof beats and whinny of a mount behind me. I turned to see Billy riding his pony, pacing it in order to approach me. My heart simultaneously leapt and dropped; As much as I desperately wanted him to pay attention to me, I equally felt I could not look him in the eye. I pretended as though I thought there might be trouble back at Chisum's so that I could maintain the strength I'd need in order to help me endure the awkwardness I felt.

"What is it?" I demanded to know, attempting to keep my tone even and cool.

"John says you were out here riding on your own."

Damn that John! Did I not specifically tell him I wanted to be on my own without the guardianship of Billy for once? He always found the need to check up on and protect me!

Looking evenly at Billy I stoically answered, "I am."

"I don't think you ought to be out here on your own."

Once again a man was deciding what was best for me, telling me what I should and should not do.

"Are these John's words or your own?"

"Both. He tells me you prefer to be on your own."

I would not have minded having the courage to lie, telling him that, yes, I preferred to be on my own, and that I did not want or need his looking after. My first pouty instinct was to drive him away, but I checked myself. This was as good excuse as any to have an opportunity to spend missed time with him, and it would allow me to drop the icy, detached act I exhibited and permit him to take the lead while allowing me to save face. I could agree to his riding with me under the guise of consenting to his protection and simultaneously hope that this moment would be pivotal in closing the rift between us as I was prideful and, therefore, unable to initiate crossing the chasm that separated us on my own. And so, congenially, I engaged him.

"I only intend to stay by the creek bed, and so I'd hate for you to feel obligated to ride with me; you've only just returned from your ride with Sallie and I'm sure you must be both famished and exhausted."

He gave me a clever grin as though he saw directly through my pretense.

"You could easily get very lost out here, Lucy. You could follow the creek as you say, but I'd be willing to bet you that you'd get bored and stray from that path eventually."

"I suppose, then, that you think you know me so well," I sarcastically remarked, temporarily forgetting my genial intentions. He ignored the slight.

"Look at all those trees over there." He jerked his head toward the winter-barren grove instructing me to look and so I obliged him.

"So?"

"So, you could easily get turned around in there."

"I'm sure I'd do just fine."

"I figure you think you might. But nonetheless, there are plenty of other dangers out here besides getting lost which, I might point out, are a very real possibility. Why do you think Mr. Chisum has so many men riding and watching his land and livestock?"

I looked at him. "How would I know? Why does he?"

"Scavengers, Indians, thieves…things of that sort. And then of course there are the

Murphy and Dolan men always looking to cause trouble. They've been known to come along every now and then and start problems or steal cattle."

I turned, looking around to view the property, swallowing hard and remaining quiet, thinking about what he had just told me.

"I don't think you ought to risk running into any one of those situations," he warned.

I had to agree, "No…I suppose not."

We rode together in silence and I was amazed at how we could still so easily enjoy this quiet peace with one another so comfortably after our nasty quarrel and the distance it had caused us. I had to admit that I was excited to finally have him here with me again, though I would not tell him so; I was still determined to keep up the pretense of my authority, affable intentions or not.

We rode ahead through the leafless Dogwoods. I hadn't seen them in bloom out here yet; they appeared as large bare shrubs as we rode past them towards the taller trees which were spaced out and barren of leaves as well.

"I cannot see how you felt I would get lost here. The trees are bare and the land open. It seems as though it would be easy enough for me to find my way."

"I'm sure it does. But like I said, it's easy to get turned around if you go too far, especially when everything looks just the same."

We approached the edge of where the taller trees began and passed their threshold. He lifted a finger and surveyed the area with it, "Do you see all of these trees?"

"Yes."

"Looks all the same, don't it?"

I had to agree that they did; ashy-white, cracked trunks all identical to one another. And he had been right; I would not have confined myself to a boring ride by following the creek bed. I would have been tempted to venture out and explore my surroundings. He knew me well enough, indeed.

Not really caring, but wanting to keep him talking to me I asked, "What sort of trees are these?"

"Sycamores."

All of a sudden I grew upset. At present we could only manage a dull, superficial conversation relegated to the risks of being lost amongst the trees. I pined for the lost days in which we would speak to one another with such ease, talking incessantly, hardly any topic prohibited, learning from one another and making each other laugh in such a manner that I would be scolded by Colleen should I have been caught.

I risked a glance at him and noticed that a ray of the early afternoon sun had, as usual, illuminated his eyes strikingly, crossing over the bridge of his nose and spreading across the flawless skin of his fair cheeks. His face was relaxed and content, making it all the more evident what a pretty youth he truly was, causing me to further miss and lust after him.

"You and Sallie…" I dared. The words were out of my mouth before I realized I would speak them.

"What about it?"

I swallowed with difficulty; none of this was my business. Perhaps once upon a time I could ask without the risk of offense, but I was unsure just now if I should proceed. I was about to make an attempt over a delicate matter, desperate to search him out for a hint, some clue as to whether or not I still held any sway with him or if, to my chagrin, he cared for her. If so, he might conceivably disclose whether or not he'd like me to make the match. I played with Viola's reigns, wondering what to say next and how I should advance the conversation.

"She's very pretty," I managed.

In a lively, imitation Irish brogue he agreed, "Aye. She's a good-looking lass." He grinned at me, but I turned away.

"I could not help but notice you had bought two hearts of chocolate to give her as a present."

I looked away as I said this, still afraid to look directly at him should I become saddened in the event that he confess he had done this for her appreciation, or in the event I had overstepped some boundary. I only looked at him when I heard him chuckle lightly.

"Yeah, well…I guess it's like they say; I'm a terrible flirt."

He looked at me and gave me a deliberate, wily smirk, teasing me as he referred to my own assessment of him. At this I decided to keep quiet for the time being.

We rode for what seemed an hour when he instructed me to halt. He pulled on his reigns bringing his pony to a stop and brought his right leg over the horse's back to jump down. He then walked over and offered his hand to me, and I obliged him, lending my own hand which he took and squeezed affectionately, customarily stroking my knuckles ever so lightly with his thumb as he prepared to carefully help me down, placing his free hand upon my waste in order to help me keep my balance. These actions of his were wildly inappropriate as they were overtly intimate, but I found them thrilling and I minded not in the least as I reveled in his bold attentions.

After he had me safely down he walked back to his own horse and unbelted a blanket from his saddle—it seemed that he had come prepared. He spread it out at the base of one of the bare trees, sat down upon it, and again extended his hand to me indicating for me to sit alongside him. I grew positively anxious, marveling at the prospect of sitting so close to him way out here where we were so very alone. My body was buzzing as I was already feeling tempted by the mere sight of him.

Rather than immediately moving to sit with him as I longed to do, I stood there wasting time like a fool instead, being too busy rejoicing at the *thought* of having the chance to sit so close with him once again, as opposed to actually *taking* the opportunity. When I finally came to my senses and snapped out of my stupidity I noted that his eyes plead with me to join him which, I confess, was worth my senselessness as I was pleased to see how badly he wanted me to sit with him. Finally, I placed my hand within his once more so that he could guide me down along side of him.

I fixed my skirt as I lowered myself onto the blanket and purposefully leaned against him. I turned my face away from his slightly at first in an attempt to maintain the charade of my unflappable composure despite how rapidly my heart beat. Then I decided to look down at my gloved hands which rested in my lap as I realized that I was about to give in and relinquish the façade of my calm demeanor. Even more so, I declined to move away from his body to allow even a modicum of space between us; this close proximity I refused to pass up. As usual he was not wearing his gloves, and so I quickly removed my own, thinking back on that day on Wortley Street when he took my hand in his to help me into John's buggy and I, disappointedly, could not share the intimacy of holding his hand as I had wanted to because I wore the damn things. This time I would see to it that, should he grasp my hand again, it would be personally enjoyable. After all, I had missed the opportunity twice already today.

He sat with his left leg arched before him, his left arm resting by its elbow upon the knee allowing his hand to dangle casually over towards the inside of his thigh. His other leg lie stretched out before him flat against the blanket. He had an air of confidence about him that exceeded my own as I could see he did not need to fake it as I had. I would wager that this disposition of self-assurance had much to do with the independent, uncompromising life he had lived beginning at a much younger age which must have forced him to be so undoubtedly certain of himself. He had an easy, comfortable temperament around others which seemed to come naturally to him.

I bravely looked at him and found his eyes boring into mine which caught me off-guard for a moment, rendering me disabled. My anxieties besought me to look elsewhere as I could not bear his studying me so intently, but my heart and head instructed me to quit squandering these moments, and so this time I forced myself to look directly at him and return his gaze. Still staring at me he tilted back his hat which always made him look particularly appealing, and I, now unable to break the intense look, tried to calm the tension I felt by reminding myself that I, Elucia Grey Alexis Howard, ought to be able to look this boy in the eyes.

I could not catch my breath due to the pleasure of this cherished circumstance with Billy as my bindings made no allowances. As we sat quietly together he leaned in and hesitantly kissed me lightly upon my cheek. I turned to him, smiling impulsively, letting him see that he had pleased me greatly, but I was unsure of how to respond; if it were conventionally allowed, even acceptable, for me to kiss him back. I knew that it would be considered inappropriate because I was promised to another man, but hang that promise as it was not I who had approved the match. *I* approved of promising myself to Billy, and there was, of course, no one around but us two to see, and so no one other than we would know. But I wondered if Billy would think poorly of me should I give in and react with a kiss for him of my own.

I lowered my eyes and my face flushed as I deliberated how I should respond to his intimate gesture when suddenly I felt his hand slide upon my cheek opposite him and very gently turn my face to his. He kissed me again, fervently, and this time full on the mouth. I understood then that it was safe for me to return the indulgence, social convention be damned!

I wished I could say that my behavior was that of a decent, virtuous lady, pushing him away as he tempted my honor, but I could not. My want of him was urgent, and I believed whole-heartedly that he wasn't tempting me, but only simply wanted me the way I wanted him. I knew in my heart that his feelings were genuine, and when he stopped suddenly as if uncertain, his lips lingering only a hairsbreadth from mine, brief apprehension appearing imperceptibly in those brilliant blue eyes, I quickly lost my validity further by placing my hands upon his shoulders and impatiently pulling him toward me, making him understand that I wanted him to again kiss me, and so, taking my cue, he conceded, placing his lips against mine until he broke away for a mere fraction of a second before coming back again heatedly, the tips of his fingers lightly grazing my neck and causing me a pleasant faintness from his touching me in such a way. Despite whatever virtuous sanctity that resided within me, the inability to stop him was greater, rendering me completely and happily powerless.

When he pulled away again he looked at me, studying and taking me in. He seemed deep in thought, charting my face with eyes that seemed out of focus. My lips broke out into a smile so sudden it surprised me. I had missed him horribly, and now, suddenly, he was here, loving me. I might have insisted that my head was spinning, but my thoughts were so monopolized by my desire for this moment that I had awareness of nothing else but Billy. My mind was so diverted that I could not say that I might have noticed a dizzying spell.

He placed his hands around my waste and came back to kiss me again, but I stunned myself by turning my face from him, unexpectedly curious all of a sudden.

Whispering, I asked, "You were so angry with me—for what I am. Why show me this affection?"

He smiled and told me, "What you are? *That* girl? *That* night? That isn't who you are. I should know that better than anyone. I suffered being without you, believe me. I never should have been so prideful and foolish as to get so upset with you and done what

I did that day; I only wasted precious time. My feelings for you are so overwhelming that it turns out walking away from and forgetting about you isn't quite so easy."

I went red at his confession. I desperately wanted to apologize for the poor behavior I had exhibited toward him, for the terrible things I had said to him. I had been heartsick since that day, believing that he should think that I had meant those things. It caused me sleep that was restless; I was crushed beneath my own imprudence. How could I even begin to make amends?

"I am so very sorry for what I said to you. I didn't mean it, not any of it—"

He opened his mouth to speak.

"Please…let me finish. I've been anxious to end this complication between us."

He looked down, displaying a knowing smile and biting at his lower lip before looking back up at me.

"I know, Lucy. I didn't set a whole lot of store by what you said. I know you, the real you. I knew you were only being mean on purpose."

"You did?" I was taken aback; how clever he could be! "How did you know?"

"The way you were that day, it was out of the blue. There's no way in hell that the girl who let down her airs as you did, lying next to me in the grass, or sitting close to me, giving her secrets to me and treating me as an equal could be that way. I suspected you had an agenda," he smiled at me again, "but I couldn't have imagined what it was."

"But how I treated Phyllis—"

"I know why you did such a thing. You did hurt that girl's feelings, but, you forget that I know how grating she can be. I ain't saying it's okay, but I can only imagine what you must have to tolerate with her. Christ…she works at my own nerves!"

"Is that so?" I asked with a impishly derisive look.

He nodded, "Yeah, sure…" He looked away and down, adding sternly, "But I ain't saying it's right!"

"And so you still disapprove?"

He sniffed and then looked up at me. "I know you better than that. But I knew that something set you up to behave that way. You're by far too sophisticated to treat someone in such a way, no matter what your taste for them is. I figured you weren't quite yourself."

"But you still felt the need to reprimand me due to my poor conduct, though you admit to understanding that I was not myself and therefore doubtlessly within explicable limits."

"Lucy, I apologize if I overstepped my boundaries, but excuses or not, it made for an uncomfortable situation, and Phyllis has feelings, even if she is bothersome. I meant to make you aware, and at the same time, put an end to an ugly circumstance. But, again…I know it wasn't my place."

"No, Billy, you're wrong! As my best friend I value your guidance; I want your approval, and desperately so. I'd accept the reaction from no one else! Yours is the only opinion that matters."

I thought about what I had just said. Perhaps I should I tell him what had caused me to lash out at her; admit to him that my jealousy and disdain for her was more strain than I could bear at that moment, and that her boldness with Billy only served to increase my impatience with her—I felt that only I had the right to be so unrestricted with him. I was sure he would find this excuse logical if poorly executed, as there is never a reason for a lady to become so disagreeable; I am well aware of this rule. Then again, I doubt that Billy would accept any excuses I could offer on the matter as he admitted he would expect nothing but cordiality on my part. But clearly even I was capable of slipping and losing my self-control as well. Am I not human after all? And more hopeless than that, men did not often comprehend the wars held between women.

"Billy, I—the way she behaved with you…it was so blatant. I resented that I was not free to be as bold as she, and I begrudged that such an unbearable girl should get to exercise such freedom with you when I cannot! And that she should be able to be so straightforward without the slightest familiarity, receiving no repercussions of any kind! I found her crude. If it had been any other boy—"

"You were jealous," he teased obsequiously.

I smirked at him, trying not to laugh, when he spoke with sincerity, "I know, Lu. And I wouldn't say she got away without suffering any repercussions," he laughed.

I looked at him and found respite there, seeing his sympathetic smile. I turned my attention to smoothing my skirt because, though I wanted to smile at his deft perception of knowing me so very well, I thought better of being self-righteous just now considering that it was my self-righteousness which had placed me in such a predicament in the first place. But his empathy had alleviated the anxiety I had felt and, so, I could not help but feel vindicated. He knew, right or wrong, that my behavior was born out of the intolerance I felt for such a silly girl who had directed her attentions to the very young man whom I adored, and worse still, for all intents-and-purposes, he knew that matters were made far worse for me as I knew it was she who could be free to have him if he were so inclined to return her affection. Then I laughed at the absurdity of this concept. It was only regretful that the preposterousness of this thought did not indulge me with any influence at the time in order to help me avoid reacting so spitefully, which in turn would have helped me circumvent the rupture with Billy.

"She hasn't any couth," I insisted. "And yes…her forwardness with you, I admit, pushed me quite far. You are mine to be so acquainted with, not hers, and because of this, I lost my composure."

"Your composure was just fine, you can believe that!" he said, laughing irreverently. "You were nothing less than intimidating. Your status makes for you a personality that women must reckon with if they want your approval." He was still chuckling.

"I know it, Bill," was my lackluster response.

"But I don't want to talk anymore about what happened that night, Lucy. I just want to be here with you like this."

I gave a shy smile. I could feel the color rising in my cheeks again and I was suddenly, acutely aware of him sitting so close to me. My thoughts oddly drifted around the idea that he had had the opportunity to spend more time with Sallie, yet he chose to follow and sit out here with me. I then realized how ridiculous it was to think this. It was absurd to consider that any other woman was as important as I where Billy was concerned. I could feel how much I mattered to him down to my very soul. I *knew* we shared something special, he and I, and at times it seemed so very tangible. Finally, our bond was being acknowledged, and Billy could or would not ignore it any longer, deciding to make his feelings known to me. I realized that the argument we had was really a blessing in disguise, for without the time spent apart we may have still hid how we truly felt from one another. The thrill of his honesty was overwhelming. The boy all the girls wanted had wanted me, yet still, I wondered exactly how significant his feelings for me were since he knew I was meant to marry another and, therefore, he probably let himself believe that he must keep a certain distance from me. I knew I'd have to be subtle in my questions if I were to know the truth instead of told what he thought I wanted to hear.

"Billy?" I looked off in the distance. I would look anywhere but at him in the hopes that my discretion would encourage him to be honest.

"Yeah?"

"You told me about a girl once—a girl you knew in Sumner."

I inadvertently turned back to him and saw that he rolled his eyes, semi-amused.

"What about her?"

"You said she was your girl, and that you had left her behind."

He seemed indifferent to this. "Yeah. What else?"

"Is she still there waiting for you?"

He was quiet as he thought about my question. "I honestly don't know. Maybe."

"Do you think that one day you'll go back there to her? Or maybe bring her here to be with you?"

He shook his head, "No, I don't think I'd bring her here, and I don't have any intentions to go back to Sumner. At least not today."

I looked down.

"But you love her, do you not?"

He turned my face up to his, serious. "I thought I did, Lucy."

"Billy?"

"Yes, Bonita, my pretty one."

"I...I am..."

I put my head down as my eyes began to water, and I covered them with my hands. I was afraid to state my proclamation, and I was failing at my restrained intentions. The more information I tried to gather imperceptibly the more anxious I became to find out what I wanted to hear.

"Yes, Lu?"

I looked up and tried again, but I only managed to stutter again. "I..."

He shook his head, slightly entertained, and so I sensed that my objective was obvious to him, especially as I had a difficult time finishing my sentence. I continued to look at him; I badly wanted him to say what I could not dare. He looked over at me and mercifully said, "So now you're falling in love."

I sighed, relieved that he knew what it was I tried to say, saving me from saying it aloud on my own, and distressed that he only pointed out what he supposed my feelings were instead of declaring his own. I continued to look away, not wanting to show him my face.

"Falling?" I said with great difficultly as I began to weep quietly. "Fell, Billy. Have you not done so, too? With me?"

He closed his eyes and took a deep breath in a suppliant appeal. "Don't let's talk about that."

"Why not? If it's true, then there is no harm in our being honest with one another. If it is not, then that will be that."

"Lucy, I know I'm young, but I would bet all I had, which admittedly isn't much, that there is no other woman like you. You're the first girl I've met that I could talk to. I mean really talk to. I can tell you anything." He paused a moment and I took advantage of the break.

"So then, tell me this!"

He sighed, "Lucy...Everything about you is the opposite of what I would have expected from a girl like you. You interest me. Most of all you talk to me, not at me. You want to know about me, about my life, and you're sincere in your interest. I...I don't know. I think of you as being so much like me."

He seemed to feel as if he believed he had said something wrong. "I mean...I know you're so far above me and I'm just some nobody passing by, but there's so much about you, and me, that seem so much alike, even if they're different. There is nobody that I can talk to as I do you."

"Yes, so you've said. What exactly is it that you are trying to say to me?" Restless, I said this a bit more harshly than I had intended.

He looked at me, his expression stripped of pretense, his eyes resigned, reflecting that he had no agenda in saying such things to me. Perhaps my affluence had rendered me unimpressed by wealth, and I could see how unbelievably special he was despite his having not a cent to his name, loving and wanting him dearly, still. Our feelings for one another were completely devoid of greed and full of innocence, unlike the match my father made for me with John. All of the things that Billy and I shared with one another should have made it easy for him to give me a straight answer. God help me if he should say he did not share my aspirations of love.

"Lucy, I won't dare speak of love to you. It's ridiculous for someone like me to profess something so bold to someone like you."

"Billy, you are ridiculous for thinking something as clumsy as all that. Am I not a woman with emotions? Feelings are complimentary; money cannot buy such things! And so it isn't up to us, logically, what our hearts want. We are all born to feel freely! My heart tells me that it must be you, and I know that your heart must tell you how it is you feel for me."

I raised myself up and knelt before him, grabbing him desperately by the lapels of his jacket.

"I'm so very happy now that we have settled matters between us. Billy, you've made New Mexico my home. Now that I have you, life here is not only bearable but very beautiful. You are beautiful to me. And now I've admitted to you how I adore you, so can you not feel comfortable now in telling me what it is you feel?"

Looking at one another he leaned up and again placed his lips upon mine which I welcomed with enthusiasm. He pulled me back down from my knees and placed his hands upon my face and his lips upon other areas: beneath my right ear, against the taut-ness of my neck as I turned it to subtly let him know I wanted him to go there, and then finally beneath my chin before finding my lips again.

"I do love you, Lucy," he whispered in my ear.

He unbuttoned his jacket and my hands were curled into fists as I clung tightly to his vest, pulling him close to me as if to keep him from moving away until, finally, we noted the time and discovered that we had been gone for nearly two hours. Reluctantly, he packed up his bedroll and belted it upon his saddle as we prepared to mount our horses to head back. He lifted me up onto Viola and I then watched him climb expertly onto his horse.

As we approached the house I noticed Sallie sitting on the porch surrounded by most of the boys; Minxie, Steve, Josiah, and the Coe cousins among others. I took a sly look at Billy to see how he would react to this scene, but I found him looking the other way as we passed by the group. Sallie, however, had looked in our direction and waved, happy to find Billy coming back in from his ride with me. We approached the stable and, after helping me down, he took the horses inside and I waited for him to settle them and reappear. Upon exiting the building he offered me his arm which I accepted and together we walked toward the assembly gathered around Sallie. As we drew near I saw that she held a book.

"May I inquire about the book you are reading, Sallie?" I asked.

Proudly, she replied, "Pride and Prejudice," as she looked at Billy, smiling keenly as if this should be meant to impress him—as if he would know the significance of a Jane Austen novel. This caused me to decide to demonstrate my own knowledge of the subject in order to both challenge and put her in her place.

"I have read it," I remarked, "But I cannot tolerate her narratives as they often tend to drag on; how dreadfully she bloviates. I find her writing tedious and experience boredom in reading her pages, though I must admit to having a slight interest as I find her stories are quite progressive. It's only too bad that she tends to lose her audience as they must sift through a great abundance of print."

"Do you? Find her progressive, I mean? I find the opposite to be true, myself. She seems to condone propriety and is reproachful by the lack of it. I find much truth and honesty in that. I could not find a grain of liberalism within the pages as she seems to adhere to societal guidelines."

A point to Sallie for attempting to match wits with me and keep the pace. It is too bad I meant to take her down.

"I can assure you, it is there, but it is not contained within the lines themselves, but rather between them. She is progressive in that she mocks the superficiality of class, writing of class differentials and the triviality of all that goes with it, such as love having no place between two people divided by a societal gap. Austen seems to disfavor this as she scornfully acknowledges it as an unfortunate and disagreeable truth. She is sardonic in her narrative and dialogue. Austen also finds no sense in a woman having to rely on a man as an invalid might a nursemaid. That perception is quite enlightened. In fact, allow me to correct myself as I ought; if one pays attention to her works, one should easily discover how she ridicules societal hierarchy, passing it off as nonsense."

It was silent as Sallie seemed as if she would graciously accept her defeat. But after putting her head down in embarrassment, she remained quiet for a moment before making an acerbic attempt at a rebound. Sarcastically she stated, "You are quite observant."

I responded with my own derision. "I ought to be, as I am exceptionally educated and have read Austen works nearly all of my life. I am now utterly bored by the topic."

The boys remained quiet during and after my repartee with Sallie, and I took this opportunity to make my exit.

"If you'll all excuse me, I must change for dinner. Sallie, perhaps we can talk more about the book at a later time, when I've nothing better to do."

She nodded with false civility as she let out a gasp of aversion. It was not difficult to doubt that she was only too happy to have me vacate the premises after she had made this exceptionally clear. I didn't mind, and I could not blame her. After all, I had brazenly belittled her intelligence during our confrontation and embarrassed her before Billy and the others.

Throughout dinner Sallie and I were seated next to one another under advises of our self-appointed betters in an effort to help advance an age-related friendship. We sat exchanging pleasantries and nothing more, though I attempted to make amends with polite conversation, feeling regretful such as I did as it was ill-mannered and unladylike of me, after all, to challenge her in front of her admirers. Perhaps I should have allowed her the simple triumph she intended to impress Billy with as I knew there was nothing that I need prove to him, and therefore, it was unnecessary for me to chasten her. Was I truly so unnecessarily covetous of Billy that I was willing to construct competition with another female over the smallest of matters due to my love of the boy and, therefore, invent my own compulsory want to needlessly impress him? In contemplating the matter, I wondered, too, if Sallie was honestly such a poor sport, as she was nothing but curt with me as we sat dining despite my best efforts to conduct a cordial conversation. If so, I decided that she should perhaps better equip herself with sharper wits, and I had also come to the conclusion that I had indeed did her a favor as perhaps her earlier humiliation would inspire her to try harder in the event of any future debates. Then again, for one woman to undermine another in front of potential suitors was a perilous thing as it made the loser seem simple or feeble-minded, a trait found unattractive in a woman by a man. This would be a shame for Sallie, and I should have held my tongue, but then I looked at Billy and decided if one of us should come out the victor and receive the spoils, then let it be me.

# 6

# 1877, December

I waited for Billy to take me to the ring with him. I had been passing the time riding Viola in the yard when he finally came in from the fields; I had not changed into the riding attire I wore when we practiced.

"Hey Lucy!" he said with a smile.

Broadly, I smiled back at him.

We rode back to the McSweens' together so I could change. When we had reached the house we dismounted and went inside.

"Did you know they don't have any violets?"

I turned to look at him, unsure of what he was referring to. "I'm sorry. Violets?"

He seemed uncertain, taken aback by my confusion, but replied, "In town. In the shops…there aren't any. They aren't in season, at least that's what I'm told."

Still confused, I laughed a little and asked, "Am I to believe this is a misfortune?"

He took his hat off and approached me. "You like violets. You said so. You like to wear their scent, but you can't get it here. I thought I could get you flowers, but all I could get my hands on was this…"

He held out his palm and in it was a spool of ribbon—as close to violet in color as possible, perhaps a bit darker in shade. I looked up at him, enchanted. My eyes were inquiring.

"For your hair. I thought you could use it for that, or for something else," he took in a nervous breath and lowered his head, shaking it dismissively as though he were making a fool of himself, which couldn't have been farther from the truth; he had endeared himself to me even more so, and I was enamored by his sweetness.

"When I asked for something violet, this is what I was shown."

His expression longed for my approval, but he needn't have worried himself. I approved a thousand times over!

I laughed ecstatically at how well he had tried to please me and accepted his gift. I turned to admire it when I heard him say, "It's quiet."

Innocently enough, as I played with and wound my brand new gift of ribbon around my fingers I gave him details.

"Everyone is in town tending to their own matters."

Billy's countenance was thoughtful and he asked me when they were expected back. I found his particular look and question strange as the facts were boring enough, but I continued to answer him.

"They'll be gone a while."

"Yeah? How do you figure?"

I furrowed my brow at him, considering his interest in the matter odd, as if it were of some importance to him that the house should remain empty.

"Alex and John are at the store handling business matters, and all of the women have gone to the market for supplies and are planning tea afterwards and..."

Instantly, I grew self-conscious as I gave these explanations, pausing briefly as I studied Billy, suspicious of his objective. I now understood that his face did not reflect interest in the reasons why everyone had gone, but rather, it gave the impression of his being elated at the prospect of being alone with me. I wondered if this were true, and if his questioning me was an attempt to calculate the duration of the household's absence, but then I dismissed my reservations as silly; I did not believe he concealed any wicked intentions that should cause me anxiety. After all, John himself had assigned this boy to me, putting him in charge of my welfare when John did not need him elsewhere, and I've never felt safer than with him. Still, I could not deny that my usual ease with him had been somewhat displaced. He had never before caused such a nagging sensation in my gut as he did just now, a misjudged awareness that I could not suss out tugging at the corners of my mind. Surely, this feeling was my mistake.

Still, I continued, "They will have tea at the café while they wait for Alex and John to finish reports, and then all will have an early dinner together at the Wortley Hotel."

"And what about you?"

"What about me?"

"Don't they expect you to eat?"

"Yes, of course. John's cook will come and prepare my dinner."

"When?"

"Six o'clock. Why should that matter?"

"Why didn't you go into town with them?"

"Because I am to spend today with you as planned; as usual you are expected to stay with me until everyone comes back."

What my senses had tried communicating with me became plainly obvious. It was as though I were slapped in the face—it was so shockingly blatant! How I could have misinterpreted the situation I couldn't say, other than prior to that day at Chisum's, Billy had always been a near perfect, cautious gentleman. But by allowing him to seductively play with me as he had, I felt absurd and stupid that I could be so daft! My faculties had failed me and I silently scolded myself! Until now our secret ardor had been relatively faultless between two innocent youths wholly devoted to one another as we had to steal little moments here and there. However, this being the first time we would have true privacy, of course he would mean to take full advantage! He had never held back from what he wanted of me before, and I knew he knew me well enough to know that I would not resist him, so why should he not plan to have his way with me now?

I now understood my mistake in imparting the plans and whereabouts of the house's occupants. If I had not done so, I would have gotten through this day intact. I had unintentionally encouraged him to do as he pleased by presenting him with the chance to do so, and I realized that I had somehow inadvertently yet deliberately given the impression that I expected he spend his time alone with me by suggesting that it was in fact expected of him as usual! The trust I had in him had caused me to blunder so carelessly when I allowed him in here alone with me while I redress, and a man I had been intimate with at that! And his gift—I had accepted it! But no…surely he had intended nothing egregious by the small gesture. He would have given it to me no matter what.

In his eyes I could see his thoughts working out the opportunistic details in his mind. I had unwittingly made a precarious offer in my naiveté, for what other purpose would it serve in his mind to point out how utterly alone we both were here? *Innocence!* I thought, *only innocence*! I now felt foolish in having ignored my initial instinct as I should have both trusted my feelings and knew straight away of Billy's intentions considering how entirely well I knew him! I was more than aware of his sly reputation with the girls, and had I not been subject to and experienced his desires for myself? Of course he would do with me what he wanted if it pleased him—hadn't he already done so! My woman's intuition shrewdly picked up on the perception that my clueless innocence had either overlooked or refused to recognize.

But then my thoughts shifted from shock to perplexity. Despite the complete disbelief I had toward my own imprudence, I now only stood there bewildered considering how I had not once thought of running from him to preserve my virtue for all of my self-reprimanding. In fact, I felt just as curious of the situation as I was startled. I was taken aback, mortified even, by my own willingness to make excuses by believing I was ensnared now and that there was *nothing* I could do to dissuade him. I was willing to stay and chance a scandal in the event he should approach me in a most indelicate manner. I had no plans to refuse him. In truth, I found the expectations of how to conduct myself as a lady in public of more concern than whether or not I should entertain his actions, and I could always secret away the deed.

Quickly, he took his advantage and, when he pulled me to him, I was too astonished to contest him. A thought of John passed fleetingly through my mind. He had taken to staying here at the McSweens' as well as me, and with Billy here, assessing me intimately, it felt too close for comfort.

My hand in his, he took me to the couch and pulled me down to sit close to him. It was hard for the two of us to find time such as this where we could be completely alone and play out our feelings as we did just now without the fear of prying eyes. He said nothing, he only looked at me and, seemingly without his realizing it, he stood up and pulled me along with him again. I followed him mindlessly, drifting in a surreal state of interest. I followed him without argument with the strange thought that I refused to be entirely unhappy.

My back was to him and his arms were wrapped around me. He kissed me softly, gradually moving his lips from place to place upon my body. I remained still, enjoying this. We hadn't much time before the house would be occupied. Reluctantly, we rose from my bed and broke apart to dress. I took an evening dress from my wardrobe, leaving my riding dress in a heap on the floor. He helped me snap my corset back into place as it was too tightly laced for me to do on my own. He kissed me and professed his love again; telling me he wished he could have me for himself and promising that he would never stray far from me.

He told me he could fix it, what he had done. When I asked him what it was he meant by this, he told me of what I could do to help ensure he would not get me into trouble. I became upset at his suggestion, expressing emphatically that I would never do such a thing. If God saw fit to give me the child of a man whom I loved and who loved me, then I would be nothing but happy with such a blessing. I would not turn to whores tricks, I told him bitingly. He conveyed a look of contentment, promising me that he would want nothing more, but still, imploring me not to be foolish. I ignored his plea. I refused to sink to the level that he was asking of me, angry that he should suggest it.

Once we both were dressed he stoked the fireplace in my room. It was relatively warm already and I wondered why he should do this when I saw him bring his duster over. He had laid it out over the bed before having me and, it, covered with the blood of my virginity, went into the fire. There, I saw who I had been burn.

○○○

"Where can I get my hands on some violets?"

Billy and Minxie were hunting with the Coe cousins, hanging back to talk.

"Violets? You're not goin' all frilly on me now, are ya Bill?"

Billy laughed, "Hell, you know me…you never know which way I'm gonna turn," he laughed again, "Actually, Lucy likes them. I'd like to get her some."

Minxie looked at Billy, surprised. "Ya gotta be kidding me, Bill! What is it ya fink you're doing? Ya know all the bleedin' guys are talking—"

"I don't care what all the guys are doing, or saying…they can take a flying leap for all I care. Shoot…Lucy's my friend and she's all alone out here. We enjoy each other's company, that's all. We've grown close as friends, and I'd like to acknowledge that. I want to please her with a present from me." Billy grew quiet and thought a moment. "You know, I'd never known anybody like her. She's different."

"Yeah, she's different! She's the bloody boss's *wife*!"

"Wife-to-be..."

"Oh Lord, Billy!"

"What?"

Minxie shook his head in frustration. "Ya don't see it? What ya just said only proves me point"

"Yeah? And what's that?"

Minxie shook his head again, this time in stunned amusement. "Ya don't see her as his 'wife', Bill! Calling her his wife-to-be....well, read between the bloomin' lines, goddammit!"

Billy thought about this and realized that Minxie had a point. He ought to be more careful when he spoke of Lucy, and to that end, he'd try not to speak of her at all.

"Yeah, Minx, I catch your meaning. Still...We're...Well, we are who we are. I'm not gonna stop talking to her because the hens will cluck."

Minxie laughed, "Right. I'll respect that, Bill. Seems ya got your mind set to it, no matter."

"It's because she's a woman and I'm a man that makes our friendship all so offensive."

After saying this Billy thought back to the afternoon he spent with her in her bedroom. They were not simply friends, but everyone couldn't be the wiser.

"She's been cordial and understanding with me. She's never condescending, and a girl of her status ordinarily wouldn't bother with a guy like me. But she likes me, and I like her. The only trouble is, where do I get the flowers? I can't go into Tuntall's, and I sure as shit wouldn't dare go to Dolan's."

Minxie looked at Billy and considered him. He decided to ask him a personal question to fell the bad feeling within his gut.

"Billy...I want your honesty. All the men here look her way. I can't believe ya have a perfectly innocent relationship wif that girl."

Billy stared ahead and contemplated whether he should confide in his friend or not. He concluded that Minxie could be trusted, but he still needed to consider the idea of betraying Lucy and cheapening what had happened between them. Any other girl would make no difference. He felt that it could work in his favor to have a friend to keep his back, and this made all the sense to him, but he wouldn't divulge all the details.

"Minxie...I hope you're not suggesting she ain't a proper—"

"Christ, no! I'm talking about ya having less than admirable ideas."

Too late. Billy looked down, defeated. "It's true that I have feelings for her that are more than friendly...."

"I knew it! Ya son-of-a-bitch!" Minxie said with a hint of laughter.

"Minx, I think it's complicated. She doesn't love John, and he doesn't love her. The first time I saw her I...She never once judged me, do you know that? I don't remember the last time somebody looked at me and didn't figure I was up to no good."

"How do ya know she don't love him?"

"She's confessed as much to me. *She* should know. There's something there that gives us comfort with each other. I want to have her company. I enjoy it, and she enjoys mine."

"Ya don't have the marrying sort of feelin's for that girl?"

Billy looked at Minxie seriously, the humor draining from his face.

"Minxie?"

"Yeah?"

"I do love her. I never met anyone like her. I couldn't help falling for her."

"Cheese and rice, Billy! It's always the bloody same wif ya! Ya couldn't leave this one alone? Just this one? If Tunstall finds out...."

"He won't find out...*will he*?"

Minxie caught his meaning. "No, he won't. Not by me. But if ya fink you'll be able to duck that flirtatious behavior—"

"I'll do all right."

"And what about the others—in town?"

"What about them?"

"How will you be able to hide the fact that there's only one girl that owns ya? Are ya suddenly gonna to be able to hide from the fact that you've paid attention to nearly every girl in Lincoln already? Sooner or later your affections're gonna present themselves. I know ya well enough now to know how anxious ya're when it comes to the fairer ones. Near as I can tell, you're damned, Bill. Ignoring them will seem odd behavior, and paying them attention will put ya past Lucy. Will she tolerate that?"

"Yes. She has as much to lose as I do. She'll understand. She needs to hide her feelings just as I do, else John would become suspicious. She won't risk it. Besides, my flirtatious behavior may just work to my favor."

"How so?"

"Maybe it won't look so suspicious, me treating Lucy so fairly if I'm treating them all that way," Billy smiled at his own cleverness.

"Heaven and hell...I guess ya both got it all figured out, don't ya?"

Billy heard sarcasm in Minxie's voice. He understood the problem he had created and the trouble that both he and Lucy could find themselves in, and now he had involved

Minxie. He didn't care about himself, other than being driven away from her, but he did not want her ruined. He couldn't conveniently break the spell she had cast even if it was life and death. After making love to Lucy, he could not see beyond her, and he knew this was certain.

# 7

## December-February, 1877

I put a candle in the window so Billy would know it was safe to come to my room. Colleen would come in and help me prepare for bed and then leave me to myself for the rest of the night. I tried to wait patiently for his knock, but I became more anxious as I longed to see him. Finally I heard the light rapping and the door cracked open. He stood there, his face uncertain.

"She's gone, we're alone. Hurry and close that door!"

He did so and came towards me, upon which I jumped down from my bed and ran to him, leaping so that he'd catch me, his guns pressing into the backs of my thighs as he held me up and kissed me. He walked us over to the bed and laid me down there. My nightgown was raised up above my knees after having my legs wrapped around him, and he bent down and kissed the insides of each thigh, sliding his fingers up and down my calf softly as he did so, making me giggle uncontrollably.

"I love you, Billy. I'm so glad you came. I confess I feared you might not."

"Nothing will keep me from you, Bonita, I can promise you that."

He slid his arm beneath me and lifted my body to position it further upon the bed. He climbed next to me, placing his arm across me, just below my breasts. He removed his hat and carelessly tossed it so that it landed by the bottom of the bed. I ran my fingers through his hair and leaned in to kiss him.

I slid my leg over his and played with the buttons of his shirt. I leaned my head in just beneath his chin and nuzzled him there. He stroked my back with his fingers before pressing me tight against him.

"Where do the men think you are?" I asked.

"In town, I guess. I rode with them and turned back. They were in an excited mood—I doubt they noticed me separate."

"And if they wonder where you are when they come back?"

"Don't worry about that. It wouldn't be all that unusual. Believe me, what I do is of no concern to them."

I believed I understood what he meant, but I didn't press the issue. All that mattered to me was that he was here sharing my bed and no one else's."

He untwisted the ribbon holding my braided hair and let it fall free, running his hands through it, and then again placed his hand on my exposed thigh. I put my hand to his face and looked at him contemplatively. "Your eyes are beautiful."

He smiled amused, and turned his head to playfully bite my thumb.

"Billy?"

"Yes Bonita."

"I don't have to stay here."

"What are you talking about?"

"I don't have to stay...*here*."

Billy looked at me, perplexed. He was silent for a moment before asking, "What are you driving at, Lucy?"

"I can show you."

I climbed out of bed and crept swiftly across the hardwood floor towards my wardrobe. Billy sat up, interested. I opened the doors and knelt down by my luggage chest. I snapped it open and pulled it apart. Billy quietly came off the bed and knelt beside me in anticipation. My luggage chest yawned wide before us. I placed my hand within a notch set in a panel as if to open a drawer, but it instead opened on a pair of hinges. There, my safe was presented. I turned the tumbler, deftly selecting the combination. The safe yielded, revealing the money and fine jewels held within. I peered at Billy as he studied its contents, his eyes wide with amazement.

"We can sell these things," I offered.

He reached in and pulled out a sapphire necklace that lie loose. He held it up and admired how it glinted in the firelight. "What are these, Lucy?"

"Sapphires; my inheritance. I have so much more, tucked away within the drawers here inside the safe. Jewels worth more than what you can imagine. I wouldn't expect you to obtain what they're worth, not out here, but they could fetch more than enough for us to start our own life—"

"You want me to sell these?"

"We could build a house and make it ours. I know you and Jim talk of owning your own farm someday. You could have that...with me."

He smiled at me skeptically but affectionately.

"Minxie and Jim could come, too. You could have what you want; I can give it to you."

"Lucy...I can't believe all that you have here. This is unbelievable. I never seen so many riches!"

He lay down on his back and played with the sapphires, captivated by them.

"I don't care for these things," I told him, "I've had finery all my life—it means nothing to me. I've only had you for a short while. To me, you are what is precious, flesh and blood. Not these hard, cold stones."

Without taking his eyes from the stones he smiled.

"You would have the opportunity to turn them into currency," I pointed out.

"How do you figure?"

"John now has you with him when he travels."

"Except for when he leaves me with you."

"That will change."

"Yeah? How so?"

"Because from now on you will insist that you go with him always, as will I. I've seen the way things are here, I am not blind. Things get worse every day. When you travel with him you could attempt to pawn these off…in an unfamiliar town. And you can go off on your own out there at every chance!"

"Yeah, and get arrested for stolen possessions," he snorted sarcastically, "Do I look like I should be in possession of things like this?"

"Billy, I have money here, too. Did you not see it? Five-thousand dollars' worth. We could go now and use the money to travel away from here. With my fine clothes we'll not be suspicious. And we could dress you as well. We would say that we are funding our way through the west. We could acquire so much with all of these things! Even my dresses and gowns! We could turn a fortune's worth of everything! And with such terrible greed out here we'll fare all the better! They'll turn a blind eye if it brings them wealth!"

He sat up with a start and, disbelieving, asked, "Are you listening to yourself?" Then he stared soberly at the sapphires pooled in his palm. He whispered so low I very nearly missed his words, "Lucy…I can't…I couldn't do that."

"Billy, why? Do you not want to make a home together? A home that is all yours? And mine? We could make a life together, Billy. Isn't that what you want? And there's more! I have a land deed by proxy, to be signed over to John upon our marriage. Over one hundred acres!" Out loud I contemplated to myself, "Of course, Alex is the executor in this matter and keeps the deed in his possession, but I could do my best to locate its whereabouts…"

He chuckled, "Usted está loco; You're crazy!"

We sat quietly a moment, both in thought, when he asked, "How come it's you who has land to sign to John? I thought the business was between him and your father."

"It's been given to me for the purpose of my giving it to John as my wedding gift to him. It's to be signed over to him after we've exchanged our vows."

He thought on this a moment and then, "I thought it's you who's supposed to be his wedding present."

"Well that gift has gone to hell now, hasn't it?"

He laughed a little then smiled knowingly at me.

"My giving myself to him is only to ensure that our union is secure, to entitle him to the gains."

Upon saying this Billy's face changed. He lost his smile and I could see the muscles working in his jaw as he ground his teeth.

"If I wasn't sorry for what I done before, I'm really not sorry now."

Now it was I who smiled at him and, hoping I could use his anger to my advantage, said, "We could take it—I could sign the tract of land over to you, they'll be less likely to ask questions if a man decides to sell his own land—"

Laughing now he said, "Hang on there, señiorita—you're dreaming…"

"—we could gain even more!" I could hear the desperation in my own voice as he refused to take me seriously. "We would make a fine life, you and I. Wouldn't you want that—with me?"

His eyes lit up at me as if he thought he had offended me. "Yes! Yes, it's what I want. But I don't want to do this anymore. I've been stealing to live since leaving Silver City, and I refuse to steal from you so that I could have what I want. I'd like to make my own way. Being here has finally given me a brand new, honest start. Besides, even if we did take these things and run, they'd come after us!" he pointed to the contents in the safe, "They'd come for you and them," he peered at me, serious. "And what would they think of me if I took you and your money? You're set to marry another man. They'd think me a crook and a good-for-nothing maggot! I don't want to be with you like that, like some miscreant. And what sort of man lives his life off a woman anyway?"

Without a beat I answered, "John Tunstall."

"What?"

"John Tunstall lives his life off of a woman. And my father lives off of me, too! Why is it that you think I am with him? What have I been telling you? It's for what I can get them both!"

His lips broke into a smile and with a small laugh he pulled me close to him, kissing me on the forehead. "I love you for saying that. Well, you can be sure that none of your things make me want you all the more, Bonita. You'll do just fine for me as you are. I don't want you for what you have."

"It's as though I am a carcass being fed on by a couple of vultures!"

He laughed, "How very dramatic."

"I wouldn't want anyone to think poorly of you, but if we start over someplace new, it wouldn't matter. I'm not at all concerned for what they'll think of me here or back home! And I know already, Billy, that you love me anyway, but don't miss the point. It hasn't anything to do with why you want me, but rather how I can give us both the freedom to do as we please. And you wouldn't be stealing a thing from me. I would share it with you. It would be yours. We won't take all of it if you fear them coming for us. We'll take only enough to get us away from here. It is a big country, Bill. We could get lost easily."

He looked at the sapphires again and I continued attempting to persuade him, "For as long as I can remember I've prayed for you. What if my prayers have been answered? What a small price to pay if that were true! There is nothing I wouldn't give up for you, and I will promise that, if you take me away, should you decide you no longer want me I will respect your feelings. I would only ask that you promise to stay near me. I am happiest when you are close."

He was affected by my plea, but nonetheless, resolute. "We don't need to leave for that, I'll stay by you. I have no intentions of straying from you. But if you think you can tempt me because I've been a cheat, then you are misled with me—"

"That isn't true! I don't think that!"

"I ain't running with you. I won't make a life with you that way. I know you've lived your entire life according to what men expect of you, and I am sorry for it, but you can get that thought out of your mind."

"I don't want you to feel sorry for me! I want you to come away with me without your conscience being so terribly occupied with thoughts of dishonor. Sometimes the ends justify the means. Maybe you can think on it a while. I can only tell you that I would not be sorry to leave any part of this life behind."

"I believe you truly feel that way, mi corazón,"

I looked up at him without pretense. "Will you promise me that you'll at least consider it? I marry John in June. I'm not a fool, I know that there could be consequences! You are a young man, I realize your heart may change, but as I've asked, you only need to stay near me. I promise to concede to your feelings if you promise to do that. I only pray that you please decided to take me and let me leave this place."

He seemed to fold emotionally at hearing my desperation and held me tighter against him. "I ain't fickle, Lucy. I'll want you always. I will. I may be young, but I've had a lifetime of losses, and I can tell you that I've learned a valuable enough lesson— I've been without anyone to care for me for so long, and now there is you; you've given me back some of what I lost and I'll be forever in your debt. And I wouldn't be here with you now, like this, if I didn't know I'd love you forever. I'm risking my neck to be here with you like this. Do you understand what they'd do if I were caught?"

I considered this. "They'd make you leave."

"Yeah, they'd make me leave on a string. I'd never have laid a hand on you because of who you are if I didn't feel...if I didn't feel as you do, or if he loved you, or if you loved him. You're not an ordinary girl that I could just play around with."

I kissed him with honesty. "You do not need to explain this to me, I already know."

He was governing me as they all did.

"Don't you see? You are doing the same thing they do to me. You are determining what's best for me and making my decisions for me. It's true the reasons are different, but the sentiment is the same. They want wealth, and you want peace of mind. Either way I am a pawn in the game of others. I will die here like this, Billy, never having the freedom I want so badly. And it is a cruel thing to tease me as you do by loving me and then taking it away, you need to know that. I won't be as happy as I should be. Even if you stay with me here!"

"I didn't realize that it was cruel."

"Billy, I can't do anything unless given permission to do so. I'm a prisoner here. Please see me for what I truly am! If you love me I beg you—take me away from here! We can easily go where they could never find us!"

I could see his face softening. He looked at me with great compassion, and I could see that my anxiety worried him. He held onto me, smoothing my hair in an attempt to comfort my hopelessness. Suddenly he pushed me back at arm's length. "Lucy. I would not have shared your bed if I meant to leave you behind. I want you to know that."

I lifted my arms to grab a hold of his. "Billy...John pays me no attention. He loves his sister, did you know? He agreed to marry me for what he could gain, but he's been sullen ever since hearing of her wedding to another. He dares not look at me at all in the way a man set to marry should. He does not look at me as you do."

Billy looked at me strangely. "His *sister*?"

I had hoped these things would lessen John in his eyes. I went on, "He would have married me and then moved me to London to be near to her, taking me even further from home."

He continued to stare oddly as he thought about what I had just told him. Shaking the thoughts off he said, "Lucy, I'm not a good man. I've done things..."

I waived my hand in dismissal. "I know all about your past, it's immaterial—"

"You don't know half as much as you think you do."

"But Billy, you're not that person anymore. You were given a chance for something better and you took it. You were only surviving, out here all alone."

"I am by far more flawed than John."

"That is not necessarily so. Consider the context. Anyway, it doesn't matter—I love you, not him! I don't care anything about what you've done, only that you realize it and are not proud of it, and that you want to be better than that. I can only imagine what it is you must have had to endure to survive out here. I am not ignorant to the difficulties here, but I'm glad for whatever you had to do to stay alive so that I could know you.

Sometimes I'm terribly frightened, Billy. What man gives a present of guns to his fiancé? There is something menacing in that. I don't want to stay in Lincoln, and look here," I nodded towards my valuables and money, "We can go from here and build a better life. You wouldn't be subjected to thievery or the nefarious plots of others; you'd have a real chance to go straight. And I wouldn't be subjected to marry a man who cares for me not at all. There's something practical in it for us both, not just emotional. We can beat them all at their own game and leave them to their own devices. They've all made their bed—we shouldn't have to lie in it with them. You and I can both start over!"

"Lucy, a lot of women out here know how to fire a gun, and not just a pistol, either. They learn to be able to protect themselves from the dangers. It's not all that strange."

"And is this the sort of life he wants me to live? He must create a business in a place such as this and I'm meant to fire guns because my life could be in danger?"

Billy was pensive as I stood up and peered through my wardrobe and located my sable cape to be worn during the Christmas festivities. I pulled it out and showed it to him.

"Do you see this? This cape alone is worth more than ten years pay of the average well-paid man. This would be enough to keep us for a very long time." I then showed him the sable hat with the wide diamond band. "I have so many things here that we can turn into a comfortable life, far from all of this fighting and petty discrimination! Before long there will be bloodshed. I am not silly and immune to all that goes on! And I don't have to be as the women are here—raw and earth beaten. You and I will be sophisticates!" I smiled proudly.

He stood instantly at the sight of my things, taking the cape from me and running his hands over it, his face in awe. "Good God, but this is fine! Do all you people dress like this just to impress?"

I walked to him and snapped my fingers before his eyes. "Focus, Billy! Yes. Dressing less wouldn't do. I must always keep a step ahead of others. Fashion is a game," I thought to put it to him in a way he might understand, "It's very much like the game of poker. Whoever holds the highest hand wins. I have many aces in my wardrobe."

He laughed at my silly analogy.

"I'm terribly bored and tired of all of this. This would be worn once and then…" I looked off in disgust. "Billy, please…I know that eventually you'll want to move on."

Without looking at me, still observing the sable cape, he said, "That isn't true. Not with you here."

"And if I weren't?"

He looked thoughtful, though he was only vaguely listening. "I don't know. It's the first chance I've had where I could make a decent living." His head snapped up. "Wait…what do you mean? Why wouldn't you be here?"

"What if I left? Would you follow me?"

"You mean force me to leave with you? Don't be ridiculous, I know you'd never do such a thing to me. You're only saying that because sometimes you're a brat." He turned the lot of his attention back to the cape, brusquely replying, "I'd drag you back here anyhow. Anyway, don't you listen? I told you, it's my chance to do better than I have—"

I felt a rage within me. "It is not! I have shown you the way to making a magnificent life, but you make excuses! And did you promise that girl in Sumner you wouldn't leave?"

He gave me a look of disappointment and antipathy. I immediately wanted to take it back. I was becoming more and more distressed, spitefully punishing him as if he were to blame for my discontent, unintentionally goading him and succeeding at pushing him too far.

Shamefully, I quietly said that I was sorry. I rubbed at my temple and his expression relaxed, and I continued to say petty things to turn Billy's loyalty away from John. "He is not the man you think he is. He's kind and practices benevolence, but he holds Americans in low-esteem. He only tolerates us."

"And so what, so long as he pays? Anyways, ain't you only barely American? What do you care?"

"'Anyway', Billy," I corrected.

He rolled his eyes at my correcting him and snorted. "Oh, so? Can't you give it a rest?"

I ignored him. "He thinks he's smarter than the 'Micks'. I heard him say so. Are you not a Mick?"

Billy looked up at me incredulously, and then let out a laugh.

"And I'm a girl, feeble-minded and frail." I picked up the poker by the fireplace and began swinging it about angrily and absentmindedly.

"Hell…I've been called worse," said Billy, "I can't let attitudes like that come between me and my grubstake. Anyway, I'm sure he only meant to refer to his enemies."

He was impossible! He finally let go of my fur cape, laying it upon the bed only to reoccupy himself with the items upon my dressing table. He picked up my sterling silver powder box and opened it, examining its contents. "What's this stuff?"

"Are you not listening to me?" I asked, annoyed, "Why would you want to toil in the fields and place yourself between such a man and a bullet if I can hand you your 'grubstake', and more, in a matter of days?"

"I supposed I'd rather earn it. Besides, Tunstall did me a good turn, I owe him. Nobody's ever treated me like that. He gave me a job, a whole horse, and outfitted me and all."

"A good turn?" I scoffed. I swung the poker carelessly. "Now who is naïve? He figured twelve heads were better rolled than one! He may be docile in his ways as he is, after all, a gentleman, but he's a businessman first and foremost. All you were meant to do was point your finger and testify to the fact that Jesse Evans and his bunch stole those horses! He thinks of you all as philistines. It did not concern John much that you were involved, only that you held the key to getting the lot of you punished."

Silence, and then, "What's a 'fillasteen'?"

I ignored him. Then he said, "I never did have a free ride, Lucy."

"Well he pays you to lay down your life for him. That is all you are to him, don't you get it?" I sniffed in abhorrence and said sarcastically, "You are to protect His Majesty. How much does he pay you for your life? It seems to me you must think yourself worthless."

Despite my nasty remark, he only looked at me and grimaced passively. "You're only being mean and saying such things because you want to get your way."

Disregarding his comment I went on. "I confess…he is impressed by you. If things were fair enough here, I have no doubt you'd go much further than the others…"

He was barely paying me attention again. He was holding my sterling silver hair-brush now, running his fingers over the engraved pattern.

"*I* pay attention. They do not realize that I know, but I am well aware of how ominous things are here. They've been this way since before I've arrived but have gotten much worse. John uses you because you're good on those guns. You're his personal body guard—you are expendable to him. Sometimes I hate him when you accompany him because I'm afraid of what will happen to you; I resent him."

He stood still and looked at me with intrigue. I do not know if he knew what to make of me.

"A warrant for Alex's arrest was sworn out, did you know that?" I asked.

He nodded.

"I'm afraid the hill we climb is beginning to raise much steeper."

He walked over and put his arms around my shoulders, embracing me to him and resting his head atop of mine affectionately.

"I didn't realize you were so aware, niña. Things are difficult, they've always been, but what can be done?"

"Why can John not back down? His pride will kill him! If they don't manage to run him out, they will dispose of him. He's a fool!"

"Hell…I wouldn't let anyone run me out. He has just as much a right to operate here as anyone else. It's the Santa Fe Ring who's doing it to everyone."

"Whoever is at fault doesn't matter, only that they do not play fair! Men being creatures of pride…I can't bare it. You are prideful, too. This is why you'll decide to stay no matter what."

He put his forehead to mine and sarcastically said, "I just love those little pearls of wisdom of yours." Then he kissed me there and said, "Lucy, I realize that your marriage is nothing but a business deal, and that's good enough for me; it's all I need to know to be with you. But I wish I could make you understand that I'm not at all keen on making off with you and going on the run. That is not who I want to be for me or you, regardless of your situation, and I can see that it's pitiful. I understand you, I do, but I won't make some sort of fugitive out of you. I love you too much for that.

"I think it would be terribly romantic."

"I think you read too much."

I frowned at him.

He said, "You can have everything here. You can have your life and have me, too. I won't be happy with you marrying him, but I can take what I can get. I always have—I don't know anything else. You deserve better than me; you deserve to marry somebody better. I'm not a good man. I could be, but if I give in to you and do what you want, if I turn out now—"

"No, Billy!" I pushed him away from me. "I gave you your out! I gave you your chance at being a better man. There are no excuses here! I've shown you the way!"

I sat back down on the floor, laying the poker next to me while Billy placed his hands upon his hips, lost in thought as he stared into nothingness. He took a deep breath and sighed, "Lucy, all you're doing is talking in circles. I told you a'hundred times by now that I'm mostly thinking of you and your reputation, and your being with the sort of man who doesn't have to steal you away and has something to offer you. We're young. I'm smart enough to know that one day you'd wise up and resent me for taking you away—"

I stood up and stepped in close to him, peering at him with a precarious intensity. He was making me unbelievably angry!

"Resent you? I already resent the man I am set to marry, and he can offer me what you cannot, at least in the way of material things, and I have told you 'a'hundred' times that I do not care for those. *You* can offer me what *he* cannot, and something much more valuable at that! I have told you that I am only interested in your devotion. Can you be so dense?"

Scowling, he asked, "Can *you*?"

I looked at him a moment. "Oh…I know! I get it! I know exactly all about you! You're used to this sort of risk. You've been running around with those dangerous broods so the perils haven't any meaning to you. You can't distinguish between them and a life without them, can you?"

Despite my irritation and offensive denotations he smiled and showed off his gleaming teeth, his overbite giving him an adorably innocent look as he pressed his thumb against it as he contemplated me. I was still so angry with him, but I could not resist and so I backed down.

"I know that I idealize matters; that I let things get away from me. You never promised me anything, and I never asked you to. I don't know what it is I'm saying, I am only as you said, angry. I've asked too much of you and became upset when you didn't respond the way I wanted you to. I'm sorry—please don't discount me as you did before."

Still smiling he crossed one arm over the other and propped his chin up with his free hand. "Okay, Lucy. We'll do it your way. But we'll wait it out. That's the deal. John gave me a chance. I have to stand behind him. I owe him that."

I turned away from him and put my hands up to my eyes, rubbing them. Men were absurd! I found it vexing how loyal they could be to one another, yet be so capricious when it came to the woman they claimed to love. I owe my family, but I would break my obligation without a second thought to be with this man—this boy. He's lived this way for quite some time. This life was all he knew. Truly, what did I expect? He lived by the gun. But I might yet turn him away. I asked, "What exactly do you want to wait out, and for how long? It's a trick you play to placate me. When John comes tumbling down, you'll come tumbling after! If they kill John, you'll avenge him. If you die defending him, you can't go with me. I appreciate your loyalty to him, but your decision will be poorly fulfilled."

If it was tricks he wanted, I would execute for him one better, but I would sink low again upon the fear of losing him forever.

"What if you owed *me*?"

He gave me a peculiar look.

"Well, what if you did?"

His look turned to suspicion.

"Think about it, Bill. You've lain with me. That in itself obligates you to me. And what if—"

"What if what?"

"What if I'm with child? Then what would you do? Make me 'wait it out'?"

I admit, it was a cruel game I played, but I was desperate. He stared at me in disbelief. I could not tell if it was from the audacity I had exhibited or if I had touched an angry nerve.

"Are you?" he asked pointedly.

"Am I what?"

"With child. *My* child?"

I remained silent for a moment and looked at him, then turned away with guilt disguised as a haughty air. "How should I know? I could be for all you know. It would be too soon to tell."

"But either way you want to cheat me into doing what you want. Is that it?" he asked.

*Yes.*

Not wanting to face my shame, I very quickly attempted to turn the tables and so I said, "You consider my carrying your child as cheating you?"—I waved my hands about emphatically in my haste to nullify my shame and confuse him—"Why is it when a man plants his seed it's the woman who is held in contempt when it takes root? You ought to be ashamed of yourself."

He was speechless at my behavior, and I cannot say that I blamed him. I was abashed and wanted to redeem myself, but still I pressed him. "What am I to you? You say you owe John, but what, then, do you owe me?"

"You want me to *owe* you?"

"No," I whispered.

His face and stance softened, but regardless he felt bound by his own sense of duty, and a man will follow through with that.

He walked towards the bed and lay back down, elbows spanned out as he rested his head upon his hands and looked up at the ceiling. For what I was about to say I prayed for God's forgiveness, for my desperation had made my character ill.

"I prayed he'd die."

"Who?"

"John. I prayed he'd die."

"What are you talking about?"

"He had contracted small pox this September past while away in Vegas. I prayed he would die."

I covered my eyes with my hands again after repeating this for the third time and felt the tears spill out from beneath them. What a horrible person I could be. How selfish had God intended me?

"Lucy...it's late. Come here with me and sleep."

I very nearly ran to him as I could not be with him quickly enough.

He placed his arm around me. "You are not feeble-minded and frail."

I looked up at him questioningly.

"What you said earlier," he said, "about being a girl who was feeble-minded and frail. You're neither of those things."

"No?"

"Nope. Not even a little bit," he sat up slightly and looked over at me. "You're shrewd and strong willed," he lay back down and, laughing quietly said, "I find you extremely complex and interesting, though you play rough. You get downright mean. But a girl like you...an eastern socialite? You ain't like no western girl I ever known. Shit... you got guts. I believe the only thing that saves us all is that you've been raised proper and with manners," he laughed at the thought. "Still, you're like a trapped badger. You've ruined me for other girls. They're all the same and boring. But you, now *you're* exciting. John is a goddamn fool."

By January, things had reached an unrelenting crescendo. The Christmas celebration had been cancelled due to all of the hostility. Because of Brady and Dolan, and the entire Santa Fe Ring, all had to suffer.

There was often an awful buzzing about the house that I could not bear. Letters being received and sent, private meetings between John, Alex, and Chisum, the men worked up into an excitable and agitated state. I prayed in vain for a match between the two factions, that they could come to some conclusion satisfactory to all. I knew I was a fool to hope for peace as the terror of the impending head this battle would reach was swiftly approaching.

The warrant sworn out against Alex detained him under house arrest until February 2nd when his arraignment would be held in Mesilla.

January passed with a measure of panic, despair, and then, at times, cool heads prevailing. But with the arrival of February, the preceding months were proven to be tame.

John had penned an open letter of complaint in January to the editor of the Mesilla Valley Independent swearing upon Sheriff Brady's incompetence in collecting taxes and pilfering of the tax payers. This did nothing to quell the ill feelings of both factions. Indeed, it only served to ripen the wound that was already festering in Lincoln. Brady began attaching John and Alex's property. John's store, among other assets, was seized. I begged and I begged Billy to leave with me, but to no avail. I got down upon my knees each night to pray that God would grant within me a child to provide leverage, but there was nothing to be done there, either. God just didn't listen!

One afternoon I lay with him in the field, hidden by trees. We rested there on the ground next to one another, our faces very close. By now it was devastatingly clear how dreadful things would be in Lincoln. Defeated I said aloud to no one, "I don't want to marry him."

He leaned closer but remained silent. I said, "Oh, I envy the woman who will marry you. She will love you and resent not one minute of the life she will have."

Billy responded frankly, "I won't love her."

I raised my eyes to him. "John does not love me," I glanced back down, "But I could stand it if I at least loved him."

And then, morbidly distraught, before I could stop myself, I grabbed at him and begged, "Don't make me marry him! Don't let me, please!"

He looked sadly at me. "I won't go anywhere. I promise. I'll be right here..."

I stared up at the sky as though catatonic. "Your promise is an empty one. I wish it were not, but nothing rightly holds you to me."

"Is there anything to hold a husband to his wife? What the difference? Husbands leave their wives all the time."

"Yes, there is. There is the promise before the law, family and friends, and above all, God."

"Well…I don't have any family. I'm not sure I can properly say I've got friends. Can't I just promise you before God?"

"He wouldn't recognize it. And if a husband leaves his wife, the law and those who witnessed the promise, and God above all, would know him for a scoundrel."

Perplexed, he asked why God would not recognize it. I sighed and told him to never mind.

"No, tell me. I want to know. How can he pretend it didn't happen?"

"Don't blaspheme!" I rolled onto my other side, away from him.

"Blaspheme?"

"You're calling God a liar."

"No I didn't."

"Pretending is for liars."

I could hear the exasperation in his voice when he said, "Well, then I don't know what! Husbands' promises matter, even when they leave, and God pretends—doesn't *recognize*…" He looked over at me to be certain I accepted his correction. "…a promise if a priest and other people don't acknowledge it?"

"That is true."

He turned away again and rested his head upon his hands, saying nothing more. I asked him why he said nothing. He responded, "I only cannot win this argument." And went back to being quiet.

After a while of not speaking I asked, "When John takes me to Europe, after we are married, will you forget me?"

He leaned up on his elbow and looked at me funny. "No, of course not!"

"How can you be sure? I will be gone a long while."

"Are you going to forget me?" he asked.

"I never would."

"Okay then." He lay back down and stared into the sky.

There was an incident in particular that involved Billy and caused me great distress as always whenever he was involved. While John's store was being occupied, Billy and Fred Waite, another of John's men and one of Billy's close cohorts, stopped a delivery of food to the Dolan men who stood guard at the store, instigating them to scuffle. I had overheard this as I sat outside of John's closed office, hearing him scold the two and demanding that their instigative behavior cease less they give Brady and his men all the more reason to resort to violence.

Billy was no longer the same boy I had known three months ago. His temper was volatile when provoked, especially by Brady and Dolan, and the "House", as their store was called, the building where the offending Ring convened. I could dispel this in him whenever he belonged to me for a few small moments of time. But I feared for him more and more and began to recognize in him the outlaw he must have been before coming here. How was I fool enough to see only a docile creature that didn't belong in such a life? He had tried to tell me this again and again, but I would not listen. Perhaps the quiet, introspective side I had come to know was his true nature, but hard time out here on one's own at so young an age would instill in one such passion. And so there it was; there were two sides of him.

He maintained his good moods during the seemingly short, fortunate moments when Brady was not the present issue, and therein did I recognize the boy I first knew. But his trigger finger was always at the ready, as was the hardnosed look he put on. He could seem course. If I did not know him as well as I did I might be frightened. I could only say that I should want to pull him away from this and resigned myself to endeavor at trying harder so that I may never see that fractious man in him again, only the sweet-natured youth I knew he could be.

He came to pass me by one chilly afternoon as I sat out on my bedroom porch reading. Because of the fracas with The Ring my lessons were ignored. He smiled, and without saying anything, dismounted and sat close by me. I deliberately stiffened to demonstrate my displeasure with him. This only seemed to amuse him as it most often did, making me all the more full of ire.

"What is it you are playing at, Billy, with Fred Wait, down on the street?"

"That's none of your concern."

I looked at him and squinted with resentment. "You *would* dare say such a thing!"

He looked at me, impassive.

"Do not treat me as though my life is not impeded by all of this!" I demanded.

Emotion returned to his face and he removed his hat and hung his head, "I'm sorry, Bonita. I didn't mean it that way."

"You might have gotten killed, instigating as you have done."

"I already heard this from my employer…your fiancé? You remember him, isn't that a fact? Why aren't you so concerned with him?"

I fumed over this statement, yet I saw through the façade. He meant to incite me, and so I chose to disregard the question.

"And don't worry a tick about me, I ain't. I'd like to see any one of them try to put me out." he said, arrogantly.

"The things you say to me! You live for this, don't you? Full of, what is it they say? Piss and vinegar?"

He laughed heartily at this. "That's right! It's what I'm good for, Lu."

"No, it is not. What do you know of what you are good for if you can refuse such attractive advances when they beckon you? I have only laid out the plans nicely for you, but you're looking only for prime real estate six feet under! You'll live only for bullets and blood."

Amused, he asked, "Is that what you think? I've only explained myself to you a'hundred times. I'd have thought you knew me better."

"Tell me how."

"You already know it. I have a responsibility and the skills to fulfill it, that's all. I'm making a stand with the rest of them. I won't turn tail and run; I'm not a coward. That isn't who I am. I can't expect you to understand."

"Goddamn it, Billy Bonney! Sometimes I *hate* you!"

I stood up and walked away from him. I refused to look back as I knew I would find a smile of entertainment stamped there across his face. He took pleasure in provoking me. It would have incensed me further only to see that I was underappreciated and taken lightly.

John rode to Chisum's ranch for help. John Chisum still sat in a Vegas prison, and his men refused to help John's cause, trying to stay out of the fray. This caused John a great disappointment and created more distress for me. How could my father leave me here with all of this going on? I was afraid to leave the house. Brady and his men had already come in and taken inventory of the McSweens' things. I feared for my own belongings, but to my great amazement, they left them alone, acknowledging that they did not belong to the McSween's. They could not have known what my things were worth, then. It should have been impossible for that to be the case, but if they had, they could only have taken them for sure. They would have taken anything of value and made excuses for their actions. Why play fair with me and no one else? They must not have given my things a second thought, the nitwits.

I admired Billy for braving all of this, but I would not admit it to him. While it was terrifically attractive to know a man who held no fear, it was much more attractive to have a man who was breathing. I should make amends with him, though I was unsure if there were any to be made. Everyone was on edge. The sum of the others could only imagine that I would be in a complete shambles over this ungodly matter, Billy included, and so certainly he would have forgiven me my ill-temper. Still, I wanted to talk with him; I needed him to sit with me a while.

"All of this because of competition?"

"Yes."

"And does death truly fix the situation for them if they cannot drive Alex and John out?"

"Yes."

"How could this be so?"

"The Ring, Brady...they're the men with all the authority. They won't try themselves. No one will hang if that crime is committed."

I snorted, disbelieving. "And so, death it will be. Or do they not know the extent of the dangers these men present to them?"

"I believe they might."

"Have you *told* them so?"

"Yes."

"And they would not listen?"

"No."

"Hells bells! You know this land better than they ever will! You know these *people* better than they ever will! And still, they refuse to listen to reason!"

"Well, Bonita, you know it as well as me. They think they're smarter than us locals."

I sighed in disgust.

"Billy...how can you stand to back these men up? How can you tolerate what fools they are?"

"Pecking order, I guess. They're the men with the money. It's their land, their possessions. I'm only a hired hand here waiting to get paid. I have no say anyhow."

"Billy, is it the money you want, to earn your living?"

He rolled his eyes and fussed, "Let's not go down that way again. And yes, this is my living. Something I have a hard time making, and I'm proud to be useful doing something I'm good at."

I sat beside him and rested on him. He brought his arm up around me and turned his head into the side of mine and nuzzled me. So I could not get him to go with me, no matter how hard I tried. He would not let me take care of him.

"I can't understand why John hasn't sent you away from here," he wondered.

I leaned back to look at and consider him.

"Things are feverish. They are truly fools not to listen to reason, especially where you're concerned. Why is he willing to put you in danger? I've told them all I know of these men, and these men have proven my knowing by being so relentless. That Englishman is the one who looks to live six feet under," he was irritated. "You should let me take you to Chisum's ranch. You would be safer there."

"I wouldn't go, Billy. I would stay here where you are."

"Now you're a fool like the rest of us," he said, smiling.

"If you put that thought in John's head I'll not speak to you again!"

"Lucy, that'll only encourage me."

I looked at him feigning discontentment.

"I admit I resent him for not insisting you go; I can understand why you feel the way you do about him. I would never allow you to stay here. If I were him, I'd insist you leave. It angers me that he allows you to stay through all of this."

"What shall we do when it all mounts, Billy?"

"Make war, I suppose."

John sent me off to Chisum's after all. Alex's home was being prepared for an assault, and I was packed off to go as it was the safest place.

I spend most of my days in a fret, trying to keep my mind occupied but finding it difficult. Colleen stayed by me most of each day as I wept often, and just as often, was inconsolable. She only did not know that it was my pining for Billy for which I wept.

I was miles away from Lincoln and could not know what was playing out there. I could only sit and wish that things had been different. In all the places of this great space of ours we landed in a town fraught with envy and greed, run by evil men. A tiny dot on the map, Lincoln was. What fortune had brought me here? I contented myself by imagining it was Billy, to be with him. But I also imagined how I may have met another had I been placed elsewhere. But that thought comforted me not, as I knew now of Billy and no other would do. I couldn't know if I should begrudgingly be thankful. I had to see it all play out.

Sallie would chatter away about "William", and though on the inside I screamed for her to be quiet, outwardly I spoke to her about him with a good temper and charm. I no longer wanted her to have him, and though she was a lovely young woman, the thought of my previous attempt at making a match between them upset me and brought the hope that she would leave me be. Sallie seemed oblivious to the serious trouble in Lincoln. She only knew of a few altercations that needed smoothing out. I may well have been as obtuse as she, had I not been so close to the affray being fed truths little by little through overheard conversations and the honest pillow-talk of Billy. I envied her a little over this matter, as I would prefer ignorance over reality. While she mindlessly chattered away, asking me again of William's potential and telling me how she would consider him a possible suitor should he soon find his position, I only sat and pretended to care. The majority of my mind was monopolized by the fear that at any moment bad news could arrive, and please let it not include Billy. And if it should not, I would not give him to her anyway.

I remained way up the Pecos at Chisum's for longer than I expected, as the days passed frivolously, my mind preoccupied with dreadful thoughts, when finally the day of my worst fears arrived.

Fred Waite rode up in rather a hurry, dismounting and bounding the stairs in seemingly one leap. He threw open the door, frightening us ladies, as only Sallie, Colleen, Hannah, and I were present in the immediate household. I hurried from the kitchen, passing Sallie, who stood with her hand to her heart as Fred had given her a good fright. I wiped my hands upon the apron I wore as I was spending my time attempting to learn the fundamentals of baking to pass the time and attempt to keep the horrible thoughts I conjured at bay. I was covered in flour, and as I wiped my hands upon the apron, puffs of it spread out around me. My forehead was marked with the powder, as was my hair, and I would have to confess that, despite my worries, I was having much fun making such a mess, forgetting for the time being that horrors abounded. But upon seeing Fred standing there, hat in hand, face sullen, practicality took up residence in my mind. The look on his face caused my heart to quit and stomach to drop.

No sooner had I approached him did the others form a bond behind me.

"My apologies," he started, seeing at how he gave us a scare. "Ladies," he acknowledged, "Miss Howard, may I talk with you?"

His voice was uncertain, his head down. He could not look me in the eye. I nervously wiped my hands across my midsection again as I did not know what else to do with them, lowering my own head as Fred did as I waited to hear whatever terrible news he brought.

I slowly walked to him, oddly aware at such a time as this that I was not decent to receive. I also could not help in realizing how funny a thought as that should come into my head just now. Perhaps it is the mind's way of salvaging some semblance of normalcy in the face of upheaval. I swallowed anxiously, awaiting his words. Someone was dead. Perhaps they were only hurt. Severely, maybe, but only hurt nonetheless.

Fred gently took my arm and took me aside for the sake of privacy.

"Miss Howard, I…" He trailed off and stood silently. I wanted to shake him and yell for him to go on, but I could only remain silent as my cultured composure insisted. In my mind, I offered Fred compassion for dawdling so, as I could see plainly that he was upset and nervous. After a few moments he found his voice again.

"I'm so sorry, Miss Howard. I run here as fast as my horse could carry me. I haven't all the facts so that I could light out as soon as possible to reach you."

"Go on, Fred." I encouraged, steeling myself.

He looked up and opened his mouth. It was wordless. He could not make the sounds necessary to inform me as to why his presence was needed here. In that moment I again felt sorry for him, seeing how innocent and concerned he seemed. I had forgotten my own fears for a second's worth of time.

"Early this morning, John got a bunch of us together, fed up with Brady and the Ring. He wanted to retrieve his mounts; rightfully his. But…we were caught up by Brady and his men…"

"Who went with him, Fred?"

He only stood quietly, and so I repeated the question with forcible exasperation.

"Who went with John, Fred!?"

"He took myself and Richard, also John Middleton and Henry Brown, the kid… and Widenmann…"

"*Billy?*"

He nodded slowly. I feared I might faint. Fred Wait would certainly come here all this way to tell me something horrible had happened to Billy. They all knew how I adored him. I tried to remain collected.

"What happened, Fred? Say it!"

"Well, Brady and his posse caught up to us. We broke off and so did they, chasing both our party's. They come after us fast and persistent!"

"Who chased you all down?"

"I only saw Buck Morton, Jesse Evans, Brady, and Frank Baker…"

*Morton and Jesse Evans?!*

My ears pulsed with the blood pumping voraciously through my heart. Evans and Morton! And Billy! They'd killed him! They had it out for him!

"Fred…tell me, now! Who is it that's been hurt?"

"It's John, Miss Howard. He's…"

"He's what? Fred, tell me, please!"

"They got him. Those sonsabitches got him. I'm sorry…forgive me."

He put the back of his hand to his lips to stifle whatever pain or anger that lingered there.

*John is dead.*

"Fred…where is Billy?"

He looked at me, eyes wide and puzzled.

"Fred?!" I snapped my fingers at him to attract his attention.

"He…he rode with us…"

"I know this! Where is he, Fred?"

I was now suffering for him to spit it all out.

"He's been detained. They kept him to get his account on matters. He told me…he told me to tell you that he was okay."

*Relief.* John was dead, but Billy was okay. And what's more is throughout all of this misery he was still concerned enough with me to ensure that I knew he was all right! God forgive my sinfulness, but I was grateful for this small comfort.

I was suddenly aware of the weeping behind me. Colleen came to me and placed her arms around me, but it was not I who needed comforting. Out of the four of us I was sated. I was sorry for John, very much so, in fact. But John was a fool. I knew it was only a matter of time, and so I counted the days until I would hear this very news. I was prepared for this. My truest concern was that Billy did not come to the same conclusion all because of his need to stick by John's side in all of this. And in my thoughts, I wondered if Billy would come away with me now, for what was there left to stand for? I did not own any of John's holdings; his life here was gone. But I recalled the accusation I made—that Billy would avenge John's death, and that he made no effort to refute the charge.

"Fred...take me back with you."

"I can't, Miss Howard. Richard said he'd come for you soon enough."

"Hang Richard, Fred! You will take me with you, now!"

"But Miss Howard, he would be awfully mean to know I disobeyed."

"You disobeyed *nothing*. You *obeyed* me. Do you understand?"

He nodded nervously. Viola was brought with me for recreation and I gave him instructions to bring her to me. "Have my horse saddled as quickly as possible."

"Miss Howard, we won't arrive until late. It truly would be better to leave in the morning."

"When are they burying John?"

I was terribly aware of how callous I sounded.

"I believe they plan to do so as soon as possible I guess."

"Then I believe the circumstances call for me to leave immediately. No one will fault me, and to hell and back if they do!"

Fred and I rode together at a fast pace. He bade me to slow on occasion so as not to tire the horses, but I was in too much of a hurry. The sky was growing dark and I rode Viola hard and true, outrunning Fred. Viola was a prized Thoroughbred. I rode until she steamed and frothed, until finally I saw the lights of Lincoln before us. I loved my Viola dearly and felt the guilt of pushing her so hard, but Billy was all the more dear to me.

Once the lights of Lincoln appeared I finally slowed her, though I felt farther than ever as the home-stretch is long! I would swear that it took equally as long to get there from this point as it did to ride all the way from the Pecos Valley.

When I arrived at Alex's I handed Viola off to be watered and cared for, yelling hurried but deliberate instructions for her.

When Fred and I stepped up onto the McSweens' front porch I could hear the men crowded around back, down below in the yard despite the degree of the home's walls; voices angrily rising and falling. Fred broke off and walked down the opposite side stairs and around back to join them, telling them of my arrival no doubt. I went directly through the house. As I stepped outside onto the porch in back I could only manage to barely make out the figures of men as they were grouped and crowded further out in the yard, not knowing who was who, but the voices died down and I knew that heads were turning in my direction. One broke from the assembly, approached and climbed the steps and came towards me. As he stepped into the light of the porch I could see it was Billy. We stood looking at one another for what could have been an eternity when finally he warily removed his hat and held it there in his hands. I could see his face, his eyes sober and sad, his expression mournful. Until now I had only been able to think of getting to him, but I never once imagined actually seeing him. I was afraid that he would be absent. So panicked was I that I believed he might be taken from me, too. Now that he stood there before me the grief within me rose ruthlessly. I had not cried until that moment, upon which I finally had fallen apart.

He moved to me quickly and held on to me as I sobbed into his chest, concealing my face, my strength ebbing. He tightened his grip so as to hold me upright as my knees went out and slowly moved me to a nearby bench. He carefully lowered and sat by me, and I wept uncontrollably, sobbing from the pain that had hit me suddenly. He kept his arms around me and put his head to mine, his warm breath calming me. *His breath…* proof that he was here with me and alive.

I was crumbling, but my thoughts were firmly sound and I knew it was he who held me. I was sorry for John, but it was Billy I wept for, and I know he knew this. I'd ask God's forgiveness, but I wasn't sure there was any forgiveness to be given. I did not want John, I never did; and he never wanted me. As far as I was concerned the sadness of his death equaled that of a dear friend. I never felt that I had dishonored him in any way. I only desperately wanted to cling to Billy, and to his credit, he sat so very still, holding me closely and tenderly. And after all of the events that had happened, I did not give a damn if the others looked on at this as inappropriate. This was a horrifying day, indeed, after months of emotional torture, and I would not play silly games where my heart was concerned.

Richard approached us and tried to delicately remove me, but I only clung tighter, as did Billy.

"Elucia, please. This is not the time—"

"Let her alone, Brewer! She isn't going to let go!"

Richard was stunned at Billy's tone. "Bonney, let her go. This isn't becoming. John's not yet cold—she ought to grieve for him."

"She *is* grieving! Look at her! This is where she wants to be so to hell with all of you and your goddamned gossip! Talk all you want; I ain't letting her go!"

If my eyes were not closed with pressure raging behind them, and if my throat were not so thick with misery, I would have turned to Richard Brewer and told him to go find business elsewhere; that this did not concern him. Must everything be done accordingly? I was sick of my actions being placed beneath a microscope because I was a woman and because of whom I was at that! I wanted to be with Billy. Once I saw with my own eyes that he was okay, only then could I grieve for John. It is not as though I was not full of sorrow. Even now I recalled him; his character, his kindness.

All of this in spite of the fact that I did not want him and relished in Billy's warm body beside me.

But, suddenly, it occurred to me how drastically my life would change yet again. I did not mean for this to be about me, but I would be cheated of everything! After all, John and I were only entering into a business deal. With him here Billy would remain and things would be as close to right as rain as they could be. With John gone I hadn't even the luxury to imagine the comfort of having Billy with me. The irony of this all fell upon me swiftly. When John was alive, I did not want the life he was meant to afford me, but now that he was gone, the uncertainty of my place here was of great concern to me. The weight of it fell upon me. As imperfect as it had been I was content in knowing that I had some piece of what I wanted. I was sorry for the loss of him; John. He did not deserve this. He may have been of an acquisitive nature, but he was only attempting to eke out a place here which was his right in observation of the pursuit of happiness, but because of depraved greed he was dead. It should not have been this way. John wasn't a bad man. He only wanted to search out the success he was entitled to here in this opportunistic land of ours. Murder is a poor deed abused for the removal of opposition, whatever the cause. It was felonious! John's life for Dolan's and his continued success? Dolan was a coward! *Did* John believe it could truly end this way? I know that he often wrote to his family in London alluding to the awareness of all things dangerous here, promising them that he was "still alive", but did he guess that it would truly happen? Do any of us truly believe we'll meet our end over such trifling circumstances?

I wept a lifetime before Billy leaned in to me, telling me that I should rest. When my condition proved hysterical they sent for the doctor, who had given me a capsule of bromide salts to help me sleep. They laid me down, Billy placing his head close to mine like so many times before all of this. Tears still fell from me and he wiped them away tenderly.

I remembered hearing him say he loved before sleep temporarily ended the misery.

# 8

## February, 1878

John's body was brought in from where it lay on his land, shot down, and laid out in the McSween parlor. I slept through all of this, finding John lying there in state upon waking. The horror of seeing him lying there should have felled me at once, but rather, I could only stare, indifferent. I could see the damage done to him, his head corrected with sticky plaster but betraying the wound upon close inspection. I heard them talk plenty of his violent death, and so the sight was surreal, making the ruin of his face seem both strange and expected.

When Richard approached the body and swore to John's corpse that he'd get them all I knew for certain that it was all far from over, and this sunk my heart further. There was nothing I could do but wait for more blood.

Billy had given a coroner's inquest telling all that he knew and what he had witnessed—his anger plain. Because of his cool demeanor, I did not want to interfere with him just now—I knew my place as a woman, to let the men handle their matters as they would.

But my limits would be tested, as proved by Constable Atanacio Martinez. He was burdened with the task of serving a warrant for the arrest of those named responsible for John's murder, and his hesitance had made me irritable. The man was weak and faltered, stumbling over himself at the prospect at having to face Brady with a warrant, selfishly worried for his own well-being, though I suppose that I cannot say I blamed him. I still labeled him a coward. A constable afraid to deal a warrant! What some men won't do to make their livelihood, yet when their duties rear up they tuck their tails between their legs out of fear. Perhaps he should have been a cobbler, then.

Listening to Martinez argue against his responsibilities, there was an unmistakable edge in Billy's voice as he told him that "he'd better take the chance of his life" or else he'd kill him outright himself. Martinez smartly took Billy at his word, for in his tone, I would have believed he'd do the same to me if it were I who had hesitated and stood in his way.

Martinez, Billy, and Fred walked down to Dolan's store to make their arrests only to be arrested themselves. Hearing of this, my anger broke loose, yet for all of it that welled up inside of me I could not yet manage to break protocol and corrupt my composure. And for all of the mourners in the parlor I must keep my manners. Knowing I could not scream, I walked quickly to my room, picked up my porcelain wash pitcher and threw it to the floor, throwing the basin after.

○○○

Martinez, Billy, and Fred stood there, starring down the barrels of the loaded weapons leveled at them. Brady refused to allow that any arrests be made, claiming that his posse had only done their jobs, and that it had been John to make a move towards them. He then proceed to arrest the three of them. On what grounds one could not say, other than because Brady was a bastard.

Billy's anger at Brady intensified wildly at this. Brady ordered the surrender of their weapons, and when ordering Billy to surrender the Winchester that John had given him as a present, calling him a "little sonofabitch," Billy said, "You old sonofabitch, you take it!" Taking it from him, Brady and his men arrested them and marched them down the street in front of the entire town, adding insult to injury as he subjected them to this humiliation. Brady had sealed his fate then, though the arrogant fool could not have known it.

Martinez was released, but Billy and Fred sat in jail, missing John's funeral. This did nothing to curb the hate inside of Billy for Brady. This latest issue maddened Billy all the more. Brady was a walking dead man now.

○○○

I was not prepared. I did not have a mourning gown; the best dress I could manage was a black calico dress gotten from town—it had to be purchased from the Murphy store, which made for an incredibly vehement insult. I must wear the dress every day.

Colleen helped me dress and stayed by me, holding me steady as we approached the parlor where John lay. We sat next to Alex and Susan. Weeping could be heard throughout the room, quiet as a kitten's mew. I had no tear to let out as I had resolved myself of all weeping and would weep no more. I had made my mind up that John was willing to risk this, being too much of a fool and too proud to move on. I decided that he had brought this upon himself and, selfishly, me. Perhaps it was admirable that he stood his ground, as I had come to understand, but the end result made his attempt futile. I was confused over this matter as it should have been clear that John could not have won out.

A chilly panic passed through me; Billy had not come back. Word made its rounds throughout the angry crowd that he, Fred, and Martinez, had been unjustly arrested, the former two locked away, still. What charges could Brady have held against them? They had done nothing! But I reminded myself that those being dealt with were godless, wicked creatures—devils incarnate. Would they murder him, too? And *Fred*?

Oh, these were uncertain times indeed! My mind ran rampant with all of the worst cases it could imagine. This was hell on Earth! Hatred manifested within me, brought on by the fears nestled from the deepest depths of my heart, and there it began to grow and froth acidically due to the plausible probability of harm finding Billy, and I could feel the lethal animosity within establishing itself, increasing ardently and threatening to turn me into the most pitiable of beings as my contemplations befitted murder. My tolerance had been pushed to its very limitations; no woman, lady or otherwise, could have sustained this treachery, and to be robbed of the very person who could soothe me as a result of all this petty, egotistical nonsense brought on by legal criminals was more than I could stand! I could only hope that Brady had not dispatched of Billy as he did to poor John! I would kill him myself, outright, if this were to be so! Misfortune had placed me upon this downward spiral through no fault of my own, but I would rise to the challenge and descend it with ease and the grace borne to me!

It occurred to me now more than ever that Billy had been right; life in this place hardened a person. Well then, so let it happen to me. I wanted justice where, seemingly, there was none to be found, but I knew that I could create my own, and this I would do if I could. I had lost all concern, all except for Billy. The greedy bastards ruined what life and happiness I might have had here with my precious boy, and all of this misery for profit and reckoning! When I found John buried, I would deal with that depraved Sheriff Brady! I was certain that he had kept them locked there simply to be cruel. Woe to that wicked man and all of his wicked followers who would meet me now!

Yes, perhaps I was but a silly, angry girl, but still I would not be swayed by anyone to relent. I would not listen to what others considered reason. There *was* no reason here! It existed in no one's vocabulary—it did not exist in any form. Chaos was the order of the day; rules made to befit those who had stolen control.

I had taken it upon myself to leave the sullen quarters of the McSweens' to collect my thoughts along the dirty streets of Lincoln as I could no longer tolerate the disquiet prescribed by the angry voices that convened all around me; solace was scarce and un-founded within the walls of my living space. I felt provoked and had it in me to leave this house directly and expand my breathing room.

Colleen insisted she go along with me to which I replied that she was more than welcome to commit to herself to my simple attempt of self-succor if she could stomach it as her own fear of this town unsettled her terribly. Either way, I would march on, unde-terred. I would no longer be a hostage of my own fears and the preferences of others who intervened on my behalf. I did not concern myself with my own safety—it was not the same issue it once was to me so long ago during the trek I had made to this raw, wasteful place. I had seen and done plenty and had now been distanced from that innocent, naïve girl from what seemed like so very long ago. I wanted out of my own skull and was determined to run from there lest I began screaming and was unable to stop, and I would go about my way without aide of any gunman to walk before or behind me. I was tired of the intimidating pretense; I did not care how threatening the streets of Lincoln were. And anyway, wasn't the treacherous threat removed with the death of John? What should I have to fear? And so I left without informing anyone of my plans as I would be halted in my tracks to be sure, told not to go for fear of some war springing forth at the sight of me. I wanted out.

As we strode down the street many faces turned our way, not all of them friendly. I did not walk in my usual dignified manner, but in a manner that was purposeful, my shoulders squared, jaw set, and my face, overall, determined. After all that had been done I cared not for my reputation. What could reputation matter in the pit of hell? Civilization was a foreign concept in Lincoln County. One faction murdered a man outright, the other would murder in retribution.

And there came Brady with his merry band of slaughterers walking directly towards us on the very boards which Colleen and I tread, my resentment swollen to an extreme degree. He tipped his hat petulantly, mockingly even, sneering insolently in my direction as he neared. He unhinged me! The insect! Now my anger found traction and broke through my learned refined disposition.

"You lousy, no good crook!" I shouted, my outburst surprising even myself. Colleen gasped and held fast to my arm, communicating to me that I ought to reel in my emotions and remember myself and the danger this man meant.

"I am your superior, Brady! Believe that, you sniveling coward! You ought to lower your eyes when in my presence you mongrel, not dare to look at me so impertinently! Do it again and see if I'll not gouge those eyes out!"

Brady only laughed, amused and unmoved. I could see him steel his back, about to put me in my place, no doubt, when I held out my palm instructing him to hold his tongue; my face grave with meaning. At this he seemed both bemused yet entertained, but if this creature thought that I was simpleminded and entertaining, I would prove him a rude awakening. I was smarter than he, and he was no better than a snake. That alone placed me much higher above him, whether he allowed himself to realize it yet or not.

"I'll not be intimidated by you, Brady. You are nothing to me! Less than a bug!"

I looked at him with resolve and went on, spurned forward by his being staggered. Colleen only stood silently as she was caught up in fright, her fingers squeezing painfully into my arm.

"Your convenient authority may be great here in such a little town—a speck of dust on a map—but I've seen legitimate law, and I've seen it work competently, which is more than I can say for your due course. You have destroyed the lives of many in order to fulfill your greedy coffers, fattening your pockets. You have ruined the plans of men much greater than yourself! You are an arrogant, blind boob! You've hindered my father's plans with your small-town, smalltime, petty grievances in order to gain control of what is not rightfully yours. He placed me here for a reason, you sick, twisted puppet! You think John was in your way? Wait until you see the ungodly reign of terror that should befall you now as you stand between true grit and eastern prosperity.

Brady and his men began to laugh amongst themselves gleefully at this scene, yet I believed I recognized uncertainty within Brady's eyes. Yet they were enjoying the spectacle I now made of myself and so he remained silent.

"You haven't any idea of the determination of a true entrepreneur, and one from the east, no less. My father is a true soldier, seeing and causing more bloodshed than you can imagine, and his partners will eat you alive, I promise you. You think you have a band of men? He has an army, and in high political standing! You are but a babe in the woods—primitive and uncivilized. You have not the machinations of the most immoral industrialist who knows a thing or two of building a true empire; educated men, unlike yourself, Brady, who would steamroll you as soon as look at you. That is *my* faction! You have created much more trouble for yourself and this...*Ring* you serve than John ever could have with the underhanded, murderous action you committed by killing him, you simple nit-wit!"

Brady's expression retreated into something resembling apprehension, and I saw something of alarm flicker there in his eyes if only fleetingly. They all stood, he and his followers, mouths agape at my bravado. I shook inside at my foolish nerve and stood shocked that no one made a move against me. I knew for certain that I had overstepped the limits, the diligence of regret edging in, but I can only imagine that it was their confusion at being addressed in such a manner by so young a lady that had stunned them into inaction. Brady chose to ignore my threats, but only for show, at least for the time being, for I could still see the glint of uncertainty behind those beady little eyes. He would avoid a confrontation with me, a mere woman, made clear by his account of silence, but, yet, I was still a woman who could quite possibly make his life a living hell. I could see his mind at work, bearing all that I had said and weighing his options as to how I ought to be dealt with.

Before I could stifle my voice as I should have, I could not help but proclaim, "You are a wretched man, and God can only help you now!" administering the verbal coup de grâce of my criticism and simultaneously setting in motion the wheels of action that Brady might take with me.

Terrified of what I had done, I made my attempt to pass but, before doing so, I turned to him yet again.

"Brady, you exercise a crooked power—that is clear enough."

He'd had enough entertainment and walked on by as though we had not met on the street, laughing with his men and playing at pretending to ignore me. I yelled after them, "Might I recommend you take your own men and place them properly within their own cells, leaving one free for yourself. You are not a good man, William Brady. You won't live forever, and you will be judged. And forever, for you, will come soon enough!"

At this I finally broke him; he turned and opened his mouth to ask, "Are you threatening the sheriff of Lincoln County, miss? It would be unwise to threaten the law."

"Law? There *is* no law here. There is only the Santa Fe Ring. Leave me out of your fraudulent little games. You shouldn't want to shorten the already short time you have left."

# PART II
# The Regulators

# 9

## February, 1878

I kept the indiscretion to myself. I felt regret in angering Brady—and fear—but as many men often did, I believed he'd only thought of me as silly.

The men stayed now with Alex and Susan alongside me and Susan's sister and her sister's family—John's home and possessions had all now been illicitly taken, seized by Brady and divided amongst himself, Dolan, and the whole of the Santa Fe Ring. Richard was appointed as special constable by Justice of the Peace, John B. Wilson. In his fold he took thirty men, all had either worked for or loved John, or were out for blood and justice. He also procured Billy, deputized him and all. This set me very ill at ease. I once again asked Billy as nicely as I could to simply go, to just leave—I told him they were all going to die. But he would not give up on this and lose the opportunity to vindicate John and all others who suffered under the thumb of the Ring, and he would not let go of the perverse outlook he had of himself—that he was nothing more than a hired gun and good for nothing else. I had set such high sights for him, and how I hated to watch the lights that I had carefully plotted out for him grow dim.

I heard the incessant shouts of justice and morality: Restitution? How righteous! I had covered my ears against the insanity of these simple men, but, oh…how I could not turn a blind-eye, no matter how desperately I wanted to, as there Billy was, too, calling out for a massacre. They were conveniently mistaking justice for truth: That they were angry and wanted an eye-for-an-eye. The only one among them that I believed meant to bring justice to those who had intimidated and propagated against John without respite and killed him in cold blood, despite how naïve I thought him to be, was Richard. Upstanding, honest Richard. The rest only bought into it as an excuse for what they believed was owed bloodshed.

Soon after John had been laid to rest I had received a telegraph from my father calling me home. I would have given anything to stay, but the McSweens' were not my family, New Mexico was not my home, and John, who lay cold in the ground for two weeks' time, had not been my husband. There was no reason to stay here now, and my own excuses held no value.

I hadn't an opportunity to speak with Billy during the days that had passed since burying John; his time spent setting his mind to murder with the others. I had only brief encounters with him, moments of occupying the same time and space, but today I saw him alone, standing on the porch.

I watched him briefly in silence, the transformation in him strikingly evident though he only idled there. His demeanor and stare were that of a grown, wizened man, and not that of a boy. Had he always looked this way, hard-edged and emboldened? Had I so romanticized him that I failed to notice this, my eyes opened only with the occurrence of these recent events? As I stood there watching him, I wondered if I should dare go to him. There had been a lapse in our friendship as of late, it was obvious enough. Our disagreement over this trouble and his thirst for blood was a deterrent which caused us a silent rift; but my spirit felt closer to him still—nothing had changed there. I was in awe of him just now, the way he stood and the conviction of that stance, and as always, the way the mid-afternoon light fell across his face. I moved towards him and he turned to me without smiling. I held in my hand the folded telegraph I had received from home, playing with it nervously.

He nodded toward my hands, "What is it you got there?"

I looked away wordlessly and stretched out my arm to hand him the folded piece of paper. He took and opened it, reading its orders. The look on his face barely changed, betraying only the slightest hint of discontent. He leaned back against the house and nodded his head in appreciation of what the telegraph meant, and his face registered a complete lack of surprise. He looked back to me, my face down but eyes lifted, meeting his. He tapped the piece of paper against the open palm of his other hand absentmindedly, his sunlit eyes set in resolution as he studied me.

"I'm meant to leave a few days after you and the others go from here." I said.

He nodded again, relaying what he had already understood would happen.

I spoke to him. "You won't go without saying goodbye to me." It wasn't a question, and it wasn't an instruction. It was only matter-of-fact.

He nodded and spoke back, "I won't."

While I had him here to myself I wanted it to be as it was before. I longed for the days when we would sit and read together, discussing the passages within the books, or when we'd ride off and sit down in some secret place, leaning in close to one another in private conversation. I wanted all of his attention, but John, in death, had the lot of it. I wanted him to talk to me as easily as he had done countless times before, but I could see in his eyes and rigid posture that he would rather not, as if doing so would break his determination. The feeling of this was palpable.

"Billy—"

"I didn't do what I was supposed to."

I looked at him oddly, not understanding his statement and surprised to recognize him once again as his face softened into some semblance of the boy of only a few weeks prior.

"What were you meant to do?"

He set his jaw and bit at his lower lip, looking at me earnestly and helplessly. I waited for him to go on.

"I was meant to defend him."

"What could you have done?"

He shook his head in thought, "Stayed nearer? I was too far behind; I ran in the opposite direction—the wrong way."

"Fred told me…he said that they chased you."

"And I ran…"

"What should you have done, then?"

He didn't answer.

"I don't think anyone knew what they would do—" I offered.

"We knew. Men don't chase you down like that unless they mean something by it. And they were firing." Humor flowed into the corners of his lips, "That tipped us off somewhat."

"Billy, I imagine that it was chaotic, that you had to run to…*mobilize*?"

He laughed sincerely at my ambiguity, and then nodded, "There was confusion all right. They came up on us so suddenly…"

"So then you did nothing wrong. There was disorder and confusion. You did only what you thought was best, what your instincts implored you to do."

"I should have run with John and Middleton. We broke off in different directions. They chased both of our parties, but once they had us figured out, that John wasn't with us, they took off in the other direction. They took off after John. Middleton had fallen behind…but then he took off after them. He then came back and we went with Brewer and Widenmann to…mobilize." He looked up at me, amused at his jest. I stepped closer to him.

"Billy, you weren't alone in attempting to control the situation."

"Control the situation…I love that highfalutin New York talk, Lu. I'm gonna miss it."

"I saw what they did to him, Billy."

He looked at me, his face grim. "No, you didn't."

"I saw his face—"

"But you didn't see the way they did it to him."

He came away from the wall and stood closer by me, looking down at the telegraph still in his hand.

"This is real good, Lu. You can get out of this place now—get a second chance to hopefully get what you want." His face was brave. "Your father never should have sent you here. If it were up to me I'd have sent you back a hell of a lot sooner…If it was my decision."

"Is that so?"

"Yeah. It's so."

"Billy, I have what I've been wanting."

His face began to change. He was losing a bit of his composure.

He shook his head idly, "Me? Yeah, that's…I don't think I'm the best thing." He shifted his tack, "I let John down in so many ways. I'm not…right." He looked up at me.

"Because of me?"

He tilted his head up and smiled a little, his eyes luminous.

"I don't have any regrets…if that's what you're asking. You were never his; you were mine."

"I *am* yours."

He smiled at me. "Right. You are mine."

"So then what?"

He took in a breath and looked away. "I know I didn't have any right to do any of what I did. I don't know…I couldn't—I can't help myself. It's not an excuse, I know." He looked back at me. "You're this incredible thing. You're nothing like anybody I know," he moved closer, "I didn't want to pass you over. I knew I could love you the way you wanted when he couldn't, and so I did."

I only looked at him, wanting him to go on. I didn't want to interrupt his confession with my own thoughts on the subject.

"He just took you for granted, I think. I mean, how he could not feel for you like I…" he rubbed the back of his neck nervously, trying to find the words. "But he deserved you, I don't. He had the means to deserve you. Believe me, I never for one second had the daring to believe there was ever anything there for me with you, not even when you insisted there was." He stood silent for a second, then, as if to himself, he said, "I only wanted to know it for once."

"Know what?"

"You. What it's like to feel that way and realize it. I feel it now, and I believe I just might feel it forever. I don't want to tell you these things because I know that I'm not what you would really want, or what you should have, no matter how you feel about it now. You're only imagining it…I think." He nodded at this as if to emphasize that it were true and to help fool himself into accepting it.

I leaned into him and pressed myself against him as hard as I could. I breathed in his scent and cried a little as quietly as I could while he put his arms around me firmly.

How he could tell himself these things I didn't know. He wanted to be selfless, I understood that much, and so I allowed him his foolishness. All I wanted was him, and I know he knew that was the truth.

"I knew you'd marry him. I took you from him as a man; I took away his right as a husband. I'm trying to be sorry for it."

"I only would have married him because you would have let me."

"You should have the life you always had. I wouldn't ever take you out of it. I would see you marry another man before I'd ever be willing to take everything away from you so I could have you for myself. You don't realize what it is you think you want."

"You've been telling me this for two months now. You don't have to explain it all to me again only so I could tell you that you are wrong."

He laughed a little and embraced me tighter, pressing his face down and nearer to my own.

"I still have that money," I told him, "There's still time."

"I got something to do. Even if I were willing to take you away I wouldn't have you be with a man who runs from responsibility."

I wanted to laugh bitterly, like a mad woman. Responsibility, he said. Was he listening to himself? None of this was his responsibility to take! What have we done to let men believe that they must fight and die for such imagined causes—could they now no longer discern what was real and what was illusion? A man had died in a small town bidding war that was created in a microcosm, and John had accepted this. All had known the odds were stacked in the house's favor; the house refused all bids, and the bidder had known, but with prideful fervor failed to observe. I was reluctant to scream this at Billy, to shout it out until it exercised, like a demon, all nonsense from his mind, and I purposely failed to do so as I knew I would be screaming in vain. Instead I went on.

"Then you wouldn't have me be with anyone at all, for either way, you'll be taken from me and I won't have anybody else!"

"I've been here before, in this situation. They need me—I'm capable. This is what I'm good at."

"Not like this. You haven't been here like this. Even I know that much. You were merely going along before, now there is a bloody purpose that will drive and end you!"

I turned my face up at him as he held me, and I could see he was sad, too. Oh, how wonderful to be a man! To have such emotional fortitude! To never have to construct a barrier against pain by feeling the blows as a woman must, because nature constructs it for a man. Women must treat the blows each as a brick, hoping, praying, one day, you will finally get enough to enclose your heart so that it can be spared more pain. My pain spilled here for all to see, while his remained collected and concealed.

"Just tell me…I would like to know. Did you ever at least imagine taking me away from here, to pretend to have a different life, with me? Tell me the truth, knowing, as you do, that you cannot help yourself where it concerns me."

His eyes turned attentive, searching out an answer somewhere among the dust and sky that lay all around. He fixed his eyes on something in the distance as he spoke to me, "Why would a person want to know a thing like that…If it don't matter?"

"Why would you think it should not matter to me? It would be something for me to recall, happily—freedom, while I should waste away in captivity. To know the answer would give me the right to think on it and have it to imagine. If you tell me 'no', then I'll know I am where I was always meant to be. I can accept that, as I've had all of my life to learn to accept where I am to go and live in darkness."

"I think knowing a thing like that would a haunt a person."

"I am already haunted. Will it haunt you, too?"

His eyes squinted—he seemed daunted by this question. He didn't speak for a few moments, and I waited there, listening to his heart beating, as I knew as a certainty that the circumstances of his life here would soon end it. I wanted to remember the sound of it—I wanted to remember him. Young. Beautiful. Alive. I wanted to catalogue his heart's beating as an archeologist catalogues relics and artifacts of eras gone by so that I could call upon it one day when, soon enough, we would see how this would all end and remember that once, he lived.

"Yes. It will haunt me."

He pushed me away from him gently, and without looking, walked away. I had my answer, and so, his unhappiness will bring me joy when I should think of him when we are apart, as I will know that I am not alone in my sorrow and lost in all that could have been, feeling the despair of it. His unhappiness meant that he loved me, too.

As he walked away I called to him in a last desperate attempt, "I could be your last chance, Billy!"

He turned to face me, taking steps backward, "And I would be yours. Be careful of what you wish for."

# 10

# March, 1878

**W**ho kills a horse? What could be the purpose of such a callous act if not only to convey good measure? This could only mean that Brady and his posse of assassins had every intention of killing John—the slaughter of John's prized animal sent this message most clearly. It was overkill. In realizing this, their reasoning of self-defense was inconsistent with the fact of truth! If John had pulled his gun first and they shot to deflect their own harm, why go out of their way to shoot his beloved animal if not merely to perpetrate an affront to the man? If witness accounts of John refusing to pull his gun did not prove their boldfaced lie outright, then surely the need to destroy such a blameless, beautiful creature should drive the truth home; that they shot that horse to symbolize the outstanding hatred of the man who dared oppose such a crooked enterprise. A hate so great that it must be met with added insult to injury, even in death! They made his murder into an art form!

A horse was no threat, leading one to wonder what other violent lengths the Ring would lay out against humanity to suit their whim and, at the same time, declare their power. What evil in a godless territory such as this!

The Regulators had gone; Billy sharing my bed the night before they left, promising that he loved me and always would. When morning came, from his pocket, he produced a small gold ring with a delicately intricate design and slipped it upon the finger that once boasted the diamond ring that had secured my impending marriage to John. I admired its simple beauty and the significance of what it would forever mean to me—a declaration of our unbreakable bond.

"It's all I have left of my mother," he told me.

At this, words failed me, and I could only look at him with astonishment and wonder. When I found my voice I told him, "I could never take such a precious token from you, Billy, no matter how deeply I treasure the evidence of your promise."

He touched my face and kissed me sweetly on the lips. Smiling, he said, "My mother gave it to me with the condition that I would give it to the woman I wanted to spend my life with."

"But, Billy…you have denied us both that future. You will regret this and wish someday that you had it to give to the woman you will one day want to make your wife."

"Whatever happens, you are the woman I want to spend the rest of my life with—marriage has nothing to do with it. Nobody will ever match you; this ring belongs to you. No matter who I marry, I will consider only you to be my true wife."

I could feel the hot, glassy slickness of my eyes, though I was too stunned with bewildered emotion to allow them to weep, and we looked at each other in silence.

"You gave me something precious once, and so I give you this. We have sworn an oath of love to one another, and we have both now done what should bond us eternally under God—even if you don't believe it to be recognized." He smiled sadly.

"I recognize it within my heart...that is all that matters."

"Is that so, now?"

My tears fell and, placing his hands on each side of my face, he wiped the drops away gently.

"We will both always have this shared secret as true lovers often do," he said, "and now you'll know that you've gotten what you've always wanted, even if I'm not there beside you. This ring will remind you that we belong to each other, that you are desperately loved as you desperately love. You'll know that no matter where I am, I will long for you as you will long for me."

His eloquence astounded me. For someone who often spoke so dreadfully common, he could use his words brilliantly when he needed to.

"Billy, please...let me ask you this one last time—leave this place with me. We do not need to be apart. I can give you what you so desperately want, what you've been missing; stability, a home, a family...I will give you children. Many children! And you will give me, every day, the one thing I want more than anything in this world, a man who loves me truly. Can you not see how fate has brought us here together? How can you ignore that?"

"Bonita," he ran his hand through my hair affectionately, looking at me with an expression of adoration and sorrow. "I've explained this all to you. I can't walk away from this. I can't allow the terrorization of the Santa Fe Ring to go on. If I do nothing about it I'll be even less than the sort of man you deserve. I know you can't understand it, but please don't ask me to walk away from it anymore. It's a duty I need to fulfill. I want to stand up and fight back—"

"Okay...I understand, Billy."

When he left I cried uncontrollably knowing I'd never see him again and fearing that he would be taken away completely by this irrational endeavor. But all things considered, I did understand him, and I hated to make the self-confession that I admired him for the strength of character he embodied. I was, for all intents and purposes, proud of him.

I had spent much of my time helping Colleen gather and pack my belongings, unhappy to go home to New York despite leaving what could only be considered hell on earth. Out of all the jewels we tucked away, the most valuable, my most prized possession, rested around my finger, and I would turn my mind to that and clutch it tightly to my chest when the sadness of leaving overwhelmed me.

Another telegraph had come from my father informing me of a new suitor. This time I was to marry a man thirty years my senior, assuming negotiations reached an agreement. One of the contracted stipulations provided that I be seen and, upon eyesight, appear congenial. I was warned not to arrive in mourning. Otherwise, I knew nothing more of this old man.

The day before I was to begin my long journey home I sat myself down on the porch outside the room I had inhabited here one last time to read and lose myself in a world more agreeable than my own when Rob Widenmann approached me. This man was most certainly a friend of John's, but shameless in his own depiction of the depth of that friendship. Upon John's death, he began his campaign to ingratiate himself into the fold of the Tunstall's by taking it upon himself to write John's family abroad in England constantly and peddle himself as one of their own. How John's family, his father especially, viewed these appalling advances I could not say. I could, however, comment upon his brazen impositions upon myself as he not so subtly suggested that I pen a letter to the Tunstall's myself and express proof of his intimacy and loyalty to John.

In truth, though I was aware that Rob and John maintained a close enough relationship that stretched back to their travels together to New Mexico, I could not lend credibility to whatever it was Widenmann believed himself to be in John's eyes. How close must he be if he found it necessary to force recognition of his role in John's life? Rob Widenmann was an opportunistic interloper as far as I was concerned, and I refused to encourage him or help him curry favor in any way.

Because Alex held in his possession the deed to the tract of land that John was to inherit from my father upon our marriage, I began to explore a lost opportunity in my mind—if John had been murdered after we had been wed, the land would have been passed to me, and then could I have had the life I'd longed for, supposing that Billy would come to be with me? What poor timing. I shivered at this ghastly thought of mine and chastised myself. Poor John lay dead and cold in the ground and I could only wonder what might have been if his death had only been realized after our nuptials. I could not forgive myself for such a thought.

We started out southeast towards the border, progressing to Chisums' ranch for a day or two's rest along the journey, and happily I had found that we had crossed paths with Billy and some of the other boys. We embraced one another tightly, Billy kissing me tenderly but ardently, pleased to have this moment and hold me once again.

With them were two prisoners whom I recognized immediately: Frank Baker and Buck Morton. The hatred that existed there between Billy and Buck did not seem apparent as the prisoners were put away in separate bunkhouse rooms of their own, serving as a makeshift jail and keeping them out of sight and guarded. Nonetheless, I sensed something remiss; I would be a mindless simpleton to not discern the tension behind the easy demeanor of the deputized Regulators, knowing as I did all that had been done. There seemed only one way for this to play out—the end to result in payment of blood by both Morton and Baker, for the toll of anger resounded amongst all of John's devotees.

Buck was the suspected triggerman in John's execution, and I placed my bets that he had more to pay for than only this. Buck emasculated Billy and made life miserable for him not all that long ago. The two simply hated one other. By now I knew him only too well, and this led me to the belief that, though Billy was outwardly self-possessed, just beneath the surface he hid a murderous intent. I could see this plain enough through the congenial façade he practiced for the sake of decorum among those of us who were of a fairer disposition. The others, I knew, shared his keen temperament, which, to be sure, only served to resound the hate all around even more so as their raw emotions played off of one another.

And so no, I did not think Buck Morton and Frank Baker had very long to live. My suspicions were justified when Sallie and I brought provisions to these men as they sat solemn faced in their respective prisons. Morton asked Sallie to help him in writing some letters, one of which was addressed to his sweetheart, Buck having Sallie promise that the horse bridal he had braided himself would find its way to her after his death. For all the anger I unleashed on Brady and my own abhorrence of these men, I felt haunted by the prospect of their impending demise.

Guarded by Fred, Frank Baker asked if I would sit and spend time with him as he sat lonely in his room. Billy objected to this, not wanting me in the presence of either of these base men, but even more so, and in a cruel measure, he meant to deprive of Baker any privileges of comfort, especially the luxury of sharing company with a woman and having him shown any of the kindnesses the fairer sex could offer. He refused my having a visit with him. Vile though I found these men, I could not find it within myself to deny a doomed man a last request. I implored Billy to relent and allow me to sit with him, but was met with his adamant reply of "no", and a reprimanding, his pointing out how Baker and Morton murdered, in cold blood, my intended.

"It is only a small thing," I countered, "allowing this man my company and, after all, could any be sure that Frank had intended to commit John's death?"

I explained to him that the Christian thing to do wouldn't be to deprive these men of solace (though I confess, I would not dare bother myself with Buck Morton as my loyalty to Billy would keep me from him), and finally, at this, Billy yielded, but he insisted that, though I could sit and speak with Frank, he would come with me, not wanting me alone with the prisoner. I conceded that this was fair, my concession having more to do with my pleasure of Billy's concern for me rather than my concern for allowing Frank any comfort. I borrowed a bible from the Chisums' so I could read its passages.

Frank was dismayed by his current predicament. He had said that he did not expect to live very long. Despite his reprehensible crime this saddened me, and I was surprised by this, amazed that I could feel something for him, though I suspected it was only my humanity that allowed me to look upon him with mercy. We discussed religion, and he asked did I believe in God? I assured him I did, and when he asked what I believed happens after we die, I recited to him the very beliefs I was raised upon—that we would achieve life everlasting and be reacquainted with lost loved ones. To Billy's credit, he remained quiet and respectful of our conversation.

Frank told me how he had always admired me and, wouldn't it have been nice if he could have known me as a friend? For his sake, I agreed it may have been pleasant, indeed. He then apologized to me and offered his condolences on my loss of John. At this latter statement, I could have slapped him, and I turned to look at Billy and saw him menacingly raise his eyes to Frank.

Frank asked me to help him pen a letter to his family and I agreed. I wrote down his words, helping him select his prose carefully, ensuring that his last words would be both fine and brave. In an effort to console him, I pointed out that he would be taken back to Lincoln tomorrow, unharmed. Again, I shifted my gaze to Billy at saying this, but was met only by the sight of him with his head bowed towards the floor. He betrayed nothing and remained silent. Frank thanked me for my kindness, but assured me that making it back to Lincoln alive was a small chance. I couldn't tell him I understood this to be true as well. The men here who would escort them under the law would abuse their opportunity, of this I was sure.

I had left my conversation with Frank feeling upset, and rather than calm my sadness, Billy only mocked me, telling me to "Quit that bleeding heart!" He took me back to the house and, as we walked, I furtively looked at him and noted how he only stared straight ahead, the stern set of his jaw, and the determination of his walk. I knew that Frank's nerve in offering his condolences to me had served to heighten his anger.

When night had come I could hear the clatter of men throughout the house, walking to-and-fro loudly and aggressively, making an overt, obscene ruckus involving drink and vows of revenge. I lay in bed thinking about Frank Baker and death through the clamor. I was haunted in thinking how delicate the balance between life and death could be. I placed myself in Frank's doomed shoes, contemplating my own mortality and imagining what it must feel like to no longer view life as an endless supply of days for the foreseeable future, but to know the expiration of my life as it failed to exceed my grasp; to know beyond a doubt that, though I may wake tomorrow, I would not see the day after. To that end, I wondered what it was that Frank Baker was thinking of if I, safe from his fate, could lay here and think of nothing else.

There was a soft knock at my door, barely discernible above the commotion in the house. I wondered if I had imagined it when it sounded again. I rose from my bed and walked my bare feet across the chilly floor to answer it. I opened the door only slightly, dressed as I was in my nightshift, finding Billy standing there. He lifted his finger to his lips and pressed through the entrance into my room, forcing me to step back.

He seemed distressed, and when I asked what the matter was, he told me Frank Baker had confided in him that I was to be murdered on sight on orders from Brady. I did not know how to respond to this allegation, and in the wake of the thoughts I had been entertaining regarding my mortality, I could not help but feel fear. Suddenly, ironically, it would seem that I was indeed in Frank's doomed shoes after all.

"Can you be sure he speaks the truth?"

"No, but I can be sure it won't be risked. They know where you are and which direction you'll take. It would only be a matter of time before they caught up with you. Where are your things?"

"Most of my things are being held in the stables with the vehicles. Why should Brady want me…" Good God, I could not manage to give voice to the last word—dead.

"Baker says you threatened him. He says he could not in good conscious keep secret what he knows after your kindness, and he says he could not abide the death of a woman; he wanted to repay your compassion with a good turn—he feels he owes you. His affection for you and the interest of saving his soul won't allow him to go to his grave without the confession. I told him it was no matter, that he was going to hell either way."

"Billy! You didn't say such a thing!"

He only stood and stared at me plainly. "Never mind what I said to that ringster shuck! Why couldn't you have kept your big mouth shut? What made you do something so stupid? Why'd you get involved at all?"

Threatened Brady? I did, yes. Such a low man indeed! Could I, in truth, be surprised that such a fiend should order my death? Would I have minded myself that day on the street if I had considered he might not value my life as an innocent, and an innocent woman, no less? Could I truly be surprised that he viewed me as I viewed him, as no more than a crushable insect?

"I was so angry, Billy. Do you think you have cornered the market of anger? He had locked you away—away from me! He killed John, and I hated him!"

Billy recanted the harsh words he had spoken, accepting that it was because I loved him and could not help it. Though he would not say so, I suspected that a part of him loved me for this.

"Okay, Lu. I get it. Still—"

"If he were plotting my death, why not have it over with already? He's had the opportunity to do so easily if he wished me dead."

"No, Lucy...not in Lincoln. The death of a white woman, and a woman such as yourself on the heels of John's death, *your* fiancé, would have put Brady in a very poor position. They already hate him, his being involved in the murder of someone important to the citizens of Lincoln. With John, he had the excuse of defending himself. What excuse could he make with you?"

His tone said I was a stupid, ridiculous girl.

"Fine, but I am no longer in Lincoln...he could have taken his opportunity at any time after my departure and had his hands washed of it, making it appear as a misfortune of events."

"And he will, but you're still too close to Lincoln, and currently you're put up here at Chisums; you're protected well enough. Brady may be foolish, but he's not altogether stupid. Baker says he gave orders to make it look like your party was attacked by savages and far from Lincoln at that."

In my fear I began to extend the defense of my actions. "Do you think the lot of you is exclusive in your anger? Do you think that because I am a woman I am untouched by the misery of violence, especially when it directly affects me? That I have no right to voice my own opinion, directing it at those responsible? He is an evil man! It didn't help me that he put you in prison, causing you to miss John's funeral, especially when I needed...I needed you there, Billy. I wanted you there. He took John, and then he took you!"

His face softened and he nodded his head. "I know, Lucy. I'm sorry I wasn't. I wanted to be, and I only thought of you while I was stuck in there, and I was angry at the insult of their making me unable to say my goodbyes to John."

"Don't apologize to me—you could not have helped it."

We moved to the bed and sat upon it in silence a moment before I spoke, "What am I meant to do then, Billy?"

"You come with us."

"Come with you? I'd love nothing more, but I know that it's impossible!"

"No, it isn't. If we let you leave here they'll track you easy enough. If Baker is telling the truth, and I believe he is, you're safer with us."

"Perhaps I should stay, then, until this passes over. I'll be safe here!"

"This isn't just going to pass over, Lucy! You'll be a prisoner here, and if he wants you dead he'll get his way one way or another. There will be a war here, and Chisum's men are not guaranteed to hold the line. Brewer feels you ought to remain here, but we talked him out of it, though he's still unconvinced. We don't think staying here is the best thing for you. You've gotten yourself into quite a mess. You should have known better; Brady is a powerful man and a killer over the most trivial of things. What makes you think murdering a woman would mean anything to him?

"We're going to head back to Lincoln with the prisoners by way of the El Capitan trail; we suspect Brady's men are perched along the direct route waiting for us all to ride in so they can ambush us, and we'd be bound to run into the posse he sent after you."

"You mean to take a detour? Why head back to Lincoln anyway if it's so dangerous? You expect to give these prisoners over to Brady but suspect he's planning to ambush you? What is the point? He'll kill you all on sight and set those two free. You may as well just take the direct route and get it all over with!"

"Taking a direct route to Lincoln is suicide if they are waiting there for us. Yes, they'll take the prisoners then overtake us. Getting the prisoners into Lincoln past Brady's posse will sabotage their plans to waylay us and accuse us of starting war when we ride in with no trouble. We'll ride in and deliver the prisoners, legal. Whatever they do with them after they'll be unable to cause us anymore trouble and come after us as wanted men."

"Suddenly you don't care if those who murdered John will more than most likely be set free?"

He didn't answer me, but then I caught something in his expression. He was speaking in terms of legalities, but his thoughts were of a sinister nature.

"They are dead men, aren't they?"

Ignoring my question he told me, "Tomorrow you will get your things—only what's necessary. After we leave Lincoln you'll go directly to Sumner where you'll be safe until it's passable to continue on south."

I tried a different approach. "But none of you are actually intending on going to Lincoln, are you?"

Again, my question went ignored.

"What about Colleen?" I asked, "And the others? Will they not be in danger?"

"It's you they want. I don't know what you said, Lucy, but Brady's breathing down your neck."

"Why me? Why would it make a difference to Brady to get me?"

"Because he's petty, Lucy! And to make an example. That's what all of this is about; they're the Ring! It wasn't a very smart thing to do, shooting your mouth off! What the hell did you say?"

"I attacked his pride. But I spoke the truth!"

"Let me see if I can get this straight—you attacked his pride with your own. Is that about the sum of it?"

I ignored this.

"What will I do with all of you? I can't go out there, Billy! Not like this. I cannot cross the dessert with the lot of you and your prisoners as part of some…posse. I wouldn't even begin to know how to manage! And it's dangerous! I won't go!"

"Maybe…maybe there is danger, but it's an avoidable possibility at present. There is certain danger here, I'm sure of that."

He placed his hand upon my arm. "You will so, go. I'm staying here with you tonight, and in the morning we'll rise early and ride out."

"What about Colleen? I cannot leave without speaking to her! Without saying goodbye!"

"She'll know soon enough. Right now you're my concern and we need to get you, and us, out of here."

"We can still both go, together, you and I, just like I asked—"

"No, I belong here with the Regulators. I swore an oath and am part of a pact. We're going to take you someplace safe until we can get you out of New Mexico, understand me?"

I nodded obediently, but I was worried.

I lay down in my bed and watched as he went to the corner of the room and pulled a rocking chair over next to where I lay. He positioned himself on an angle towards the door and leaned back, propping his boots up on the bed and leaving his gun belt intact around his waist.

"Are you going to be terribly uncomfortable like that, Bill?" I asked.

"I reckon so, but I want to be prepared should there be any trouble."

"I'll be all right. Please, lay with me and get some decent sleep."

"I'll be all right right here."

During the night I was woken by the sound of him fidgeting in the chair, not sleeping well and trying to get comfortable. Perhaps, too, he was trying to remain awake. I slid over to the other side of the bed and persuaded him to lie down which he did now without protest, on his back, tucking his arms behind his head, still leaving his guns belted. I turned on my side towards him and lay close, placing my arm across him and feeling comforted by the weight of him beside me and the warmth of him so near. We both fell to sleep, waking before the sun had risen.

Billy allowed me to pen a quick letter to Colleen after waking and ask her not to fear for me. I was not to say where I would be taken. John Chisum understood the case and would provide further explanation regarding my bewildering departure in addition to supplying the caravan with extra men to help ensure Colleen's safety through the treacherous desert and in the event the party would meet with a nefarious gang of Brady's.

In my letter, I assured Colleen that I would be well taken care of, and that in light of the evils facing us all this was the best course of action. I lied, telling her I was not afraid and that she, too, should not worry for me.

Brady! My death would be nothing more to him than a symbolic gesture exercising the audacity and power of the Ring, attempting to prove that its power was great. Imagine, dying for such a great power in a place that not even a map would recognize! The proud jackass! He wanted only to make an example out of me, did he? Was he scoffing at the misfortune I had promised would befall him? If he truly meant to end my life out of spite and his errant arrogance, then such a war would be waged on him and the great Ring; a war so grievous that The Ring would be stamped out with less effort than a campfire! He would look directly into the face of the devil as he dragged him to hell when my father's wrath found him! It was clear that the man was senseless. Only a foolhardy man, and one full of such overconfidence as he, could dare turn a blind eye to true vehemence. I was too great a figure not to be missed—if my blood spilled, so too would his, and the precious Ring would burn. But though vengeance may be brought down upon Brady, I could not argue that it would be far better to survive this, and by doing so, keep Brady blissfully ignorant. The irony of all this was, with my death, this war would be over, wiping out the Ring and potentially saving countless lives, not the least of which could be Billy's.

I brought this to Billy's attention, but was met with cool infuriation, as though he wanted to strangle me for suggesting such a thing. He was not thrilled in the least with my arrogant observation. Then he impatiently reminded me of the fact that pinning my death on Brady would be difficult to prove as my death was meant to look as though a poor, unfortunate accident by crossing with the presentable dangers that progressed outside of Lincoln and under the blazing sun of the desert. Savages were to be blamed. In all likelihood, no one would even think to consider that it had anything to do with John's own violent death.

Billy left me to gather the clothing and riggings that I would need from my stored effects. He had come back with both sets of my English riding outfits, guns, and boots. I had a special corset used for riding that I must wear which he had failed to bring, prompting him to go back and search it out. While I waited I brushed and braided my hair and dressed as fast as I could.

When he arrived I found that my riding corset was a bit loose and I needed his help in lacing it.

"Billy! The money! Go back and take my money; it's in the safe—"

"Forget that, we need to go. We'll make our way without it."

"But we could use that, all of it! It will help ensure our survival—"

"None of that will ensure anything, and we don't have time. It doesn't matter—it's yours, just as it would have been if I had not known what I know. Nothing has changed, Lucy. You're going back to New York once we figure out how to get you there."

I disagreed, but I kept the argument to myself. I knew the value of money better than he, and I hadn't any intention of going back to New York. In my hesitancy to go, I found optimism and decided that I was granted an extension in which I could attempt to change his mind about me. I knew there would be vast amounts of trouble ahead and that we could have used that money to bribe whoever stood in our way. He really, truly, did not covet wealth or anticipate its many forms of worth.

When I was fully dressed and the sky had lightened, he took me down through the house and I saw that the men were ready to head out. Viola had been saddled and prepared for the long journey we would make through the desert. Again, I grew anxious. Knots were forming within my belly—I was terrified as to what all could happen to me out there in that wasteland. My head was filled with horrors. White women, especially golden haired women like me, I had heard, were considered a valuable prize amongst the Indians of the land. I was all but certain I'd be horribly scalped, my hair taken as a trophy. I did not relate my fears to Billy, knowing I should stand brave with the Regulators and not add to what I imagined was the certainty of their aversion to a woman riding alongside them. I would not whine, though I imagined the journey would be absolutely insufferable—I would grin and bear it, for I could be a good soldier, too. I knew how to use my guns, and because of Billy, I was quite adept for a woman so young, who should, for all intents and purposes, never know anything of such a horrifying ordeal.

I was sure if they could avoid harboring a woman under such severe conditions they would have. I did not want to justify whatever it was they must believe of my being present and a party to this; I would not make my presence miserable for them; I should make them forget I existed. And though I feared the journey I was about to make, I forced within myself the belief that this was preferable to the suffocating life waiting for me in New York.

Still, despite it being their idea that I accompany them, I felt as if I was an unwelcome party in all of this, and of course, how could it not be so? These men would need to worry over me in addition to keeping control of precarious situations. I knew I would be in the way no matter how small I tried to make myself, and so I decided I would steel myself, stiffen my back, square my shoulders and set my jaw firm, readying myself to prove that I could be an asset. I was determined to be of no hindrance and resolved to pray to God for our safety.

We set out northwest toward Roswell to mail the letters Morton and Baker had written, the postmaster eyeing us avidly. We then moved north towards the Captain Mountain trail. We rode in silence and I was ordered to keep my position in the middle of the posse, with Josiah to my right and Frank McNab flanking my left. Frank was an employee of John's and was there when he was shot and killed. Billy placed himself in front of me to my left, keeping this position so he could watch me and keep his eyes on the prisoners, while at the same time scanning the land's layout as we rode on. Adding to my frayed nerves was the worry of malevolent savages who might be out to get us, especially me.

A man I had known of in Lincoln, Frank McCloskey, had joined our party sometime before we had reached Chisum's ranch. I recognized him as an occasional employee of John's as he took all available work and odd jobs when needed. John was always happy to help out a man who was willing to pull labor, paying no mind to the dangerousness of such trust; Frank's drifting meant that he had worked under Dolan as well, and he wasn't well liked by the boys who were loyal to John, and I could not suss out the reasons why except to say that McCloskey not only seemed to be a neutral party, befriending the enemy as a hazard, but did not seem to have a particularly vested interest in bringing these men to justice for John's death. Naturally, this did not sit well with the Regulators.

On our way back to Lincoln he insisted on riding next to Morton, the two speaking to one another as if old friends, sometimes whispering. The others viewed this behavior as untrustworthy and treasonous. Even *I* knew that this conduct was treacherous under such perilous conditions. The others were incensed as the general consensus of social order here was not to engage the murderers in pleasant conversation; they were being brought in for their unlawful, unjust behavior in the violent death of a beloved friend and for breaking the law, yet McCloskey gabbed on, exchanging pleasantries with the captives and ignoring the ominous stares which surrounded him.

McCloskey was now the enemy, too, and the air grew copious with tension when he was overheard comforting Morton, McCloskey telling him he would not let anything happen to him, and that the Regulators would have to go through him first. These words were fiercely unappreciated, and McNab and Billy shot McCloskey a look of fury. The comment had been made in a brazen effort to display arrogance among the men of Mc-Sween's faction, but McCloskey's foolish mistake had ended him. My eyes grew wide at this empty-headed fool's statement and the attention it brought him. I felt certain that I would witness men die today.

We had travelled only a few hours when I was made irritable by the heat and the countless layers I wore despite it being only early March, which most always meant agreeable weather for layering. I suppose the rules of weather were different out west here in the desert. The binding of my riding corset restrained me unbearably. It was not meant to be used as a practical application under such impractical circumstances; traversing the desert as opposed to a short ride for pleasure. Lost in my own thoughts over this matter, I was looking down, staring absentmindedly at the mane of my horse, silently cursing my discomfort and scolding myself for listening to Billy and leaving behind all of my money. I was so distracted that when the first shot was fired I didn't recognize the sound. My horse fretted and bounded sideways, upset, and I saw McCloskey fall from his mount dead, Frank McNab's gun smoking and pointed where McCloskey had sat only a moment before.

Morton and Baker took off, fearful for their lives, their horses pitifully slow. The Regulators screamed to one another to catch them. Billy took off like a shot after both men with Josiah close behind. I felt incompetent in the midst of all the chaos, not being able to draw my eyes away from McCloskey's lifeless body and the bloodied, splintering hole in his head, nor could I manage myself as all of this was happening, feeling as though I were not truly present, and no sooner did I gather my wits in a feeble attempt to make sense of it all when another shot rang out. I lifted my head towards the direction of the report just in time to see Morton fall to the ground, Billy with his gun in hand. I watched as Billy fired again, this time felling Baker. Charlie Bowdre, Sam Smith, and Jim French reached the point where Morton fell and upon their horses they proceeded to take their own shots at his prone body as Billy fired a few more times into Baker's.

I was horrified by what I was seeing. My head and gut went numb before my stomach turned, causing me to lean quickly to the side of Viola as it contracted and spilled its contents to the ground in a horrible lurching manner that pained the muscles of my abdomen, neck, and upper back. It was all so disturbing, and I did not know how to react to this slaughter. Murder! My mind repetitiously screamed this abhorrent word, over and over again. *Murder! Murder! Murder!*

The rest of the men each took turns firing into Morton, the alleged triggerman in John's death—I could only stare, shocked and useless. Pressure had built up in my chest and my throat closed. I clapped my hand to my mouth which hung agape in horror. Somehow, through all of this, I temporarily caught my bearings and begged myself not to scream or sob, but to no avail. A small, stunned whine escaped through my lips and my tears spilled over helplessly. I put my head down and I covered my eyes—I did not want these men to see this, how weak I was, and despite the awfulness of the scene I was wickedly thankful that the men were preoccupied with manslaughter, eliminating both any chance that their attentions might find me like this and any dismay over having to concern themselves with a hysterical woman.

Though I closed my eyes against the horror I could see a vision of Buck's lifeless body as it was desecrated with glee, helpless against the attacks. I cried so hard for this, for him, and in this instance it did not matter what sort of man he was when he had lived, only the fact that he lay as a rag-doll, refuse for the men to play with.

Though overwhelmed with hysteria, I was aware of Billy standing by me now, reaching his hand up to help me from my horse as I leaned over the side and quickly began losing my grip. I was shaking uncontrollably as I took his hand to let him help me down. I was falling, my body so unstable that he had to use both of his arms to catch me firmly. Once on the ground, blocked from the others behind Viola, I allowed myself to cry quietly but intensely against his shoulder as he placed his arms around me fiercely.

"What have you done!?" I managed to choke out; my words thick and strained from the stress of heavy weeping.

Charlie and Richard rode over and dismounted near us. They were joined by Fred, Frank McNab, and Josiah. Jim and Sam remained by the bodies, prodding the dead men with their boots and checking their pockets for anything of value. They were speaking to one another but I could not hear what it was they were saying—it was inaudible; they were much too far away and I was much too upset to make sense out of anything. Richard began to shout at Frank.

"What the hell were you thinking? These men were to be taken into Lincoln unharmed; we're the law! We're commissioned to return the prisoners!"

Frank remained cool and snidely replied, "You blind, Richard? What the hell do you think would have happened if we took them into Lincoln? You think they would have paid for what they'd done under the 'law'? They'd of been turned right back out again and we'd have been dead men."

Richard was beside himself. Richard Brewer, the only truly decent, honest man in the bunch; he wanted to do right and abide by the rules. I wondered what his anger could mean as it seemed to me that the Ring would make the endeavors of the Regulators null and void.

Logistically, though I despised it, I could see the death of these men was necessary, and truth be told, preferential to what would have happened had the boys taken them back into Lincoln. Perhaps what placed him so on edge was that killing Morton and Baker was not like killing any other, ordinary men. The Ring would pay restitution—we all knew that. But it seemed, regardless, they were damned if they did, and damned if they didn't.

"And you, Bonney…you goddamned lunatic son-of-a-bitch!"

Billy paid no attention.

"What the hell are we supposed do now? And her," he nodded his head at me. "She was supposed to be taken to Sumner! This was supposed to be an easy undertaking; we were to take these prisoners back to Lincoln and take Lucy directly to Sumner! That was the plan! She could've been killed! You've compromised her safety!"

"I'm fine, Richard," I said, hoping to quell the argument.

He ignored me and shouted, "You're all ignorant! You, all of you, just caused an all-out war!"

Charlie spoke up, "We can still get her to Sumner, Richard. Since we won't be going into Lincoln we'll have a head start, head that way—"

"She was spotted with us in Roswell!" said Richard, "Word will spread—Sumner's only a stone's throw up the Pecos River for Christ sakes—"

"We don't know it for sure that anyone knows who she is. Who's gonna tell anyway?" Charlie challenged, "Who's gonna know…"

"*Everybody*! This sort of news travels fast. We hole her up in Sumner we could be asking for trouble. You all broke a mess and drug her down with us!"

"They were told not to run, Dick," Billy answered snidely.

Richard glowered at him, "We're finished, do you understand that? These two— these three deaths are gonna cost us."

Smugly, Billy responded, "You got it wrong, Brewer; they started this war when they murdered John! The way I see it, Rich, the prisoners fled; we did what we had to. Isn't that what you had hoped for when we found them back along the Peñasco? That you wished they hadn't surrendered so you didn't have to take them alive? I heard you say it! Well they ran, Dick!"

"Don't you condescend to me! My orders were to take these men alive! When we found them you needed to be restrained from killing them flat out, Bonney! I knew you couldn't be trusted! You just couldn't wait until you had your chance! They were dead men as soon as we caught up with them, contesting to kill them there and then—and you would have!"

"You know damn well they'd have shot us on sight had we taken them in to Lincoln honest! We're not any worse off than we would have been had we kept them alive! Either way we'd be done for," he laughed, "except now there are three less bastards to worry about!"

Richard was so angry that it became clear he could no longer find any comprehensible words. It seemed he could only simply say, "Fuck you, Bonney!

Richard yanked his reigns instructing his horse to turn and go where the bodies lay. He didn't look back.

I looked at Billy who was still looking at Richard insolently as he walked off on his horse. I stepped in to him even closer as I received a chill. I tried to reconcile this Billy and the boy I had known before all of this happened. This side of him was spiteful. But I knew he was right when he said those things to Richard. Still, he captivated me as much as he troubled me.

Richard instructed us to head to the Gutierrez ranch to arrange the dead men's burial and decide on our next move, agreed upon by Josiah and Charlie as the latter placed a fresh bullet in his gun's chamber.

Billy asked if I was able to ride as I stood with him, shivering uncontrollably still, my hands clenched into fists and clinging to his duster. I could not answer him; the words stuck in my throat. Instead I shook my head against him. I did not want to be on my own.

"All right, Bonita, come on…"

He climbed up on his horse and reached down for me to grab his hand so he could raise me up. Once atop his horse I sat behind him, my arms around his waist holding onto him so very tightly. I allowed myself weakness just this once. I swore, however, solemnly, to maintain my composure the next time.

Richard turned to ask Billy, "Can you trust people in Sumner?"

Billy nodded before spurring the horse on.


We reached the Gutierrez ranch, owned by a man named Francisco. Richard handed over the dead men's arrest warrants and related to Gutierrez where the bodies would be found.

I sat outside on the front porch, distraught. I watched Fred and Charlie take the horses around back to be watered and fed when Billy came over to me and sat down, placing his arm around my shoulders. Now I tensed at his touch which did not go unnoticed. Nuzzling into my neck he said, "Talk to me, Luce."

He was here now to comfort me, but I was unsure of how I felt about him. I was not afraid, but the manner in which he could be so swiftly cruel distressed me. I was reminded of the way he rode after those men without hesitation and shot them both dead.

"So…what? Are you angry with me?" he asked.

"You murdered those men with ease. You wear that badge and yet you mock it by using it as an excuse to kill your enemies."

He leaned back, amused. "I wanted all men dead, and now they are. Besides, it was their doing; they shouldn't have run."

"They didn't die because they ran, they died because you wanted them to. Otherwise, they would have heeled. You were faster than they were, their horses ran slowly— they were exhausted. Any one of you could have caught up to them and brought them back."

"Don't tell me you feel sorry for them, Lu. Or is it you're feeling sorry for Baker? They were evil men, all of them *are* evil men."

"And what are you, then? Aren't you evil after what you had purposely done? You were supposed to serve the law, not yourself."

I made to get up, but he held on to my arm forcing me to remain.

"You know damn well the deal. You've heard all about it, and I know you're smart enough to know it on your own. Still, let me tell you how it works…we take those men back to Lincoln, Brady lets them loose, and for our trouble they kill us. And Brady would do the same to you! They killed John and told that he made to fire on them—they told a bold-faced lie and gotten away with it! John wasn't armed, and he sure as hell wasn't stupid enough to try and kill a posse of armed men, and *everybody* knows it. He was one man against six. He wasn't a violent man."

This last statement stuck me like a pin.

"And you are? Violent?"

"I can be. Why is it you think John placed me as he did, a hired gun to go where he went? I was there to defend him, Lu…and you. Wise up! I ain't the simple boy you've made up about me in your mind. I told you all about me! You knew this of me! I explained it. Do you understand now?"

I felt a little desperate by his statement.

"It was hard to imagine. Only now do I see it. But yet I do not believe you are a killer. I know that, even if you don't! You've fooled yourself into believing you're worth nothing more than this. You may have a little wizening up to do on your own. You told me if you brought them in past Brady's posse, they'd have no excuse to murder any of you; they'd be unable to testify that they needed to defend themselves against you."

"Yeah, I know it, what I said. But Lucy…even though they would have let us get out of Lincoln, they'd have come after us eventually—they wouldn't take us before the people in the town. And then they could have made up any old story they pleased."

I grabbed the arm of his that held me, yanked it from me and stood. As I walked toward the house I turned to him. "John was a hypocrite. He'd have you do his dirty work, would he? And he was given a face full of dirt in the end. If that's what awaited him, an innocent man, what awaits you, I wonder." I turned back to walk into the house, feeling sorry that we had had this conversation. Maybe it was the tension. Maybe it was my seeing what Billy truly was. Or maybe it was because I loved him still, despite his dangerous nature.

I walked into Richard as he came out and told us he was heading back to Lincoln while the others were moving on to Patricio. He went around the back to get his horse, and I looked at Billy, asking him where I was expected to go. He said that I would still go on to Sumner, but just now I was to go with him to Patricio. He did not feel that I should be on my own in an unfamiliar place after what had happened if he could not stay there to help settle me. He told me trouble would not be far behind once the Ring found out about Morton and Baker, and probably McCloskey, and if they should make their way for me as Baker had attested, he felt I'd be better placed with him and the rest of the Regulators, and I was relieved at this because I felt he was right, and anyway, I did not want to be away from him.

It took half the day to get to the little town of San Patricio from the Gutierrez Ranch. We had woken early, had a decent breakfast, and bade goodbye to Mr. Gutierrez and Richard as we parted ways for the time being. Though the weather was chilled, I again grew uncomfortable as the sun bore down on me from the winter sky. If only I were not wearing my corset—it made it difficult to breathe, which in turn caused my body discomfort and allowed its temperature to rise from the strain; it was the primary factor of my awkwardness in what otherwise should have been a comfortable climate. As soon as we made it to San Patricio I'd do away with the thing completely, proper or not.

Once we reached Patricio we found the residents having a small celebration in honor of St. Patrick, the town's namesake, and though the population was mostly Mexican, the Irish inhabitants paid their respects to the Irish priest holding festivities throughout the entire month of March.

It was here that I began to relax into some semblance of comfort within my current predicament. We engaged our horses in the livery and made arrangements at a tiny adobe-style boarding house with a crudely made sign that read The Old Ruidoso, a makeshift lodging for travelers which was restricted to about five small rooms. It housed a storage facility that could be converted should more than five souls need a place to stay. It had a boarded porch that ran around the entire length of the rectangular shaped building. Only two rooms were available, and these were lent to Billy and me, along with Charlie and Fred. The others found refuge with locals who rented rooms in their cabins to passers-by as a means of income.

Once we had taken our belongings to our room I yanked at my corset and removed the damn thing, feeling immediate relief. Billy made a crude comment, pointing out how much easier it would be to get to me from now on, to which I replied that a gentleman would not make such a remark. He only laughed at this, citing that he could be a gentleman in public, but in private he could not make such a promise.

After we had settled our things he took me to the local blacksmith and purchased for me a pair of spurs. I had asked for these specifically as I wanted the added protection they could allow me. If a man should put his hands on me I could rear my legs up and stick him. Once they had been adjusted to fit my boots I delighted in the tiny jingling sound they made as I walked. The boys found this endearing as, to them, spurs were merely used as a practical means. They agreed, humorously, that perhaps having a girl around could prove interesting after all if I were to find amusement within the mundane.

A parade of dancing women moved along the street to an Irish tune that played as they lifted and fluttered their layered, colored skirts, and I stamped my feet along so that I could play with my spurs. I was fascinated as I watched the liberty of these women as they danced by; I couldn't imagine behaving in such a manner in my own skirts under the watchful eyes of my contemporaries. The thought of doing such a thing made me laugh out loud.

Vendors had set up their carts along the streets, inviting the crowds to gather and observe their wares. I of course was no exception, reveling in my new found freedom and running from cart to cart, my senses all amok with wild abandon. For the first time I could behave as I could not before, and the physical freedom I relished was priceless, corset-less and be-spurred as I was, and suddenly the things that were so familiar to me before were now new and exciting. I had bought a balloon from one of the vendors, playing with it and marveling in its brilliant simplicity as it floated above me, no bells and whistles, just a plain item defying gravity through science. I was never allowed such a thing as it would have been considered gauche for me to handle one. So elated was I in this small exhibition, keeping my eyes upon the inflated little article, that I took a misstep into a large, puddle filled depression, causing me to stumble and release the toy, watching with disappointment as it floated helplessly up, up, and up.

Fred bought and gave me a Jew's harp, an object I had only come to know after arriving in Lincoln, which proved to enchant me, but became a source of great irritation to the others as I took to twanging the little instrument, speaking and answering questions through the vibrations it gave out. This went on for the better part of an hour until finally it was snapped directly from my mouth when Billy had grown entirely fed-up.

I became a fount of entertainment for the group, no longer the matured Thor-oughbred they had come to know, but a mere foal struggling to find its footing in its new world. I was learning to live by a new set of rules, where simply walking along the crowded boardwalk proved trying as I frustratingly implored many large, gun-toting men to *excuse me, excuse me, excuse me.* I walked along as I often did, always expecting and being given the right-of-way as a lady; my way paved. These people did not see me as a young lady, but rather as a boy, as is how I was now dressed. My mistake in forgetting myself resulted in a very large man pushing me against a wall and threatening me when I bumped into him. He placed his hand on the grip of his gun, and as fast as he had done this the boys were on him holding him back. Only then did the man see my long golden locks gathered in ribbons on either side of my face beneath my hat. The man apologized, lifting his hat and going on his way. I was bewildered; this shocked and frightened me. I realized I would need to adjust to my appearance and act accordingly.

Another vexing incident happened when I had scolded some children playing a game of Bounce Eye directly in the footpath of human traffic after one of the small orbs found its way precariously underfoot, the marble that put it there nearly taking out my eye. What irony! I stood covering my almost plucked eye as I berated the men for stand-ing by laughing at me, bawling that I did not find the danger posed me by an errant marble funny at all!

My greatest travesty, however, came about when I actually upset an apple-cart by way of erroneously leaning against a broken section of railing on the walk, falling down onto it. This brought louder peals of laughter from the boys and more bawling from me, though I cannot say that the irony of what I had done was lost on me, either.

But not to be outdone, when we visited with the local pinhooker to see about a horse as Henry Brown's went lame just outside of town, we were introduced to a sorry looking nag named, of all things, Lucy. This time, to their credit, considering how much fun they had been having at my expense already, the men tried as best as they could to stifle their laughter and were having a hard time of it as they realized my good humor was wearing thin. I looked down at my boots in embarrassment, moving to sit down upon some crates nearby when I broke out in a smile of my own at the communal jest, attempting to conceal my amusement by keeping the brim of my hat low and lowering my head. I could not truly be angry as the joke was in too good a nature. When they had seen that I was not upset but in fact was entertained, they howled merrily until they cried from laughter.

As the sun began to sink low into the desert, dusk setting in, the town focused entirely on dancing during the evening baile. Billy and I danced for hours, the girls standing along the sidelines peering from behind their fans attempting to get his attention which was all on me. To make it clear that he belonged to me, when we had finished dancing an Irish set, I leaned my face in towards him and displayed my cheek. Standing behind me, holding both of my hands in his, he leaned in and kissed me lightly there. I closed my eyes and reached up to touch the place he had kissed me, smiling openly as those around us clapped, hollered, and whistled gaily at this gesture and all the fun being had.

We both had decided to stand along the crowd and watch the others dance as we chose to stay out of it for a while. Leaning into my ear he whispered, "Why don't you and I go back to our room where you can wrap those pretty little legs of yours around me?" I blushed at his forwardness but admit that it got to me in a most improper way. I did my best to feign offense but he disregarded this knowing I was only playing a game. With his arms around me he began to back up, pulling me along with him until we receded from the glow of the lights that lined the crowds and were swathed in near darkness, illuminated by the moon only. He spun me around and ran, pulling me along behind him until we reached our room, locking ourselves behind the door for the rest of the night.

After nearly a week Richard arrived in Patricio with news from Lincoln. Governor Samuel Axtell was in Lincoln investigating the trouble, but he spent his time in the company of Murphy and Dolan, refusing to hear out any testimony given by McSween and his partner, David P. Shield. Any fool could have known without further explanation that this alone was poor news indeed. Richard went on to say that Axtell had removed Wilson as Justice of the Peace and revoked all legal processes issued by Wilson, which voided all of his appointments, including the deputation of the Regulators, making them wanted men after the murder of Morton and Baker. The warrants issued by Wilson for those responsible for John's death and presented to the Regulators were now nullified and useless.

And it wasn't only the Regulators who were affected by this, though granted they bore the brunt of Axtell's retroactive proclamation. Oh no…by this process he invalidated marriages, bastardizing children borne of those marriages, he liberated murderers and thieves set to be hanged. In other words, they were making a mess of things and bringing harm to the citizens of New Mexico for the sake of the Santa Fe Ring and bringing down the faction that dared oppose them.

The Ring's reach was far and void of consequence except where the people of New Mexico were concerned. Axtell declared the processes of Judge Bristol of Mesilla, who was in the Ring's pocket, honorable, and Sheriff Brady and his deputies the only enforcers of his rule. Axtell swore this was in the best interest of the people, but the people knew better. The Ring was about as subtle as an earthquake. It appeared that the Santa Fe Ring's monopolization of power was all encompassing. They could kill whoever got in their way and seize their property as their own so long as it pleased them. We were all pawns; a cast in Dante's Inferno. Lincoln County's welcoming slogan ought to have been ordained as "Abandon all hope, ye who enter here."

Richard thrust a newspaper into Billy's hands, the Lincoln Gazette. I could not read his face as he read the article; it was poker straight, his expertise at playing the game serving him well. But Richard's look was troubled.

"Do you see now?" he asked Billy, but the question was posed to all of us.

"What is it?" I asked. Billy just kept reading and Richard remained quiet. "Billy! What the hell is it?" I shouted.

He peered at me with a look of uncertainty and concern. Still, he remained silent, frightening me as I've never seen such a look on his face. He looked down and away and handed the folded paper to me. All men remained silent as I read.

In the wake of the death of John H. Tunstall, one of the foremost merchants and cattle proprietors of Lincoln Co. New Mexico, Justice of the Peace John B. Wilson was relieved of his legal duties by Governor Samuel B. Axtell, who retroactively dissolved all of Wilson's previous issued proclamations, rendering the legally deputized gang, known by many as the Regulators, sent to serve warrants to those thought responsible for the death of Tunstall, as outlaws and wanted men.

Elucia Grey Alexis Howard, Tunstall's fiancée, was spotted in Roswell with the Regulators and is wanted for questioning in the deaths of Buck Morton, Frank Baker & Frank McCloskey, employees of Lincoln Co.'s most prominent business men, Lawrence

G. Murphy and James J. Dolan, who were believed to have taken part in Tunstall's death but proclaimed innocent by Dolan himself.

The residents of Lincoln are in a state of shock as Ms. Howard's station is one of wealth and refinement, coming from one of the wealthiest and finest families in the east. Her behavior is objectionable at best and has proven her to be an enemy of the people rather than her previous position of stature known as The Lady of Lincoln.

It is believed that in an act of retribution, the Regulators took advantage of and used their previous deputation rights by Wilson and the warrants signed by him as a means to exact their own form of vigilante justice on their unsuspecting prisoners under the guise of their being brought in for trial.

Shortly before the deaths of Baker, Morton, and McCloskey, Ms. Howard had threatened Sheriff Brady after the burial of Tunstall, and with the full back-patenting of the Regulators, it is feared that Sheriff Brady will serve as their next mark. Any compassion extended to Ms. Howard for her tragic loss has been revoked and replaced by a lack of sympathy from the good citizens of Lincoln Co. Ms. Howard and the Regulators are to be brought in as outlaws and served a sentence of justice befitting of their crimes. A posse has been assembled by Sheriff Brady with orders to bring the outlaws in. They are considered armed and dangerous, and if seen it is encouraged that the good citizens of New Mexico take word to authorities as soon as possible and are warned not to approach them in an act of heroism.

That last bit—such sensationalism! And I was now wanted? What I had found in the eight months' time I had spent in New Mexico was that it was an absolute nightmare. In this place it was one horror after the next. Yes, I had threatened Brady, but not once had I threatened his life. On the contrary, he had just threatened mine ostentatiously, and my presence with the Regulators was only meant to ensure my safety against Brady, of all things. Did the people really buy into this tripe? It would seem that no matter which tack I took, Brady would be able to find it convenient to twist the truth to serve his own ends. I would wonder how the self-made authorities of Lincoln could think such a thing of me, that someone like me could ever be a danger, but I knew better than to ask myself why. They were now the self-serving law of the people and creating false sentiments at that; they were shameless liars. My only concern was, did the people themselves believe this? Did my refinement not speak for itself? How could I be considered The Lady of Lincoln one minute and a dangerous outlaw the next? It hadn't made sense. Surely any fool could see the nonsense in that! After the death of John it seemed so apparent that the citizens of Lincoln County themselves had had enough of The Ring by the way they all carried on. Surely they must realize that The Santa Fe Ring made the rules and created trouble where there was none to be found. Surely, after the near riots I had witnessed upon John's death, the people could not truly believe that the Regulators were murderous bandits, that The Ring was pulling at their sadistic strings! And I could not help but notice how Morton and Baker were only presumed innocent of John's death! My rage at being fingered as an offender of the law was irrevocable and growing at an alarming rate! I was brought from my heated reverie by the sound of Richard's voice.

"Now do you all see? Bringing her here has caused us more trouble! We should have left her at Chisum's! She would have been sufficiently safe there!"

"You don't know that!" Billy retorted.

"Shut the hell up, Bonney! You can't see the forest for the trees where she's concerned!"

"Watch it, Brewer!" replied Billy, "What the hell do you know about it? We don't know if she'd have been better off at Chisum's! We know for a fact that there was a possibility they were coming for her! You'd better believe they'd have paid a visit to Chisum, and how long do you think his men could have held off Brady and *his* men? What makes you think they wouldn't have turned her over in order to avoid the trouble? Look at that article—they're quick to blame her as taking part in Baker and Morton's death as ridiculous as it is! Seems to me they're gunning for her just the same, just as Baker said!"

Jim, Charlie, George, Fred, Minxie and Josiah also objected to Richard's outlook. John Middleton agreed that, yes, more heat had been placed upon the Regulators with my presence, but regardless, they were after them whether I was with them or not. He conceded, however, that they did the right thing attempting to play it safe by taking me with them. He offered that they escort me to the train depot, but this idea was ruled out straight away as the six who disagreed with Richard believed that not only would it be risky for us all to make the journey across the desert plains out in the open as the hunted prey we were, but also that the Ring's power spread far and wide, and there was no way of knowing if there were men stationed at the depot anticipating my arrival, assuming they believed the idea was to get me back to the east.

After listening to the arguments I spoke up. "Quarreling about this is going to get us nowhere. Richard, this is where we are now: It no longer matters what we should have done, and it's my life you're all up in arms over so it's only fair I get a say in all of this. I agree with the others, and I trust Billy to decide what is best for me—he wouldn't misdirect me and risk my safety. I know he holds my security in the highest regard. Whatever he should decide for me, I will follow him. I appreciate your concern, Richard. I do. I love you for it—I love you all for it. I realize how difficult it must be, bearing the added stress of having a woman to protect in addition to all else, but I am not useless!"

Minxie placed his hand to his temple and rubbed there, "What wif all these sixes-and-sevens it's givin' me a bleedin' headache! It's too late; clearly the girl is one of us now, no use in complainin'."

I went on. "Richard...we must stop pointing fingers over whose fault is what, and I would appreciate it if I were not at the center of these problems, no matter how well-meaning you may be, the situation is what it is; I'm here and that's all there is to it. If I can stand it, so can you. We need to be productive now and figure out our next move instead of arguing over what can't be undone."

I had hoped my oration would mean the end of this particular argument, but still, I knew it was a fool's hope and that I had not heard the last of it. I truly did appreciate their concern, but it put me in an awkward position. The last thing I wanted was to be looked upon as dead weight, dragging these men down due to the supposed fragility of female weaknesses which society had burdened upon me. I was stronger than they could ever know. I would make it clear to them all that I had as much mettle and gumption as they. I had become quite an extraordinary shot for a woman of these times because of Billy at John's request. I was afraid, but in my short years on this earth, I had been taught through my dynamic breeding to bury my emotions deep and do what was expected of me. I would do no less here and treat this all the same, and I would take from it as much optimism as possible, such as the freedom it would allow me. And freedom, as everyone knew, was worth dying for. It was either this or a captive life that would surely kill my spirit. I was perfectly willing to risk my life for liberty. Perhaps that was something these men would never understand of me. Whatever fright and shock I had felt at the sight of Morton and Baker's violent deaths I would feel no more. The news I had gleaned from Lincoln County would see to that.

# 11

## March, 1878

We left Patricio for Fort Sumner the day Richard arrived, but before leaving, Billy and I had gone back to the room we had hired and I clipped the article from the Lincoln Gazette while we were packing our belongings, which, by all accounts, were not much. I had fully intended to write my father as soon as we arrived in Sumner to explain my predicament and plead with him for help. The Santa Fe Ring was a microcosm of power and the men could not combat the Ring fairly because of this as they were at a disadvantage. I may have been a feeble woman as far as they were concerned, but I was holding a few cards of my own. It would seem I may have something to offer after all. If anyone could help get us out of this mess it was I as I had a direct line of access to eastern affluence and supremacy, and my father knew many, many men in great positions of power. It was a glimmer of hope in a seemingly hopeless situation.

We travelled to Sumner by way of the Rio Hondo, picking up the Rio Pecos and following along its path. Once we hit the Pecos it was a straight ride through, but it was a long expedition. We had to ride nearly one hundred miles, which meant spending at least two nights in the desert. This would be my first experience sleeping out in the open, and it was not entirely unpleasant as our circle was well lit by a warm fire, the men telling interesting stories, many of which were unsuitable to my ears as they often forgot my presence, giving me a deliciously devious sort of thrill as I was sick to death of being handled with kid gloves and the boring chatter of ladies.

They talked also of plans to not only evade the posse sent by Brady, but the chances of ambushing them instead. They spoke much of strategy in bringing about the fall of the Ring, and to hear them tell it, it did not seem at all so impossible, though as they say, things are easier said than done. The Regulators were made of many men, though the Ring had quite a few more and ruthless at that! But there was the tale of David and Goliath, after all; anything was possible, I suppose, and it was my personal belief that good had a decent stake in triumphing over evil. Billy had insisted I sleep next to him closely when it was time to bed down as if I would mean to lie anywhere else. Two men were posted so as to keep watch while the rest of us slept to ensure our safety and make us less vulnerable. After a few hours they would wake two others to take over guard while they received some sleep of their own. The incorporation of a safeguard comforted me, allowing me the belief that I could sleep easy, though I already believed I would sleep soundly enough as I lay next to Billy.

But still, I was not looking forward to roughing it out in the dark open land; it was taxing, to be sure. The sounds of the desert night unnerved me, though I was ensured that we would be safe from the creatures of the night on the plains as they roamed about. But most of all, it was the savages who made me most anxious. The men took advantage of my uneasiness and having themselves a good laugh over it, deliberately telling me tales of Indians who captured white women, especially white women with the color of gold in their locks like me, which would make me all the more desirable, and sold them across the border into slavery in Mexico, scalping and murdering the white men who were with them. But they told me not to fret over being sold into slavery, as there was no telling if they may decide to scalp the women after all. The men delighted in rattling me, and they were making a damn good job of it, until Billy, who I may say often abused any opportunity to amuse himself at my expense, barked at them to quit it. He found they were going too far in alarming me this way, especially with this being my first time in the intimidating, dark, virginal open space that I was not accustomed to, and knowing how absolutely terrified I was of savages. Even he did not have the heart to frighten me. I trust he held a bit of empathy for me as he had once found himself a frightened boy alone in the blackened desert night not long ago when he was only but two years younger than I. He was so very protective of me; whenever he *would* tease me, it was relatively harmless and not in such poor taste.

During our first night out in the desert, the men spoke of Brady and their plans to remove him from office. I was confused as to how they intended to overthrow him from his position when they hadn't any power or authority to do so, but then it was made clear to me that they hadn't any intentions of taking any legal measures considering that their legal rights had been revoked. I must admit I was not shocked in the least. As far as I was concerned, Brady could burn in hell. I only worried for the boys. What if they were hurt or killed in all of this? Suppose any plan they conjured backfired, as it was likely to do, and instead of cutting down Brady, they were either cut down themselves or caught and hanged?

I imagined that if I were going to be a part of this congregation I would need to put an end to worrying so much as women are wont to do, or at the very least not show it. My predicament as a lady was exceptional, and these were men with a mission and ready to die for the cause they felt was just. I would learn to respect that, even though I bided my time and held out as long as I could before I would inevitably beg and plead with Billy to run again and take me with him away from all of this. Right now, though, I knew he had a rage inside of him that he had to satisfy. No amount of begging would abolish it, not even my own.

One of the most horrific measures for a woman spending the night in the desert with a group of men had to do with one's natural call of duty which, unfortunately, I had to do often, attributing this to my nerves. This was always an embarrassing struggle for me as I was too frightened to go on my own, which meant I would need to have Billy take me while the others snickered. They would wink and make lewd comments about what it was we were planning to do out there in the dark. Sometimes Billy would be playful, placating by smiling and winking back, but most of the time he let them know he was unhappy with disrespectful behavior towards me. Just because she's out here with us in britches, he'd say, don't mean she ain't still the lady y'all knew back in Lincoln, to which they would all shamefully shut their mouths and keep quiet.

It was undesirable to go walking around in the black vastness, especially with only a small, weakly lit lamp to guide the way when one was trying to stay concealed, so Billy told me that I would need to learn to curb my many undertakings, such as drinking too much water, as they pertained to the call of nature before it was time to sleep.

We found a large rock which I ducked behind. I popped by head back around to look at him, telling him to move farther away. He argued with me, telling me to quit being so damn modest.

"Lucy, I'm standing far enough away. This ain't any time for you to be worried about your pride," he said.

"I know. Billy...*please*? I promise to try and hold it more if you promise to walk a little bit more away."

"I ain't gonna hear nothing," he swore. "Besides, don't you think it's a little late for you to be embarrassed in front of me considering I've seen everything you got to offer?"

"But a lady can still have a small amount of privacy, can't she? Please?"

"Yeah, all right," he conceded as he stepped a little further away, but not before he flippantly warned me to watch out for any poisonous critters that like to bite.

In the dark this was no easy task! I wish I had asked him to loan me the lamp. Lowering my pants and squatting, I could not see beneath me, and not only was I afraid of spraying allover myself, but God forbid a scorpion happened by unseen! Or a rattler! I was also an exceptionally bit chillier with myself exposed in such a way, which did nothing to help me hurry along! All I wanted to do was finish my business and hurry back to camp. I heard a sound behind me, the sound of a rock releasing itself to the ground from the boulder perhaps, but I yelped in shock just the same. I heard Billy coming for me.

"Get out! Stay away! I'm fine!"

"Okay, then...just checking up on ya darlin'."

There was a note of amusement in his voice. I'll just bet he made that sound all on his own just to tease me.

When I was finished and able to yank my pants back up as quickly as I could I stumbled back out through the darkness and we walked back towards the men, hearing Sam Smith telling a story about The Red Ghost of the Arizona desert. My interest was piqued, despite my unease of the shadowy darkness of the New Mexican desert, the camp fire glowing upon and casting odd, eerie shapes over the natural objects of the desert landscape that surrounded us, coyotes whining somewhere out in the dark and the high moon cascading a pale glow upon the shapes in the surrounding areas set much too far outside the parameters of the campfire.

"He trampled a woman to death! He did!"

"Naw," said Fred, "that's a bunch of bunk Sam! He trampled a woman to death and the woman she was visiting with didn't see nothin'?"

"She sure did! She saw the Red Ghost riding off with Death on its back is what she saw!"

"There ain't never been, nor will there ever be, a Red Ghost riding around these parts, Sam! You're haywire!" said Jim French.

"I swear to ya! I swear to all of ya! It's a true story! The Beast of Death is out there!" Sam asserted.

"What is this story you're all talking about?" I asked a bit apprehensively.

They all grew quiet and looked up at me.

"Well," began Fred, "Sam here is talking to us about demon beast who goes riding off all over the Arizona desert flattening everyone in its path with some...ghost rider driving it. Oh, I forgot the best part!" he laughed, "It wears a cow bell!"

All the men laughed vigorously, save for Sam.

"It's true, Lucy, it's true!" Sam maintained. "It's the devil's beast!"

"Well, I must admit that it doesn't seem terribly imposing, Death using a cow bell to announce his presence, that is..." the men laughed again. "Why would a beast of the devil roam around Arizona?"

I heard a collective groan from the group of men at my question.

"Aw, the hell with y'all! You're all just lame!" Sam complained.

"It ain't nothin' but a bunch of hokum, Lucy!" said Jim.

"Why don't you let her decide for herself, Jim?" Sam protested.

Despite my proclivity for being terrified of the desert after sundown, I encouraged Sam to go on. "Tell me about it."

Sam espoused a look of smug arrogance.

"If you ask me, I think God sent that thing because of all the evil being done."

"You complete dipshit!" chimed Henry. "You mean to say that some innocent woman was trampled to death because God saw fit to teach all us sinners a lesson?"

"Not just her," Sam corrected, "others, too!"

Jim French spoke up, "…and then, nitwit, there's the matter that you say the beast was sent from the devil. Last I heard the devil don't do dealings with God and carry out his work!"

Riotous laughter erupted at this. My concern over the matter began to fade as not only were the hard-bitten men unconvinced and amused, but also because I could not help but find the story to be a ludicrous rendition only a religious or unenlightened rube would defend.

"Yeah?" Sam spat back, "Then what about all those people God drowned in the Great Flood cause they was all evil? I mean, not all of them coulda done wrong. I'm sure plenty of innocent people got drowned just the same; just like that blameless woman got trampled. But all the same, God works in mysterious ways! Hell, maybe he is in cahoots with the devil after all!"

More riotous laughter.

"Sam," began Jim, "you best watch that mouth a'yourn 'fore you find yourself trampled by some ungodly devilish beast for blaspheming as you just did."

"Whatever," Sam replied, "Y'all just keep laughing yourselves silly, believing there ain't nothing out there so's you can sleep at night. I'm getting some shut-eye. See y'all in the morning—if the beast of death hasn't gotten any of ya first!"

He walked off to lie down upon his bedding, and, admittedly, I began to worry a bit.

"Where would he come up with a story like that if there wasn't some truth to it?" I asked.

"Don't tell me you believe that godforsaken suspicious little fool, Lucy." George said.

"No," I made an attempt to sound undaunted. "I just wonder, as stories usually have some grain of truth."

Josiah, who had remained quiet during the entire tale, finally explained. "The U.S. Army strapped some poor soul to a camel because he was too afraid of the animal to ride it. See, camels could handle the Arizona terrain better than the horses could, so they came up with the idea of importing camels to the area and using them instead. When they tied the soldier to the animal it took off. He was unable to free himself and he died right there, right on top of that animal, dehydrated and starved to death."

"That's awful!" I exclaimed.

"Yeah, sure. But that's all it was. Most people didn't recognize the animal, as you can imagine they wouldn't expect to see something like that running around these parts. And seeing a figure riding it, dead as it was, rumors spread that it was some sort of… unearthly creature. They finally shot it dead, but by then, the body had decayed and fallen off long before. That's all there is to it."

"So why is it that Sam believes it was something sent from beyond?"

"Because Sam is a religious moron who believes that truth is what people need to tell themselves in order to sleep at night. They had tracked it and taken a shot, but the thing ran off, leaving behind a decayed head, if you can imagine that."

I shivered at the thought.

"But they finally shot and killed it," he finished. "So there's nothing to worry about. No demonic beast with a dead rider is out there just looking to trample you to death."

I laughed at this and looked at Josiah. We smiled at each other, silently agreeing that Sam was a simple fool.

"The hell with all this noise!" exclaimed Frank. "Pardon me, Ms. Howard," he bowed his head towards me in apology, and I nodded in acknowledgement.

"Nobody touches Brady," Brewer.

"Yeah?" Billy sarcastically asked. "Well Brady didn't mind touching an innocent man and his wife." Meaning me. "Killing a woman is as low as it gets and just plain cowardly as is, let alone killing a man because he posed a business threat."

"You listen up, Billy! Quit shooting your mouth off! I said nobody touches Brady!"

"I agree with Billy," chimed John.

"Brady's gotta go," agreed Fred.

"I make the decisions, and we ain't going after Brady. I'm through with this conversation." Richard stood and walked off to lie down.

As I tried to sleep, I heard strange noises and envisioned a headless rider coming to trample me to death. I tossed and I turned, disrupting Billy, who irritably asked me to quit fussing about, but, try as I might, I could not. I would have risen and walked away to sit alone by myself so as to leave him be, but considering the thoughts of impending doom that ran rampant throughout my mind I could not. Damn that Sam Smith! True or not, that camel with its decaying rider was real enough here in my mind and the vastness of the night as I lay at my most vulnerable. Finally, Billy sat up and shook me on the arm, prompting me to sit up alongside him.

"I know how difficult it is for you out here like this, but I need to get some sleep. If you're gonna toss and turn like a goddamned sidewinder I'd just as soon you slept on your own."

But this I would not do. I promised him I'd keep still and he lay back down again taking me at my word. I lied down again and shut my eyes, feeling his arm come up around me, trying to imagine good thoughts, but I kept coming back to that damn camel and dead man riding it. But I dared not move! I forced my body to lay as still as a statue while my mind raced like a horse, picturing myself crushed beneath the hooves of a camel accompanied by a god-awful, rotted corpse. Finally, thankfully, I fell asleep, though I cannot say that I had such pleasant dreams. If I could, I'd punch that Sam right in his mouth so hard that I'd knock his back teeth down his throat!

We arrived at Sumner in the early afternoon. We rode along on the Portales, and with Billy leading the pack of us, he looked back at me and whistled, which was my cue to spur my horse forward and flank him so we could ride in side-by-side. I thought of the girl he left behind here. I wondered who she was and, even more, what she looked like.

So many of the locals flocked to cheer the Regulators and to Billy with their greetings, thrilled to see him, and I noticed how the girls gathered to gaze upon him, equally as thrilled. Which one was the girl he had told me of? This, I refused to ask, though I desperately wanted to know the answer. I could not allow myself to stoop to such a level; a woman of my stature never yielded to such frivolity. It was unbecoming for a woman to allow a man the awareness that she was in competition for his affections, and further more inappropriate to allow him to know with whom it was she was in competition with.

It was a rule that, whenever a woman was in the company of a preferred gentleman, she would assume the role of the pursued. A lady of such means as my own would never permit a man to recognize that she felt threatened, and in truth, I could not muster the emotions of jealousy as it were; it simply was not an option, both because of my erudite social upbringing, and because I could not imagine Billy wanting any other as he wanted me. My virginal blood bonded Billy to me above all others, and I know he knew this. I knew also that he loved me beyond all else, his mother's ring upon my finger was proof enough of this. But I also knew that men, especially young men, would seek out or accept female propositions if offered, and I was not fool enough to believe Billy was different than any other young man. If he were to share another woman's bed, this would not affect me in the least, so long as it was my bed he came back to. In the world I had come from, men had mistresses. It was an accepted fact; wives often turned a blind eye, even if society had not. Then again plenty marriages where I came from were arranged based on financial gain rather than true love. Even many of the marriages based initially upon love ran thin, and bridegrooms often sought appreciation elsewhere.

But no matter—Billy was a young man and I would allow him space to sow his wild oats. I would not risk his resenting me for attempting to hinder his natural male inclinations any more than he would risk my resenting him by making me a poor farmer's wife. Obstructing him would only drive him into another woman's arms for good, and I needed him in my life no matter what the circumstances may be. A bleating shrew is the last thing a man finds attractive, and seldom, if at all, does it ever work. And if he were to lie with other women, it would be best to allow him to get it out of his youthful system now so that I may have all of him later. Most of all, none of this made much difference to me because I had his heart—no other woman ever would. I would bet everything I owned on that one fact, and having his heart was the thing I coveted of him above all else. What care was there where his body should be lead, so long as his heart knew its way home? A woman, we love so very easy. But a man, his love is difficult to capture. Catching a woman's heart doesn't take much. A man need only pay her attention and treat her as though she were the only woman he noticed, and for this, a woman fell easy. But to capture a man's heart…that was something! Regardless, I had always taken pride in how the young girls flocked to him like moths to a flame. It made him all the more beautiful to me.

We lead our horses to a large house and dismounted where some Mexican men and boys came along and took them away, after which I turned to Billy and asked him where it was they were taking them. He told me they would be taken to the stables. I pointed out that our belongings were strapped to them, and he assured me that nothing would be taken, that all of our things would be exactly as they were. He then lectured me, telling me that I would need to learn to follow his lead and not worry so much so long as he was not, and also, that I would quickly need to acclimate myself to the environment of the west and pay better attention to the many more, very real threats to be concerned with, and that I should learn to decipher which was what.

He winked at me and walked away towards the opening of the house when a young girl ran out to him, jumping up and throwing her arms around his neck. She kissed him and he kissed her back, swinging her around in the excitement of the moment at seeing one another. He put her down and spoke to her in Spanish. I could not understand the words, but I could understand his doting nature, elated expression, and the extra-mellifluous harmony in the words which he spoke to her. This was her. I sized her up and understood that, in a barren land and simple setting such as this, she would appear to have an exotically pretty face, but truly, she was rather plain, and upon being placed back onto her feet I could see her confidence was fragile. Her body language proved to me that she was nothing if not shy and somewhat withdrawn. Perhaps this was an attribute that Billy found endearing.

These Mexican women, they often yielded to their men, regardless of their own views. This was understood amongst the civilized classes as I had heard it discussed in social circles. They never argued or offered their own opinions to their husbands, even when an insightfully issued slight-of-hand word could provide a better end to the means. But a civilized wife tended to agree with her husband, despite her dissatisfaction, and then deftly, artfully, bent him to her will by employing pretense. It was always best to allow the man to believe he made the decisions and knew what was best.

I wondered if there wasn't something to their sort of marginal local accordance, some trick, perhaps, and then, I rejected the thought outright as I would refuse to bend to any man's will unless my own best interests were at its heart as well. If I did not agree with a man's decision, well-meaning though it may be, it would be rebuffed. I decided that God had made me too strong of will and mind to accept any man's approval or permissions outright without argument, unless I agreed wholeheartedly—that was my New York way of life. But here, I would let things be my way without question. I would do as I pleased. I would let this set the tone and underscore my feelings toward this girl and her relation to Billy versus my own. I would be the absolute and complete antithesis of her. I would not allow him control over my emotions, not unless his desires were my own. Where she would swoon, I would stand firm. If she should blush over his advances, I would remain impartial and challenge them (though admittedly, this would be difficult). I would separate myself from her in every way and be her opposite. What man wouldn't become bored by a woman who would do his bidding at every turn? A man, especially one so wild as Billy, needed a woman who could keep pace with and push him to his limits. This is what a man like Billy, who lived to love life, would find stimulating. I'm unsure as to why I considered all of this if I feared no woman upstaging me where Billy was concerned. But perhaps it was because she embodied what he adored—she was one of his beloved exotic señioritas. He had quite the soft spot for those.

Billy went through the doorway into the house and she followed. I stood there alongside Minxie, Fred, Henry, Sam, and John. Richard and Jim went off to see about the horses. When Billy came back out he came towards me.

"You're set up to stay here. We're heading back into Lincoln."

"Lincoln!? Are you mad? What is there that needs to be done?"

"Don't worry yourself about that."

"Don't you tell me not to worry myself about that, Billy Bonney! Do not talk down to me like a child! Why is it you all are leaving and I must stay?"

"Don't argue with me about it. You don't have any business in any of this. You were well aware that we were bringing you here, and there ain't nothing else for you."

"I don't have any business in this?" I asked, pointing to myself. "Maybe you ought to consult with the Lincoln Gazette then!"

He placed his hands on my arms affectionately and leaned his forehead against mine.

"Lucy, I need you to trust me. You know as well as I that rag got it all wrong. You know we've got business. You know that. You're to stay here so that I know you're safe."

He kissed me tenderly and hugged me close to him.

"I know you must be confused," he began. "Here you are—we're putting you through hell, I know. You shouldn't be involved in any of this, and life out here is rough. I know you're not meant for it and it must be hard. I ain't ignorant to how trying this must all be for you."

"But it's not, Billy! Yes, it's very extreme compared to the life I'm used to. But still…I don't want to go back to that life. I want the freedom I have here!"

His smile was conciliatory. "I know you think that now, but I promise you that will change. As trying as things have been, they can get worse."

"I'm willing to get used to it."

"There isn't anything out here for you."

"But you're out here!" I protested.

"And if something happens to me? You don't want the sort of life you'll have to live to survive. I don't want that for you. I want you to be okay; I want to know that you'll be okay if God or the law sees fit to take me."

I didn't know how to answer, so I simply said, "I'll figure that out if it comes to that. But I don't want to think on that just now."

He kissed me again, this time on the forehead and then my lips. He thought me ignorant, and I suppose I was. In my world, I was experienced. But In this world, his world, he was the expert. And I could not hold it against him for wanting to keep me safe from the horrors such a place could present. I've seen plenty already in such a short span of time, only the tip of the iceberg, I'm sure, and to someone like him and the others, this all was old-hat. Things happened here. Bad things. None of what I experienced was anything new to them; it was only new, and terrifying, to someone like me. But I should do my best to conceal that from them all.

"That girl…" I began.

"What about her?" he asked suspiciously, oblivious to my simple curiosity.

"Is she the one you told me about? From Sumner? The girl you love?"

He smiled what I thought of as that "Bonney Smile", the grin that let on when he had something to hide.

"I love you. Do you believe me when I tell you that?"

"Yes, Billy…I believe it. I really do. But the way you reacted to her when she ran to you…"

"I have affection for her. I still care deeply for her. But, Lucy, nobody else is you. There never will be."

He hugged me close to him again, firmly. He rested his head on top of mine before bringing it before me and nuzzling my nose with his own.

"Lucy…I know you know that I ain't no stranger to women. But you really need to settle down…"

I waited for him to go on.

"You've broken me in. I get this pressure, right here." He pointed to the center of his chest. "And I get these… feelings—"

"Butterflies."

"—whenever I see or even think about you. And if you ever repeat that to any of the men I'll kill you!" he laughed.

"I never tell anyone what is said intimately between us two," I looked up at him and smiled. "But Billy…"

"What is it?"

"I don't want to go away from you. Truly I don't. I'll brave all of this just to be near you. I know you want me to go back to New York because you're afraid for me; I know you want what's best for me, and I believe in my heart that it is truly why you want me to go, and not because you do not care for me. But you need to know that it is not what I want. And I need you to know that the life awaiting me back there is no life at all."

"I know it. We can talk about it later. Right now I need you to get set up so we can get out of here."

"Billy, I don't speak Spanish. What am I to do?"

"The Maxwell's speak English. Paulita speaks it well enough…"

"Is that the girl? Is that her name?"

"Yes, that's her name."

"So I am to share a roof with Paulita while you are gone? How do I do that? How should I refer to you when I speak of you?"

He snickered, amused.

"Don't worry about it. I ain't hiding you. No man in his right mind would hide a girl like you. You're meant to be displayed out in the open. You decide how you want to handle it, having to share living quarters and what not. But don't bother about how you refer to me. I can promise you that I won't ever hide you from any woman. Hell…I want everyone to know you're my girl."

I positively beamed, looking down to hide this from him! But I then had a thought, "Even like this?" I looked down at myself pointedly so that he would understand my meaning.

"Lucy, don't forget who you are. I haven't. You're still every bit the grand lady to me as you were when I first saw you. That is how I see you when I look at you. Though I can't deny you're the cutest little thing to walk around in a pair of six-shooters and britches! I'll be, but you're a real cowgirl!"

He smiled broadly at his little joke, and I confess I had appreciated the remark.

"Billy?"

"What is it?"

"I'm not stupid. I know your plans. You promise me now that you'll come back here for me."

"I'm always gonna come back for you, Bonita."

I was shown to my room and my things were brought in. There was a desk with a looking glass set above it, and I sat to compose the letter I had intended for my father, but after I had only been sitting for no more than five minutes, gathering my thoughts, I was pulled away by a large woman speaking rapid-fire Spanish at me. I thought I had done something wrong, that she had been yelling, when it occurred to me that, after hearing it spoken so much, especially from Billy, it was simply the style of the language. It turned out that the woman had an interest in showing me how to help prepare supper for the men, though I tried to mime that I had just been preparing to sit down and write a very important letter when she began to speak a decent stroke of broken English to me as she explained that we must prepare a meal for the men. I quickly explained that I did not know how to cook, let alone cook Mexican dishes, and for many at that, to which she only laughed at my ignorance, and after a long pause of poking fun at me in Spanish for, by what I can only guess, being a woman unfit for a man, she declared that she would take me under her wing and show me the process of cooking a proper Mexican supper to make a woman out of me. Her name was Adora Espinoza, and in being a plump, large woman, I supposed that she must have cooked and eaten many Mexican meals in her day.

Adora showed me how to make tortillas first. After mixing all of the ingredients I had to handle lard with my bare hands to help with the dough, which I then preceded to pound at it with the flats of my palms in order to mash it all together well, which, evidently, I did incorrectly. I did not know there was an incorrect way to make dough. Adora showed me how to knead the mixture and ply it properly, pulling off little pieces to roll into balls. I looked to her to see if I was doing this right as I was certain the Mexicans had their own special way of making a dough-ball. Adora nodded approvingly. She explained that the dough needed to sit for a bit, and when I asked her if I should stay and help, she politely declined. This was fine by me; I was not born to cook, and I had a letter to write.

I sat at the desk and began to pen my letter. I placed the pencil to my lips and thought. How should I explain my situation? How could I convince my father that, though I remained his ever loyal, loving daughter, my defiance of his instructions was not deliberate, that it was not my intention? I had not meant to be disobedient. Could I manage enough confidence to persuade him to consent to my current position? I did not think so.

My father feared nothing, and I did not know enough about of the politics of Lincoln in order to educate him on the matters of the injustice which endured here in New Mexico, nor the possibility, no, probability, that my life hung in the balance because of them. He was a powerful man, my father, and he would not receive such news of my considerable but necessary rebellion favorably, and at the hands of poor hired farm hands, no less. He could not know or believe the seriousness of the situation unless I could relay it to him proficiently. With these considerations I began:

Dearest father,

I beg you forgive me, your eternally loving daughter, for disobeying your great authority in sending for me to come home at once to New York. Here in the County of Lincoln, responding to the death of our dear friend, John H. Tunstall, war has broken out over the territorial rights of property and the unlawful murder of our dearest Harry. Though he was to be made my husband under God and by law, the war hasn't to do with me other than the corruption of what is known as the Santa Fe Ring and its desire to see to my death alongside my contracted life's companion in order to exercise its power. A bounty has been placed upon my head, and I fear that I may have instigated such a low action in that I could not withhold my tongue, lashing out with such fervent anger towards the town's sheriff, William Brady, as he is the sole instigator of this most unfortunate event which has cost both John and me. This I should not need to regret but for the fact that Sheriff Brady's pride had been stung by the sharpness of my tongue, and I must lament that I am stuck here in New Mexico as the army of The Ring is many and my life is now in peril due to Sheriff Brady's bidding which is vengeful and full of resentment.

I am enclosing an excerpt from the Lincoln Co. Gazette. In it you will come to know of my predicament and of the deputized men known as the Regulators who have been engendered to stand against The Ring's corruption and its crooked men who hold self-appointed positions of authority. This is proving an arduous task as great men of federal law have visited Lincoln and have been charmed by the The Ring, revoking the powers of deputation from the Regulators for their attempting to bring to justice yet only a few of the men in the pay of The Ring; the very men responsible for dear Harry's death. I, too, have been named a suspect in these matters. It would seem that Sheriff Brady will not rest until I have been put in my proper place, which as far as he is concerned, is six feet below the ground.

I am kept here in the safety of these regulated men, unable to travel and make my way to the train depot as there is much fear that I will not make the journey safely. As your beloved daughter, I implore you to send help however you can, be it men or funds, the latter of which will be of great value for its ability to hire council so that we may be represented by an honest man and therefore stand a fair trial and reasonable chance. As you will read, I am now considered a wanted participant of this war and am considered an outlaw as Sheriff Brady himself has accused of me involvement with the Regulators while my association with them is only meant to serve as protection from the true enemy and keep me safe. This is the very reason I remain here in New Mexico. Please, father, I beg of you to send financial resources!

I also beg of you to take these matters seriously and talk to no one of my whereabouts. In order to keep our position safe I will remain vague in my correspondence. Know only that I will retrieve letters sent by you to the post of Roswell, Fort Sumner, and San Patricio. It would be best if you would submit three copies of each letter you send by post to ensure I receive word from you as soon as possible. Please address each letter to Mrs. Inkwell so that I may keep my identity safe. I will check each of these post locations as often as I can.

All my love,
Your ever loyal and loving daughter,
Elucia

When I had finished writing, Paulita walked through the door to let me know it was time to eat. I thanked her and folded my letter, preparing it for the post. I turned to find her still standing there, looking at me rather oddly.

"Yes?" I asked.

"You wear the guns," she observed.

I simply looked at her as oddly as she had me.

"I never see such a thing as that," she continued.

How the hell should I respond to such a statement? Did she mean to be catty, or was she innocently making an observation? In all of my good breeding, I summoned my sobriety in an attempt to direct this predicament in the direction which I wanted it to go.

"It is a necessity. I must travel with the Regulators, and so I must dress accordingly. It is a simple matter of survival."

"Do you shoot them? Your guns?"

"I have."

"Do you like to dress as you do? As a man?"

*Catty.*

"I don't dress like a man. I dress like an heiress. Have you heard of those? I am from the east, from a very prominent social family. These clothes I wear, they were tailor-made special for me in Europe. I have two pair, one in the colors I wear now, and the other in black and blue. I wear them because I must, until I can make my way back to New York and all of my fine lace, silks, satins, and furs. I wonder if you have even seen such fabrics as those. Does that answer your question?"

She bowed her head, seemingly in shame. Perhaps she did not mean to offend me and only asked the questions she had out of curiosity. I reigned in the venom I had spat. I was not familiar with these people; it was possible they were rough around the edges where polite society would be polished.

"Have you never seen a woman dressed this way before?" I asked civilly, in an attempt to show that no harm had been done.

"No. I am… I think I mean to say, surprised, that Billy finds you as he does."

This statement worked upon my nerves. Clearly, giving her the benefit of the doubt was a hazard of my affluent upbringing and learned good manners.

"Billy knows me as the finest woman he has ever seen. Up until the past near month I dressed far better than any woman outside of any eastern border."

I turned to play with the letter I had written and folded. "Anyway…seeing me like this gives Billy a thrill. He finds it, how do I mean to say? *Stimulating*."

"Supper is ready," she said.

"You said that."

"A place has been set for you. I trust you will find your way to the table."

Before Paulita left the room I turned back to her. "Just how does Billy tell you he finds me?"

"He says you are his Señiorita Bonita."

Still unsure of her, I was, however, positive I had the upper-hand, and I would be careful not to let that slip. She was jealous, this I could see. Her tells were showing.

The way these Mexican women ate before their men astonished me. Upper-class women always filled up before dining in a party, especially when gentlemen were present. We ate like birds. It was uncomely for a woman to stuff herself full of food. But I could already see how these people had such an incredible passion for life; eating, laughing, and talking—with a full mouth, no less. Such manners would be considered beyond rude at a table back east; there was no ceremony. One would think these people have never eaten before!

I could see it, why Billy had such a love for the Mexican people. He had spent most of his childhood with them, and it was true that that would have been enough for anyone to develop a fondness—he lived as they did. He was full of passion for life, and the Mexican population personified that passion overtly.

Their language was expressive, their dress the same. The women wore lose fitting blouses and skirts that fluttered and flowed. From what I had understood, they even often wore no shoes during the warm months. They were free in every way and exhilarating to be around; they danced and sang nearly all night long as though if they stopped they would lie down and die.

When the evenings fell, the Mexican boys all took turns dancing with me, and because of Billy, I could manage most of the dances. They flirted with me and kissed me upon the cheek adoringly. I took no offense to this as I found it endearing and part of their culture. They were an animated and communicative people indeed. The young boys spoke words to me in Spanish, and though I could not understand the words, the body language was unmistakable. If I had been the type to open myself up to just any man, my intuition told me that Billy would not approve if I were to go along with whatever it was they wanted to do with me.

One night, as the music and singing carried on, I needed to drop myself down to sleep. I entered Pedro Maxwell's house and went to my room. The house was quiet, but the streets from Beaver's to Hargrove's saloons were alive with music and laughter. Paulita's door was closed and I wondered if she was in there, asleep.

I crept down the hall in case I should wake anyone otherwise, though I couldn't see how it would matter with the commotion outside. I opened the door to my room and upon entering I reached into my bag and took from it a shirt of Billy's that I used to sleep in since I had left John Chisum's in a hurry. As I prepared for bed I sat at the desk and stared into the looking glass. I began to brush and braid my hair when I heard the door creak open. It was Paulita. We stared at each other for what seemed an irritating amount of time before she asked if she could come in. I said "yes", and she sat upon the bed. I turned to look at her, waiting for her to speak up. Her timidity annoyed me. I was ever more certain a man would draw boredom from a lifetime of women like this.

"I love him."

I nodded.

"But he loves you."

"He wants me to go home to New York. So you can have him all to yourself when I'm gone." I turned back around, bitter. I was certain the quiver in my voice was quite discernible.

"Every girl wants Billy to herself. Even with you gone, I still will be only one among many."

"And then so maybe we have that in common." This was bullshit! I knew how dear I was to Billy, what I meant to him—that he only saw me. But I had a humane need to try and make her feel better.

"No. Billy is a flirt notorio. This...this is truth," she exhaled and gave a small chuckle, "But you...you are his querida numero uno."

"I am unsure of what you mean."

She laughed, but it was not malicious. In fact, it seemed she found my ignorance to her language charming.

"You are his only," she answered.

"And you know this because?"

"I see the way he look at you. I also hear the way he talk about you. He also tell me to see to it that you are taken well care of."

"And so... you don't like me much then, do you?"

"I don't know you. But...Billy loves you. You cannot help it, I know this. I can see for what it is he likes."

"And what is it that he likes?"

I knew the answer to this. I did. I didn't need any other lover of his to tell me what it was he saw in me, but I wanted to hear her tell me all the same.

"I don't know how to explain. Maybe...it is okay to say that you are so much more like him. You are pretty. You see what he sees. You teach him things. You know him best."

"I know him best?"

"You spend all the time with him. What you are to him is obvious. I'm sure there is plenty else, but those are the things I see. How can he get bored with a gringa rubia like you?" I could not help but see a small smirk escape her lips at saying this. "Especially when a girl like you should bother to look his way?"

"What is a 'gringa rubia' exactly?"

She smiled and laughed again, and so I let go of my question, saying, "Well, Paulita, I can offer him things that will ensure him a good, decent life. I can love him and give him so much more if it pleases him."

She nodded slightly at this, then stood up and moved to leave the room.

# 12

## April, 1878

By the time the men came back I knew what they had done. Word spread fast when a man of the law was killed, no… murdered, in the line of duty, especially when that man of the law was none other than one of the bastards who had created this goddamn mess of a war.

I ran to Billy and jumped on him, throwing my arms around his neck. He winced but held on tightly. Noticing his discomfort, I leapt down and, hearing a small groan of pain, I saw that he was favoring his left side.

"What's happened to you!?"

"One of Brady's men got me—"

"You were shot!? My God Billy, what the hell happened in Lincoln?" I instinctively lightly placed my hand to his side.

"I'm fine. It barely touched me. Got Jim good, though!"

"Jim! Is he dead?"

"No. Well…I don't know. I don't think so…"

I looked at him incredulously.

"I'm sure he's fine," he tried to assure me. "The bullet winged me and hit him in the leg." He limped off towards Pedro Maxwell's and I, of course, followed him.

"You're sure he's fine?" I asked in disbelief. "What the hell does that even mean, Billy? You're sure? You're only *sure*? You didn't bother to check?"

"The last look I got of him he was being drug off to hide. I took the hell off. Anyway, you were here—waiting for me," he smiled at me with that charming smile of his, a hint of humor edging his words as though I ought to be thrilled he had thought of and come back for me.

"Billy…"

"What? I had to get the hell out of there, Lucy! I didn't have any time to play nursemaid. He was already being taken care of. I had to go! I'd've expected him to do the same if it were me."

I stamped behind him as he limped in through the Maxwell's door. Paulita was concerned and made such a fuss, calling for a woman to come and look after him. Billy was enjoying the way she openly fawned over him, but I knew plenty well enough by his good humor upon his arriving at Sumner, and by his own admission, that he was only skinned and that he did not need so much attention paid him, and so I stood back and watched the ludicrous charade unfold. He did not need the extra care; he only enjoyed how it entertained him so.

As his hip was tended to, the torn material of his pants cut wider so the woman could go to work and clean the superficial wound, I stared at him intently. He returned the stare.

"What is it you're looking so ornery for?" he asked me.

"Where is everyone? Where are the others? Did you leave them behind as well?"

He rolled his eyes and melodramatically lolled his head to face the other way.

"Anyway," he went on, "I brought Minxie back along with me."

"And now you've involved Minxie…"

"Minx's been involved. Damn…We all are! What the hell is it that's got stuck in your craw?" The woman tending his wound starkly instructed him to remain still.

I didn't answer; I had nothing to say, and though it was true that I was positively outraged that he and the others made things all the more worse for us by setting up Brady, the truth was I was staging a preemptive strike. I must tell him about the letter to my father, and once I had done so, he would be displeased with me. He may even be angry. He may be *very* angry! And then there was the fact that he was changing due to the severity of the situation, which was becoming more and more terrifying for me. My dear boy had been shot, nearly killed, maybe. Jim—dead, alive? I didn't know. And I didn't want him to leave me again. And I didn't want to leave him and go back east. Either I would need to change along with him and dig my heels into this mess, forcing him to keep me here, or I was going to have to let him go. Out here it was blood, tit-for-tat, and for the first time I forced myself to see, to really see, that first one of us would drop, then one of them, then one of us, and so on and so forth, and I would need to choose this to be with him. And here he was, at ease, laughing and behaving as though he had just rode in for a pleasant visit. For an outlaw who had just murdered a man of the law and cohort to The Santa Fe Ring, and who had been skinned by a bullet, he seemed far too relaxed, to be sure.

"I wrote my father."

He jolted and glared at me.

Again he was ordered to stay still.

"¡ Sí, está bien!" he waved her off, "You what?"

"I sent him that article, the one from the Lincoln paper that Richard brought back with him."

His jaw dropped and he stared at me. "What the hell did you do?"

"I told him I wasn't going back." I lied, wondering what he'd say.

"Oh, the hell you ain't!"

"The hell I ain't! I *ain't* 'goin' back!" I yelled in return.

"The hell you say…What'd you say to him?"

"I only said that it wasn't safe for me to come home. That I would have to wait. I'd only written and shown him proof of what was happening here. I asked him…" I drifted off, fearing that what I was about to say, that I had asked for his assistance, would only irritate him further.

He looked at me expectantly.

"I asked for his help."

His eyes drew wide and he stared at me as though deaf and dumb. "Does he know where you are?"

"No."

Billy drew back into his chair and settled down. I looked at him attentively, watching him skim the nail of his thumb against his teeth, thinking. He winced again as whisky was poured over his leg.

"How's he supposed to help?"

"I asked him to send money."

"That all?"

*No. I asked him to speak with friends in powerful positions to provide us with leverage.*

"Yes." I am a liar. If he knew all of the truth he would send me packing, stuffed in a crate nailed shut by his own hand if he had to. He was distrustful of politicians and authority. I could not blame him, as they have only proven to be trouble, but it was my father. If he could not be trusted to help his own flesh and blood, then no one could.

"How's he supposed to do a thing like that?"

"I've asked of him to send three letters, one each to Patricio, here, and Roswell. I gave him a fake name to address them to. He can send it that way, or tell me where I should go to collect it."

He sat and looked at me a short while, saying nothing. I crossed my arms against my breast and placed my own thumb against my teeth, nibbling at it as I waited for him to say what he would. He seemed serious in considering whatever it was he was thinking.

"We're going to Patricio. We leave today," was all he said.

"Patricio?"

"That's what I said…"

"*I'm* going to Patricio?"

"You're the reason I came back," he smiled haughtily, then added sarcastically, "Besides. We gotta catch up with them boys I left behind."

We headed back toward Patricio by the same route in which we had come to Sumner, down through the Rio Pecos with Minxie hauling the pack-mule. We were planning to stop along the way in Roswell but set up camp much more than a few miles out when night began to fall. Minxie and Billy set up the cooking implements and placed mutton in the pot to boil over the campfire, making me sit and watch it while they went off to fire rounds. When they came back Billy was carrying a fairly large rock.

"Look what I found," he extended his arms, offering it to me. When I reached out my hands I saw it was not a rock but a creature of some sort and immediately I recoiled. He laughed hysterically.

"What is it!?" I shouted.

He looked bewildered. "It's a tortoise. Haven't you never seen one of them before?"

"Take it away from me."

He looked at the Dutch pot with the mutton. "Haven't you been stirring that?"

He put the thing down a little too close and I slid away from it as far as I could before it slowly sauntered off. "The water's all boiled down and it's stuck to the pot!"

"You only told me to watch it!"

"I didn't think I'd need to explain that you needed to stir it around."—he gestured wildly with his arm, stirring the air emphatically—"Jesus Christ! Well, I hope you like shitty mutton."

"No thank you."

Minxie muttered miserably, "Shite."

"No, you'll eat it," Billy ordered. "You have to. Go over and refill the canteens while I scrape this shit off the pot."

I took the canteens and glanced around for that ugly tortoise. I had not seen it so I continued on to the river, happy to have something to do I couldn't possibly spoil. When I came back and sat down I was given charred pieces of meat on a plate. It was rubbery and dry and awful. I put the plate down after I took a small bite and he gave me a look of condemnation as he chewed upon his own scraps with difficulty. I picked my plate back up and nibbled at the parts I felt could be savaged, which, I may tell you, were not many.

"You only told me to watch it," I said again, meekly.

He remained quiet and looked down at his plate, his face betraying his annoyance as he pressed his lips together tightly. He rolled his eyes to the sky and again began eating his ruined food. So far I was not making a good impression of being a party to all of this. I began a new subject.

"Why take me to Sumner only to take me back to San Patricio?"

He looked up from his plate at me and stared. He inhaled and exhaled deeply. He and Minxie glanced at one another pointedly sharing a private thought before he put his plate down in the dust and walked over to his horse. Opening his saddle bag he took out a folded newspaper and brought it over, handing it to me. Again, it was a copy of the

Lincoln Gazette. He pointed to a selection and said, "I'm afraid you really are one of us now, darlin'."

Minxie snickered a bit and Billy gave him a look of derision.

To sum up, the column expressed that I was "...obviously of impure stock and not the supposed lady of the east as presented to the citizens of Lincoln..." Indeed! "...easily adulterated by the immorality and wickedness of the Regulators as under their influence...a supporter and participant of the gang..." It was nearly the same drivel the rag presented prior!

They gave a description of me right down to my guns and publicized my family name, listing the admirable Gen. Addison W. Howard as my paterfamilias. I went pale at that, Billy noticing, even in the fading, near blinding brilliance of light that marked sunset in the desert as the sun hit the earth.

"That's right. You're in trouble." Billy playfully accused in a sing-song manner.

My throat dry, I managed to croak out the fact that I still couldn't understand why I should be taken along. "You told me I'd be safe in Sumner."

"Yeah, well, I guess you missed the part about your description, right down to those fancy model three's John had given ya."

"So?"

"How many young, petite, blond cowgirls you think are running around here showing off guns emblazoned with horseshoes? You know—the Irish symbol of luck and all that?"

*How droll.*

"Ya are pret-ty obvious, here, poppit," Minxie offered, no help at all.

"I don't see how it matters. As I understood it, Sumner was the one place you were certain I would remain safe until I could leave New Mexico."

"So now you want to leave New Mexico?" Billy asked as his eyebrows rose in mock curiosity.

"I simply do not understand it at all!" I cried, losing patience. "If they are looking for me aren't they most likely to find me with the likes of all of you!?"

"The likes of us? Yeah, sure, that and all. And if you ain't with us, when word spreads all about you, you'd be all on your own."

"You can't trust those people, then?" I asked, confused.

"I can trust most of those people, but I can trust myself better than I can any of them. And I can trust The Lincoln County Regulators better than anyone else. So you stay with us for now. I can't leave you there on your own now."

I gave him a hard look.

"What?"

"What did you do in Lincoln? Did you kill Brady?"

He looked down, coyly, then back up at me with his Cheshire grin.

"It isn't funny, Billy—"

"It is a little…"

I stood, humorless.

"Naw…I didn't kill him. Well, who the hell knows? I might've."

Minxie laughed.

I looked at Billy with exaggerated incredulity. "What does that even mean?"

"We set up behind the Tunstal store's corral wall. We was all firing. Hell…he bucked out in a smoke. How the hell should I know who did him in? Maybe we all did."

"Right. Ya should of seen the bleedin' look on his face, Lucy, sittin' there in the middle of the street peppered wif lead," said Minxie, pantomiming Brady's reaction as he crossed his arms over his belly and feigned agonized confusion.

"You're disgusting!" I spat. I looked back at Billy. "But you didn't shoot him exclusively?"

"Does it matter?"

"Are you dense!?"

He squinted at me. It was a very distinctive look, this one. It was the look he gave when he was about to go around the bend; one never knew if the look was merely innocent or a prelude to something unpleasant. I may have withdrawn such a bold comment had I been anyone else. As it were, however, I was not. Anyone else and he may do his worst. Where it concerned me, however, the worst he could do was ignore me, pick up that plate of disgusting mutton, and start shoving it back down his gullet.

"You killed a man of the law!" I shouted.

"Yeah, a man of crooked law—"

"Crooked law," Minxie repeated, muttering through a mouthful of dried out mutton.

"—the only kind of law up there in Lincoln," Billy agreed as he removed an equalizer from its scabbard and ran his hands along it seductively, popping the chamber open and spinning it. It whirled efficiently, as hushed as a lullaby. He kept those guns so clean they operated like poetry incarnate. "I got a bullet with a name on it for each and every single one of them bilkin' swindlers."

We reached Roswell by noon.

"I'd like to check the post," I said, taking off before Billy or Minxie could say anything. I had decided that it would take some time for any mail to arrive as it had not been all that long ago that I mailed my letter, but I was anxious. Once I reached the postmaster I asked if any mail had come for me. I had given him my pseudonym and found that a letter had in fact not arrived. I did not know whether I was relieved or disappointed by this.

I headed back around to find both of the boys docking our mares and unloading our things.

"Here, give me some of those," I offered. I was handed my bags and my Winchester and strode off.

"Hey!"

I turned to see Billy staring after me with a dumbfounded expression on his face.

"Where you off to?"

I checked myself. "I don't know. The hotel across the street?"

"Uh, uh," he replied, "We're staying someplace else.

"Where?"

"There's a parlor—"

"Hot bloody damn!" Minxie exclaimed. "Some ladybird tail would be just about all right!"

"I am not staying in a brothel, Billy! A house of ill-repute?" My disgust was only outstripped by the disbelief that he would assume such a thing.

"Yeah? Then I guess you're sleeping out in the street, then."

"What's that supposed to mean?"

"We ain't got any dinero...not unless you want to make some for us." Minxie and Billy laughed.

I caught his meaning and punched him fairly hard in the gut and pushed Minxie. Minxie stumbled and Billy grunted, grabbing his belly and slumping over.

"Jesus Christ! I'm only fooling you, Luce."

"I do not appreciate that sort of humor!"

Again, Minxie laughed at my quickly slipping virtue.

"We don't have a choice. I know the lady of the house, she'll put us up."

"Bloody hell yeah!" Minxie shouted. "We've not got any dinero, like the man said," he said glibly, taking his things and running off.

"I don't share the same side of the street with houses like that, let alone associate with its inhabitants," I replied.

Billy looked at me heatedly. "You'll do it, or you can find yourself on the next train eastbound! You want to stay out here you'd better lose that hoity-toity little attitude of yours right quick! You want to stick around, promise me you'll brave, whatever just to be with me, but you don't want to manage any of it! It's all just talk. Hell, you know what? You need to go the hell back to where you came; you don't belong here."

He started to walk away from me and I only stood there feeling weighted down by my things, watching him go. Before he left the stable he stopped and turned back to face me.

"Trust me, Lucy," he held out his hand to me, indicating for me to come to him and follow. His look was sincere and understanding. If I were going to commit to this as I had promised to myself and to him, then this would need to be part of the deal. One foot before the other, I told myself. I took his hand and followed.

I looked up and read the sign aloud; The Swann's Nest. Ilse Swann's place, Billy explained.

The place smelled of rosewater, and of all things, lavender!

We both put our things down. I looked around me. There was a parlor off to the side where two men stood playing billiards, and a smallish table where four men were ensconced in a game of cards. There were mirrors everywhere, and pictures...my God, the pictures! Women in a state of undress, posed suggestively!

A scantily clad woman came down the steps from the second floor and I instinctively and self-consciously crossed my arms across my own breast at the sight of this, putting my head down and moving away.

"You new here?" Billy asked.

"Yes. I reckon this ain't your first time."

"Ilse around?"

"Sure thing, sugar. She's with a client."

"Yeah? She still doing that?"

"If the money's good and the client's an old friend. You know how it is..."

Billy nodded and turned his head to look at me. I was standing, cross-armed and all, close to the door and peering out the window. He smirked and turned back to face the woman.

"When she's available, you'll let me know."

"Sure thing I will."

I turned to see her wink at him and I grimaced. He looked at me and grinned.

"What's so funny?" I asked disdainfully. He merely shook his head.

Other than the men in the side room it was fairly quiet. I looked to see a young woman, maybe my age, maybe younger, preparing drinks. She brought the tray to Billy. Refusing, she came towards me and I contemptuously turned away from her.

I heard muffled laughter from someplace in the house. I looked up above me as if I would find its source. I went back to hovering near the door, soothed by the sight of it. *I could walk back out of it at any time*, I thought.

We waited in silence for maybe a half-hour when one of the bawdiest women I had ever seen came in and hugged Billy wildly. Her face was painted up and her hair was piled higher than I'd ever seen, ringlets tumbling down, their color an unnatural blond. Her breasts billowed abundantly from her tight bodice.

"Billy! Where the hell you've been sweetheart!?"

"Getting into it…"

"I know that's right."

I watched this sight unfold with utter contempt.

"Who's your little friend?" she asked, interestedly.

They both looked at me, I looked back, defensive. Billy walked over to me and put his arm around me as if I were his buddy.

"This here is none other than Lucky Lu of Lincoln County."

"Who?" she asked. Instead of answering, he only looked at me, eyes alight with fun. What a sport he could be.

"Ilse, we need to be put up. We're running short but I can get you back."

Ilse nodded at me, "She's a pretty thing."

"Aw, no. She ain't for sale."

"She'll fetch a price…" she placed her hands on her hips and looked at him, chin and eyebrows aloft, trying to tempt him to reconsider.

"Yeah, but… just the same…"

She was trying to negotiate me! What a life this was! Ilse walked over to me, my arms still crisscrossed. "What d'ya say, honey? Are you gonna let this young man argue your value? I can help get those pockets lined," she smiled at me. "I got a good eye for these things, you'll do well!"

"No thank you," I replied quietly, as politely as I could. I turned my body into Billy's for comfort, bowing my head down. He put his arm around me, squeezing my upper arm affectionately.

"Well, all right then. But you just let me know if you change that mind. A young pretty thing like you could do well out here. Think about it."

She looked over at Billy. "Fine, Bill. I trust you enough. Third floor. It's quiet up there; been slow."

She looked at me again, a bit longingly it seemed.

"That's fine Ilse. Thanks darlin'. Knew I could count on ya," he flicked a dime at her and winked. She caught it, expertly. He tipped his hat, picked up both of our things, handing me my rifle only. Ilse looked after me, thoughtfully. I looked back at her, knitting my brow, combating her thoughts with my own.

"Hey, sweetheart! Come here," she called. We both turned. "Her," she said, pointing at me. I stood stark still, Billy prodding me. "Go on," he whispered. He left me to go up the stairs.

I still hadn't moved, watching her cross the room.

"Come on, I ain't gonna hurt ya," she assured me.

I began to move slowly towards her as I watched her open a drawer in a small side table.

She took something from the drawer, brought it over to me, and coaxed me to open my hand. "It ain't a damn rattlesnake, sweetheart!"

I opened my palm and she dropped a very small, leather drawstring pouch into it. "What is it?" I asked, suddenly intrigued.

"Queen Anne's Lace seeds."

"So?"

"So, take them after you fuck that boy."

"Excuse me!?"

"What...?" she let out a small chuckle. "You think I don't know when a woman's been plucked and by whom, especially when he's standing so nearby? I'm good at my job, darlin'."

She stared at me, considering me again.

"You aren't from around here, are ya darlin'?"

I shook my head, to which end she peered down at the pouch in my hand and said, "Take 'em a few days after. Make sure you chew them right and good. They taste somethin' awful and can cause your bowels to freeze up something' terrible, too, but they'll keep you right," she patted my belly with her palm.

I closed my hand around the pouch tightly and walked away, fast, looking back as if she were the goddamn boogyman himself. I ran as quickly as I could up the stairs to the third floor. I called for Billy, and when he answered I ran into the room and slammed the door behind me. I threw my rifle on the bed and sat in a chair by the window, propping my head up with my hands as my elbows were supported by the window sill.

"What's got you so bugged out?" he asked.

"Nothing," I replied. "I think maybe..."

"What?" he asked, expectantly.

I changed my mind. "Nothing."

I looked out the window at the town below. If one would have told me months ago on that train out to New Mexico that it could be even worse than I had first thought, I wouldn't have believed it.

"Come over here."

I turned to see Billy sitting on the bed.

"What for?" I asked.

"Just come on."

"I don't think so."

"Why not?"

I turned to look back out the window and heard him get up off the bed. He walked over to me and kneeled down upon one knee. "Is it because you're in this good old fashioned whorehouse here?"

"Maybe. And I think you ought to know that I am not interested in any parts of you just now."

He grabbed my hand, and as he stood up, he pulled me up out of the chair. "That's too bad, 'cause I've been just dying waiting around for you," he leaned in and kissed me and I pushed him away, moving to the other side of the room.

"I ain't kidding, Lu. Get over here!"

I looked around the room but was seeing past its walls into the other rooms in my mind's eye. I crossed my arms around myself again and turned around and around, imagining the things that went on through those walls. It disturbed me that I was not only merely within the vicinity of a brothel, but here within its walls, in one of its rooms, no less.

"What is it that's going on with you?"

"I don't want to be a whore."

I had begun to shiver. I put my hand to my lips and looked wildly about the room. My eyes began to water and my throat closed up. I let out a gasp of desperation, and, coming up behind me, he put his arms around me, talking to me gently.

"It's okay. You're okay," he whispered. "We just happen to be here now—it doesn't mean you're a whore. You just need to get used to this for right now. You are here with me. Look at me."

I did as he told me and I looked at him.

"Breathe," he told me. He pulled me slowly backwards, still held by his arms, towards the bed. We might have been dancing slowly as we had done so many times before, just like this.

"I think I might be ready to run," I whispered, panicked.

"No, you're not," he replied. "Let it go. Let all of it go, just like you've wanted. You're here with me; I'll never lay your spirit low."

"You paid that woman."

"I gave her my marker."

"You took me upstairs."

"You came on your own."

"She gave me this." I showed him. He took it and frowned.

"It's a whore's trick, Billy. Do you not see? I would never..." I looked at him. "I would not presume to abandon a gift from God between us two. Only a whore would do such a thing."

"So you've said."

Devotedly, he kissed me. "Lucy, I love you saying that. But now, like this, out here? We can't take any chances, and you know I have a hard time staying away from you. I don't want to stay away from you. Do you want me to?"

"No, Billy...I don't. I really don't. I never did."

"Then just for now, you do what you need to, whether you want to or not. Otherwise, it would be no good without the precaution. We're all doing things we're not proud of."

On this point, I could not disagree, but to be with his child—it would give me the security I needed.

Palming the seeds, he put his arm back around me and resumed taking me to bed, whispering in a near hush to my ear, "I've been waiting for this; I've been waiting for you. You're mine, and only mine, do you understand? You are never to lay with another man; do you understand that?"

I nodded obediently.

"Look at me and say it."

I turned to face him. "Yes."

"Now... you can give me what I want, or I can leave and get you out of my system easily enough. I'll leave you be if that's what you really want."

"No...I don't want you to go. I need you to stay with me. I'm sorry."

"Don't be. I understand, Lucy. You're bearing a lot of the burdens you were made to reject, but always think on how you're with me, okay? When you're with me, it's okay."

When it was over, and he lay sleeping, I took a blanket lying at the bottom of the bed and wrapped it around myself, gently easing myself from the small bed so as not to wake him. The springs yawned, relieved by my shifting weight, and I checked to make sure I hadn't disturbed him.

I stood and went back to the window. The sky had begun to grow dark and I watched the people who remained outside in the slipping light walk up and down along the street. I could hear the sound of pianos as their tunes floated up into the air, conversations mingling with chords of stringed instruments playing from somewhere. A gun shot sounded down the block and I looked toward the sound, my head responding as though a man had snapped his fingers to gain my attention.

I looked back at Billy's sleeping body. I dressed quietly, determinedly. I was thinking on what he had said, about my learned aversion to the very things I would now be presented with. In a desperate attempt, or more likely, a fit of madness, I decided I would deliberately face this way of life, no matter the task. I needed to dive in head first—I needed to allow things to shock me in order to build my strength of character, and so I decided to make the effort to behave the way I observed others in these towns, even if it was to be at my own risk.

When I was dressed I left the room, easing the door shut behind me. In the hall I fit my boots on so that I could reattach my spurs, mindful of the noise it would incur. I walked down the quiet hallway and descended to the second floor. Once there I could hear the muffled sounds of feigned female passion and the grunting of men getting off on it. I forced myself to endure this, defying the desperate resolve to cover my ears before moving on. When I had reached the ground floor I saw the young girl from earlier sitting on a stool. When she saw me she swiftly stood and went for the bottles of liquor set up along the sideboard. I mindlessly placed my hands upon the grips of my guns and ran my fingers along the bullets in my belt as I watched her. She walked to me, holding her tray, and I took the toxic liquid she offered. I tipped my foot back, my spur jingling, and lifted the glass to my lips as I poured the stuff down my throat, feeling it burn and wanting to cough it back up.

I wiped my lips and croaked, "How old are you?"

"Fourteen," she replied.

"Where are you from?" I asked.

"Here."

"This building?"

"I reckon."

"Do you have any sense? I asked where you are from."

"Here."

"Roswell?"

"Yes."

"Are you a whore?"

She shook her head.

"You will be."

I slammed the glass back down on the tray she was still holding and walked towards the front door before stopping. Perhaps I should go out the back— it was the most appropriate thing I could have done being a lady, such as I was, or, used to be, but wasn't this the point, to stare down the bluntness of the west and morph into one of its inhabitants? And after all, I had come in from the front—I was never a back-door kind of girl to begin with. In order for Billy accept me here, I would need to shed all that I was, all of the worries of what others should think of me; of my propriety. I didn't want to be that girl anymore, and if I were to convince him that I belonged, I would need to take the appropriate measures. And then, suddenly, I realized…I was standing in a goddamned whorehouse, worrying whether I should exit through the front or back. I didn't think it mattered much anymore how I left; the damage had been done. My concerns, invalid.

I walked the darkening streets and followed the sounds of laughter, music, and light coming from a saloon set up across the street. Once inside, I stood before the door and studied all of the people. Card games, faro, saloon wenches working the room and attempting to squeeze every ounce of pay out of the men who bought into their racket.

I scraped my boots along the wooden floor and slid over to the side of the ba-twinged doors so I could continue watching. I hadn't any money, so what was I to do? I thought I should attempt my sea legs, and so I approached the bar. The barkeep walked over to me, curious.

"What can I get ya little girl?"

"I haven't any money, but why don't you give me some of that whisky you got back there?"

"No money, huh?"

"That's right, sir, no money."

"Tell ya what…I'll let you go on upstairs and earn some," he said, laughing at his own joke.

I laughed in a very bitter, snide sort of way, and in a snarky manner matching his own said, "Third time I've heard that said today."

"Yeah?"

"Yep. Now I'll tell you what…" I placed my hand on my gun, deliberately draw-ing attention to it. "…you can give me what I asked you for, or I can beat the wits out of you for it."

I had heard the Regulators speak this way plenty, barking orders and taking what they wanted from the places they patronized, but the barkeep only stared at me, the men on either side of me looking at one another, astonished.

"Shit, girl," said the Barkeep. "You got brass ones for one so goddamned tender." He laughed and turned, grabbing at one of the bottles bearing the brownish fluid that I had asked for and poured it into a glass. "On the house, little girl."

I picked up the glass and attempted to drink it down, but instead choked on the taste and bits of grit, spitting it back out. The men all laughed.

"What the hell did you give me!? Is this a joke?"

The man to my left spoke up, "Nobody asks for whiskey, girl. You talk tough for one so ignorant. You got yourself a glassful of rotgut there. 'Round here we call that varnish."

All the men around me laughed.

"You outta be arrested for serving that swill, mister," I insisted.

"Giv'er a Sangaree, on me…" the man to my left said, laughing and throwing a coin on the bar. "I like you, girl."

For the next hour the men around me paid for my drinks, my favorite being what they called a "champagne flip".

I pushed through the batwings and onto the boardwalk. I was full of it, filled to the gills. I felt a hand slide down the back of my jacket and pull me backwards.

"Billy!"

Things were hazy; I could not make out his expression. Was he angry? I didn't know.

"Did I just see you come out of there? I must be seeing things because that can't be. What are you doing out here on the street all by yourself?"

"I just figured I'd...get used it to, I mean to it."

"Good God, let's go, swillbilly."

"Going to where?"

"To take a bath."

After we had bathed, we sat upon the building's steps. It felt terribly cold, only April in New Mexico, after all. I had left the madam's parlor without my coat, and not had I even so much as brought my gloves, an accessory I never went without. Billy had brought my coat from the room while I had been soaking myself in the warm water of the tub.

We sat with our coats wrapped tightly about us, leaning intimately into one another, something we had not done in what felt a very long while. I was still giddy from the alcohol, and instead of going back to the room to lie down, he felt that it might be best if I sat out in the chilly air for a bit considering my condition of disarray.

He asked me why I had left him, and I could only answer that I was, and am, very confused.

Listless and head whirring, I began, "I have been telling you that this is the life I want, but it's not particularly so." I stared about, clouded, and went on in earnest, as though I were delivering an elegy. "It's the life I know I must trek through; tread the muck and the mire, as it were, to get to the life I actually want." I shook my head lazily before him, my mind in a reverie, fluttering my hand about before me, thoughtlessly gesturing to help my point along.

Thoroughly entertained by my dizziness he asked, "Which is?"

I leaned unsteadily into him and, grabbing him about the collar said, "Oh...someplace with *you*. *Anywhere*. Even here, if that is what I must do." Again, I raised my hand, epic in my drunkenness, as I placed my other hand to my heart to demonstrate my resignation to my plight.

I shivered terribly. Holding my hand, he then took the other and brought them to his lips, breathing upon them to warm them. "I should have brought your gloves..."

"I'm fighting for my independence, too, Billy. But I need only to find my footing. I am somewhere in between what it is I want and must abide by to have it. I am trying to bridge the gap. I am."

"Lucy," he laughed, "I adore you, you do realize that?"

I smiled and conceded that I did, in fact, know this.

"You have so much strength in you. I'm well aware that you're above all of this and shouldn't be placed in the middle of it all. If you're so determined to go along with all of this, you need to get used to this life; you need to trust me."

"I do trust you, Billy. I trust only you."

"I don't like any of this. I still think of and remember you the way I first saw you, the lady you are. I don't see you in this way. And I do want you with me very much…"

He looked down, putting my hands to his lips again to warm them. We both only sat there, our heads tucked together against the chill of the night air.

"Come on…we need to get you out of this cold air now." And then, "Never do that again, Lucy. Not ever. I don't want to find you off someplace like that alone, again."

# 13

## April, 1878

"Not Much Mary Ann"
—Andrew "Buckshot" Roberts

**A**fter landing back in Patricio we near immediately took off for Blazer's Mill, but before heading out I saw Jim French there with the rest of the men. I ran to him, throwing my arms around him enthusiastically, happy to see that he was alive. I looked back at Billy who winked and stood smiling.

"What happened, Jim?" I asked.

"Didn't you ask your boyfriend?"

"He says you were shot in the leg and couldn't ride out."

"Yeah," he looked over at Billy. "Sam stuck me under the floorboards of that bed there in the store."

"Get the hell out! What then, Jim?" Billy asked, waiting to be captivated by a good tale.

"Well...I lay there on my back with two six-shooters, listenin' to them goddamn Dolan boys kicking around, looking for me."

"Ya tricked them out good," Minxie pointed out.

I was struck dumb by this story.

Jim's face grew somber. "Last I heard Peppin managed to arrest Alex, a couple of his house boys, too. And Widenmann."

"Under whose goddamned authority?" Billy exclaimed.

"That's the bitch of it all, Bill. You know authority don't matter up there."

"Yeah...don't I know it."

A thought occurred to me and my wits returned. "How is it you two managed to get shot?" I turned to Billy. "I thought you said you were behind the corral wall."

Jim began to answer and I saw Billy give him a sly look, shaking his head slightly. I looked back at Jim, my expression insistent upon him ignoring Billy's want of discretion. Jim looked between us, uncomfortably caught in the middle.

Feeling now that he must explain he said, "We ran out after Brady fell...their side was taking shots, you know how it is," he said, attempting to blow it off and make it seem less alarming that it was. He shook his head and waved his hand dismissively, as if I had indeed "knew" how it was.

I looked to Billy with an air of consternation. Commenting on my expression, he said to Jim, "This is what I was wanting to avoid." He looked down and sucked his breath in between his lips. "We was trying to get the warrant for Alex's arrest—Brady was carrying it," As an afterthought he said, "And I wanted my gun back."

"Were! *Were*, Billy! We *were* trying to get…! Quit speaking like an ignorant imp! And that last part is just plain stupid."

"Yeah…thanks Jim," he said, scratching at the back of his neck absently, his sarcasm overt.

Just then Richard rode up.

"What the hell is she doing here?" he bawled. "You're like the green on a damn bad penny!" he told me. "You were supposed to be in Sumner!"

"She '*were*'." Billy responded, droll in his summation; I smirked at his being fresh.

"She was supposed to stay in Sumner!"

"She was," Billy concurred. "But she didn't."

"Roberts was spotted up the Rinconada." Charlie panted, catching up to the crowd of us.

George and Frank Coe were ready to start out after him, and once all the boys were gathered we started out immediately, Minxie staying behind. We headed up the Ruidoso, spending the night on the Rinconada.

As the campfire burned, the remains of a stray, slaughtered steer were cooked. Billy nudged my arm and pointed out to where I could see a shadowy gathering of people in the fading light as they passed by on horseback.

"Apaches," he said.

Upon hearing this, I blanched and he got himself a good kick out of it, funning me being his reason for pointing them out in the first place. He intended to alarm me for his own pleasure; he told me on purpose!

"Stand down, Lu…they won't bother us," he assured me. "There's plenty of us around." He clapped me on the back and got up, leaving me to sit there, panicked.

We arrived at Blazer's Mill and the men rudely demanded supper of the inhabitants. Feeling shamed by their bad manners, I managed to eat only a little, though I was urged to eat more. Refusing, I left the table and stepped out to see to Viola, petting her along the black shading of her sleek face.

"My pretty little Dapple Grey," I said with affection.

She nudged me approvingly, nickering, and I slid my hand along her snout in appreciation when I heard a state of agitation from around the side of the house. I peered around the wall to investigate, finding that the men were all standing there, guns undone and at the ready. An older man I did not recognize sat with a rifle propped on his lap as he stared down the Regulators as they surrounded him. I watched with terror, but fascinated nonetheless, both wondering and worrying what it was that would happen.

I could see Frank Coe speaking to the old man as if the two were old friends. I heard him say, "You will not be hurt, upon my word, if you surrender," to which the old man responded that he did not believe this, refusing to give up his disposition. He then made a comment I could not hear to the crowd of men before him and a shot had been fired by our side, prompting an all-out firing match. I backed around the corner of the house as the bullets flew, sidling up close to the wall and getting down on the ground, using my arms to shield my head against the skirmish. When the volley had quit I very slowly emerged, still in a crouched position, to peek around the side of the house again and view what remained of the fray. Some of our boys were scattered, prone on the ground. I was jolted by this horror, and witnessed Richard walk off, dogged by the haunting resolution of the promise he made to John, citing he would get every last one of them before his last breath was due.

"Where the hell is Lucy? Billy's unmistakable voice shouted.

"I'm here!" I returned, rushing out to him.

"Get back!" he intensely commanded, his tone startling me into retreating. I watching him come towards me as he held his arm—I could see that he was bleeding there. I opened my mouth with the intention of asking him if he was okay, reaching out to touch him, but the words did not come. The fracas was so chaotic, the air so thick with the acrid smell of gunfire and kicked up dust that it clouded my eyes, fogged my mind, and coated my throat so that I could not even manage to ask something so simple as if he was all right.

When I had gone out to Viola, I had untethered her as I planned to ride her around a bit while the others finished eating, anticipating that they'd sit around talking about the war and their plans for it which was always an unhappy topic with me.

Now, always a fair high-strung, Viola bolted at the sound of gunfire. Unfettered and confused by the frenzied disorder, she bucked back and then forward, trotting far enough out to stray near the firing zone, which truly, could have been just about everywhere.

"Viola!" I went to run to her but Billy grabbed me and forcibly slammed me back against the wall. I reached out in her direction as I tried to get away from him but he held me fast against that wall.

Bullets flared again, blazing by and hitting the edge of the house causing splinters to spray and skin us both. I heard Viola whicker abnormally and squeal wildly before watching her go down. I kicked at Billy and nearly broke free but he had pushed me back hard.

"Stay put, goddammit!" he yelled directly into my face, his eyes stark as he ordered me.

He put his good arm around me, buckling me, and pulled me with him down to the ground. I kept struggling to look towards Viola so I could at least see her, but Billy shielded me, hovering over me as best as he could to keep me safe and from being hit by the gunfire.

When the firing stopped again Billy lifted his head and turned it, peering out and squinting through the dust in an attempt to see what was happening. While he was distracted with this I slid out from under him and ran to Viola who now lay in the dirt making such horrible gasping, whining sounds—sounds I had never in my life heard a horse make. I knelt down beside her and frantically laid my head upon her side, scared for her, when Billy grabbed me again and began to pull me back. I fought him off, his wounded arm's strength waning and unable to get purchase of me. I looked up and to the devil's delight I had done so at such an unfortunate moment—I saw the back of Richard's head explode, a surge of red spraying thick, bloody mist that mingled with the unsettled dust, gore marking the ground with bits and pieces of him. I stayed still, hearing nothing after witnessing this sight—not Billy screaming at me, not Viola shrilly crying out, not the other men yelling...I only saw Richard, face down in the dust, his gaping head wound explicitly visible. I raised my hands to the sides of my face, pushing my hat back and squeezing them against my ears in shock, my eyes staring, bewildered. It was all over after that.

Reality came back quickly enough and I hurriedly knelt down and placed my hand upon Viola, feeling her flank rise and fall with each shallow breath, her lungs struggling. The others ran towards us and the horses, hollering about getting a wagon for our wounded and getting the hell out. As they scattered about, preparing the horses and other necessities to leave, the sooner the better, I remained kneeling by Viola, talking to her, telling her it was okay.

Billy watched me pitifully, but with a grave, stern voice said, "She's hurt, Lu. She's hurt real bad."

I was crying over her body now, sniffling audibly.

"You got to put her down, Lu."

I looked to him, wide-eyed and irate. "She'll be fine. Billy, she'll be fine. She only needs her wound to be tended to, it's her leg. It's only her leg!"

"Her knee's been blown out, Lucy! And she's caught one in her breast. There's nothing to be done for her."

Men were rushing all about us in a fit of confusion, and we two sat there as though displaced, ensconced in this small tragedy within a larger one. I barely made a move except to sooth Viola, deluded.

"You put your horse down, Lucy!" Billy yelled, knowing my thoughts and how he needed to get through them to me.

"Shut up! Don't you say that to me!" I pushed him and slapped at his face. He grabbed a hold of my arms and held them so tight it hurt.

In a blatant, unforgiving voice he said, "Do you see what's going on here? We don't have time for this! This is your obligation to take care of! Take your gun out and put your goddamned horse down! She's suffering, Lu!"

"I won't!" I cried. Leave me here, leave me alone! You can go and I'll stay!" I looked at him maliciously. "It's what you want anyway! Leave me with my horse! Nobody asked for your opinion! I certainly don't care for it!"

"Nobody has to ask for my opinion. I'm not leaving this horse here like this and she's your responsibility. You take your fucking gun out!"

The boys who could stand stopped running about and gathered around us to watch the scene unfold. Steve Stephens, Big John Scroggins, Henry Brown, Fred Wait, Jose Chavez Y Chavez, and Charlie Bowdre, who tended to his wounded abdomen by pressing his hand against the ache there. He was barely able to stand, and only by the grace of God did the bullet deflect from his buckle, leaving him in pain, still. Josiah, shot through the leg, managed to stand with help from Henry and Fred, watching the scene as well.

Billy leaned in to me, close to my ear, whispering, "Lucy…she's your horse. She's down. Put her out of her misery."

I only sat quietly with my hands curled into fists and wrapped around me, holding me like the child I was as I rocked back and forth.

"We don't have time for this!" argued Henry.

Billy held up his hand to silence him.

"Billy," I begged. "Please…leave me. I can't do this. Don't make me."

"Do it!" he yelled.

I shook my head and wept, still holding on to myself. Charlie, who took pity on me, said, "Jesus, Billy…don't."

Billy placed the hand of his good arm around my throat, just below my jaw, applying enough pressure to cause me to stand up along with him. He looked me in the eyes firmly and, with a tremendous lack of both patience and empathy, but with an understanding that had broken my heart all the same despite the angry thoughts I had for him, he said to me, "You want to be here? If you can't even kill a horse, you can't kill a man. If you want to survive out here, you can't look the part, Lucy, you have to play it. We lost our captain. We lost Brewer. Roberts blew him apart like he didn't matter nothing to him, and he didn't. And now you want to sit here crying over a horse! Now, your horse is in pain, she's done for. Take that fancy horseshoed Schofield out of its scabbard and go to work."

I fell apart and grabbed at his jacket, holding on to him, barely able to stand.

"Billy? Please? I can't!" I sobbed. He grabbed my arms, pulling me off of him, and then pulling me back down to the dust. He took the gun from my left hip and placed in within my right hand. At first I refused to hold the gun, but he placed his hand over mine and secured it, squeezing it against the grips. He cocked the hammer and, without removing his hand he guided mine, gun at the ready, placing it directly upon Viola's brow, squarely between her eyes.

"Pull the trigger," he gently commanded, still covering my hand with his own, not letting go; letting me know he was with me.

"Show me that strength of yours. Prove to me what you've been preaching at me. Prove to me that you can be brave. This is the right thing to do, I wouldn't lead you wrong."

Viola's cries had gone from a piercing desperation to a mere gasping, her once magnificent lungs expended, her nostrils stirring up dust before her and emitting a ghostly vapor against the cold. Her breathing was labored, the full weight of her body bearing down upon her as she lay, helpless, on her side. I still sat there, gun in hand, poised against Viola's skull.

"I'm here with you, Lucy. I'm right here," he said, gently. Lovingly, he painfully managed to tuck a stray lock of hair behind my ear with his wounded arm.

"Pull the trigger and be done with it. Your horse needs you now. She's suffering; she's scared and she's dying. To not do this would be cruel. Trust me. You are hurting her far worse by refusing what I say."

All the men stood watching silently. Billy remained quiet, staring at me, urging me with his eyes and trying, I know, to give me some of his own strength. I closed my eyes, preparing to do what I was told must be done.

"No! Open your eyes, Lucy. Open them!" he demanded.

"Jesus Billy," came from somewhere around us.

After what seemed a lifetime, I obeyed and opened my eyes, and I pulled the trigger, screaming as I did so in order to help summon the ability to do what felt impossible. I watched the blood spray over her and pour from her, seeping to the ground, the life going out of her by my own hand. As Viola lay silent, the men stood with their heads down. Not over the death of my horse, but over the burgeoning death of my innocence.

"We need to go," Josiah softly said, attempting to be respectful towards my aggrieved state of being. I stood, and Billy slowly stood up alongside me, still peering at my face. Peripherally, I could see him watching. Without so much as a glance towards him I walked on and away from him, letting him know beyond the shadow of a doubt that I hated him. I walked away from them all towards the readied horses and the wagon that was prepared to pull our wounded. I chose a horse, Middleton's, I think, as he was placed in the wagon and hauled off to be treated. The others quickly gathered my belongings from my now dead horse and hurriedly exchanged them for Middleton's, placing his along with him in the wagon.

We moved out like bats out of hell.


"Christ! Ya made her leather boot her own damn horse?" Minxie asked, incredulously. "Why'd ya let her do it for herself? Why didn't ya do it for her?"

"Can you really ask me that? How can you not know the answer?" Billy looked away.

"Billy…it was only a horse. Ya could've done it for her and spared her—"

"Spared her? Spare her and spoil her? No…she can't be spared anything."

"Why the bloody hell not? God, it must've been awful for her."

"It was awful for me. I'm the bad guy now."

"Still, why couldn't ya have just done it for her, Bill?"

"Because, it was her responsibility! A man kills his own horse! She'll learn one of two things: Either she'll finally get it; it's ugly. She'll realize she can't hack it out here and go back to where she belongs, or she'll learn to stand as a man. If she stays she'll need to learn that lesson. You know how difficult it is out here. If she insists on hanging about, then, woman or not, she ought to be exposed to the reality of her decision."

Minxie began to nod in understanding. "Okay. Fine…I get ya straight. You're right."

"Yeah, well I only hope to God she understands it soon enough. She hates me, Quinn, for what I made her do. She won't talk to me. I only did it for her own good. She has responsibilities just like the rest of us. I won't always hold her hand, play at being her goddamned nursemaid! I only want to teach her. I want her to toughen up. That is *my* responsibility."

"There's no way she hates ya, Billy-boy."

"You weren't there. You didn't see the fallout. Right or wrong, she blames me for being so cruel."

"She'll get over it. You know she will."

# 14

## April, 1878

After the skirmish at Blazer's we took off and headed back into Patricio. A few of the men, Josiah, Charlie—recovered from his near fatal wound—and the Coe cousins, had scattered by the day after, leaving for their respective homesteads to lay low for a while.

Despite my persistence in harboring resentment towards Billy as I did, I still took his cue and drove up to ride in next to him, though I did not acknowledge him otherwise.

Upon our entrance into the little town we were greeted with much appreciation and gratitude by the residents who were shouting cheers at us and for God to bless us all, reaching out their hands to touch any one of us, many of them making the sign of the cross upon their person as though God had answered some prayer. I was taken aback at first. Though they had paid us such attentions before, never had they paid it so exceptionally. It was so very much unexpected that these people should acknowledge us in this way. The Regulators were a well-known gang amongst the towns, counties, and placitas of New Mexico, but such fanfare was unanticipated—they had become their incendiary device against their oppression. I was amazed, mesmerized, if confused, by their response.

The Regulators' heads were hung low after the battle at Blazer's. Word had spread ever so quickly by word of mouth alone that Bill "Buckshot" Roberts whipped the Regulators but good and all the boys knew it. This was in no way respectable publicity for the intimidating reputation the Regulators had commanded. One old man not only held off more than a baker's dozen of feared men who were by far less than the half of his age, but he had put a few out of the stand, devastatingly injuring them before he was taken himself. John Middleton, shot in the chest and expected to die, though he would recover, George Coe lost his trigger finger, Josiah shot in the leg, and Charlie nearly laid low if not for his oversized belt buckle. These were men who were regarded as some of the most dreaded in the territory. Now they would retreat, tails tucked thoroughly and rightfully in embarrassment. Had they fallen, or only lost the battle and not the war? I knew word of the trouble would spread far, talk of their disaster front and center, but I realized that the Regulators would not give up so easily, regardless of the beating they took. I had decided they had only lost the battle after all, even if they did get their man when all was said and done.

Richard was dead and buried long before Roberts succumbed to his own mortal injury. The old man had even held up well enough to continue the fight solid whilst mortally wounded, and he still clung to life while suffering severe pain for about a day's time. As we were leaving Blazer's Mill I heard them speak of burying Roberts beside Richard when his body finally gave out.

Making matters worse, upon our arrival, Minxie hit us with two pieces of distressing news, the first of which I had fully expected; the papers reporting that the Regulators had fought undefeated, but dishonorably so, with the people in general feeling as though they'd fought an unfair fight: fourteen against one.

*Ha!* I thought, *Unfair? Roberts held well enough all by himself! He might as well have been fourteen men all on his own!*

Well, what could the ignorant public possibly know? After all, a fight needn't had been executed, not if Roberts had given up as he was respectfully called upon to do. Instead, he intended to make a fight of it. I suppose the people can feel much better knowing that one old man put up one hell of a fight and handed all fourteen young, fierce men their asses.

Minxie also disclosed that troops were coming out of Fort Stanton. Billy, dismissing it as old news, was corrected. Ignoring my request that he respond to only me and acknowledge my plea for help, my father, instead, went over my head entirely and responded in full military fashion. I knew it was a gamble to write, and I had lost, putting us all in danger.

Instead of sending funds or someone to help our case, a two thousand dollar reward was placed upon my head. I was to be brought in alive only, and as one could imagine, this made our precarious predicament much tauter for being wanted men, and in remembering my fear of telling Billy of my communication to my father back in Sumner, I was all but certain he must be angry with me over this matter though he said nothing. I was as discomfited by my father's snub as the Regulators had been upon Roberts' already legendary one-man stand during the gunfight at Blazer's against their small army of men. I had caused us so much more trouble that it could not be measured unless one could measure it by the gold tendered from my father's coffers.

While I had been off with the boys on the Rinconada, my father had already begun his mobilization to remove me from New Mexico and place me back in New York. The bounty on my head was too great to resist, and I had become celebrated. I was not hard to spot in the least, and the guns I carried were a dead giveaway. Instead of being livid as he should have been for all of the extra trouble I had caused us, Billy took to referring to me as Lucky Lu out of affectionate pride, this moniker being picked up by the locals.

How he could be so laissez-faire upon the whole ordeal was beyond me. The bounty my father had placed on me put us in a state of even greater mortal danger than all combined killings of the past month.

Two thousand dollars was a great deal of money to these people. This act of my father's, of which I felt was betrayal, could not have come at a worse time. The Regulators, once quite the menacing "posse of assassins," were in danger of being reduced to the likes of a bunch of near peckerwoods, as they might say in in these parts, being laid out as they were by one tough old bird. I'm certain that Dolan and The Boys appreciated this greatly. And as there was a reward placed upon their heads as well, the amount placed upon my own served as a grand surplus indeed. We were in for it now, to be sure. We were worth a fortune to most of the people of New Mexico, the whole of us, and rumor might persist that perhaps we were not so dangerous after all, leaving any near damn sucker to mortally misjudge the Regulators and attempt to take us all for our reported value.

Fearing what anger may bear upon me over the news concerning my father, Billy surprised me by pointing out that perhaps it was not the worst thing.

"That money might just be your insurance, Lu," he had said. "Only a fool wouldn't be so careful not to harm you with two thousand dollars on the line. And those guns are a guarantee that you're the real deal. If anybody wants to collect on your head, they'll have to bring it in capitated. Your father has just assured your survival."

I was impressed with Billy's preferred grasp of reckoning regarding the situation.

"But Bill…my guns will mark you all out as well, as it is no secret that I am to be found with the Regulators. Though my life may be spared, should I be caught, it would give the rest of you away. I could not abide by this—you know that!"

I thought to remove my guns to make my identification all the more difficult, but he disagreed, responding that as long as we were in a familiar town and under the protection of its inhabitants we should have nothing to fear. He also reminded me of how my guns were a personal guarantee of my welfare. He also made the remark that a gunfighter never went without his guns, and I was to wear them always, come hell or high water.

"Under the protection of a familiar town or not, two thousand dollars will cut those ties," I countered.

He looked thoughtfully at me. "You might be right. Still…there ain't anything to be done at present. Besides…we all have rewards on our heads and have for some time now, and it's made hardly a difference to these people. They value us for who we are; their freedom is worth more than money."

I suppose I understood, as their longing mimicked my own. There was no amount of money that could have me turn back.

I marveled at how quickly word of mouth could spread; word of us all. I was assured that this was in no way a surprise in the least considering how desperate the situation was here in the territory. The people had been longing to push back, but being cowards, they had only to wait for those to come along who could do what they themselves could not, and so, we were on the docket for discussion among the citizens across the territory.

○○○

Gen. Addison P. Howard
New York, New York
April 10, 1878

Dear General Howard:
You are forthwith advised to cease and desist in offering the reward you have tendered upon your daughter's life as well as to disengage the regiment you have procured from Ft. Stanton in the attempt to bring her home to New York alive and unharmed.

As it presently stands, Mrs. McSween and I are Ms. Howard's legal guardians and are unprepared to relinquish this charge in the best interest of your daughter's wellbeing and in favor of her security. In this sense, she is currently a resident of New Mexico. This fact, should you ignore my counsel, will result in your being held in contempt and violation of the law should you continue to have your daughter sought out under the large bounty you have offered, as her capture will constitute kidnapping, which, as you must know, is an egregious offense of the law.

Our relinquishment of guardianship would mean to allow you to continue upon your own free will to do all there is within your power to bring your daughter home which, by offering such a large amount, should place her life in even greater jeopardy as the fiercest men residing within the territory will take up arms in the hunt and most assuredly create a war of minutia within the war that already rages wildly, which may result in your daughter's death as well as those entrusted to guarantee her safety as they will fight to keep her as they consider her under their protection, and therefore, their responsibility.

I have begun to maintain business with a lawyer by the name of Montague R. Leverson, an Englishmen acquainted with our western customs, who implores you to heed my advice as good authority.

The bounty in the excess sum of two thousand dollars which you have generously offered in the interest of Ms. Howard's safe detention, which is to result in her safe return to New York, is feared to do more harm than good as she will lose the benefit of anonymity amongst the towns here in New Mexico which is, I assure you, a tremendous advantage. I fear this benefit has already been unduly breached by your proclamation.

Both the life of your daughter and the lives of the men tasked with her safety have been placed in a further precarious situation by your most gracious offer of good intention.

I fear you may have misjudged the sentiments of the men in charge of your daughter in the midst of this war being carried out between the faction of Tunstall, myself, and Mr. John S. Chisum, and the faction of Mr. L.G. Murphy and Mr. J.J. Dolan, as the latter faction is corrupt and untrustworthy and earnest in their malevolent intentions. They have heinously ordered your daughter's death on sight and, I can promise you, they mean to carry it out. They have a large posse comprised of their own men who are well acquainted with these orders. Offering such a substantial reward, inviting all to participate, will only serve to assist the Dolan men in their ability to locate Ms. Howard easily as, at the very least, they will need only to sit back, gaining from the expended efforts of others pursuing Ms. Howard as throngs of many will seek to pocket such an extensive amount.

In addition, the bounty will most certainly result in piquing the financial desperation of good men who will only find themselves in a situation of which they will have no hope in combating as they will no doubt find themselves face-to-face with better armed, competent and adequate men.

I urge you also to think of your family and its good name, as this public search you have heralded will bring about a scandal to you and yours and serve to ruin Ms. Howard's reputation, who only finds herself unable to escape this war due to the confines and orders given under the Murphy/Dolan faction for her life's end.

Perhaps you might think about changing tacks and use the money as a catalyst of goodwill in an attempt to buy Ms. Howard and her sentinels a fair trial with excellent legal representation as they find themselves within an unfair position.

Once again I remind you that Ms. Howard will remain our ward, and therefore, you are entreated to withdraw the reward you have offered.

May I also remind you that the Lincoln County Regulators are doing you a tremendous service by keeping our beloved Elucia in the realm of safety. I implore you to turn your mind to that matter and consider my request of funds for legal action.

I remain your loyal friend,
A.A. McSween.

OOO

I was still brokenhearted over the death of Richard and Viola and it did not go unnoticed by Billy that my manner towards him was very casual and matter-of-fact rather than my customarily harmonious and intimately familiar conduct—my behavior was stunted rather than naturally mellifluous as was ordinarily typical of me. This was not by design, but rather forced upon us both by his means to the ends of building my western character. My still being distraught over what had happened at Blazer's Mill only served to add to my emotional displacement.

When George Coe had had his trigger finger shot off, Billy procured carbolic acid to help seal the wound and stave off infection, and in seeing this I began to truly understand the life that I had intentionally wanted to sell my soul into. The incongruity of western living was a mystery to me. The way these men took everything in stride, taking care of matters such as sticking the remaining stub of a blown off, open wounded finger into a jar of acid as though a common, every day action, felt curious and strange. Billy's own wound was not so bad—his arm was still tender—but all-in-all, he was lucky, the bullet only skinning him. The both of us wore scratches upon our faces from the splinters and mortar that had struck us there. He was thoroughly impressed, amazed by Roberts' determination and spirit. What impressed me was how these boys could be so comfortably at ease about the whole debacle.

We had taken our residence at the same boarding house we had occupied prior in San Patricio, despite being offered and welcomed avidly into the homes of the Patricians, gratis, as we were beginning to become infamous and had sympathizers in nearly every town, Patricio's inhabitants being our principal supporters. We refused their kindness as Billy wanted to be alone with me and spend time with me privately. Only Minxie took a kindly offer, staying in the home of a señiorita with whom he had a special interest.

At this point in the game, we would have taken one of the rooms around back of the Old Ruidoso for purposes of safety via concealment from the street despite both back rooms being unavailable. We'd have forced out whoever had hired the rooms. But for the sake of anonymity after the trouble at Blazer's Mill we didn't cause a fuss. In fact, the fight at Blazer's Mill had such a devastating effect on egos of the Regulators, made worse by its being recorded for all to read in the local papers, that the last thing any of us needed was any more attention drawn to us.

I had gone to our room and sat upon the bed there quietly during the afternoon to reflect on and contemplate my position, listening to the town's patrons move about outside, up and down the street, going to wherever it was they were going, moving from one simple prospect to another, something I wanted to envy but, for the life of me, could not. As much as I wish it were not so, their lives seemed boring by comparison.

I watched the human forms move to-and-fro through the window which, though its curtain was drawn, was still fully functional as the curtain was made of sheer, cheap lace.

I heard the familiar sounds of Billy's footfalls approaching the door to the room. Stopping before it a moment, I could see the shadow of him beneath the door before he entered. His movement was hesitant, and so I knew he was looking to make amends, to set things right, as he felt, correctly, that things were very wrong between us.

I hadn't any trouble accepting his case, and allow me to note that, indeed, nothing between us was truly out of order, only bent in some way. We had crossed a bridge together, he and I, and I wished to burn it behind us. We would only have to figure out together how our friendship was to work on this side. We must find how it would fit. But he needn't have been terribly concerned as I would have liked it very much if we could mend our fence if he so too felt it needed to be done, and his concern was reassuring. I wanted the scales between us even, and so, for whatever it was in which he needed resolution, I would oblige him, and not entirely without good reason on my part; he was my guide, my mentor; he always had been, and it was my duty to allow him to teach me. I must learn to stand firmly against the adversities and the challenges presented to me on a near constant basis in this territory, just as he had instructed me. And I suspected that, with time, shock would no longer pervade my sensibilities, but rather my instinct would be intact upon first blush soon enough. I had already begun my journey into the new role I was to inhabit within this society, and Billy was doing the right thing in forcing my hand in matters. I was forming to fit now. I was beginning to leave behind my delicate nature and exchange it instead for the raucous nature of the vicious social disorder that reigned supreme here, and I would need Billy to continue to help me find my way. We must make our peace.

Opening the door, Billy stood there looking at me. I looked back, and with excited interest, I positioned myself to sit over the side of the bed. I could see that his wound had begun to seep, staining his shirt. He would need fresh bandages.

I smiled agreeably and serenely, showing him that I was in a state of happy surrender and relieved to see him here. I opened my mouth to speak first, but before I had obtained my words he walked quickly and dropped to his knees before me, placing his head in my lap and grabbing both my hands in his, twining, untwining, and then twining his fingers with mine again and again, desperate to touch and connect with me. He laid his head down upon its side, his expression lame and sad.

"Forgive me, Lucy…" he whispered. "Forgive me, please…" he begged.

Gently I pulled my hand from his and stroked his head with the tips of my fingers as I often did when comforting him, smoothing the hair by his temple and running my fingers over and around his ear, wanting him to feel the tremendous affection I had for him.

"What have I to forgive you for?"

"For what I done," he whispered. "For what I made you do. I know how badly I hurt you, and I'd rather die than ever hurt you."

I placed my lips next to his ear. "My sweet boy…" I whispered, caressing his cheek.

He grabbed my stray hand and again put it back into his, desperately holding on.

"I know how much you loved that horse."

"Not as much as I love you, or loved Richard. You were in the middle of that fight, too, and I realize that I am blessed to have only lost my horse. I have not been angry with you, Billy. I did not mean to imply…"

"Don't say it…"

"You must know how upsetting the circumstances that I've born witness to have been for me; it had not one thing to do with what you had me do—I was merely overwhelmed. You had me do what needed to be done, there was no other way. Do you think I cannot realize that? I didn't want to let go, and you forced me to accept what I would not. It makes me understand that you love me enough to push me so hard. You are a fine teacher. I'm grateful for you."

He looked up at me, his misty eyes blinking optimistically.

"This is all so unreal, Billy. If anyone should ask for forgiveness, it is I, and so I am. I must find my nerve. You men do not have the time to deal with the histrionics of a woman. I know this."

He laughed into my lap, light and subdued.

"You love me in all ways, and I know this is why you push me so. You take care of me so well, and I will follow your lead; it will only be slow going for me at times; I must learn to relive my life. Do you think you can be patient?"

He raised his head. "For you? Yes! And I know it, that you have to learn new lessons. But, I admit, as much as I want you to stiffen up that back of yours, I'm afraid you'll lose your heart. Promise me that won't happen. Promise me you'll be able to walk the line."

"I promise. And I *will* grow stronger. I want to please you more than anything, and I know, also, that my life depends on it."

# 15

# April, 1878

Gen. Addison P. Howard
New York, New York
April 21, 1878

Father,
I see you have ignored my request completely and have spared no expense in your usual attempt to once again crush me beneath the wheel of your authority.
I wish you the best of luck in your quest to find me.

Your loving daughter,
Elucia "Lucky Lu" Howard

Our fame was extraordinary enough now so that I was often recognized right off by my guns. In Patricio, the people continued to love the Regulators and welcome them with open arms, trusted to protect them from prospective trouble.

Billy, of course, warned me that there was always the exception, but I did not heed his warning as my rebelliousness was beginning to know no bounds. My patience was wearing thin, and upon hearing of the regiment sent out of Fort Stanton to find me under my father's request, I told Billy that I would offer a big "fuck you" to any impending bounty hunter no matter who the source may be; regular man or soldier alike. I would not let them take me without a fight. Billy told me I was beginning to talk a little too big for owning such a little pair of britches.

Leaving our room I was on my own and headed toward the local general store in order to obtain some sweets and locate, hopefully, a good book to read and carry along with me. My guns were twisted around so I could allow one to show through my coat as I was taught to do, and I felt competent to walk the streets of Patricio alone, safely.

The more our fame grew, the more female admirers Billy acquired. He had plenty before, but the influx was tremendous. I could not say that I was jealous, not even in the least. But I could dare say that I was irritated as many of these women were aroused by his outlaw status, the very status I shunned in him and tried, in vain, to beg him to outrun. These women only encouraged his position, the ghastly cows! This, I hated them for!

We argued about this, Billy and me. I objected to dealing with the unwanted and unnecessary aggravation these wanton women incited in me as I was already so fraught with the distress upon the grim duty of war. He'd only laugh and tell me I was ridiculous.

"I will not suffer your indiscretions at my expense when the cost of my sanity has already run the funds dry!"

"Need I remind you that you were willing to sacrifice your sanity?"

"Do not preach at me, you son of a bitch bastard! I have forfeited all of it for *you*!"

"No, you have done that for *you*."

"I have done it for us *both*! Will you abandon me someday and run off when my back is turned?"

"I promised you my heart, but we had an understanding otherwise."

"Oh, yes, of course. The understanding that I can never truly have you," I said with scorn.

He looked at me severely.

"Was this the same promise given by you to Paulita?" I asked sarcastically. "Am I to turn out the same as she?"

"You know better than to push me, Lu. You've pushed me far enough already."

"Oh yes, do not push you where your precious Paulita is concerned! Do not push you with the promises you have made to us both. And so there we are! Whatever makes your shame easier for you!"

He came to me angrily, causing me to almost retreat. But instead I proudly stood my ground. When he finally approached me he grabbed me roughly and pulled me to him, kissing me passionately before taking me to bed.

And as the new throngs of women attempted to gain Billy's attention I turned to my own bag of tricks. I sucked on cherry flavored candies constantly so that Billy would associate this with the taste of me, and naturally I wore lavender perfumes and fragrances, always, so that he would be reminded of me every time he picked up on the scent, which, in these towns, was a popular one amongst the ladies of the evening; the fallen ones. Despite my previous disappointment of lavenders popularity amongst the low-class demographic, I now realized how fortuitously it worked in my favor as the scent was revealed everywhere which made it near impossible for him to escape me, which in turn might cause him to develop a sudden urge for me. I would always be around so long as the scent of lavender held out.

When I had arrived at the store I found Nathanial Hawthorne's Scarlet Letter on a shelf and I picked it up. I had read this book, but it had been quite a while, and as it was the only novel available, it would have to do. Also, I thought, I could read it and appreciate it much more by relating it to my current life's precarious position. I was almost guaranteed to get a kick of out the irony. Me, the virtuous harlot!

The candies were in jars at the counter, and before finalizing my shopping by selecting the confectionaries I intended to purchase, I decided to browse around the store a bit longer. It was a tiny place, unlike John's store. The maneuverability in such a place as this was difficult at best.

As I wandered about, carefully and slowly, I couldn't help but notice a small gathering of men outside the window of the store who were gawking at me. I made my best effort to ignore them. They did not worry me, though I found their behavior quite rude and much too gratuitous. Eventually the door opened, the bell chiming, signaling a customer, and I heard boot steps approach from behind me. I turned around to find a slightly built, fairly tall figure of a good-looking young man standing there, grinning from ear-to-ear, light blue eyes twinkling with excitement. Yes, he was certainly easy on the eyes.

"You're her!"

"I'm sorry? I'm *who*?"

" Lucky Lu!"

"Says who?" I asked, irritated.

"Recognize those guns, and..." he reached into a satchel he was carrying and began rooting around. I placed my right hand on the handle of my gun.

"Whoa, girl, it's okay. I ain't lookin' for anything that's gonna hurt ya. I just wanted to show you somethin'."

I was annoyed by his presumption. "Who says I was worried?"

"I didn't mean to imply..." he shook his head anxiously. "I apologize."

His accent was off the charts southern, and unlike Billy, he spoke with a glaring twang. But I must admit, where it otherwise would have, it did not irritate me in the least. There was something about him that I found charming, and so his flawed speech characteristic was forgiven. Perhaps it was his open countenance, or his obvious, gregarious nature.

"Where're you from?" I asked.

"Mississippi," he said dismissively. "Look at this!" he exclaimed, pulling a worn, yellowed book from his pack and handing it over to me.

On the cover was a blackened silhouette of a person. I could see that it was wearing what looked like a bolero hat tilted low over the face in an unflappable, cool manner. A long black line protruded from the outline of the face where the mouth would be, tipped with a shade of orange and complete with billowing, grayish smoke swirling above it; a cigarette that hung casually from the lips. I could see that this figure was meant to be a girl as there was the unmistakable appearance of a ponytail which wrapped around from the base of the neck and hung down over the shoulder and down the front, long and lengthy.

I looked up at the boy. "So?"

"*So*? Read the title!"

Lucky Lu:

The Socialite Sweetheart of the Southwest: Debutante of the Desert

*Clever*. I frowned at this but skimmed through the nickel pulp nonetheless. This boy must have read it over-and-over again, multiple times, as his excitement over the matter would suggest. The book was near flimsy with use.

As I flipped through the pages he spoke, "It's so fascinating! What I read about you, I mean. You really a Regulator and all that?"

*Honorary*, I smirked to myself.

There wasn't any way I would distance myself from the Regulators in this instance. I wouldn't let a strange man think I hadn't the protection of the Regulators, and so I remarked, "We'll, I could tell you this: if I weren't, there's no way I could take all of New Mexico on all by my lonesome," I smiled at him with facetious exaggeration. "What's your name?" I asked.

"James. James Moffey. But my friends all call me Jim."

He stood there nervously, hands on his hips, smiling eagerly at me. I went back to flipping through the small book.

"Where did you find this, James, if you don't mind my asking."

"Oh, no…'course not—not at all. We, my friends and I…" he pointed towards the window where the other boys still stood. "That's Rufus Bach, the one holding his hat in his hands; the one with the reddish colored, blond hair. And that other one, standing next to him, is Engel Brauer. The other one, standing there looking through the window at us is Finnegan Flynn, but mostly we call him Finn…"

"James!" I snapped my fingers at his face. "I didn't ask about your friends!"

"Oh…I'm sorry. I apologize. It's just…" he frowned a bit.

He took his hat off respectively, as if suddenly remembering that he was wearing it, and worried it in his hands fretfully. I felt a trifle guilty for a moment, barking at him as I had. I could tell straight away that he was merely an excitable sort and probably couldn't help going off on a tangent or two. But then he bounced straight back.

"Well, I can't believe it's you! I've been reading all I can about the Lincoln County Regulators! I couldn't believe they'd been riding with a woman!"

"Do you find something wrong with that?"

He looked at me, regretfully. He replaced his hat and began to nervously rub at his forehead, his eyes growing wide. "No, ma'am! No, not at all! Just fascinatin', I guess."

We looked at one another quietly for a moment.

"I ride with them for protection," I asserted, wanting him to understand my meaning.

He nodded, comprehending, and said, "Gosh...you really are just like they say!"

*How was this something he could possibly know? How could he know anything about me, truly, through what a trash rag said?*

"Which is?"

"Oh, well...that you're real pretty," his face flushed and he stared at the floor. "It's all in there." He pointed to the pulp book.

Despite my unsympathetic conduct towards him, I had to admit that I truly liked him immediately. His personality was friendly, if exaggerated, though I suspected the exaggeration stemmed from his nervousness. Otherwise, I found his anxious demeanor pleasantly engaging.

"So, like I had asked, James, where did you find this?"

"Oh, right...I'm sorry. Down by Seven Rivers. My friends and I, we stayed on at the Beckwith Ranch?"

He smiled widely at me and went on. "In there," he nodded and pointed to the book, "they say that you're the gunfighter's darlin'."

He smiled wide and let out a small, excited chuckle and blushed.

"They say you're the Kid's girl, and that you're real classy and cut a real smart and feminine figure among all the men. The women, even..." he trailed off, unsure as to whether or not he had offended me in discussing my feminine figure. He took his hat off again and stared down at it. I decided to help him get himself out of his self-inflicted, foot-in-mouth dilemma.

"What about them? The women, I mean."

*How is it I could still manage to cut a classy figure among the women*, I wondered.

He looked up at me appreciatively, seeming to have forgotten his previously embarrassing blunder.

"They got to pullin' up their sleeves, like you do."

I never could stand having to wear long sleeves.

"I've seen many women along these parts with exposed forearms out in the streets, wearing their gloves and all just like you do. I guess they're settin' a trend by you," he declared with unmerited pride.

"Yeah? You think?" I asked, curious and interested as I instinctively looked upon my arm.

"Oh, sure thing," he nodded. "I noticed it after learning of it in that there book."

"Seems like an odd thing to notice for a guy, James," I said, teasingly, flirting a little.

"Aw, yeah, well…" he blushed. "You pick things up here and there. The women find you fascinatin'."

I couldn't help but smile at his awkwardness.

"Do you mind if I borrow this from you for a day or two?"

"Ordinarily I'd not let it go, but I'd be only too happy to oblige *you*, Ms. Howard. I plan to collect as many of those nickels and dimes on you as I can find!"

The young man was enamored but delightfully so. I don't believe he realized that he had that sort of effect in the least; just an honest boy from Mississippi. He certainly wasn't playing a game by which he'd try to win me over by flattering me, telling me what he thought I wanted to hear. In fact, his honesty was astoundingly apparent. I appreciated this in him. Of course, only a fool would attempt to mislead me, knowing who I was and that I rode with a dangerous crowd.

I placed the book in the pony-express satchel I had slung across my person and began my way towards the counter to make my purchases and secure my supply of cherry candies.

"Can I buy those for you?" Jimmy asked, eagerly.

Being a lady, one of the rules, depending upon the context of the situation, was to never allow a strange man to buy you things of any kind—it was unfitting. But this boy was unthreatening and only too happy to please me. I found his behavior far too adorable to turn him down. I selected a large amount of cherry sticks and discs to which Jimmy commented, inappropriately I might add, on my rather large selection. I frowned upon his overt, improper observation, but his remark was meant in polite fashion, and so I overlooked the statement, all together realizing that he could not have known the better and was only still too excited.

We left the store and walked out onto the boards. His friends looked our way and leaned in to one another, discussing something privately.

"Are you with Billy?" he wondered loudly.

I had ignored the question. I was not in the habit of discussing Billy or his where-abouts with perfect strangers, no matter how friendly and harmless they appeared to be. I turned to him.

"It was nice to meet you, and thank you for your thoughtfulness," I held up the brown paper sack of confectionaries in appreciation (I had to be careful not refer to this purchase as a gift). "It was a real pleasure speaking with you as well," I smiled and held out my hand, and he shook it without taking his eyes from my mine.

"I'll bring your book back. I can promise that to you. Where can I find you?"

"The boarding house in the front of town. The Old Ruidoso? We're around back, room four."

"All right, then."

I walked off, parting with him, and headed back to my room at that very boarding house. I couldn't wait to read what this book had to tell and show it to Billy.

When I showed Billy the book he laughed with pride, telling me with a wink that I was now certified. I flopped on the bed and lay down on my stomach to read the tale of myself with Billy coming to sit next to me. I discovered that I rode out courageously from the confines of my highborn life in the east, breaking from eastern social convention and going west and from town-to-town to carry out my plan in sharing my abundant wealth with the poor.

"Hey Billy, listen to this!"

"What's that, Bonita?"

"They say I'm 'the Kid's lady'—"

"Damn right ya are…"

I popped a cherry disc in my mouth.

"A mysterious party of the Regulators. What does that even *mean*?" I joked.

We had good fun with that and laughed.

"It says that I have many lovers, including the Kid—that'd be you—and I lure in thieves and men of otherwise poor scruples with my legendary beauty, and then I shoot them down for any valuables they may have on their person and distribute what I find amongst the poor communities. And apparently I earned my name, 'Lucky Lu', by escaping all of my gunfights unscathed."

"I gave you that name!" he said, playfully irked.

"Well did you hear the part about my legendary beauty? I'm legendarily beautiful!" I rolled onto my side and threw my arms out wide histrionically. I propped myself up by my elbow and placed a hand to my heart in a swooning fashion. Sighing, I threw my head back and closed my eyes, dramatically basking in my literary affirmation.

"Aw, but darlin', you are legendarily beautiful," Billy said, leaning over to kiss me.

"Here's a good one!" I shouted excitedly. "'I've challenged men, my beauty giving me the edge as it stays the hand of the beast, allowing me to cut them down.'"

I laughed so heartily my stomach hurt, Billy chuckling along.

"Where do they get this stuff?" I wondered aloud, snickering and shaking my head in amused incredulity. At one point I was described as Goldilocks amongst the bears of the west. I could no longer take the ridiculousness of it all as my eyes were watered and my belly cramped from laughter.

Billy took the book and began flipping through the pages, looking at the artist's renderings.

"These ain't half bad. Look at this one; they got your eyes wrong."

Indeed they had. A few of the pictures were done with a hazing of color, and they had painted my eyes in a very fashionable, brilliant color of green, whereas my eyes were brown hazel, more brown than anything.

"Where'd this thing come from, anyway?" he asked.

"Somewhere down by Seven Rivers," I answered, still flipping the pages.

"Who's been to Seven Rivers?"

"I met a boy at the general store. He approached me; said he recognized me and started talking to me, showing me this."

"Who's this boy?"

Impishly, I teased him. "Wouldn't you like to know…."

He rolled off the bed. "You're damn straight I want to know. Who is he? I want to know everybody you relate to, especially men who give you things."

I smiled at him. "Is this you being protective of me, Bill?"

He turned to look at me and, winking, he replied, "You bet your legendary sweet beautiful ass, Bonita."

I smirked and said, "He's just this nice boy from Mississippi. He was real pleasant, perfectly harmless. I liked him."

"My, but you are trusting."

"He's staying here, around back in room four."

"So he walked right up to you at the store? How's it he recognized you so rightfully?"

"My guns, is what he said. I imagine he put the puzzle together when the rest of me matched up with them. I have been described in the papers, as you well know. You yourself told me my guns give me away."

"Yeah, okay. That's right, I have. And there's a price on your head, so let's just say I'm uncomfortable with it."

"He's very nice. I truly did like him instantly. I promised I'd give him back the book. You can come along with me and see for yourself."

"Think I will…"

"I think you'll like him. He's perfectly agreeable."

"You got some sort of fondness for this boy?" he teased. "Some sorta, I don't know…*infatuation*?"

I felt my cheeks go hot with color and I punched him on the arm for spite. He flinched and I heard him gasp.

"Dammit! You wacked me right where I'm bruised!"

"I'm sorry, I am, but it serves you right! You should not make such fun of me like that."

"Believe me, I'll remember that for next time."

"Anyhow, no, Bill. He was just pleasant is all. His friends, however, I couldn't say. They seemed a bit rough around the edges. Of course I didn't speak with any of them, but I think they may be of a lewd nature."

"What makes you say so?"

"When we walked out together they pulled themselves in real tight, staring at us, whispering and laughing. I'm plenty familiar with that sort of behavior in men."

Billy scoffed and said, "Let's get on with it so I can meet this kid."

We left the room and walked around back. Jimmy and his friends were standing outside their room on the roundabout porch, talking. I could see that Jimmy was taller than all the boys even as he leaned against the wall smoking a rolled cigarette. When he saw us approaching he smiled immediately, involuntarily, pushing himself from the wall and standing up straight as an arrow as he was greeted by my presence. He removed his hat and walked down the porch away from his friends to meet us.

"Howdy, Lucy! I didn't expect to see you already! I'm glad for it, though!"

I looked over at Billy to catch his reaction at Jimmy's enthusiasm. He appeared unmoved. Jimmy looked to Billy and made a dangerously wild assumption. "Holy damn! You're the Kid!? You must be! It's a pleasure to meet you, sir!"

Billy looked at me and enthusiastically snorted at the idea of being called "sir".

"How'd you know a thing like that?" Billy asked.

"Oh, I know it must be you. You're with Lucy, so it's gotta be you!"

Billy took this in stride and accepted the child-like exuberance the boy couldn't help but offer.

"Well, there's plenty of us with Lucy. Anyway, call me Billy, that'll do just fine."

Kneading his hat nervously again with his fingers, Jimmy replied, "Well…okay then." Then, as if trying on a new pair of shoes or shirt he said the name out loud to himself. "*Billy.*"

Billy gave me an odd look before looking back to Jimmy. "So you're the boy Lucy here's told me about, I suspect," Billy eyed him, attempting to detect any fractures within the boy's seemingly pleasant countenance.

"She told you about me?" Jimmy asked hopefully, staring at me pleasantly.

"Don't get all excited there, friend. I only asked her where she got that book from and she told me."

Billy and Jimmy each stood there a moment staring at one another, Jimmy smiling amicably, Billy's smile patronizing and distrustful.

"So, I didn't catch your name," Billy explained.

"Oh, I'm sorry, I guess I didn't give it."

"Yeah, that'd be my guess, too."

"It's James Moffey. But my friends, they call me Jim."

"Okay Moffey, what is it you're all doing out in these parts? Just passing through?"

"Just passing around, actually. Moving from place to place, and then back again. We're just real casual like."

A voice then sounded from behind Jimmy.

"Passing *around* the law."

The other boys all laughed at this crafty repartee, with the exception of Jimmy, who frowned and seemed nervous. I recognized the boy who had joined our discussion: Finnegan Flynn. His was a perfect example of what I explained to Billy about being rough around the edges. That accent of his—it was nearly identical to Jimmy's, but his drawl was by far more lazy. He was a real character, coming off as a real tough piece. Whether or not he did so because he wanted to impress Billy was something I could not tell. And honestly, it didn't matter. Billy was indifferent.

"That a fact?" Billy asked him.

"Yeah, so what if it is?" Finnegan answered, impertinent. "You all the Regulators?" Finnegan sucked upon his cigarette.

How boorish he was.

"Well, the two of us are not us *all*, but you'd be accurate to presume we're part of them," remarked Billy, snidely.

"Yeah? Well, why is it you gotta girl running around with ya's? I mean, that's a bit unusual, ain't it? I hear tell she's got a lotta men. She there to lay with? That I could understand. To keep her around as you all do she must be one fine lay. I'd see fit to keepin' one myself for reasons such as those, but odds are I'd tire of her and shoot her dead before she had a chance to whine about it. You know how women are—always talking and bitching about something or another."

I looked at Billy, his hand dangerously close to his Colt. I looked to his eyes and saw nothing there as they stared at Finn, unblinking. With the exception of his twitching fingers, Billy didn't move a muscle, and Finn either didn't notice how dire his situation was, or he was putting Billy to the test by ignoring his fierce intimidation, showing off how unimpressed he was with the Kid.

Finn went on. "But I'd sure be interested to know this one you got in the biblical sense, so long as you'll be taking her back along with the rest of ya before she tries my nerves. Ideally though, it's not a bad idea to drag a whore around with ya; makes things convenient."

I continued looking at Billy, my heart nearly bolting from my chest as it beat so terrifyingly fast for not knowing how violently Billy would react to this remarkable insult. He stepped past Jimmy and put his face close to Finny's.

"Lucy's a lady. I hear words like that come from your mouth again and I promise you they'll be your last. As it stands I'm giving you a break because Lucy hates it when I lose my temper. So I won't kill you, long as you apologize to her."

Finnegan dragged long and hard on his cigarette as he stared at me, squinting against the glare of the sun which had accompanied our gathering in the past fifteen minutes as it was on its way down into sunset.

Inhaling his allowance of smoke, Finn held it then exhaled, taking his time before speaking.

"Gee…I'm real sorry, Lucy. I just suppose I jumped the gun a little. You must be as pristine as the Virgin herself, I'll bet."

Before anyone could react Billy pulled his gun and cocked the hammer, putting it directly into Finnegan's face, right between his eyes.

"Apologize!"

I put my head down while Jimmy stared wide-eyed at the confrontation between Billy and Finnegan.

"For God's sake, Finn, apologize, *please*," I begged in a small voice as I stared down at my boots. *Please God, don't let Billy kill anybody else*…I could stand Finny's insult so long as it didn't get Billy into any more trouble.

"You deaf? I just did," he returned.

Inwardly I flinched. Finnegan's cocky response, I knew, would try Billy's patience even further.

Billy yelled, "*No*! Apologize the right way—and mean it! Look her in the eye!"

Finnegan behaved like a fool. He did his best not to betray the slightest bit of fear, but I could see that his knees faltered a bit and he lost his balance, making out as if he meant to shift his weight. But his cigarette was quivering in his fingers.

"I'm sorry. Truly," he looked in my direction and apologized again. "Lucy, I'm real sorry. I just ain't never seen a girl ride with so many men and get some fame under her belt without playing what God give'er to offer. My apologies," he nodded at me, and Billy, satisfied, replaced the hammer, putting his gun back into its scabbard.

"Damn," said Finnegan to Billy. "You're high-strung, ain't ya?"

"I am when it comes to assholes. You don't know her reasons for being here, and it would be in your best interest to remember that and treat her like a lady."

Finnegan nodded and said that would be fine.

"So," Billy began. "You boys are 'passing *around* the law'? What's that supposed to mean?"

"Killed a man," Finnegan replied glibly, obviously proud to lay this fact out to the regulated Kid himself as though it were a prestigious badge of honor meant to impress the notorious boy who stood before him and who had threatened his life. Finn was attempting to hint that he could be a killer, too. "He had quite the nerve and all to steal my horse."

Billy simply looked at him, unimpressed. Noticing this, Finnegan challenged Billy, looking directly into his eyes with menace before taking another toke from his cigarette and throwing it to the ground to crush it beneath his boot heel.

Jimmy stood quietly. By the expression on his face and the sweat that had formed upon his brow and around his open collar I could see that he was alarmed, and that he hadn't trusted Finnegan to open his mouth. The other boys, Rufus and Engel, had approached, but I could not know how long they had been standing there, for this was the first time I took any notice of their presence. Before now I was caught up in what was happening between Finnegan and Billy.

"Well, it was nice meetin' y'all—makin' your acquaintance and all that," Finnegan said, sarcastically adding, "The Lincoln County Regulators, I'll be."

As he walked away the other boys followed. His style immediately set him on Billy's unlikable side. Jimmy spoke to Billy and offered his apology for what Finnegan had said about me.

"Finny doesn't seem to have any carin' for what others might feel—he just says what's on his mind. But he don't mean what he says so much. I know it was...it was wrong to say what he'd done, but in truth, he was being honest. He just don't know, or doesn't care, when to keep his mouth shut," Jimmy rubbed the back of his neck as he struggled to explain. "He's gotten us into some real bad scrapes talkin' like he does. I tried to tell him it don't go with social particulars..."

"I'll bet," replied Billy, disdainfully. "You can go ahead and chalk this up to another real bad scrape that he's gotten y'all into. But there ain't any need to apologize for your friend, Moffey. You don't need to worry so much about handling him. I'll take care of it, you can believe that," Billy put his arm around my shoulders and brought me close, lifting the brim of my hat with his nose and kissing me by my temple.

Jimmy seemed uneasy by what Billy had just said, and I felt bad for him. Jimmy seemed like a real nice sort, after all.

"We're heading off to meet up with the other boys to get something to eat. You're welcome to come along, if you'd like," I offered.

Jimmy looked at me and the smile I had begun to associate with him returned. He seemed truly excited. "Yeah? Really?"

"Yeah. Really," Billy replied.

"Oh, I would definitely love that!" Jimmy gave a twittering laugh over his excitement at the invitation.

"Get washed up and meet us over at the Kavanaghs'. You know them?" I asked.

Jimmy shook his head and replied that he did not.

Billy instructed him. "Their house is just three down on the left after you turn down White Cat Road. There's a U.S. Flag posted over the porch."

We started back to our room when I turned to Jimmy, remembering, "Oh, Jimmy! Your book! Here…"

I held the book out in an effort to hand it back to him. He smiled at me again and said, "I want you to have it. It's yours."

"No, I wouldn't take it from you. You said you liked it so much."

"And I do, but I like you more. I want you to have it, really. Think of it as a gift, from me."

Kitty Kavanagh was a devout Roman Catholic Mexican woman who had married an Irish Protestant. She changed her name from Catherine to Katherine, and married Dylan Kavanagh, a Confederate soldier during the Civil War, when she was eighteen. They had been married nearly ten years and were still very much in love. They had three young children, one girl and two boys, who were all raised Roman Catholics as their mother had been.

Their house was clean, dry, and tidy, but small. Henry and Fred had been staying on with them, and the Kavanagh's were only too happy to welcome any of the Regulators as guests despite the family's need to make do with what little they had. They were honored to have us and refused any compensation, but one or the other of us would find a way to slip a dollar amount here and there amongst their belongings. Many of the men paid for room and board in homes elsewhere.

Billy knew the Kavanagh's well and he would not turn them down when invited to supper as this would be impolite. He would bring me along with him, but despite the invitation I had extended to Jimmy, I now felt concern with having him there with us; one more mouth to feed. But Billy would explain and of course we would see to it that the family was repaid their generosity.

Upon entering the house Kitty beamed at Billy, "¡Billy! ¿Cómo estás? ¿Quién es tu invitado?" (*How are you? Who is your guest?*)

Billy hugged her with fierce sincerity before answering in Spanish, "¿Cómo estás cariño? ¿Crees que tienes un poco de espacio extra?" (*How are you, dear? Do you have extra room?*)

"Billy! ¡Sí! Cualquier cosa por ti!" (*Of course! Anything for you!*)

Billy tipped his hat, "Gracias, preciosa!" (*Thank you, beautiful!*)

The Kavanagh's were extremely generous people. Their adobe-style Mexican kitchen was very compact, but we managed to fit the number of us at the table just the same. The kitchen was rustic, and though I had become accustomed to the provincialism of the homes of the west, I still found the small quarters unnerving.

I sat, squeezed in between Billy and Jimmy; Jimmy on my left and Billy on my right. Jimmy sat quietly with his head down, staring at his hat which he placed in his lap, his lips poised in a polite smile. Billy's head was turned away from me as he spoke with Henry and Fred, his left hand resting tenderly upon my thigh to let me know that I was on his mind while his attention was given elsewhere. I adored this particular gesture, this trait of his. He always found small ways such as this to show his affection for me whenever he could not be open about his feelings. I turned to Jimmy.

"Jimmy," I said.

Jimmy lifted his head and looked at me, expectantly.

"You mentioned to me that you're from Mississippi."

"Yes," he grinned reservedly. "I'm from a place called Tupelo."

"Does your family still reside there?"

He went quiet for a moment, looking down again and clearing his throat uneasily. It appeared as though he were suddenly troubled. It was clear that he did not want to speak of Mississippi, and so I changed the subject. "Where is it you intend to head to from here?"

"Oh, I couldn't be sure. Like I mentioned, we're just drifting, is all."

"It would seem one could not drift so forever. I do hope you plan to settle yourself some place, soon."

Looking at me, he suddenly blushed and smiled. "I can't help but notice that you've been calling me Jimmy," he happily pointed out.

I felt a little mixed-up by his statement. "You told me that your friends call you Jim."

"Oh yes, they sure do, but not like you say it," smiling, he added, "I like it, '*specially* the way you say it. You've only called me James since we met…until now, that is."

"How do I say it?" I wondered.

"Don't know. I just like how you call me Jimmy," he thought a moment. "It makes me feel sorta special," his face colored.

"I see. Well…I have a habit of playing variations of men's names as I see fit, so I'm glad you don't mind."

"Mind? Oh, no! Why, I'd frame it if I could."

Billy looked at me and I looked back at Billy. He gave me a funny look in regards to Jimmy's bizarre testimonial, furrowing his brow and smirking as if to suggest that Jimmy was a ridiculous, hopeless little Nancy boy and all soft on the inside. I turned away from him and gave my attention back to Jimmy, blowing off Billy's inferred cynicism.

Kitty and her daughter, Rosa, walked around the table setting down the plates and dipping sauces for us. I offered to help as it seemed I ought, but was turned down as I was their guest. They put out a plate of tortillas, piled high, and plates filled with chicken and pulled pork, bowls heaped with beans and corn and other vegetables, and a plate containing jalapeño peppers was served. Kitty and her children took a few small ones to eat with their supper, as did Billy.

Billy had sweetly fixed a plate for me with food I could stomach. I had an aversion to these spicy dishes and he knew exactly which Mexican fare I had trouble tolerating. After he had finished selecting my meal, he offered me butter for the bread he had placed on my plate.

Silverware clattered and scraped against terracotta dishes, and a mixture of Spanish and English conversations went around the table. With everyone so ensconced in discussions with one another, I took the opportunity to talk with Jimmy given that all the chatter had provided some semblance of privacy.

"Are all of your friends from Tupelo, like you?" I asked.

"Just Finny. We grew up together. We's just like brothers, he and I. Tupelo was too small, so Finny says to me, he says, 'Jim, let's turn outta here and make our way out west. We could make it to California and stake a claim and even find a gold or silver mine.'"

"But instead now you're running from the law…"

"I suppose so. It's true, what Finn said, about killing that man. But we left Tupelo for the west just the same. Now we're just drifting. But I reckon we could still make it to California, yet."

"I hope you'll pardon my saying so, but you don't seem anything like Finny, or those other boys. They seem like a few real hard cases. How is it you're friends with them?"

"Well, it's like I said…Finn and I grew up together, and the other two we met along the way."

Nodding, I contemptuously said, "This place is a hotbed of troublesome activity after all. I imagine it would be best to pass through here with such…" I looked at him, searching for the right word for the sake of accordance, "challenging men as your friends seem to be. In fact, I can even attest to it."

I arranged the cloth upon my lap curtly as I carelessly cast a disapproving look around the table at my friends who had dumbfounded me as I saw they casually looked back, hearing what I had just said. I had not realized the table had grown so uncharacteristically quiet. They sat staring with interest in me and Jimmy's conversation, but I sensed an idea that they had a specific interest in what it was that I might say about them next.

"You're only passing through Patricio then?" I quickly added, awkwardly turning back to Jimmy.

"Well…" he looked at me and around the table with uncertainty as the men seemed poised to cause him discomfort no matter what he should say to me next.

"Go on, Jimmy, she ain't gonna bite your head off!" said Henry in a raised voice. "She's seen the devil out here—she damn near shook his hand—so there ain't about nothing you can say to her that's likely to offend."

With the exception of Billy, who seemed less than pleased by this truth, the men laughed and I gave Henry a nasty look as Jimmy replied, "It's just...well, I wouldn't mind staying around here so much," he stared at me with a self-effacing smile that lacked pretension, and as he studied me, his expression was full of honesty, though his eyes seemed far away, as though he had drifted into a pleasant thought, and I found that I was fond of and impressed with him for his exploitive daring towards the Regulators and his lack of embarrassment in being confronted by their deliberate, ill-mannered conduct. It seemed, at least at present, they had a complete inability to rattle him.

An exhalation of petulance came from somewhere down the table and only then did he decide to switch tack. He shook his head, saying, "I reckon that's about right, Lu. Finn and I don't seem to have so much in common. I'd bet you got me there!" he nodded his head for emphasis and I turned from him to snub Billy for such poor behavior on behalf of them all, but my attention was called upon when I heard Kitty insist that Jimmy eat more. I looked at Jimmy's plate. Most of what was placed there was nearly gone. He accepted Kitty's offer and went about piling on more food. He looked, after all, to be one who didn't eat often.

Once supper was finished we thanked the Kavanaghs and I headed back to my room at the Old Ruidoso. The boys wandered off to find the others and play faro in order to make us some money. Jimmy, as far as I knew, went along with them.

Back in the room I sat down with a piece of paper and a pencil I had bought at the general store:

Alexander A. McSween,
Lincoln New Mexico
April, 10, 1878

Dear Mr. McSween,

I, Elucia Grey Alexis Howard, of sound mind and body, do hereby give you permission to sell the property specified in the deed of which you now hold within your offices. Mr. J. Chisum shall be the property's rightful recipient now that our beloved John is gone.

I should like to move the sale of the land at $2.50 per acre. The deed states the land is made up of five-hundred acres which should bring me a price of $1,250.00, less the %10 of the wages owed you.

I should like for you to sell this land as quickly as possible,

The funds from the sale are to be set up in an account under my name at The Exchange Bank in White Oaks.

If Mr. Chisum expects to use this war as leverage to bring down the selling price, please advise him that I have no intention of lowering the price whatsoever. He can either have five-hundred acres, or he can pine for it when another buyer purchases the tract. I am certain to find another fit buyer as there is no shortage of businessmen in the territory or heading out from the east to stake a claim. From what I understand, Mr. J.J. Dolan would have interest in the property, and I will not hesitate to make him an offer should Mr. Chisum decline.

Sincerely yours
Elucia Grey Alexis Howard

I drifted off to sleep and awoke to the door being opened and shut very loudly. I grabbed for one of my guns.

"Shh, shh, no, it's just me, Lu, Billy. Look, I have something for you."

I rubbed my sleepy, bleary eyes, wondering what time it was when Billy came and sat by me upon the bed.

"What time is it," I asked.

"Nine-thirty. Look…" He pointed to a section in a paper he was carrying.

"Yeah, so?"

"So, read it!"

"How do you expect me to do so when there's nary a light in this room?"

"Here, let me fix that up for you."

His eyes were adjusted to the dark better than my own as he had been awake in the darkening hours all this time. He opened the bedside table and pulled out a box of matches. Removing the glass chimney from the oil lamp he then removed a match from its box and flicked its head against his thumb, lighting the wick, the glare hurting my eyes. He replaced the chimney and sat near to me on the bed again.

"What is it? Could this not have waited?"

"I suppose, but you're up now. Read it."

I waited for my eyes to focus, rubbing them and shaking the sleep from my head.

"You might get a kick out of this. Hell! I know I did!"

My eyes were still unadjusted, and Billy, impatient, grabbed the paper back from me and said, "Here, let me read it to you."

Gen. Addison Howard of New York, father of Elucia "Lucky Lu" Alexis Grey Howard, has withdrawn the two thousand dollar reward offered for his daughter's safe return to New York in April as Alexander Anderson

McSween, Esq. of Lincoln Co., lawyer and personal friend of the Howards, advised Gen. Howard that he had turned his guardianship over to the McSweens', and therefore, to pursue his daughter via monetary means by issuing compensation to the individual(s) responsible for her return would place him on the wrong side of the law as Ms. Howard is now a bona fide citizen of the New Mexican Territory. Mr. McSween also provided certainty to Gen. Howard that the reward was not only more likely to result in more bloodshed, but place his daughter in further danger.

Mr. and Mrs. McSween have agreed to relinquish Ms. Howard's guardianship back to her family through the proper legal channels. This system will be extensive for the Howard family, but would remove any chance of dubious relations from all parties involved.

One of Gen. Howard's primary concerns is that his daughter is being kept in the company of the Lincoln County Regulators, one of the most feared posse's in the territory. Gen. Howard fears that his daughter has been taken by this gang of men as their captive. Mr. McSween has assured Gen. Howard that his daughter has been placed within the custody of the Regulators to insure her safety as they are most qualified, being able-bodied, capable gun-fighters. This plan was put into motion when Ms. Howard's life had been threatened in earnest by the Santa Fe Ring as her caravan made its way south towards the train depot of the Union Pacific and Mr. McSween believes absolutely that Ms. Howard's life was spared due to the diligence of the Regulators. Mr. McSween explained that the Lincoln County Regulators had been under Mr. Tunstall's employ and had been deputized men until Governor Samuel Axtel removed their legal status as a result of their attempt to bring in two of the men responsible for Mr. Tunstall's death.

Mr. McSween allowed that the Regulators are indeed a fine bunch of boys, and that Gen. Howard should feel at ease that they are the group of men handling his daughter's safety. Mr. McSween explained the corruption that is the Santa Fe Ring and how its arms enfold the town and its inhabitants, and how the Regulators mean to correct that corruption while keeping Ms. Howard safe as the people embrace the Regulators as the peoples' champions.

At present, Gen. Howard is anxious to regain guardianship of his daughter so that he may bring her home. Judicial proceedings are expected to take place this upcoming August. As it stands, there is no longer a reward placed upon the return of Ms. Howard, and the dogs of the military have been called off.

My father called off the militant arms and staid the bounty hunters—the news had me staggered! I asked if we were free from worry in that regard, providing the news had been widespread enough, and Billy assured me that it most likely was, considering he was quite certain that my father would see to it that it hit every newspaper within range of Lincoln.

"Come on! Put those boots on; we gonna go celebrate!"

I smiled at him and leapt off the bed, pulling my boots on and buckling up my guns. Once out the door we passed Minxie who followed alongside us and entered the batwings of The Keeper's Inn. Billy and Minxie stepped over to the side by the faro table near the entrance, and I stood and took note of Henry Brown, Frank MacNab, and Big John at the bar with drinks. Fred Waite and "Dirty Steve" Stephens were each sitting at different poker tables. I spied Jimmy standing at a table behind Finn and next to those other two friends of his, Engle and Rufus. Jimmy looked in my direction, smiled, and waved. He leaned down and said something to Finn then walked towards me, and as he did so I could hear Finn loudly complaining, losing another hand apparently to the same man.

"It's nice to see you here! How are you?" Jimmy beamed.

Billy, suddenly behind me, proudly placed his hands upon my shoulders and said, "She's a free woman, ain't you heard?"

"A free woman?" Jimmy furrowed his brow, confused.

"Completely free!" replied Billy. "She's a full-on citizen of the New Mexican Territory. Just like me!" he leaned in and kissed me on the cheek impishly.

"Well, that's nice to hear, then, I guess," he cleared his throat. "I'm happy you're here."

I bent my head in appreciation of his comment. There was a house band playing in the corner—the place was alive with music, lights, and laughter, and I was in such a pleasant mood! Billy turned back around to buck the tiger.

"So…you're a free woman now. What's that mean?"

"It means that my father has no control over me. At least not until August, that is. He was out to drag me back east, but, turns out he can't do that legally just yet." A feverish laugh that I did not recognize escaped my lips.

"Oh." Something flickered in Jimmy's face. Perhaps I only imagined it as the look was fleeting, but I was certain that his smile waivered. "Well, I'm dreadful glad to hear you'll be sticking around, then," he said honestly enough.

He asked if I'd like a drink, and I told him I would like a sarsaparilla. He walked off to the bar to get it for me and I turned towards Billy. "So? How goes the game?"

"Already won," he smiled back.

"What about the others?"

"They ain't doing too poorly neither."

"This game has me absolutely confused."

Enveloped in the game he quipped, "Well, lucky for you, I grew up playing it."

I laughed at his sincerity. "Truer words were never spoken."

He quickly flicked his eyes back-and-forth between me and the game, attempting to keep his attention on both when he said, "I see the way that Moffey is with you. That friend of his, what was his name? Fred?"

"Finn."

"He's a real problem. Moffey's just fine enough, but that other boy's a flaw in any friendship you intend to have with him. Be careful and watch out for that one…Finn."

I mock saluted him to let him know I caught his meaning and walked off to meet Jimmy who was back with a full glass for me.

We walked off together toward an open space by a window near the band. I took a sip of my drink and set it down beside me on the sill and Jimmy and I began to play around with a two-step.

"He never takes his eyes off you, does he?" he asked.

I vaguely turned my head towards Billy asking, "Who?"

He nodded in the direction I had looked. "Billy."

"No, he does not. The situation is a bit difficult for the lot of us, and I bring extra worry, my being a woman and all that goes with it," I rolled my eyes lightheartedly and smirked. "They're concerned for my wellbeing, but I can understand that."

I put my head down and watched our feet move to the rhythm of the music.

"I figure he's got somethin' on that," replied Jimmy.

I looked back up. "What's that?"

"Takin' that extra care with you. I know I'd never take my eyes offa you," he smiled pleasantly.

"Well, the others take good care of me also, but Billy, he takes extra special care of me. We grew close in Lincoln."

"He really has you sown up, doesn't he? I barely see you without him."

"Well, I can't say that I blame him. I'm here for the same reasons they are, technically anyway. He doesn't like me to be out of his sight often."

"Why's that?"

"What? The reasons we are here, or why he doesn't like me out of his sight."

"The first thing."

"J.J. Dolan and his army of crooked politicians in Lincoln, that's what. They killed my fiancé."

"Oh. I'm sorry to hear it."

"It's okay. I'm sorry it happened—it was brutal enough, but my heart was spared any true pain."

He looked at me strangely, and so I answered the question he seemed to be asking with his eyes.

"We were arranged to be married; I was sent here by my father. That's how I had come to meet Billy and most of these boys—most of them worked for my fiancé."

He nodded to let me know that he followed my story. We heard Finn over the din and turned to look just as he called out the man he had been losing to as a cheat and a fight ensued. The two arguing men were told to take it outside, and so they did, and I picked the conversation back up.

"It came down to war, really. I was called back to New York, but the word was put out on my life."

"You mean this J.J. Dolan guy put a bounty on you?"

"I guess you could say that, only it's a little more involved. There's a circle of men in Lincoln, called the Santa Fe Ring. The town sheriff was a part of it—he's the one who put the word out on me."

"Was?"

I ignored the question.

"After they had my fiancé killed to remove the competition he presented, the boys here and Billy, and quite a few others, were deputized. The sheriff placed Billy and a few of the others in jail when they went to him to present warrants for the arrests of those responsible for murdering John—that was my fiancé's name, John—but instead of allowing them to serve their warrants, he tossed them straight into jail instead. They meant to make an example of me as well, wanting to punish me after I called out the sheriff as a coward for doing such a thing. An even longer story made short, the Regulators took me for fear of the threats made by The Ring."

"Wow! Sounds like an awful place, Lincoln."

"Well…it's the west. They get to make their own laws out here," I sniffed, disgusted. "So I never made it to the train back to New York, The Lincoln County Regulators got to me first. I can't complain, though. I wanted to be here, with Billy. Once I met him I didn't want to go back."

"If it's not too presumptuous…"

I waited for him to go on but he grew quiet and contemplative. We stopped moving and I asked him, "What is it, Jimmy?"

"Well, I wonder, are you and Billy… You said you were very close and all, and seeing how you're always together, I thought, maybe, you and he might be…"

A gunshot went off outside and Jimmy muttered "shit", letting go of me and running towards and out of the door.

I hurried over to peer out and see what the fray was all about, finding myself standing near to Henry, Minx, and Billy, who were still focused on playing faro despite the disturbance. Things like this often happened; guns went off all the time—it was never really worth quitting what one was doing to have a look.

I saw Finn standing over the body of the man he had called a cheat, screaming and pointing at him with his gun, though the man looked as good as dead to me. His friends, Jimmy included, pulled Finn away in an attempt to get him out of the sight of others.

That was the last I saw of Jimmy that night. I thought it would be the last I'd see of him for good, but the next day after the dawn grew into noon we were all sitting on the porch outside of the boarding house watching the funeral procession of the dead man when I saw him walk over.

"Howdy," he raised his hat.

I was mindlessly chewing on a pencil and looked up, surprised to see him standing there. Billy and some of the others looked at him as well. I looked back to the people following the casket and saw a woman in black wailing into a handkerchief, two small children trailing her.

I looked back at Jimmy. "How is it you're still here?" I asked. "Where are your friends?"

"Took off."

"You didn't go with them?"

He shook his head. "I'll catch up with them soon enough."

Minxie was leaning on the railing watching the crowd of mourners. "Blimey...the whole town's out there, ain't they?"

Though the rainy season was still off by two months' time, and it was fairly cold, the sky remained a dark shade of gray.

"Do you suspect it will rain today?" I asked Billy.

He shook his head. "Just cloud cover. Don't feel like rain...or sleet."

I nudged Billy over and slid along with him to allow a spot for Jimmy. He thanked me and sat watching the procession along with us.

"Anybody know his name?" I asked aloud. I didn't get an answer, but I saw Dirty Steve out there with the funeral-goers. I suspected that he must have known the man.

The Constable, a sympathizer, Jose Chavez Y Chavez, approached us. He lifted his hat. "Any of you boys responsible for this?"

The boys all shook their heads in response, and I looked down, knowing who it was who had done it along with Jimmy, who only stared straight ahead.

"Chavez, I never really got a good look," said Big Jim.

"Man's name was Gavin Greenfield. Near as we can tell from a few witnesses he was in an argument over a card game," replied Chavez.

"Ain't that a damn shame?" spat Henry. "Man can't sit down and play a game of cards without the ante going up to the grave after," he shook his head cynically.

"If any of you know anything, I advise you to say so. You know you're all pretty well known in these parts; you might be interested in keeping the fingers pointed the other way. I sure am—don't need any trouble from this place to add to any woes." Chavez stood a moment trading pleasantries, considering, then tipped his hat and walked off.

I looked at Jimmy, who looked the other way.


"Billy…"

"Yes Bonita?"

We sat inside of our room, each respectively occupying ourselves; Billy reading the news and I reading my book. I wanted to ask him something, but he hadn't looked up from his paper when he answered me, and so I thought about changing my mind. But it bothered me so that I knew who killed that man and said nothing. I knew that Patricio was a safe place for us, and that Chavez was right: That if any of us knew, it would be best to say so. I did not want any kills under our belt if we had not been responsible for them. I did not want to disappoint Jimmy, and though he would have nothing to fear as I would not so much as mention his name, my loyalties lie with Billy and the Regulators. We had to watch our backs, and our plight was too important to ignore and risk being cast out or accused.

I was about to turn around and think upon this some more when he finally looked up and at me and said, "For God sakes, what is it?"

I stared at him a moment longer, wondering if I should make an excuse to give myself more time to think, but I decided Billy would know what to do.

"That man? The one who was killed the other night?"

"Yeah, I remember. What about him?" he turned his attention back to the paper.

"What if I know who did it?"

He looked up at me as if startled. "What do you mean 'what if'?"

"It was that Finny guy. The one who insulted me on the street."

"Yeah, I know which one he is. I told you that one was trouble."

"What do I do?"


Billy walked me to the Constable's office and we spoke to Chavez. At Billy's urging, I told him what I knew of the murderer, and Chavez did not hesitate to get a gathering of men together to ride out after Finn. He asked if I knew where he might be. I told him that I did not, that if I did, I would most certainly tell him. I told him that I knew he had been in Seven Rivers not all that long ago, which Chavez concluded meant he may be headed north, still. He thanked me for the information and I curtsied to acknowledge his thanks.

When I told all that I knew Billy and I took a walk along the street when he remarked, "Well, that's a dead giveaway if I ever saw one."

"What?"

"That little thing you just did in there," Billy gestured and bent his knees, sure-footed, mimicking me.

"Well, it's ridiculous when you do it. Why is it a giveaway?"

"See something like that and you know a person is a tenderfoot. Try to avoid that and act like you know what you're doing out here, wouldja please?"

"Should I tell Jimmy? Maybe let him give his friend a heads up?"

"No, don't you say anything. I don't want you involved in the mess."

"Then why bother making me tell at all?"

"Hell, I don't want this on your conscious, either. I wouldn't want it on mine."

"But, if it were you, wouldn't you want to be warned by a friend that a posse was coming to hang you?"

"I reckon so. But the guy killed a man over a game of cards. He ain't a good guy. I can't rightly say I care much for what happens to him, especially after the way he spoke to you, and in front of me, no less."

"Billy, if it had been you and someone kept information from me that could help me protect you…"

"I understand—I know," he placed his hand affectionately upon my shoulder. "But still…"

I agreed with Billy, but told him that I did like Jimmy very much, and out of respect for him, I wanted to allow him to warn the friend with whom he had grown up, even if that friend truly *was* lower than a dog. Billy said he understood my feelings on the subject and agreed that Jimmy was decent enough. I knew he could see it troubled me to keep a secret like this from a friend who might benefit from it.

"I'll tell him, Lucy. Okay?"

I smiled at him in thanks. It wasn't about Finny. I couldn't have given a rat's piss about him. But Jimmy, he must have seen something in Finn to stay by his side all of these years. I only wanted to respect my friendship with Jimmy by allowing him to respect his friendship with Finn.

"Wow…I can't believe you told," Jimmy removed his hat and bowed his head in astonishment.

"No?" responded Billy, with acerbic glee.

"Someone like you who knows what it's like—"

"I ain't *never* killed a man over a card game. I don't know what any of that's like."

"Sure…but there's the other part. The law! I know the law wants you all desperately—suppose I let slip where they could look you up?"

Billy stepped into him and Jimmy fell back. A memory of mine was piqued from that night in the saloon when Jimmy and I danced together.

"Suppose'n you did?" challenged Billy.

"I wouldn't. I ain't stupid. I know better than to do a foolish thing like that. But all the same…"

Billy put his face dangerously close to Jimmy's. "We ain't nothing like your friend. Anyway, put it this way, Moffey, I told you, so now you can go on ahead and warn him that a posse's been sent for him—if you get to him first."

Jimmy put his hat back on and turned to go.

"Jimmy! Wait!" I watched him stop and turn back around to face me.

"You knew about the money, didn't you? You read so much about me and all… you knew, didn't you?"

He looked at me, his eyes perplexed, but then I saw a glimmer of reckoning in them. He removed his hat again and hung his head in shame.

"And you want to lecture us about honor among thieves," I said bitterly. "I genuinely liked you, Jimmy." I folded my arms and turned to walk away.

"But I wouldn't have!"

I turned back around and faced him.

"Finny…he wanted to. I did, too. I'd've done it, until I had the chance to meet you and talk with you."

"You're breaking my heart, Jimmy," I angrily retorted.

"Before I knew you, what did I care? It's a lot of money, Lucy. We were just drifters without any roots. That money could have bought us quite a lot, and it wouldn't have harmed you, turning you in—"

"But it would have harmed my friends! You could have gotten them killed in your selfishness!" I yelled furiously, but Jimmy kept on talking, though this statement of mine cowed him even further as I saw his shoulders slump impossibly low.

"But after I saw you in that store and said your name; when I talked with you—I couldn't believe it," he proclaimed. "You were standing there right before me, and you were so real, and… and I…" His cheeks flushed red. "But Finny, he figured we hit pay dirt." He grew quiet.

"Well don't leave me hanging here, Jimmy. *Did* you hit pay dirt?" My question was scathing.

Jimmy stood there looking more and more ashamed and visibly growing more afraid of Billy as he kept glancing at him, afraid he might find any wayward moves. But still, Jimmy went on. "Finny knew we couldn't take you, that we weren't capable of the sort of fight it would mean. We were only four…"

I placed my palm to my forehead in realization. "That's why you asked if Billy was around!"

"I did too want to meet him. That was honest enough," he plead, looking in Billy's direction and being met with a cold stare. Then he looked to me without taking his eyes completely from Billy. "But after you gave me the slip when I asked if he was around, I knew that he couldn't have been far. I knew as much from all the reading I done that he was never far. And Finn, he figured, rightly so, that there was plenty more of you around. Anyway, I only asked about his whereabouts for show, in front of the boys."

"So what was it you planned to do?" I asked, indignant.

Billy stood there, watching the back-and-forth, half amused, half vexed, but he was as curious as I to know the details.

"Finny wrote a letter to the sheriff in Lincoln. He sent me to deliver it."

I looked at him incredulously. "So you're a liar, too! I thought you changed your mind."

Jimmy moved his mouth like a trout, attempting to stammer out his response. "I didn't do it! I didn't take it…I never mailed it!"

"Did that letter include the position of my friends?" I asked despondently, feeling vulnerable over my stupidity in the failed trust of a boy I hardly knew. Billy's ears pricked up.

"Yes," Jimmy quietly replied. "He wrote about all of you…he wanted all of the rewards. But Finny ain't worth nothin'! Why turn him in?"

"Aw, don't say he ain't worth nothing, Moffey. He's at least worth a hemp necktie, and a party to boot!" Billy wickedly stated before cruelly laughing.

Billy and I turned to go when Jimmy called out, imploring us to wait.

"I promise! I never mailed that letter! I didn't care about the money anymore, not after knowing you. Lucy, I know I haven't known you long, and maybe you'll believe that my fascination over you has gotten the better of me, but…"

"But what?" Billy asked, interested.

"I would never do anything to hurt her. Not ever! I would never want to have her taken away. She's…she's priceless!" Jimmy anxiously tapped his hat against his leg feeling exposed by professing to what must have amounted to what he believed was his love for me under such cruel circumstances.

I looked down, not wanting to look him in the eye. I felt poorly, caring for him the way I did. And though I was at first angry with him, I now felt ashamed. I couldn't deny that I understood his wanting to turn me in for such a large sum of money without knowing me, but… "If you were so fascinated by me, Jimmy, before you met me, why would you want to put me in such a position? Wouldn't you want to see me persevere?

Isn't that what most men want for their heroes?" I asked, a bit too sarcastically than I had meant to.

"Yeah. Well, I guess you got me there—"

"I know it!" I yelled, "I always got you there!"

"I suppose I can't consider myself a true admirer if I was willing to turn you in," he said, defeated.

He placed his hat back upon his head and turned to get going. I stared after him, feeling regretful. I looked at Billy who read my expression precisely. To his credit, his expression conveyed a look of compassion for me. Maybe even for Jimmy, too.

# 16

## May, 1878

Frank MacNab was the now self-declared and undisputed captain of the Regulators, and it was under his jurisdiction that our next course of action was to move down to Seven Rivers where a number of our posse resided. Evidently, the agreed headquarters of the Regulators was the McSween household, and Frank had sent word to Alex regarding our plan to head to Seven Rivers, but before doing so, we would make our way to the McSweens' to convene there, first.

A concern of mine was that we were heading back into the belly of the beast, but my concern was dismissed, as always, as it was agreed among everyone that I knew nothing of this situated war. It was true that I had found trouble concentrating on the mundane details—I was not particularly interested in vigilante justice; it was not the reason I wished to be here. I made no windows into the souls of the men where the war was concerned; I only wanted to be hidden away from it all. I was not devout in its supposed requisite obligation and yet, though I did not understand these men and their need to pay back blood with blood, I would follow them still despite the danger—I would rather be dead than return to the stifling life I had waiting for me in New York, and to me, what was life anyway if Billy were not there? If Billy had no plans to stick with me, as his mind was full of all the same hateful things as the others', then I would stick with him, pure and simple. And I had to admit it wasn't always half bad. I had already, in such a short span of time, lived the freest life I had ever known! Was it worth taking a bullet for? I would have to say, unequivocally, yes. At this point, between Billy and me, our feet were both firmly planted in this campaign, though different reasons prevailed for us both; I was far more willing to leave it all behind than he. After all, he had given his word and I had not, nor would I ever.

We rode along the Rio Bonito on our way in to Lincoln, past a ranch belonging to man named Charlie Fritz. Ab Saunders, Frank Coe's brother in law, came with us. Frank Coe took off suddenly, riding a quick racing pony that took him directly past an ambush waiting there for us. He was fortunate: they allowed him to pass, believing him to be on his own and apart from our party which is what they had camped out to capture. Billy and I had been the farthest behind in the pack. When MacNab and

Saunders caught up and stopped to water their horses along the water gunfire broke out.

I heard the shots and something within me became intolerable and mean, and I spurred Middleton's horse as fast as I could. Billy, who was riding next to me, tried to reach out for my reigns but was unsuccessful. I was being driven by demons unknown, sick of all the fighting. I drove my horse hard, wanting to kill any who fired upon us. There was an animalistic growling from somewhere within the depths of me where the fires were stoked high somewhere way down in the very pit of my belly. I was intemperate.

Without thought I pulled my right-handed pistol, and as I ran along a shot burst forth and my horse, riding at such a quickened speed, violently stopped abruptly in mid-flight and rolled as he went down fast, a bullet penetrating him and throwing me to the ground. I felt an intense pain climb from my knee to my hip as I hit the ground remarkably.

I was captured along with Frank Coe and we were held at the Fritz ranch before being taken as prisoners into Lincoln and placed in the Dolan store.

They docked me with Frank Coe for the killing of Morton and Baker, as, said they, I had been involved, and imprisoned me in a back bedroom within the store. I could not speak to Frank as we were kept apart and had not had an opportunity to report anything we might have known to one another. I had heard via my captors, speaking amongst one another directly outside the door of the room I occupied, that MacNab had been killed on the run, and that Ab Saunders lay somewhere out there, shot and badly wounded.

In my room I stood upon my bed to look out of a window set high within the wall wondering what had happened to the others and fearing that, perhaps, along with myself, Frank, and Ab, they had indeed gotten Billy. My fears grew when I overheard Frank Coe plead with our captors to get Saunders who had been left to die where he fell. He begged them to let him die in comfort and "not out there alone."

My worries regarding Billy were spared, however, when I overheard Sheriff Co-peland speaking with one of the posse-men who had brought Frank and me in. They were standing right outside my room in the yard and directly below my window which was situated by the ranch's back door. They were smoking, for I could smell the unmistakable stench of cigarillos. Also in my favor, though my door leading into the hall was closed, it was not so terribly thick and I could hear them speaking in such careless tones as they continued to hover around my impermanent prison both inside and outside the house. They were using me to bait the Kid—they had mistaken Ab for Billy. They had not even so much as taken my guns from me, nor did they have any warrant of any kind. I was not a true prisoner.

Not sure of one voice from the other, I believed it must have been Dolan who said he had it on good authority that the Kid would come for me after the other voice had mentioned that he had obviously "slipped out". I prayed he was wrong and that Billy would not come, and then I believed that any worry I might have harbored in upsetting myself over this fear was unfounded because I knew there wasn't reason enough for him to come for me. He was not stupid. Brady was gone, and the death of Tunstall was by now under a federally funded investigation, and with my father's and John's father's own money intervening—the Tunstall family offering five-thousand for any man responsible for the death of his son, and my father's expenditure's in emancipating me from the guardianship of the McSween's—my profile was too high. My father's influence with and willingness to use U.S. militia to bring me home was enough on its own to keep me properly safe. I knew that this would liberate any unease from Billy and remove any threat of my peril from his mind.

Bored, I asked if I could please borrow a silver dollar which they had obliged me with. Sitting cross-legged on the edge of the bed I practiced flipping it over the backs of my fingers between my knuckles. I had seen Billy do this very often and I found it very interesting to watch. But my own dexterous fingers, a result of years' worth of playing piano, could not sustain the balance of the dollar and the coin kept falling to the floor with a clink, after which I had to repeatedly bend down and back up again to the point where I was giving myself the vapors, the pain in my leg being of no help either. I could not suss out the balance required for this game and I quit the effort as I was not interested in focusing on trivial parlor tricks. After one spends sixteen years of one's life being forced to jump through hoops, all one longs for is the freedom to do as one pleases.

When they had brought me supper I inquired after Saunders and was told they deployed one of Fritz's wagons to pick him up. I asked if I could go for a walk in the yard as my leg ached, and this I was allowed with an escort, of course. But after a short while, an hour or so, I was told I could go free.

I was offered an escort to the McSweens', but the property being only a stone's throw away, I initially declined. My declination was, however, disregarded.

In walking down Wortley Street, slight limp and all, over the din of Lincoln's bustling inhabitants I heard a low, familiar whistle come from John's store. Not wanting to draw attention to myself and give away Billy's position by looking towards the direction of the sound, but not wanting him to think I did not hear his call, I raised my hat from my head and wiped my brow, hoping that this signaled to him that I had indeed heard.

After entering the McSweens' and speaking with Susan's sister, I went back to my room and out the door, walking quickly to the corral behind the store and ignoring the shooting discomfort in my thigh. I saw Billy standing there on the back porch, arms folded, casual. I ran to him and he grabbed me, kissing and hugging me close, telling me how stupid I was to do such a thing and to never do it again. I wrapped my arms around his neck tightly as if I could secure him in this way, so very happy that he was in fact okay.

I related all that had happened at the Dolan store; that Frank was there, and how they had suspected Billy would come for me, and Billy confirmed to me that he would not have, that I was right in my presumption that he felt any danger I was in had passed considering Brady's expiration and the new publicity regarding the matter of the war. But he thought on it and said, "Then again, I'm not so sure that I ain't selfish enough to keep you anyhow."

He pulled me into the back room of the store John once owned and put me down upon the bed that Jim French had once hidden under, the nagging desire for one another after such a trying event very strong, removing each other's' clothes only insomuch that we could do as we pleased but still make a run for it if we had to, and the pleasure expanding to our bodies so great that Billy was careless, and my not knowing my fate come August, I thought I should get my hands on some of those Queen Anne's Lace seeds.

We redressed fully and lay there on the bed together, side-by-side, hands clasped tightly together. I thought we should go, but as ever was his plan, Billy decided we ought to wait things out. I worried they might search the store again hoping to find any Regulators hiding there, but Billy told me not to concern myself as there was no reason to believe that there had been any more of us coming down the Bonito and it would have been a wasted effort on their part, especially convinced as they were that he had turned out the other way. He explained that he had made it into Lincoln unseen. I asked him how he could be sure of this, and he stated the obvious—that no one had come looking. Surely someone would have mentioned seeing any conspicuous figures roaming about the town knowing that a few of the Regulators had been picked up just outside its limits over by the Fritz ranch. I pointed out the fact that Dolan was correct—that often, Billy was never far from me. He refuted this, telling me if Dolan believed he was nearby, then he may not have let me leave so quickly.

"Frank is dead," I reported.

"MacNab? I know."

"I think Ab Saunders as well, but I can't be sure. He was most certainly terribly wounded."

He nodded mindlessly and pulled my hand up to his lips and kissed it before putting it back down between us, still holding it tightly.

We waited through the night, and when we arose we began loading up on supplies before leaving the store. When we emerged it was to gunfire. Regulators were running off in different directions mounted on their horses—the chaos was absolute. I hadn't a horse; Billy went for his, taking me with him to the McSween's stables so that I could get my hands on one.

Once Alex's house-man had set me up we took off into the affray; the Regulators were firing upon a posse of men who were firing back. Billy argued for me to stay behind, and when I disregarded his command, he yelled again for me to run and stay back behind the corral of the store. I turned to him and screamed back that I was tired of idly watching the massacre of my friends. I was tired of being placed safely out of the way; my position now was do-or-die. Admittedly, I realized my self-imposed position was all arrogance, my "do-or-die" creed fashioned by puerile histrionics, but my emotions were suffused with outrage and fury. I took a place among the fight with the Regulators, pulling my guns and firing back at will along with my companions at any man I didn't recognize, though I was reckless and unchecked—this I knew.

During the fracas I saw an unattended Frank Coe come out of the Dolan store and join in with the fighting without the slightest hint of hesitation, and I had fortuitously hit a man in the shoulder which had taken him out of the game. Eventually a regiment from Fort Stanton came and broke everything down, allowing the Regulators to flee the town.

Josiah "Doc" Scurlock assumed captain, and Billy was moved up the chain of order. Sheriff Copeland had appointed Josiah deputy with the power to make arrests and serve warrants. It would not be long until our new captain would lead us back into battle, and this time again behind the guise of legality and backed by the sheriff of Lincoln. Evidently, we had a bone to pick with the citizens of Seven Rivers. These were the men who fought the round with the Regulators on the streets of Lincoln and the men responsible for the ambush that killed MacNab and wounded Ab Saunders after learning of our planned visit to their district. They had meant to take us down, but instead, our gang had killed a good handful of their men.

Just as I had, Frank Coe had heard our captors talking to one another back at the Fritz Ranch, though unlike myself he had come to know that the Seven Rivers posse had been instigated by none other than Dolan himself, who had dispatched a posse of his own men to the Rivers imploring them to stand up to us, citing that we rode on the side of John Chisum, whom the citizens of Seven Rivers were extremely displeased with. I asked Billy to explain this to me and in doing so I found that I myself had, unwittingly, become a part of their problematic situation. John Chisum was attempting to contain the land, fencing off water which disallowed the citizens of Seven Rivers its usage and expanding his land without concern to his fellow homesteaders, and here I had only offered to allow him to expand his land further. Well, that would be too bad because I needed money for my own ends. At present I had zero sympathy for Seven Rivers. Now we would have to pay them back. In the meantime, however, we would lay low in Patricio. A number of us would go, Alex included, as he had business there against the Seven Rivers party.

Billy attempted to talk me into going to Chisum's, assured that I could now remain safe there, but I told him that that part of me was over. I was a part of the fighting if it meant being free, and I meant to fight if need be. I refused to be useless simply because I was a woman—I would not remain idle. I would not watch my friends die. I would stand up and fight alongside the boys and be a part of something greater than myself.

As I explained this to Billy he looked at me with a strange combination of gratification, dismay, and disbelief. Miraculously, I heard Billy tell me the words I had never thought I would hear him say under these circumstances—that he was pleased with me, and proud to call me his girl. He made it a point to tell me that he meant not to encourage me, but he could not deny the appeal of what I was becoming. Amused, he called me his *Guerrero Hermoso*, his Beautiful Warrior, winked at me, then spurred his horse ahead, laughing.

# 17

## May, 1878

San Patricio proved to be less than the safe haven it had become for us during this war. Because there was no longer a justice of the peace in Lincoln, Alex knew he must come to appear before the justice of the peace in Patricio, José G. Trujillo, in order to swear affidavits against the Seven Rivers mob, holding them accountable for Frank MacNab's death.

Sheriff Copeland took the warrants to Fort Stanton where the The Seven Rivers posse was being held, arrested after the dispatched military regiment broke up the skirmish in Lincoln, urging the colonel there, Colonel Dudley, to allow him to serve the warrants and bring the lot of them to Patricio for a hearing. The trouble was, Murphy and Dolan had already bought Dudley, which meant they had bought the entire goddamned military at Fort Stanton. Therefore, Sheriff Copeland was impotent in the matter of having the Dolan partisan Seven Rivers posse brought before the courts and tried as the responsible party for MacNab's death simply because the Dolan faction held Dudley in the palm of their hand. Instead, Colonel Dudley, taking his cue, sent Sheriff Copeland with a military escort to Patricio for the arrests of the Regulators which included Josiah, Widenmann, and John Scroggins amongst a few others who were arrested in Lincoln. McSween, along with his house-man, George Washington, the very same man who had saddled me on the horse that was currently in my possession, were arrested when Copeland and his escort reached the town. Billy, me, Charlie, and Minxie were fortunate, having left Patricio after dinner at the Kavanagh's.

Prior to dinner being served, Alex had taken me aside and told me, in private, that John Chisum accepted my conditions and purchased the deed for the land I had offered to sell him. Chisum, admiring my business savvy in understanding the value of that land and the demand it was in, and the audacity upon threatening him that I would accept no less than the amount asked for, paid an extra two-hundred. The money had been placed under my name in the Exchange Bank at White Oaks as directed. This information buoyed my spirits somewhat; it meant that I would have means here in New Mexico should I need them, and I had every intention of hanging onto those means and leaving them to collect interest, hoping against hope that someday Billy and I would use that money to start a life of our own. It was something to cling to.

There was one other item of discussion that Alex had wanted to talk with me about. He handed me a small, black enameled box, and when I opened it I found inside a macabre object.

"It's a mourning pin—"

"I know what it is," I interrupted. "I don't want it."

Alex gave me a peculiar look. The pin was a constant offering given to survivors upon the death of a loved one. The tiny pin boasted a design that had been made with John's hair, twisted and fine, intricate in its creation. I found it morose.

I answered the question Alex seemed to be asking of me silently. "I never loved him, and so I do not deserve any remembrance of him. You know as well as I our marriage was one of convenience, not love."

Alex nodded his head slightly and pocketed the gloomy little trinket.

As luck (or in the case of Lincoln County, misrule) would have it, the magistrate who had assigned the warrants had resigned, which meant Dudley was at an impasse. He knew the only remaining magistrate that he could bring all arrested parties to, The Seven Rivers posse and the Regulators both, was José G. Trujillo in San Patricio, a sympathizer to the Regulators. Having Trujillo as magistrate meant the Regulators would be freed and the whole of the book thrown at The Seven Rivers posse, the latter of which would be an action that would displease Dudley's informal superiors, Murphy and Dolan. It just wouldn't do. Dudley had no choice but to turn the matter right back over to Sheriff Copeland who freed all the captives at Fort Stanton. This equity served to deflate and anger us to a degree, but the Regulators were out. Adding insult to injury, however, it was relayed to those of us who had escaped this misfortune that The Seven Rivers posse had the run of the coop at Stanton while the Regulators were locked away.

The Regulators, under Josiah "Doc" Scurlock's authority, raided the Dolan-Riley camp as payback for the raid in Lincoln, rounding up all the horses and mules and driving them back to Lincoln. We left some men in their camp wounded and one dead—an Indian—and, incidentally, the man responsible for the death of Frank MacNab. While the dead man might have made his bed by killing one of our own, more trouble was brought upon us as the land no longer belonged to Dolan and Riley, but to a man named Thomas B. Catron. Catron, understandably outraged, sent several letters, one of which reached Governor Axtel, regarding the lack of law enforcement in Lincoln County. Axtel removed Copeland on some bullshit, capricious technicality and reappointed George Peppin as sheriff of Lincoln County. Once again the Santa Fe Ring had the town's sheriff as their front man and in its pocket (it might as well have been Brady), and the Regulators were once again outlaws by this proclamation. I cannot say that I was surprised. This arbitrary abuse of power was unconstitutional and, quite frankly, pissed me off. It seemed impossible to keep the game up when our faction could not gain headway or turn important, unbiased heads of state to reform the situation that was swallowing us whole.

In Lincoln a man named Frank W. Angel, Esq., was brought in to investigate the death of John and, Billy, among several other Regulators, gave yet another deposition regarding the events of John's death, and to Mr. Angel's credit, he was able to persuade some of the men in the Dolan faction to give their accounts as well, but I could not, for the life of me, see the point in any of this. It was their word against ours. To me it all seemed a wasted effort. Billy and the others, feeling the futility in this particular endeavor as well, concurred. But what else could they do? They would exhaust every tactic they could.

In addition, the Regulators were in a precarious position as the Dolan faction brought in a group of men called the Rio Grande Posse in thanks for the raid on Catron's land. They were led by the infamous, notorious, murderous soldier of fortune, John Kinney. William Rynerson, the Lincoln County D.A. and Santa Fe Ring partisan, sent for this troupe of men to overtake the Regulators, and this would be an easy feat as the Rio Grande consisted of approximately twenty men. The Regulators were in desperate need of new recruits. We took to the hills of San Patricio. We were outmanned, outgunned, and for the time being, outrun. It wouldn't take much for Dolan to finally end us all.

But while in San Patricio, before the arrests and the subsequent attack by the Regulators on Catron's land, I had again run into James Moffey. I was on my way to the bath house before we were to sit down to dinner when I happened by him. I was concentrating on our troubles when I heard someone say, "Hi, Lucy."

Shaken from my thoughts, I glanced in the direction of the greeting, at first not noticing that it was Jimmy. I was feeling confused by my contemplations and all that had happened, and with the sky darkening and my being alone and vulnerable, I felt my gut sink in as I berated myself for the folly of wandering off alone as I had so many times before in this town. I had always felt safe here, but at present, things were uncertain, always.

I bounded back a step and instinctively reached for my pistol.

"It's me, Jimmy!"

My gut eased up as I recognized him in the fading light.

"Every time we meet, you gonna go for that gun?"

"Jimmy?"

"That's what I said..."

I leapt forth and threw my arms around him, happy to see him so unexpectedly.

"I don't believe it!" I exclaimed. "I never thought I'd see you again. How is it you're here in Patricio?"

"Looking for you."

"Me?"

"Well," he looked down and dug at the dirt with the toe of his boot, "The Regulators."

"The Regulators?" I asked. I was suspicious.

"Heard you all was looking for some fresh blood."

Understanding sunk in. Suddenly, feeling the exhaustion of all the distress added to the weight of my own body, my shoulders dropped and my knees nearly buckled. He stepped forward and reached out his hands to secure me and stand me back up straight. I grabbed at and held onto him by the front of his coat.

"I can't take this any longer," I sighed, not to Jimmy or anyone in particular; into the air.

"You're all in a hard way, it would seem."

I nodded against his chest. He brought me over to the boardwalk and sat me down there next to him.

"Where are your friends? What about Finn? I thought you'd be with them."

Jimmy shook his head. "Finn and Ru…and Engle, they're not the sort I want to involve myself with."

"What about you and Finn being just like brothers, knowing each other since birth?"

"Well, there's never any accounting for taste," he said, jokingly. But I could see something amiss. There was sorrow there.

"What is it, Jimmy?"

He looked at me for a few moments, studying my face.

"You really need to ask? You know plenty enough about Finn to figure my straying from him, so…" He shrugged his shoulders and I agreed, but in jest I reminded him that he would have known Finn much longer than I, and that he still chose to stick with him plenty before now.

"Well, Finn wanted out of Tupelo, and so did I. You know how it is…people, they change. Finn was never any sort of a saint, but being out on our own, he took off in a direction I didn't want to go. Being out here," he lifted his chin for emphasis, "It's rough, and there are only a few ways to survive."

I nodded.

"Finn decided that he wanted money the easy way, and his personality is worth all the intimidation in the world—the violence out here appealed to that in him." Jimmy brought his knees up and wrapped his arms around them. He was looking down, feeling low.

We sat in silence for a moment before he spoke again. "It's like what Billy said that last day I saw you, that you all ain't the type to kill a man over a card game and don't know anything about it. Well, I ain't that type, either. I should put myself in good company."

He leaned over and prodded my shoulder with his own, smiling. I smiled back, but what he told me didn't seem like the sort of thing to inspire such a troubled conscious as he seemed to have. Call it intuition, but I had been out here long enough to know a face like that.

"What is it that finally pushed you from him?" I asked.

He looked at me again, studying me. He seemed uncertain, perhaps wondering if he should confide in me.

"Go on and tell me, Jimmy. I've been through plenty; you won't be sparing my feelings by keeping it to yourself. Tell me why you're so troubled."

"Well, for one thing, he took off with a band calling themselves The Bastards."

"I've heard of them. They run around wreaking a lot of havoc. They're out of Arizona and are in cahoots with The Painted Ladies," I thought a minute. "I've considered running off and joining them myself—The Painted Ladies," I snickered to myself.

"Those whores on horseback!? Are you kidding? You're better than they are. You must be pulling my leg."

"No, Jimmy, I've thought of it. Get myself away from all these men and their need for bloodshed," I joked.

We sat together, quietly, until I asked him again to tell me what it was about Finn that upset him so. He took in a breath and let it out rather slow, as if mentally steadying himself.

"He went to Tularosa that night, and that's where I followed him to. When I met up with the three of them, they had been sitting around, drinking in the saloon there on the main street. There was a girl in that town that Finn had his eye on, but she didn't return his interest, and being the sort of person he is, and being full as a tick, he went for her."

He stopped there and looked at me to see if I caught on to what it was he was telling me.

"He raped her?" I asked.

He nodded, mortified.

Memories of the sort of nearly unbearable pain that had been caused me at the taking of my own virginity rang like bells in my head and I winced at remembering the scathing agony of submission as if I were being ripped apart all over again. To have it happen so brutally, so cruelly, made me shudder. That poor girl—what misfortune. There was the misery and shame of it all to be certain, but to not even have the comfort in knowing it was hers to offer out of love and be accepted out of love in return, to not be lavished with adoration during the ordeal, it made it all the more troubling to me.

"I took back off to Seven Rivers after that. That's how I heard all about the Regulators and all the trouble."

"My God, Jimmy," I put my arm around his shoulders affectionately and rested my head upon his shoulder. "That's a horrible thing to do, what Finn did. Are you sure it truly happened that way?" I pulled back and looked at him.

He nodded. "And there wasn't a thing I could do about it. If I could, I would've."

"How is it you came to know of it?"

"Are you kidding? Finn bragged. He *bragged*! Told us he went in through her window and threatened her with his pistol. I was so disgusted, Lucy...she was a good girl, too. She lived with her ma and pa, and he ruined 'er. Just like that," he snapped his fingers. "Because he was angry at being refused. And he killed that Chinaman in Patricio."

"That was a Chinaman!?"

"Half, I think. Why?"

"Well, it was dark, but what I saw he didn't look like a Chinaman. His name sure didn't sound like a Chinaman's. Greenfield, wasn't it? That's English."

He looked at me again, this time intently, putting pieces of a puzzle together. His eyes seemed to twitch. "It was you...wasn't it?"

"What? *What* was me?"

"You! You told, not Billy. He lied for you. You ratted Finn out!"

At this point, I didn't care if he knew I told.

"Yes, Jimmy, I did. Billy didn't see a thing. He didn't want the death of that man on my conscious knowing there was something I could've done to help...I'm sorry."

He started shaking his head and saying, "No...No. I'm sorry. I'm the one who's sorry."

"What have you got to be sorry for?"

He looked at me like I might be losing my mind, and then a little pained at having to remind me.

"The reward money. I'm sorry I did that to you."

"Oh, Jimmy...I understand it. You didn't know me. And who knows—maybe you wouldn't have turned me in, like you said. No, I believe you wouldn't have," I nodded my head in certainty.

"No, I wouldn't have, but Finn...he would have, because of me."

"Well, the point is moot because the reward money was revoked, remember?"

Exhausted, he laughed, "Yeah, I do."

"Anyway, I'm not sorry I ratted Finn out, especially after what you just told me. If I ever come across him I'll kill him myself."

Jimmy smiled at me half-heartedly. After a few moments of silence I said, "Don't do it, Jimmy," I was suddenly aware of a brutal fact: I could not save Billy from this, but I could have another chance by trying to save Jimmy from it all.

"What else have I to do?" was his reply.

I laughed incredulously. "That is not a good enough reason to help you figure that out."

"So I should accept that *you're* serving a good cause by fighting for it and simply leave it at that?"

I put my head in my hands and sighed loudly. Again, my femininity would undermine a man into sacrificing his life. No...not a man. A boy! Another boy!

A man, he feels as though he is ill-thought of if he doesn't fight when he feels a call to arms, and he feels even worse if he does nothing while a woman does what he considers man's work. Billy could not give himself to me as a coward, and now Jimmy would consider himself one by knowing *I* was in the trenches and *he* was not. One way or the other men will find a reason to fight.

"It's an awful situation," I muttered hopelessly.

"War always is, at least that's what I hear," he smiled at his slight attempt at a joke.

"This is different. It's as though we're fighting some invisible...thing that's out in the open and everywhere! We can feel it, like air! But like air we can't get a handle on it! And even then, it can't be invisible because it's completely full of substance! But it might as well be just a big black void for all we're able to do."

Jimmy looked at me funny. "You drunk? Or maybe did ya smoke anything funny before we run into one another?"

This time I laughed. I was too exhausted to make any sense, I knew that.

"They're ferocious, The Ring. *Oh*! They use the law against us, but the law they use is crooked—it is no law at all! They bend it towards their will and there isn't a goddamned thing we can do about it. No matter how much we fight back it's always as though we're fighting blind."

We sat quietly another moment, then, holding up one finger I scoffed, "One man's death. That's all it took—one man's death! And he was willing to die for nothing! He knew—they all knew—that it might end this way and still he took the trouble to stay put. One man dies and now all this! So many now have died for nothing!" I put my hand to my head, then rubbed my tired eyes. "I ask you, if John new the consequences, and knew they might mean death, if he accepted them, then why are we all here, now?"

I spread my arms out before me as if I were yielding to Jimmy a vast and wasted empire that had been burned to the ground, adding, "It's a bear of a bitch."

He laughed at this statement, throwing his arm around me and pulling me close to him fondly.

"I wanna be a Regulator. I gotta belong somewhere, and I figure that I'd like to do something good with my life. The Regulators are trying to set things right. And you're looking for men. Well, here I am."

I had to give up; there was nothing I could do to persuade this one either. Relenting, I looked to him and asked, "Do you realize your friend's name is Finn Flynn?"

We sat together and laughed about this for a few minutes.

And so Jimmy was with us during the raid on what we thought was Dolan's property, and he was out in the hills of San Patricio, hiding out with us.

# 18

## May, 1878

As the sky began to glide into evening we stopped and set up camp. Minxie and Jimmy went off in an attempt to hunt some wild meat, and in the meantime, Billy had me come with him to practice shooting in order to pass the time. Billy spent an awful amount of time doing this and often insisted that I, too, draw on a target.

Billy told me to bring a few of the emptied cans that had been used for supper, leaving Fred and Henry there to watch over the camp. As he walked ahead to choose the spot where we would fire, I stayed behind to pick up the used cans. I went through our supplies and found a full can of peaches which I also took, bringing the armful of cans to him just as he had asked.

As I approached Billy he wore the smile I had loved on him for so long; he was happy to play at targets and have me close to him, and I smiled back in kind. I could have imagined us being back at John's, before the nightmare of this war.

"Ready?" he asked.

"I sure am!" I declared.

"Okay, first you throw a can in the air and let me fire, then you do what I do."

I threw the first can, an empty one, and he managed to shoot the can while in the air five out of six times before it touched down.

"I'll never outdo that, Bill."

"Not without practice you won't."

I handed him an empty can and he threw it up. I managed to hit it with only one shot out of six. Billy told me that this was still something to be proud of, assuring me that hitting a moving target as frail and uncertain as a thrown, empty can was difficult.

Finally, I picked up the full can. He fired upon it and, after the first shot hit, the contents splattered and rained down upon us, causing him to shout, "What in the god-damned hell!?"

Surprised, he observed his arms and shirt to see slices of peach and nectar had found its way all over him. I had been standing back only a bit and so all the same I, too, was hit full of the same sticky muck. He turned to look at me, eyes ablaze and agitated.

"I took a full can so I could throw it higher," I explained.

"I don't give a damn, Lucy. Are you crazy? Jesus H. Christ it's all over me and my goddamned guns! Good Christ! It's running down my goddamned neck!" he shouted as he walked off toward the camp, leaving me standing there alone. Enough of it was on me, too, and so I figured that I had also paid a price.

I approached him back by the camp as he went through his bags looking for his supplies with which to clean his guns.

Trying to apologize I said, "I'm sorry, Billy. I didn't consider—"

"Right…how could you have possibly known that the damn thing would explode and come down everywhere? Good God, Lucy. You didn't consider because you didn't use your head!"

He walked away from me again and I followed. He sat down upon his bedding near the fire and began to clean the gunk from his equalizer. As I looked at him I noticed that his shirt was not only covered in the sickly sweet mess, but his hat held large pieces of sticky peach as well. I tried my best not to laugh, knowing how angry he was, though Fred was no use as he howled on and on. As we sat by the fire the stuff baked into our clothing, causing us to smell sugary sweet and overwhelmingly so. Minxie and Jimmy, who had come back around carrying a small deer to skin, noticed the smell straight off.

"Good God, Bonney, what the hell is that? Ya cookin' a bleedin' pie?" asked Minx.

"See this genius standing here?" he pointed at me. "She thought it would be a good idea to throw a fairly large can of peaches into the air as a target because it would go higher."

At this last word he looked at me in disapproval. The boys found it funny, but told him that he'd better go off and wash himself up, otherwise, he and I could sleep far enough away from the rest of them. We smelled like sticky candy, and upon being told to leave he looked at me unhappily.

"I'll go get cleaned up once I get my guns cleaned up, first."

"Well, take that one with ya," we turned to see Charlie approaching on horseback. "I can see she got it on her, too."

Billy and I went down to the wash and brought with us some fresh clothes. We stepped into the creek with our boots to wash the stuff off of them. It was chilly out there in the desert by the water near dusk; it was only early May. Billy removed his shirt, quickly rinsing himself with the chilly water, replacing the ruined shirt immediately with a clean one. I did the same as he. We removed our pants and replaced them as well, dunking the filthy clothing in the water, eliminating as best we could the amassing of pests who would be drawn to the scent of nectar. I took my suede jacket, wet my fingers, and began to delicately scrub the places the obliterated peach had stuck to. Billy did the same with his hat, flicking off pieces of orange colored fruit and then rubbing the spots with water. He didn't speak to me much, just concentrated on getting himself cleaned up. Once we were finished we hung our wet clothes up on a branch to dry and went back to the camp.

I was more than thrilled to have Jimmy with us. While the others either squabbled or worked themselves into an agitated pitch of agreement over their anger at MacNab's death, one way or the other unified in the assurance that this was all far from over and feeling the stings ever more personally, Jimmy paid me a great deal of attention. He took his new role as a Regulator very seriously, but rather than foam at the mouth as the others did, he knew when to quit the debate.

Swiftly, he grew comfortable with and close enough to me that it caused Billy an obvious difficulty—it was impossible not to notice the trouble it caused him, his eyes scrutinizing Jimmy's every move.

His attentions caused Billy to become increasingly unappreciative, and I, so tuned in to the thoughts that presented themselves in Billy's mind, became anxious. I enjoyed the receptiveness Jimmy provided me to an incredibly extensive degree as he kept me occupied and entertained while the others plotted and planned, driving us all further into emotional debt and ever closer to a conceivably imminent, violent death. But, because of the strain it caused Billy, I was considerably torn between abandoning my newfound friendship with the boy for the sake of retaining whatever small amount of peace and harmony was afforded us, and wanting to hold on to my new confidant who kept me entertained and relevant.

Billy's unhappiness was so palpable that unease pervaded my senses and served to take my breath away as I worried that something unpleasant should erupt between the two, making things all the more difficult. I understood that he must have found it rather improper, so protective was he, that Billy could not help but study the friendly disposition I kept with Jimmy and find it anything but satisfactory. But I saw no harm in it. I wished myself to be the captain of my own desires and the last thing I needed was to be furthermore told what to do and how to behave, especially during such a lackluster career as a wanted criminal in the midst of a bloody battle. The thought of behaving proper was almost laughable. I found it absurd to think that my open and innocent relationship with Jimmy could be so upsetting that it could possibly usurp the real horror of what was happening, yet that did not stop it from being so. Perhaps there might have been a stab of jealousy on Billy's behalf—I would not rule it out. But more importantly, Billy had an agenda where I was concerned, and there would come a time when to challenge Billy's agenda would mean a declaration of war.

"You took me aside to complain over the way another boy should look at me?"

I furrowed my brow and squinted at Billy, peering at him as though he were mad. "The only thing more extraordinary than the ludicrousness of your assertion is your nerve!" I backed up a step, turning my body, snorting in disbelief and anger. I came back at him, finger pointed, "You screw other women! So how dare you!?"

He grabbed and pushed me up against the rock that shielded us from the others and told me to shut-up.

"Don't you talk at me like that!"

"Why?" I laughed, "You think I don't know? They're on you, always. They give me trouble and make me look a fool; they relish the opportunity to rub my face in it. And here you are, disturbed that a nice boy admires me from afar!"

Clearly chastened by the afflictions he had cast upon my emotions based on his own behavior with other women and being called out on it, discovering how his actions bothered me so, Billy changed tact.

"I'm not giving you up so he can have you! I'm not letting him take you to a place I refuse to let you go!"

"And that is?" I asked, bitterly.

"You deserve better than what you'll get here. And he's selfish if he's willing to allow it."

He stepped away from me in the same manner I had earlier stepped from him. Exasperated, he came back at me and lightly pushed me back by both shoulders again. He slid his hands down my arms and grabbed at my hands. "Look," he said, presenting my hands to me, palms up. "Still as smooth as the day I met you."

"So?" I challenged.

"So, frontier life is hard! The gloves will have to come off, Lu."

He looked emotionally exhausted. "You weren't made for this kind of life. Go back to where you belong."

"It seems to me that you're getting carried away. It's not as if he's offered me a proposal."

"You don't get it! For all that fancy education of yours you understand nothing! You won't last in a life out here."

"I've managed this far, and under such appallingly dreadful circumstances, too!"

"No, this…this is child's play! Maybe you'll catch a bullet and we'll put you in the ground," his eyes bore a glassy sheen. "Maybe you won't. But it'll be damn exciting and entertaining before it's all over. All this is to you is a game, a way to shirk your responsibilities and the chains that shackle you to them. You're caught up in the freedom of it all! You forget, I know you! I know how unhappy you were. For the first time you feel like you can breathe, but I don't think you grasp the gravity of your situation."

"Out there," he pointed to nowhere in particular. "If you survive all this, you'll be stuck, because you can't keep living like this. This excitement won't last forever."

"How dare you insinuate that I have no concept of the danger and that I take pleasure in it! And I never said I wanted to live this way—"

"Let me finish! You'll settle down into a boring life and become some poor farmer's wife. You'll be penniless! Are you capable of living a life of poverty, or is it some novelty in your head because it hasn't been realized yet?"

His eyes were full of intensity. I may have been witnessing fear in them, anger, or even sorrow. He went on. "You're always going on about wanting your freedom. Well, the life you want doesn't include that. It'll be the same for you here as it is back in New York, only it'll be worse because you'll scavenge for a living. You'll keep house in some tiny little box and chase children around in the middle of having them. You'll slave away, day after day, over the same old drudgery you'll hate. At least if you go back you can simply sit back and could change the view on a whim."

Now I saw spite.

"You can have a governess to care for your children while you do as you please and wait around for the servants to bring you your next meal. You can even ring a little bell to get their attention!"

I made an attempt to push past him, but I could not manage; he pushed me back against the rock, forcing me to listen as he mocked me.

"Out here, all life will bring you is misery, and smallpox for a quick exit, if you're lucky! No bell-ringing for it, either!"

He looked down a moment and then back at me.

"I screw other women? Okay...I screw other women. The more I'm with them the less of a chance there is for me to get you in trouble. If that happened it would ruin you completely! Then you can't go back! You'll be stuck and you'll resent me for it. And what if—"

I wanted to shout at him and tell him that should such a thing happen I would have no intention of going back anyway, but he turned away from me. He swallowed hard as he tried to recover from bearing his emotion before turning back to me.

"And what if that happens and we're just like are now—forced out here to hide in the goddamned desert, what then? That's the last thing we need in all of this."

I could see the idea of this frightened him; that the real fear was not entirely shrouded in putting him and the others in a precarious position should I miscarry in the middle of nowhere, but also in losing me because of it.

"You're running around free as you please, but you know you can always end this when you want, that's how you can stand it. When you can't stand it anymore and it stops being fun—"

"You think this is *fun* for me?"

He said nothing more as he turned and walked away from me. I did not follow immediately, allowing him the space to make his exit. In the end, what I felt from him was not anger or jealousy, but hurt. I couldn't bear the thought that I was causing him pain, knowing that there was nothing I could do to avoid that feeling in him. I realized that now. No matter how strong I presented myself, or how agreeable, or how successful I proved my resilience, he would always carry terror for me. I understood now there was nothing I could do to ease his concerns.

The sun had begun its decent and dusk flourished happily. I remained by myself for a short while, occupied with thoughts prompted by Billy's words until finally I followed his path back to camp, finding him sitting sullenly upon a sizeable rock.

I lowered myself and sat at his feet, sidling next to the left of him as close as was physically possible, hooking my right leg around his and wrapping my arms around it as well, holding to him close. I sat beneath him in complete submission, my body language imploring his forgiveness, silently letting him know that I understood his disposition and was willing to acquiesce. I knew he did not mean me any harm, but conversely, was showing his love and compassion for me. He accepted my concessionary bid, placing his hand gently behind my neck and caressing it affectionately, letting me know that all was right between us.

We had set up our camp by a fairly large cave tucked clandestinely up upon a ridge and set back into the hills. We would lay low here for a day or two before moving along and secreting ourselves away in another location which, hopefully, would include bath water. In the meantime, we were left to our own devices which meant that bickering over plans of action would be the order of the day.

As I sat dutifully by Billy's feet the scheming games began, governed as usual by the deeply passionate declarations of revenge. What irritated me most about this was how the men often looked to me as though I ought to have a care in regard to this insanity as I had made it inherently clear that I wanted no parts of this foolishness. Had I anything to say, it would have been worthless; valueless in the face of their vehemence.

As was my way, I exhibited a worn yet poker-straight face as I relied on my emotionally defensive tactics to avoid this unpleasantness and shut their bloody war talk out. Instead of listening to what they had to say, I instead turned my mind to amusing, if unquestionably impossible and terribly ridiculous, thoughts of the happier version of life I might have been privy to had John not been murdered. Once again I found the unfortunate irony in my predicament (my existence was fraught with the cruel mockery of irony). Once upon a time, marriage to John seemed a fate worse than death. But now it was never clearer to me that my very happiness had hinged upon that union. If John had not perished senselessly then life would go on as it had prior to his death, which meant I'd have Billy and, though imperfect, everything I had wanted and prayed for all these years—the love of a man whom I loved in return. With John gone it had all been scattered to the wind.

Darkness had set in and with it boredom ensued. I pulled out my Jew's Harp and as we sat in a tattered circle around the fire I began twanging away upon it. This amused Jimmy, who laughed freely at my whimsy, clapping his hands in enjoyment. The others shook their heads and groaned, irritated at the thought of suffering through my wanton playing.

After ten minutes had passed I was asked to please stop—despite my classically trained musical abilities, I had no melody or otherwise any sort of understanding of this instrument.

"Lucy," Charlie whined.

"Yeeess...?" I answered through the harp's vibrations.

"Knock it off. You're aggravating everybody."

I ignored him and pressed on, twanging away. I found a great deal of amusement in their complaining over my playing, and so long as I should need to suffer through their incessant talks of small-scale military strategy and other forms of plotted mayhem, I believed I was entitled to at least have my own occupation, even if it occurred at the expense of others.

Merrily, obliviously, I went along with my monotonous, uninspiring tune, entertaining myself and Jimmy, when again, same as last time, Billy took it from me. But unlike last time, he did not simply pocket it, but threw it away into the darkness.

"I'm sorry you were ever bought the damn thing," he looked at Fred ominously, which must have seemed decidedly Faustian as he stared from across the fire. I said nothing; instead I sat sulking quietly to myself, deciding that I would simply buy myself another next time we found ourselves in town.

We travelled to a small village known as Picacho, situated along the Rio Hondo. The Regulators began expanding their forces by enlisting scores of local men, many of whom were Hispanic, following a man named Martin Chavez who was a twenty-three year old Picacho farmer. Martin had begun a race war back in 1874, riling the Hispanics then as now to fight for their freedoms, and their loyalty was such that they were willing to follow him into battle again. Our forces expanded grossly over the course of what seemed merely overnight.

Among the men who had joined our ranks was a boy Billy's age named Tom O'Folliard. Tom and Billy became inseparably fast best-friends. Despite my exceptionally close relationship with Billy, I believed, of course, that I could not compete with Tom who, like Billy, was an orphan, losing both of his parents to smallpox. The two of them shared the reality that they were nobody's son—they belonged to no one, and it was they who could understand this, not I. And of course I was of the opposite gender, which meant there would always be a breach that Billy and I could never close regardless of how intimate we were. And then there was my birthright alone which set us far apart.

Before Tom, these things never occurred to me—they were never an issue. But now I was paranoid. Could I lose my friendship with Billy to Tom? I didn't know. I loved him so much that I was literally terrified—I wanted to trust in the bond that held Billy and me together.

Billy and I had an exceptional love for one another, and we had what I would have described as an unbreakable attachment. We shared a longing to bleed life and each other dry, and here we were both a part of dire circumstances that had us clinging to one another, but even that could be a bust since Billy tried to force me out at every turn.

With Tom entering the picture I became fretful. I was afraid that I could spend all my days and nights consoling Billy and professing my love and devotion to him until my face turned blue and it would still be to no avail as I could not understand his plight and position in life as Tom could. But then came the realization that it didn't matter if I couldn't exactly understand Billy's position—we loved each other irrevocably. I held onto this believe and brought my fears to him as I was always wont to do, and there he reinforced my confidence by avowing that I made up for the losses he suffered in life. He put me at ease immediately, telling me I was at the center of his life and would remain there for as long as we lived—no one could replace me.

While in Picacho, Tom monopolized much of Billy's time, and in fact, the only time I chanced upon him was when he diligently forced me to practice my shooting or whenever he caught Jimmy and I together sharing friendly moments that he deemed too intimate. It seemed as though Billy would be selfishly happy if I were to spend all of my time alone. One night as we lie in bed I begged him to let me have my friend as he had his. I did not want to be lonely and Jimmy made the days easier for me.

"Please," I begged. "I think he may need me, too."

He seemed to break at this. "Si…por ti, I will."

The mood was dense with angst and exhilaration as we awaited the impending battle that was sure to break; but when this would be, no one could say. But it was coming. Like the proverbial calm before the storm the inevitability of this confrontation was down our backs like a monkey one could not shake off. Anxiety was high and manifested itself in many forms; thrill, edginess, apprehension, enthusiasm, and as usual, it nearly incapacitated me. But Billy never seemed more alive and volatile, and sharing in his excitement was, of course, Tom O'Folliard. I was no stranger to the way any of these men viewed bloody confrontation—I had witnessed it from the first, and Jimmy was no different from the rest of them. He was raring to go, barely able to contain himself and in a rush to prove himself to the others. In his words, this would make him a true Regulator—his right of passage. This outlook only served to make me sick to my stomach. Celebrations arose every night with the men drunkenly hooting and hollering about the beating they were going to give "them Dolan boys".

With Billy's time occupied by Tom, the new recruitments, organizational tactics, and of course the women, I was often on my own with the exception of Jimmy keeping me company when he managed to pull himself away from the twisted revelry.

Drink flowed freely, and in an attempt to calm my nerves I partook of the poisons, allowing them to carry my thoughts away to someplace pleasant. In the dark, while dancing with Jimmy and otherwise having a grand time with him, I grabbed him by the hand and began to lead him to the place where my bed awaited. Despite my liquor dampened senses, I still found myself surprised and amazed at my willingness to want this boy in my bed as I was feeling predominantly absorbed in having my body satisfied in the way Billy often had done for me. It would have stopped there, the part of me that knew better overruling the situation, but with my inhibitions weak, it was easy to allow myself to ignore the small shred of clarity that otherwise seemed impossibly durable enough to hinder my desires as I knew I would regret my actions. The licentiousness of the deed I was about to act upon knowing Billy would disapprove caused me tremendous pleasure, both mentally and physically. The idea of going behind his back incited me. I wanted him to see that I could do it, too.

I pulled Jimmy along, both of us giggling favorably over the anticipation of what it was we were about to do; he would have his way with me and finally realize his adoration, and I looked forward to getting off by laying with another simply because Billy forbade it.

But when we had reached the home of the family who had put me and Billy up Jimmy held back, his elation now tempered. I felt my own smile wane.

"What is it?" I asked, annoyed.

"I can't do this. Christ, you *know* I can't. I want to…but I can't."

"Why the hell not?" I was incensed. What reason could possibly stop this boy from lying with me to get off? I knew that he wanted me—that he loved me. Billy would have never let anything get in the way of his having me, as he had already proven many times over, yet this was obviously not so with Jimmy as clearly he was refusing me.

"He'll *kill* me."

"Who will kill you?"

Astonished, he looked at me and I was suddenly very aware—that small shred of clarity. "Billy? Don't be absurd."

"No, Lucy, he told me. He threatened me—if I ever put a hand on you so much out of sociability he said he'll kill me dead."

I walked towards him like some sort of coquette. "You can't be serious, Jimmy. He' s said as much to me—"

"What? That he'd kill you?"

"No…that he'd kill whoever put their hands on me," I laughed ridiculously, and then I asked him, "Are you really going to pass up this chance because you're afraid of what he might do? He wouldn't dare do anything; his bark is worse than his bite when it comes to me. He's over protective, that's all. He'd never hurt you because he knows it would hurt me and that I would hate him for it. And anyway, who will tell him?"

"*Tell* him? It's *his* bed!"

"He's out all night, so it ain't exactly his bed tonight, now is it? And he won't be back for a while. You'll be gone by then."

He laughed and sarcastically said, "Yeah, well, just the same…"

"Jimmy, don't be a fool! It serves him right! If he wanted me so bad he'd be with me, not with some Mexican slut! Now, do you want to take me to bed or not?"

"I do, but not at that cost. And it's not just the fear of what he might do, or that I swore I wouldn't, but I respect you—and you're his."

"*His*? I'm *his*!? For the love of God, piss on that! I'm so sick of hearing that I'm his! He hasn't bothered with me and, in fact, I'll bet he's off screwing some Mexican whore right now! Why is it that I shouldn't be allowed to do the same? I should be entitled to determine what's best for me! I decide what it is that I want! It's up to no man to decide for me."

"Lucy, please calm down. You're drunk."

"I'm so goddamned tired of hearing how I'm too well respected for this. I want you to kiss me, Jimmy. I've *wanted* you to kiss me."

He blushed and seemed to consider this, but instead he let reason rule. "Tomorrow, you'd be sorry, and there'd be trouble between me and Billy—you know that. There'd be hell to pay. Let's not risk any of that."

I ridiculed his anxiety. "The first time Billy came to my bed *he* didn't worry about getting caught, or what would happen afterwards. He took what he wanted. Why don't you do the same, you look up to him so much!"

Jimmy put his head down in defeat, unable to explain. "Billy loves you, Lu. I believe he'd risk everything for you."

I looked at Jimmy soberly, my wits beginning to approach the fringes of my mind. What Jimmy had just said about Billy made me ashamed because it was true. Billy *had* risked plenty for me. Billy loved me, and I was playing a fool.

"Lucy…" whispered Jimmy. "I love you, too. But Billy…he got there first. Don't let's make this complicated."

He leaned down and kissed me on the forehead and then the cheek before bidding me goodnight.

Oh, damn him! Damn that Billy Bonney! It was him I wanted terribly! Not Jimmy, *Billy*! But the man I wanted was off having his fun while I was left here to suffer without him! What girl was enjoying what was rightfully mine? Well, I would see to it that I should get my way—I'd make him give himself to me!

I went in search of him and when I found Billy I advanced on him as he flirted with his whore du jour. I reached out my hand and grabbed his arm. The señiorita he currently spoke with, coquettishly covering the lower half of her face with her stupid black lace fan in a manner of seduction flashed her furious eyes at me. My indifference to this assured her that I was not, in any way, concerned with her mood as I easily lured Billy away from her.

Billy paid no more attention to the girl as he stared intently at me, wondering what it was I sought. I lead him to a secluded, darkened corner where I could speak to him as privately as possible amidst the raucous celebration that was happening all around us. As angry as I was with him for meddling in my affairs I hid it well as there was time to pout later.

Billy continued to look at me without saying a word. Curiosity was splayed across his face as he waited for me to speak, but I remained just as quiet as he. With drink coursing through me and my body vibrating I raised myself up by my toes so that I could match my lips with his to kiss him. It was uncertain at first but very quickly it became passionate. Stunned, he did not immediately place his arms around me or kiss me back. I moved in to him to fill the small space that remained between us. Our bodies were now flush with one another and, finally, when his confusion subsided, he held me tightly and began to kiss me feverishly. His arms encircled me and embraced me with such strength that it seemed he would squeeze the life from me if he had wanted to, and in my being so close to him I could feel that he wanted me. And then, just as suddenly as I kissed him, I just as suddenly and cruelly broke it off as I toyed with him. I pried his arms from me and turned to go, leaving him standing there, dazed, but knowing that when he came to his senses he would follow me.

I stumbled off into the darkness, becoming oddly aware for the first time of the crisp, cool air. As I entered our room in my drunken state my carnal need began to wane along with the height of my intoxication. I grew exhausted. I slipped out of my clothes and located my satchel, rummaging through it and locating the old shirt that had belonged to Billy which I now slept in. Forgetting now my plans for seducing Billy as my fatigue wore down my resolve, I changed and climbed into our bed, alone. Almost immediately I fell into a slumber, the alcohol luring me into a fast sleep.

I cannot say how long I had lain there before he entered the room. I was woken by the sound of his spurs and boot heels as he came to my bed and sat upon the edge, leaning down towards me. Through bleary eyes I saw that it was Billy. He kissed me tenderly and said not a word. Exhausted, and my whiskey bravado gone, I could not find the strength to take this opportunity to force myself upon him and have my way as I had wanted. I was out of it just enough not to know how long any of this lasted, his kissing me. But he continued to do so until the kisses grew deep. I closed my eyes, still hovering between awareness and sleep induced confusion, but still, I could feel my body responding to him.

I stood in the middle of the placita minding my own business, being in a particularly all-around good mood, when I felt a deliberate shove. I stumbled a few feet and, when I found my bearings, I turned around. There she was, the girl whose conversation with Billy I had interrupted last night; the girl whom he had abandoned for me.

No sooner had I turned when she spat in my face. I stood a moment and, with an incredulously loud squeal of shock and awe, I stepped toward and slapped her. Hard! Palm connecting solidly with cheek. She put her hand to her face where I had stung her and stared me down with hatred in her eyes before coming at me full-force, angrily pushing me backwards. I summoned my balance and then rushed back at her, shoving her down. We were both on the ground rolling around with one another as we pulled each other's hair and slapped one another's faces. I picked up a handful of earth and thrust it into her mouth, covering it with my hand so as to keep it there. When the struggling caused me to lose my grip she promptly spit the muck out, coughing it up; slick, brown spittle spattering forth. Finally I sat atop her, slapping at her face with both hands and repeating this action until I was grabbed from behind and pulled off of her.

Josiah held on to me and I continued to kick and squirm and demand that he let me down. I accidentally caught him in the shin with my spur causing him to yelp in pain. The boys gathered around, along with other assorted peoples who had come to watch the great display. Billy held the other girl back, yelling at her in Spanish. Tears ran down her cheeks in droves as she cried and screamed, pounding his chest and clawing at his face while he shouted at her. Josiah put me down and I instinctively patted the dust off of my clothing as well as I could, still watching the scene before me. I was displeased that he should concern himself at all with her after her actions and I made no effort to hide this fact as I scowled upon them both.

I watched her cry to him as she pointed to me and said, *Ella es tu chica muy poco* to him, to which he replied by snapping at her to be quiet. In English he told her never to do that again to me, to keep her hands off of me, and this, taking my side being more than she could bear, caused her to walk backwards from him, sulking as she said *Ella me insultó!*

He came to me and asked what had happened. I explained that I was only minding my own business when she shoved me. He told me not to encourage this sort of confrontation, and next time to walk away. I replied that I would do no such thing just as he could never simply walk away from a fight. He conceded that he understood my argument, and so I also took this opportunity to point out what Jimmy had told me—how Billy had threatened Jimmy against paying me attentions, and that it seemed quite unfair that he should get to exercise his amorous notions but not I. He appeared slightly cowed but sidestepped that particular matter altogether, going on to explain that, because it was in our best interest to get along with the patrons of the town, I ought to learn to walk away from such conflicts, to which I replied that perhaps he should spend his time paying more attention to me instead of other girls, then, in order for me to avoid another such confrontation. He laughed and agreed that I might just be right. I told him that I was always subject to this sort of problem because of his roguish behavior—I told him that this is what I meant when I said that I was made out to be a fool by the other girls to whom he gave his affection. He put his arm around me and pulled me to him as he kissed my temple and apologized, swearing that it was me and only me for him. He admitted to his horrible flirtatious ways, but assured me that there was no one who meant what I did to him and that he made that point clear to any woman he paid any mind to. He told me that this was most likely the reason they gave me any trouble at all.

So then, his love for me made me a victim.

And how could I not agree that I had lowered myself to such maddened behavior!? This was not how a lady handled disagreements. But of course, I had been exposed to the outlaw way of dealing with adversity. It was rubbing off on me nicely, to be sure. Rolling around in the dirt and pulling at one's hair and scratching at one's face was beyond frowned upon. Then again, perhaps there was another way to look at this; evidently, physical confrontation was what the girl understood.

Once the situation had calmed down, Billy came to me and told me that he should like to have my photo taken. When I asked him why, he told me he wanted to mark me forever as the warrior I had come to be. He laughed and said that I had earned my rank and that he wanted to document my role for posterity. He said I was the prettiest little cowgirl he had ever seen and wanted a photo of me to keep forever so that he could look upon it and remember. I agreed to take the photo so we made plans to have it done in Patricio when next we were there.

Jimmy was perplexed by the entire fiasco.

"I just don't understand it."

"What is there to understand?"

"You love him…"

"Yes, this is correct," I nodded to stress the point.

"…and he adores you, as you put it."

"Actually, that's how he puts it."

"Then why does he bother with other girls? Will he stop now that he sees how much trouble it causes you?" Jimmy looked at me with an expression of antipathy.

"It's really none of your concern, Jimmy."

"Maybe not. But if a girl like you is gonna belong to a man, then he ought to appreciate that. I don't understand how he can even see past you."

"He can't, he is just easily diverted. All I need do is snap my fingers and he'll abandon another without a second thought to be with me."

"So why don't you?"

"Sometimes I do. I exercised this fact just last night."

"Would this be after your drunken seduction of me?"

I ignored him.

"Why do you allow this behavior?"

"You really don't understand, Jimmy."

"So educate me. Because what I know is I'd be here with you if I were lucky enough to be him."

I smiled and blushed at his admitted interest and appreciation of me.

"I once nearly had Billy ready to take me away with him so that we could live a life together. He had told me it was what he wanted. Then all of this happened. He felt that, as a man, he had to stand up and fight. And then, when faced with his old ways, he told me that he wasn't good enough for me, that I deserved better. He told me he would never subject me to a life in which he could not take care of me properly. I've told him that doesn't matter to me, and he said that I only believe that because I've always had money, and so the thought of struggling doesn't really occur to me. He said he would do nothing that would cause me to resent him, that I was young and soon enough when the hardships came I would hate him for putting me in such a position if he were to give in."

"You think he meant all that?"

"I know he meant all of that," I took this opportunity to present Billy's mother's ring, still upon my finger, to Jimmy, explaining to whom it had belonged and what it meant between us. "He frustrates me with his assumptions. I've begged him, pleaded with him. I've explained how confining my life is back in New York, and that I'd give up luxury for freedom happily, and to be with the man I love rather than a man my family could benefit from."

"I don't know. I don't think I could keep myself from you if I was him, regardless of all of those things he's said."

"Hence his aversion to your overtures; you would have no trouble subjecting me to a life of poverty. He views that as selfish. In addition, if he wanted that life for me, he'd have me himself—and he doesn't entirely keep himself from me, either, anyway."

Jimmy looked at me, bothered by my last statement. I disregarded his expressive protest and continued the conversation.

"Those other girls," I pointed to a girl Billy was talking to across the street for effect. "They're just sex. Billy is a young man; I won't confine him to me, especially under such tumultuous circumstances. I'll let him get it out of his system and be the girl he not only comes back to, but whom he winds up with. I could turn into a shrew and demand that he commit to me, but that would only cause him to resent me. If a woman must force a man to be with her, and only her, then the relationship is doomed right off. I accept Billy's ways. My relationship with him is consensual. And the thing of it is, someone like you comes along, has a problem with it, and wants to throw a wrench in the works hoping to destroy the liaison in the hopes that he may get what he wants by slipping in through the cracks when the object of his affection is on the rebound. You figure if you break us apart, then perhaps I'll come running to you."

"Throw a wrench? That's not what I'm doing. I do want you, but I would never—"

"Then what? You don't know either Billy or me. You don't know what we have together. Back home men often have mistresses, so in that respect, it doesn't bother me in the least. I'm used to the concept."

"But I bet if those men loved their wives they'd never stray."

I spoke up as if I hadn't heard his last remark.

"And the biggest reason he won't commit to me, the reason that all of those other little reasons he's conjured up fit into so nicely and neatly, is because by committing to me he's encouraging me to stay, and he doesn't want that. Regardless of how badly he wants me with him, he feels as though it's wrong to want to keep me here. If I stay and anything happens to him my prospects will be few, and this worries him. He wants me to go back home. It's because he loves me that he can't stay away from me the way he should, yet can still manage to push me away wholly. What you see as incomprehensible actions I see as true love. It must take a lot of love for one to sacrifice having the one they want because one believes that person will be guaranteed a better life without them. And I know it hurts him terribly, too."

"Okay, perhaps I am selfish, you got me there. But it would be hard to be with someone else when you're thinking of the girl you know is thinking of you, too. Yet Billy is able to do that."

"Well, he is a man, after all."

"So?"

"So it seems to me that men can love a woman desperately, but still fulfill their needs elsewhere."

Jimmy didn't say anything to that; he seemed to agree.

"You never knew me before this war. Billy did. He has seen me as you have not. He saw me as something more than this—he knew a very wealthy girl with the world at her fingertips. I was resplendent, and that is how he still thinks of me. You only see me as this," I waved my hand down the length of my body to underscore my point by highlighting the ordinary boyishness my clothes provided me and the tattered fabric that was once fine. "I have to concede that I understand his trepidation at taking me away from that life to place me in one where the prospects are lean. He is intimidated because he knows he cannot afford to keep me in the lifestyle to which I have become accustomed, and because he's afraid that I'll stop loving him when I tire of being a poor man's wife. But I know in my heart, in my entire being, that that is not so."

I meant to end the conversation, but after a beat I said, "Besides, despite the fine poker player he is, he doesn't know of the ace up my sleeve," I smiled cockily.

"And that is?" Jimmy asked.

"I have a sum stored away, plenty enough to keep us and begin a life with."

"Why not tell him?"

"Can you imagine? If he is difficult now in his insistence that I go back to New York, knowing I have my own means to make the journey would only make him all the more persistent. Besides, the time is not in season yet. He is caught up in far too much and much too loyal to turn and run. But there will come a day when the fruit will be ripe and he will pluck it—he will be unable to resist it when he is at his most desperate. He does love me. All I need do is stand it and wait for him to give in."

# 19

## July 14, 1878
## The Five Days War

We rode into Lincoln with the intent to put an end to our fugitive state. The Regulators were going to make a full-fledged stand against Dolan and his faction, and they would kill two birds with one stone: they meant to punish The Ring for the murder of our friends, and for the nerve they exhibited in making the Regulators out to be criminals when they had, in fact, been sanctioned by the law. They would let this stand end all of the fighting once and for all. The Regulators, as well as many of those who were citizens of Lincoln, were tired of being under the thumb of The Santa Fe Ring, and someone had to put a stop to their corruption. Today would be that day.

The street was uncharacteristically quiet; many of the citizens had left town to avoid the explosive battle that was inevitable, and the men who were here to fight were prepared to do some much needed damage.

Sixty of us rode into Lincoln well after darkness had provided cover and took up strategic positions. Billy was to stand at the McSweens' ordering that I go with him as their home was a bastion, meant to withstand battle; Minxie, Jimmy, and Tom were among those who went with us. I was surprised to see that Susan and her sister and her sister's children were still present.

Our horses were corralled in the McSweens' barn and we took our places, taking inventory of our provisions as we would be barricaded, not knowing how long we would be holed up. I should have been terrified and found it odd that I was not—it didn't seem real to me. After all that had happened I had still not grasped the magnitude of this war, yet I was surrounded by ordnance and men running back-and-forth as they sized up the situation and boarded windows and, still, I could not imagine an all-out conflict and, more than that, I could not imagine that I would be a part of it. How my life had come to this state of affairs I did not know.

When morning broke the Dolan faction responded to the Regulators' audacity by sending a volley of bullets into the west side of the house. Shots were fired sporadically between the two sides throughout the day along with threatening banter; it all seemed an empty production; neither side making headway, simply yelling and taking useless shots at one another. It was clear that nothing would be accomplished with the exception that we put ourselves in the precarious position of a rattrap; we were blockaded indoors and surrounded on all sides. I spent that first day in the room I once occupied despite my explicitly being told to stay away from the windows. I lounged upon my former bed reading Dickens' *A Tale of Two Cities*. Eventually, I had grown accustomed to the sound of shots being fired.

As evening approached the firing stopped, and Jimmy and I sat aside to play the Checkered Game of Life while the others sat around exercising their own various activities to keep themselves occupied after a long day of hollow skirmishes with words and bullets.

The board was set and the teetotum spun; I made the first move, landing upon School and sent to College, receiving five points. Jimmy, landing upon Influence received five points as well by heading on to Fat Office. I went to Bravery and then to Honor, another five points! Jimmy spun, receiving nothing, while I spun and received Cupid to Matrimony. Jimmy, next, found himself at Honor by way of Bravery as well, picking up another five of his own, while I then found myself at Poverty by way of Intemperance, and Jimmy found his way to Suicide. This game was proving somewhat of a discouragement after a long day of strife.

Putting the game aside and finding ourselves in a life-altering position, it helped me to summon enough courage to ask Jimmy a question that I had wondered about since that day at the Kavanagh's when he idly chose to dissuade any communications about his family.

"Jimmy?"

As he packed up the game-kit he vaguely replied with, "Hmm?"

"What happened to your family?"

He waited a pensive moment before answering, "If I gave a gal the only thing I had left of my mother, well…I would love her, too."

With that he stood up and walked towards the front of the house to convene with some of the other men. I looked down at my finger with the ring on it and smiled implicitly.

The second day proved to be more of the same tedious taunting by both sides. However, there was an added element: A Buffalo Soldier had been dispatched to engage with Sheriff Peppin. Looking out the window I stood wondering what this was all about when a shot had been fired from the house upon the soldier. As the daughter of a U.S. General, I knew this unprovoked retaliation would cost us dearly, and in being correct, on the third day a band of officers were eventually dispatched into Lincoln to delve into the matter, and they, too, were fired upon, and again from within the very house in which I stood. Knowing we had nothing to lose was one way to perceive the miserable state we were in, but inevitably, these mistakes would expedite any end that would conclude poorly on our behalf. Initially, I would have thought that making such a daring stand against The Ring was sufficient enough, but when the Buffalo Soldier had arrived and had been consequently threatened, bringing the subsequent officers in swiftly on his heels only to be threatened as well, it occurred to me that things had become much more severe by far! Now I was really feeling the terror.

Prior to these poorly executed tactics on our part we had been caught up in a stalemate which might have gone on for days; this war began clumsily at best. But by the fourth day it appeared obvious how this all would end. Our rations were waning and worse, the house smelled of human waste as there was nowhere to relieve one's self but indoors.

By the fifth morning, neither side giving up, it was all too clear that The Ring had the advantage when a band of troops out of Fort Stanton, led by Col. Dudley, marched in, responding to the threats previously made upon his dispatched soldiers. We were overwhelmingly outnumbered, and many of the Regulators took this hint and got out while the getting was good, skipping out and up the Bonito Ford from their respective dens. But for us, locked away in the McSween house, the epicenter of this battle, there was no denying that it would be the Regulators who would succumb to the fight. I didn't know which was worse—losing the battle and facing a hanging or having to stand another day locked away with little water and food and the unbearable stench of bodily refuse as bullets rained upon us!

Declarative shouts insisting for us to surrender came from outside, the voices trailing in easily through shattered glass. I heard various expletives that trailed back out in response, above all, a "Fuck you, Peppin!" floated breezily throughout the house.

At one point Susan bravely stepped outside, approaching Col. Dudley and asking for the surrender of her husband to be procured through him and not Peppin. When her plea was denied she came back, resolved to the bitter end.

There were only thirteen Regulators in the house, certainly nowhere near enough to do battle with the Dolan faction, let alone a regimented U.S. army, and I witnessed the others falling apart on account of our pitiable condition; they felt the same as me, rightfully doubting the decision to put ourselves in such a position. All except Billy—his leadership refused to give in. His mind was working, taking stock of the situation and contemplating a way to succeed nonetheless.

Given the circumstances, Billy and I did not converse much as he was busy being in the thick of it all, but I went into the kitchen to find him and talk sense.

"Billy, we're in a real bad way here."

He looked at me, stern. "You think?"

"This skirmish would last forever if it weren't for the fact that our supplies are nearly non-existent! Soon, we won't have a choice but to give up! The troops have been called for! It's all over for us now!"

He hardly noticed me, barely paying attention. "Well, we can't just give up. We'll die before that happens," he carelessly replied, pacing and thinking to himself.

"We've been outdone!" I cried. Still, he was not paying me any attention. I grabbed him by the arm and made him see me. "So what, then? Those men out there, they're in a much better position than we are. They have endless food and water, ammunition, reinforcements—they've got the goddamned army for Christ sakes! They're in open space and we're confined in a prison. We handed ourselves to them on a silver platter! Giving up and dying would both be par for the course! Those are our only options!"

"Something's gotta give," he replied, more to himself than me.

"Yeah...us."

He looked at me disappointedly. "Luce...we fight to the end. I won't let them win, not that way."

"What difference does it make? They're going to win! It isn't up to you how they do it!"

"You think I don't know our predicament? Well, I know it! But I won't give up! Are you asking me to?"

I looked down, silent. I never considered giving ourselves over to The Ring. My only purpose for saying these things to Billy was because they were true and I needed to say it out loud.

"No," I said quietly, realizing in utter defeat that I would rather he be shot dead than swing from a gallows.

"Well, if your plan was to bring this to my attention as if I didn't know, then you were mistaken."

"What do we do? The troops—"

A shout came somewhere from within the bowels of the house. A desperate, troublesome shout. Above the noise and the commotion all around us and the chaos of my own mind, I couldn't decipher from which direction it had come.

"It's on fire; they lit the house!"

Billy's head rose immediately at this. Tom and Minxie shoved into the kitchen and looked at Billy and Alex, the latter of which I had not noticed before now as he sat upon the floor, sullen, in anticipation of our next move.

"How bad is it?" Billy asked.

"It's on fire, Billy! It's pretty goddamned bad!" I yelled.

"How bad is it?" he asked again, speaking over me at both Tom and Minxie.

"It burns slow," replied Tom, "but all the same...the candle's going at both ends, Bill."

"We gotta break," said Minxie.

I sat with Billy and Alex in the kitchen as the others ran in and out as the house burned all throughout the morning into noon; the soldiers attempted the inferno twice before it smoldered to life. More gunfire played and I cowered down and covered myself for dear life; this time, the barrages of bullets seemed so much more intense. An explosion came from somewhere within the house causing me to instantaneously fall to the floor in a fetal position, debris hurdling throughout in aftershock, a smattering of which caught me upon the side where a small portion of my face and right forearm were unprotected. Billy ran to me and threw himself around me, albeit too late as bullets flew from our side and theirs while the house burned ever more fiercely.

The crowd of us had now been forced into the small space the kitchen and small areas around it provided us. The women were shouting, screaming. All except for Susan and myself. Susan flitted about the accessible remains of her home purposefully, collecting sentimental articles and whatever intact valuables lay about. During most of these days spent within the house the group of us had done our best to respect the home, only barricading the necessary areas such as doors and windows, and making portholes in the walls from which to fire, but as the days wore on more and more things were sacrificed to the plight of survival, and now to the powder keg we were trapped within.

The McSween house was burning; their home was burning!

I found the courage to look up and see that Alex still sat upon the floor, slumped more than I would have thought possible from when I last took in the sight of him. He was holding his head in his hands and mumbling things to himself, rocking slightly back and forth like a frightened child. Billy left me and knelt down before him, shaking him with both hands to get his attention. "We'll get out, Alex! Come out of it!"

Billy, Jimmy, Jim French, Chavez, Minxie, Tom and a young law student named Harvey Morris staying with the McSween's were going to make a run for it when the dark would come to rest at its peak. I had come nearly undone, but I could not let myself betray this to the boys. I held on to my wits as tightly as I could as they devised this reckless scheme. They would run and create a diversion, Billy assuring them that some or all would be pelted with gunfire, and once the guns were trained on the group of them, the others could escape. The fear in me had become so pronounced that it had nowhere to go but out of my joints where I could not control the trembling. My first reaction was to cry and beg them not to go, but I knew! *Oh*...I knew that this was the only way out, and I had to stand it rather than fall apart.

Billy expressed to the women and children that they should leave willingly, under the control of the firing squad outside, lest their skirts make it impossible for them to run. They agreed, and as I stood and watched them leave under the protection of the sheriff's posse and U.S. Military, I found I was expected to go, too.

"I will not!" I shouted in protest.

Billy gently seized my face within his hands. "Go. It'll end for you, now. We have to run, but you can leave now and be shut of it all."

I shook my head fiercely. "I won't go, I won't. Not to them."

"Don't risk this. Don't make me live with this," he begged. "If you go to them you won't be hurt; I couldn't stand it if you was to—"

I tried not to cry but the tears came nonetheless, and they fell even harder when I saw the compassion in Billy's face as he looked upon me, the two of us seemingly alone within a circle of flames. But then his face changed; his expression altered, determined as he looked into mine. "Give me your gun belt," he commanded.

Knowing this an imprudent time to ask question, but wanting to understand him all the same I asked, simply, "Why?"

"Because you'll run faster without the added weight."

I stared on at him a moment too long before he demanded, "Now!"

I unbuckled it, and in my haste and panic I faltered far more than I should have. When I had freed myself of it I handed it over. He slung the belt over his shoulder, handing one gun each to two of the others who would run off and fire back during the diversion.

"When we take off, you count to five, but not too slowly. Wait just long enough for a cease in firing, but not long enough for them to regroup. Then I want you to run—run fast! Watch our direction and follow."

"I will," I vowed.

I quit my crying, my nerves heightened, jolting me into action. Alex was pulled up from the floor by Jimmy and Chavez, and the boys readied themselves to run towards John's store and make it down to the wash. I was to leave with Alex and his housemen.

Outside one could see long a very fair distance for the fire and I prayed that they'd make it out alive. I was more terrified than I had ever been in my life up until this very moment, and for obvious good reason.

Billy placed himself by the threshold of our exit, gun out and preparing himself for the run of his life, the others standing around and behind him waiting for their cue. All he needed to do was move and they'd follow. Like lemmings off a cliff. I shook this thought from my mind; this was the only way out.

Things moved very slowly for me, and for all of the turmoil around us things seemed strangely quiet. The heat from the flames unfazed me, the ash falling and swirling around slowly as though in a water globe.

I kept my focus on Billy, my anticipation building to an intolerable fever pitch as I waited for him to strike and make his move. Finally, he sprung forth! In a spectacular display all the men went out within the blaze and heat under a hailstorm of bullets! I stood transfixed a moment before shaking myself out of it, remembering, as always, what

Billy told me, *'count to five...run fast'*. It all went from so slow to so terribly fast all too quickly, and I am unsure as to whether or not I waited long enough, not long enough, or at just the right moment when I ran. I braced myself to get hit, punctured by the artillery that had burst forth only seconds earlier, but nothing came and I heard nothing. Almost as if rehearsed, I methodically leapt over a body lying prone on the ground without even considering it and managed to run, in the darkness, over variations in the ground all leading downhill without faltering; I was all grace and tension. All I knew how to do in that moment was to run. I ran until I hit the Bonito, not realizing I had done so until I was forcibly slowed down by the weight of water and drenched with it. I felt blind, unseeing, and almost as if I had run into him there was Billy, finding me and holding on to me, pulling me along with him.

"No one else ran," I panted. "It was just me. They didn't run!"

The sound of gunfire erupted again and I believe I knew, then, that Alex hadn't made it, that he'd waited too long.

Across the river we were reunited, all except for poor Harvey Morris, who had fallen, and the others who ran much too late. But those that ran at the first were here, worse for the wear, but here. We all stood together and watched up the hill at the blaze that was once the McSween house. There was no one else coming, no sounds in the night to indicate that any of the others who were poised to run after me were going to see tomorrow.

Jimmy was skinned in the leg and Minxie twice in the arm, but we made it out alive and virtually unscathed. There was only the yawning darkness before us beckoning us to turn from the bedlam that was Lincoln and onto the next phase of adversities that would catapult Billy into misfortune and onward into infamy.

# Readers Guide: Discussion Questions

1. Why do you think John is indifferent to the obviously close relationship shared between Billy and Lucy?

2. Lucy represents stability for Billy, and Billy represents liberty for Lucy. Do you feel they were truly in love with one another, or merely the idea of one another?

3. Lucy chooses to give her virginity to Billy out of love, rather than to the man she is contracted to marry. Do you agree with her reasoning?

4. Like many women of the Victorian era, Lucy reviles the oppression of her gender and station, as well as the idea that she is the property of men. Do you feel Lucy was naïve in preferring to live a life of hardship in order to escape this situation, or that she truly coveted liberty over wealth?

5. Billy gives Lucy the only object he has left of his late mother: her ring. What, in your opinion, does this signify regarding his feelings for her?

6. Lucy grants Billy the opportunity to leave his turbulent life behind to live a comfortable and devoted life with her, but he instead chooses to join the Regulators and fight the tyrannical Santa Fe Ring. Do you feel this has much to do with his righteously defiant personality and hatred of the Ring's brutality towards innocent men, and if so, do you understand his position?

7. Though Billy cavorts freely with other women, he warns Lucy she is not to do the same with other men. Do you believe this is his way of protecting her virtue, or do you feel there is also jealousy on his behalf?

8. In love with Lucy, Jimmy dislikes Billy's infidelity towards her, to which she explains

that it is in a man's nature to sleep with other women, and that she will bide her time until Billy is settled and resolves to sharing only her bed. Is her reasoning logical?

9. Both Jimmy and Billy are in love with Lucy; Jimmy being more agreeable towards her, while Billy is often hard on her. Considering this, who do you believe has Lucy's best interests at heart and truly loves her? Explain your reasoning.

10. If Billy had agreed to run away with Lucy prior to the breaking of the Lincoln County War, do you believe they would have loved one another as strongly as they had after suffering the difficulties of the war together?

11. If Billy were alive today and facing adversity under the benefits of our contemporary social contract, how do you think he might handle himself as a modern citizen?

www.ingramcontent.com/pod-product-compliance
Lightning Source LLC
Chambersburg PA
CBHW031053020726
47495CB00007B/1858